HARD ROAD

TO

GETTYSBURG

HARD ROAD
TO
GETTYSBURG

A Novel by
Ted Jones

LYFORD
Books

For Vonnie

Hard Road to Gettysburg is a novel. Although set against a historical land-scape, specific events portrayed by characters, and even many of those involving historic personages, are fictitious. Except for historical figures, any resemblance of characters to persons living or dead is purely coincidental.

LYFORD Books
Published by Presidio Press
505 B San Marin Drive, Suite 300
Novato, CA 94945-1340

Library of Congress Cataloging-in-Publication Data

Jones, Ted, 1937 Oct. 22-
    Hard road to Gettysburg : a novel / by Ted Jones.
       p.   cm.
    ISBN 0-89141-445-2
    1. United States—History—Civil War, 1861-1865—Fiction.
I. Title.
PS3560.05418H37 1993   92-41960
813'.54—dc20   CIP

Typography by ProImage
Printed in the United States of America

PART ONE

·······························

The Sisters

CHAPTER 1

· · · · · · · · · · · · · · ·

The more Caroline Wade endeavored to repress her listless, gloomy mood, the more depressed she felt. For the present, in pretense of contentment, she whistled softly as she packed Porter's basket. Her husband was leaving for his next circuit ride in a few minutes, as soon as the sun rose. Despite her feigned vigilance, her mind strayed from the task. She had, in one absentminded moment, placed a half-full milk glass in the basket. It spilled, naturally. After cutting away a soaked section of a peach cake, she began packing again.

Life had lost its meaning. Nothing remained to distract her from her anguish and loneliness. People seldom bothered to visit anymore— a circumstance she unrealistically attributed to the farm's isolation— and she no longer went to call. She knew the reason for their avoidance and unwelcoming eyes. It had begun two years previously, with her husband's appointment as judge of the circuit court of southern Illinois. Porter Wade always had been a harsh man, but power had added meanness to his qualities. His elevation to the highest legal station in the region simply offered the final excuse for the neighbors to avoid even superficial social attachments.

The circuit frequently lasted three weeks, occasionally longer. Caroline had grown weary of the mind-draining exertion necessary to fill the hours of the day. Not that her husband's presence eased her loneliness much. But even if his affection for her had withered, if ever it had existed beyond illusion, at least his presence provided occasional human contact. She had thought about divorce, but concluded that it was out of the question. Porter's prominent station required an absence of scandal. Divorce represented the second worst sin.

She watched as Porter quietly gathered his belongings and placed them on the floor next to the back door. For the fourth time he looked out the window and checked the weather, checked the time, then checked off in his mind the items he always carried with him. He gave attention to everything—everything except her. If possible, his avoidance of her this morning seemed more premeditated than usual. Why? What sin had she committed to merit such enmity? She certainly lacked nothing in physical features. Her social graces were as refined as any woman her age lacking training from a fancy Eastern finishing school. Never had she denied him anything he required. Although from the beginning their sexual encounters had been infrequent, she always responded when he beckoned. She had concluded, simply, that something critical to sealing their relationship had been missing from the start.

He turned and looked in her direction, but his eyes were focused on something beyond. She shifted slightly, trying to insert herself between him and whatever had attracted his attention. He turned away.

She desperately ached for someone's touch, anyone's, especially a man's.

"Will you be away long?" she asked as she stuffed the last pint jar of peaches into the basket. She knew the answer, but she wanted to hear the words.

"Three weeks," Porter replied stiffly, "you know that. Why do you always ask?"

She recoiled from the sharpness of his voice. "I just . . ." There's no point in continuing, she thought. She closed the basket and raised the handles. "It's just so lonely here without someone to talk to." She repressed the desire to express again that they should move. She knew, from bitter experience, that the suggestion always evoked his wrath.

"I have to prepare the buggy," he said as he swept by her and grasped the basket. "No need for you to see me off." He stooped to pick up his personal items, then juggled the cumbersome load. She moved forward intent on assisting, but his glare drove her back. He walked out the door.

You bastard! she mouthed as the screen door slammed behind him. Not even a peck on the cheek. Is touching me so repulsive? She flung herself onto the chair beside the table, buried her face in her hands, and began to sob. She sought relief in fantasy. As usual, she lacked the concentration to bring anything pleasant to mind. She simply had no experiences, even shallow ones, to give dimension to her daydreams.

She wiped her nose on her sleeve before lying her head on the table. Shortly, she heard the muffled sound of the carriage rolling past the window. What good is crying? she thought. No one will hear.

"Get up, horse. Get up, now."

She shuddered as a wave of melancholy washed over her. Her hand accidentally pressed against her breast, and she consciously squeezed several times, fighting the impulse to draw her hand away. The simple act of touching her body that way made her feel sordid. Depression overwhelmed her and she battled to repress the screaming rage swelling deep inside.

"I want a baby," she said softly, almost whimpering. "Oh, God, please give me a baby." Yielding to the futility of her pleading, she pulled her hand from her breast as she sprang to her feet. On one lame pretext or another, Porter had avoided her bed for more than six months. Their last shared affection had been on New Year's Eve—and that only after a raging blizzard had shut them in for a week. That night they had talked as any normal husband and wife, but by the next day all evidence of his affection had vanished. That brief interlude only made conditions seem worse. She had felt like a whore, as if she had participated in a perverted one-night stand.

Four years earlier—it now seemed a lifetime ago—she had considered herself the most fortunate woman alive. Even then, however, Porter Wade had been a petulant man, or sometimes quiet and withdrawn, but hardly ever even in temperament. He was physically handsome, almost to a fault; the local female population had generally regarded him as the catch of Saline County. Then, as now, he owned four suits of clothes, all the same: black trousers, black coats, black bow ties, and white shirts with narrow ruffles down the button line and on the cuffs. Trained as a lawyer, he also had served as the lay minister of the First Baptist Church, the largest congregation in Harrisburg, Illinois. His attire conformed to his needs in both his vocation and avocation. Even then, he had distressed Caroline by his manner of speaking of God as if He was an equal. Impulsive females frequently swooned at this self-proclaimed evidence of his superior quality.

In time, she had brushed aside her doubts. A perfect combination, she had rationalized, a noble profession and virtue beyond question— all things considered, a man destined for prominence.

No less than a dozen of Caroline's contemporaries had competed for Porter's attention. Only Caroline, shy and cautious, always yielding to the force of Porter's strong will, had attracted his consideration. Their courtship had been as proper as might be expected, even more so. They had often walked for an hour without speaking a word. His occasional squeeze of her hand, followed by a slight bow as he left her on the porch, marked the summit of their displayed affection during that period. Never did she think that one day she might yearn for such simple expressions of adoration.

A year following their marriage, Wade became a circuit judge. The last time she remembered his smiling at her was the day he was notified of the appointment. Porter had a firm view of a judge's proper bearing. Nothing in that view included gentleness or compassion or, most especially, love. Overnight, his personality had changed for the worse. His mood became sour and judgmental; he viewed everyone as being beneath him and, worse, deserving of suspicion. "Emotions must be subdued," he had told her as she placed an arm about his waist shortly after, "or else they will control us." She thought at the time that he was referring to his demeanor as a judge, but he had applied the restraint to every quarter of his life.

The role of judge held no mystery for him; he had assumed his father's former position. The old judge had died less than two months earlier. By the time of his death, the old man's scowl had become so etched in his face that the mortician was unable to remove it. He persists in passing judgment from the casket, Caroline had thought. Porter's mother, a bitter, lonely woman—Caroline's mother had been her only friend for her last ten years—had died earlier, and Caroline envisioned the same end for herself, only worse. At least the former Mrs. Wade had a son to ease her loneliness.

Caroline walked limply to the bedroom window and watched passively as a stiff gust of wind churned up a cloud of dust. Long after the buggy disappeared below the east ridge, her gaze remained fixed on the emptiness. Finally, as a shield from the sun just now rising, she brought her hand mechanically to her eyes; then she turned away as her chin dropped to her chest. Alone, she thought. Totally alone. As a tear rolled down her cheek, a despairing, involuntary sigh broke the silence. She cried often these days, and for hardly any reason. Letting her body go limp, she toppled forward onto the bed and sobbed uncontrollably before drifting into fitful slumber.

She felt nothing when she awoke—neither sorrow nor hate, not loneliness or relief. As one does with a chronic, ever-present pain, she pushed all feeling from her mind. She simply felt nothing. She had nothing important to do, so her mind wandered from room to room— a short trip in the four-room log house that confined her. I might as well be in prison, she thought as the edge of depression crept back into her thoughts. For the time, in 1838 in Illinois, the dwelling had adequate qualities, even better than most. She presently rested in her room, the front bedroom. The gleaming brass bed on which she lay, the pride and joy of her few personal possessions, provided a stark contrast to the gray drabness of the rough log walls. Her husband slept in the adjacent room, more a half room, on a single bed. A chair and a small table, on which sat a pitcher and washbowl, were the only other items in his room. Stairs on the north wall of this small room led to a loft originally intended as the children's sleeping quarters. But there were no children. Porter had slept up there as a child, before his family had gained prominence and moved to town.

The small parlor joined Caroline's room on the west side of the house. A horsehair sofa stood diagonally in one corner. A slat-back rocker next to the window provided a place for reading with natural light; a coat tree stood next to the door. This room shared with the kitchen a large, open fireplace that served double duty for cooking and as the source of heat for the house. Caroline spent most of her time in the spacious kitchen, cooking and sewing and, in season, canning the fruits and vegetables she grew in the garden or harvested from the fruit trees east of the house. Behind the house was a root cellar—she often found tranquil relief in its dark, musty confines on hot summer days—and beyond it stood the small barn where she kept a cow and three dozen laying chickens. A horse grazed in the pasture.

She had stacked the back shelves of the root cellar high with glass jars filled with, among other items, green beans and tomatoes, as well as the apples, peaches, and plums from which she baked the best pies in Saline County. Two first-place county fair awards, now gathering dust in a drawer, confirmed her status. Potatoes and onions filled the two bins under the shelves. All of this contributed to her problem: Their life-style was largely self-sufficient. She had no need to depart from her isolated existence except to buy the staples necessary for cooking, and even those items Porter usually brought from town.

A stone path curved around the root cellar and led to the outhouse tucked away behind a grove of poplars fifty feet to the west. It was a cold journey on a blustery winter night.

Twenty-five years earlier, Porter's father had constructed the main house from logs harvested from the forest two miles to the northeast. Before his death, the senior Judge Porter Wade had accumulated more than three thousand acres of prime forest and a third as much cleared farmland. Less than fifty acres was under cultivation by Porter Wade, Jr. He had no interest in farming. Except for one quarter section share-cropped by a local farmer, the land had grown over with grass. Three separate farmers rented the grassland for their grazing stock. The value of the land, complemented by the rental and annual harvest of trees by a local milling establishment, combined with Porter's salary to make him the wealthiest man in the county.

Porter had been an only child. He had inherited his family's holdings when his father died. All of this, plus the power and prestige embodied in the Wade name, had added to Porter Wade's allure for Caroline and the other young women who competed for his attention. Caroline had won the contest without really trying—a victory she now considered a curse.

Caroline sat on the porch stitching needlepoint. Four days had passed since Porter's departure. She yearned for the sound of another person's voice, even if it had to be the voice of a sixty-year-old man. She expected the mail carrier to arrive at any time. He delivered the mail every other Friday, usually about noon. The ritual seldom changed. Zack, the mailman, usually came in for a piece of pie soaked with cream before finishing the last leg of the route leading back to Harrisburg. If he had the time, he passed on any gossip picked up along the way. Zack's arrival often provided the only social event during her husband's long absences.

Off to the east Caroline saw the telltale cloud of dust signifying the movement of a vehicle along the rutted, single-lane road. She smiled broadly as she laid her sewing aside and rushed to wash her sweat-streaked face and brush her hair. She patted her hair as she returned to the edge of the porch. But something seemed different. Caroline shaded her eyes against the late morning sun. She saw two people in a buggy, not Zack's usual wagon. She strained her eyes to identify the occupants. The person on the right, a woman, began to wave as the buggy drew closer. Gradually, the form became recognizable. "It looks like Victoria," Caroline screamed with delight. "My God! It is

Victoria." Caroline pulled her dress up to her knees as she began running toward the buggy.

She arrived breathless. "Victoria, I can't believe it's you. Why didn't you write me that you were coming?"

"I did," Victoria replied with a smile. "Over a month ago. If you lived in civilization, you might receive your mail now and again."

Caroline laughed. "I thought you were the mail carrier. I'll probably receive the letter today." She patted the horse as she studied the battered old carriage. "Did you ride in this all the way from Alabama?"

"Heavens, no," Victoria replied. "We traveled by stage to Harrisburg." She looked around. "You do have a horse, don't you? Jeff must return the carriage tomorrow and will need a horse for the return trip."

"There's one in the pasture," Caroline replied, "and a saddle in the barn."

"We expected to be here earlier, but we lost our way. This territory is more godforsaken than I remembered." She studied the terrain again. "How do you stand it, living out here all alone?"

Caroline looked at the young Negro holding the reins. "Is this your boy?" she asked, ignoring Victoria's question.

Victoria turned and patted the driver on the shoulder. "This is Jefferson—I call him Jeff. He takes care of me. Don't you, Jeff?"

The man's statuesque pose seemed an extension of the wagon seat. Only his black pupils darted to the sound of Victoria's voice. What a powerfully built man, Caroline thought. Bulging biceps pushed against the sleeves of his shirt; the muscles in his neck strained at the confining buttoned collar. A worn straw hat sat squarely on his head. He offered no sign that even the simplest thought troubled him.

As Caroline dropped the hand that shaded her eyes, Jeff looked first at his mistress; then he examined the woman standing by the horse. His jaw slowly dropped as he formed a somewhat pained, inquisitive expression. "Ya'll both looks like the same person," he said finally.

"We are, sort of," Victoria replied casually. "This is my twin sister, Caroline."

"Twin?"

"I don't suppose he's ever seen twins before," Victoria said, turning her head from side to side. She turned to the black man. "That means we both were born at the same time, Jeff, from the same mother."

"Lordy me!" he exclaimed. "That must'a ripped your mama apart, or else you two was mighty small."

Victoria laughed. "Well, not exactly at the same time. First one, then the other. Actually, I was born first, so Caroline is my little sister, you might say."

Caroline patted her hair, then smoothed her cotton dress and smiled broadly. "Well, don't just sit there. Come into the house. You must be burning up after that long ride." She turned and started running toward the house. "I'll fix some tea," she shouted over her shoulder, her loose blond hair flowing in the breeze behind her. "Take the buggy to the barn, Jeff, after you drop off my sister at the house."

"Git up, horse." Jeff flipped the reins and clicked his tongue.

Caroline ran into the house and tossed a log on the smoldering coals; then she tested the kettle. Half-full. She ran back outside. She threw her arms around her sister as she stepped down from the carriage, the stiff petticoats under Victoria's green satin dress almost pushing Caroline away. "Oh, Victoria, you can't imagine how pleased I am to see you. I wondered at times if I'd ever see you again." She leaned back and looked at the image of herself, then smiled broadly again as she clasped her sister's cheeks between her hands. "Come. Come into the house. We have so much to talk about."

"Is Porter here?" Victoria asked as she examined the surroundings for signs of life.

Caroline's expression changed instantly. She loathed weak women, especially women who complained. She had endured her misery in silence, never once mentioning her unhappiness in her letters to Victoria. But she had kept her feelings contained for too long. Besides, what were sisters for if not to share joys and heartache? Of heartache she had an endless supply. She stopped, then turned to Victoria. "Oh, Victoria, I'm so unhappy. Since Porter's appointment to the judgeship, he's hardly ever here. He has changed so. I sometimes believe he hates me." She forced a smile. "But let us talk of more pleasant things." She grasped her twin's hand. "How long will you stay? Long, I hope."

"Is a month acceptable?"

"That's much too short a time." Pulling on Victoria's hand and humming softly, she skipped toward the house.

"Is it all right if Jeff sleeps in the barn?" Victoria asked. "He's no trouble, and he provided such good company on the journey."

"Come on in. The water is heating for tea," Caroline said, changing the subject. She had always been uncomfortable around Negroes.

She never quite thought of them as deserving slavery, but neither did she quite think of them as people, at least not in the proper sense of the term. She simply never gave them much thought at all. Nothing prevented Jeff from sleeping wherever he wanted, as long as he slept someplace other than in the house. She twirled and clasped her hands together. "You must be famished. We'll attend to your boy later."

"Do you still make those delicious pies?" Victoria asked. "You always were the cook in the family."

Caroline smiled. "I have apple with fresh cream, your favorite."

As the two walked into the parlor, Victoria stopped. She began breathing heavily as beads of perspiration popped out on her forehead.

Caroline looked at her with obvious anxiety. "Are you ill, Victoria?"

"It must be the sun. I've been a bit queasy the past several days, especially in the early morning." She wiped her brow and sighed.

"Well, you just sit yourself down. I'll fetch you a cool glass of milk. It's in the cellar. I'll be right back." Caroline danced briskly through the kitchen and out the back door. She returned shortly carrying a gallon tin bucket. "Fran gives the sweetest milk in the county." She hesitated, then laughed. "Fran's my cow. She's the closest thing I have to a friend since moving to this godforsaken place, although the chickens are a close second." The sadness returned to her face. "Oh, Victoria, I'm such a ninny. I committed a terrible mistake by marrying Porter. I don't know what I shall do. I want a baby so very much, but Porter won't even sleep with me now." She hesitated as she studied her sister's reaction. "Victoria, are you with child?"

Victoria appeared startled; then her expression gradually shifted to amazement, then to joy. "I don't know," she said, sounding as if she had never considered the possibility. "Do you suppose?" She patted her stomach softly and smiled.

"Oh, Victoria!" Caroline exclaimed. "That would be wonderful." Outside, she heard the clomp of horses' hooves. "That must be Zack, the mailman." She ran out the door. "I bet you have a letter for me from Alabama," she shouted.

Zack pulled the horses to a stop and looked at the two letters. "One of 'em shore is," he replied. "You been expectin' this?"

"It's from my sister, Victoria," she said, pointing to the house, "but she arrived first. She's in the house."

Zack looked sad. "Does that mean I don't get none of your pie this trip?"

Caroline cocked her head slightly and smiled. "Of course not. You get down and come on in. I baked an apple pie especially for you."

Zack tied the reins to the brake handle and jumped to the ground. "I haven't seen Victoria in, what, four years now?"

Caroline thought for a moment. "Must be that long, Zack. She left here in the spring of '34, when she married Henry Thornton. I haven't seen her since, myself."

Zack shuffled onto the porch. "I'll wait out here," he said, pounding the dust from his clothes. "Don't want to be no bother."

"Nonsense. You come on in." She waved her hand. "Victoria will enjoy seeing you."

"Zack Hart, you darling," Victoria said, shifting her attention from her abdomen to the old man standing in the doorway. Without rising, she extended her hand. "It's so good to see you."

"You too, Missy," he said. "'Cepting when ya smiled, ya both always looked the same to me." He bent down and placed his hands on his knees. "Did y'know ya had a crooked smile? It adds a certain wickedness ta your charmin' face."

Victoria reached out and touched his cheek. "I'll take that as a compliment," she replied, "and so everyone tells me, Zack. That's the only way anyone can tell us apart. You haven't changed a bit—you're as frank as always. It's good to see you, old friend." She fought back the nausea as she tried to rise. She let her body drop back into the chair.

"Here's your pie, Zack." Caroline had a new bounce in her step. "Sit down and rest for a spell. You'll want a glass of milk."

He nodded as he sipped the cream from the saucer.

"Is the judge away?" Zack asked as he munched on the pie.

"Yes," Caroline replied. "He won't be back for more than two weeks."

"Well, ya ladies'd best be careful." The old man squinted his eyes and shook his head. "I saw two men campin' down by the stream a few miles back. A couple of unsavory characters if ever I saw any. Prob'ly nothing, but two ladies all alone is a temptin' . . . Well, y' know what I mean." He licked the plate and set it on the table. A thin whisker of milk clung to his upper lip. He licked it clean.

"Thank you for the warning, Zack," Caroline replied, "but we'll be fine." She had become accustomed to the ever-present danger of being alone and seldom gave it a thought anymore. She had enough real problems without worrying about imaginary ones.

Zack extended his hands to the two young women. Each grasped one. "Better be on my way if I'm ta make it home 'fore dark. My Betty starts worryin' 'long 'bout sundown. Shore was good pie, Missy Caroline. Missy Victoria, I truly enjoyed seein' ya again."

"And you, Zack. Have a safe trip home."

"I will," he replied as he walked onto the porch and half turned to wave. "Just four more stops. You watch out now, ladies." Caroline waved as the old man turned the wagon and drove away.

Caroline returned to the parlor and pulled up a chair. She lifted her cup and sipped at the tea. "I'm dying to hear about life on a plantation, Victoria," she said mischievously. "I've heard so much about the relaxed, carefree way of life down there. Is it really true? Your letters are always so brief."

Victoria bent down and unhooked her shoes. "Well, sister of mine, that's mostly a myth. I've been too busy to get around much to see who might have time to relax. All the women I know work from sunup to sundown."

Caroline's expression conveyed her disappointment. "How do such stories start, anyway?" she asked.

Victoria leaned back and pulled her dress up over her knees. She fanned herself with the hem. "Do you mind if I shed all this cloth? It's so hot, and I'm still feeling a bit peaked."

Caroline grasped her sister's hand and led her into the bedroom. "You get comfortable and rest now, and don't worry about anything."

"You still have mama's bed, I see." Victoria pursed her lips. "I don't know why I gave in so easily when you said you wanted it." She ran her hand down the long brass post. "Oh, well, I've enjoyed the kitchen table and chairs." Before long, as they had so often done in their younger years, both were lying on the bed clad only in their undergarments. Victoria laughed. "Do you remember that time when I was giving you a back rub when you were lying on this bed, and we heard the noise out the window."

Caroline blushed. "Did you have to bring that up? You knew Jimmy Clapp had his eye glued to the window watching us, and you didn't say anything. You just sprang to your feet and shed to your underclothes."

Victoria shrugged and raised an eyebrow. "Well, he was such a sweet boy," she chuckled. "I just wanted to make him happy. It must have worked. I expected his tongue to drop out when I stretched." She slapped her sister on the butt. "But he could hardly take his eyes off your fanny long enough to look at me. Poor boy. It was six months before he could look me in the eye." She sighed. "Maggie Clark wrote me that he married Sara Gordon and has two kids now."

Caroline rolled to her back and locked her fingers behind her head. "Yes, but the youngest, a girl, died last winter. I hear he blames Sara, and they hardly speak anymore." She sighed. "Nothing quite turns out as we think it will when we're young and innocent, does it, Vickie?"

"No, I suppose it doesn't."

The afternoon slipped away as the sisters discussed the events in their lives since their parting more than four years earlier. Both girls had experienced bouts of depression following Victoria's move south. Until that time, from the beginning of their memory, they had spent virtually every waking hour together. Never had theirs been a life filled with luxury, but neither had they lacked the essential comforts available in this frontier environment. Simon Taliaferro, their father, had been the only physician within fifty miles, and he had provided a comfortable living before being beset by a series of tragedies. First, in 1832, there had been the death of their older brother in a swimming accident. The death of his only son had sent Dr. Taliaferro into deep, gloomy despair. He had just begun recovering from that when, six months later, during the harsh winter of '33, his wife, Martha, had become ill with pneumonia. The doctor never quite forgave himself for his inability to save her. Less than a year later, the doctor, too, had died. Passersby found the buggy at the bottom of a ravine, horse and driver dead.

As with most physicians, he had settled many of his fees with commodities, or even an occasional parcel of land, when grateful patients had especially appreciated his services. His holdings increased over time. As a result, the extent of the girls' inheritance surprised them. Besides the house and its furnishings, there were 823 acres of farm and pastureland—the largest parcel was 161 acres—and a full section of virgin forest. The discovery that their father had still owned a section of prime Pennsylvania farmland, which he had inherited from his father, was most surprising. All of this, in addition to the $3,920 bank deposit, provided the girls with an estate valued at $27,500. Over time, they sold the odd parcels, all located in Saline County, and the woodland, but they elected to retain, in joint ownership, the house in town and the Pennsylvania farm and house in which a cousin-once-removed lived. This endowed them with cash of just over $8,000 each, plus the steady income from the farm, to carry them through until marriage. Neither had waited long.

Three months after the doctor's demise, Victoria met an Alabama cotton farmer. He had traveled to Illinois seeking to establish a northern cotton distribution network for a cooperative of small landowners from northern Alabama. He was a widower and ten years her senior, but that had only piqued her interest. A more mature, established man promised greater security. The romanticism of it all, the idea of being a Southern lady with a plantation and servants to attend to her needs, had been more than the nineteen-year-old girl could resist. And she had overpowered Henry Thornton. After a dizzying courtship, she married him and departed to live her dream. Only later did she learn that his farm was considerably less than a plantation and that the black servant who had accompanied her husband north also doubled as a farmhand. He had never deceived her; she had presumed.

After a brief period of immature disappointment, she decided to take matters into her own hands. "I never did tell you how I entered the slave business, did I?" she asked, rolling her head and looking into her sister's eyes from six inches away. "I suppose I felt ashamed at first. Later it didn't seem important."

"I shouldn't wonder that you felt ashamed, Victoria. You know how Daddy felt about slavery."

Victoria shrugged and looked away. She refused to dwell on her questionable practices. "I used half of my cash inheritance to purchase a clubfooted black girl of eighteen, an older black woman of about thirty—none of the slaves know their real age—with two small sons, and two middle-aged field hands." She pulled herself up and clasped her arms about her knees. Caroline extended her arm and began to massage her sister's shoulders. Victoria moaned with pleasure. She threw back her head and let her long blond hair cascade. "God, I'd forgotten how good that feels." She hummed a song from her childhood. "None of the slaves was prime property," she said finally, as if eager to unburden herself to the one person to whom she felt comfortable expressing her deepest feelings. "I had long-range plans; small boys grow into men, and male slaves, properly cared for and encouraged, produce more sons. I bought the young black girl for only a hundred dollars. I reasoned that a clubfoot created no hindrance in the reproductive process. Besides, Jeff—my nigger out in your barn—had no woman, and I thought he might like her. She is a sweet creature."

"Victoria, I simply can't believe what you're saying, talking about people as if they're nothing but property."

"Well, honey child," Victoria countered, "Alabama has different standards than Illinois. I can't change the way things are, so I may as well make the best of them. Besides," she said with a mischievous snicker, "I truly felt sorry for Jeff. Every time he saw a woman, this rather substantial lump began to grow in his pants." She chuckled at her sister's discomfort. "Made no attempt at all to hide it. I offered him his choice and, after much soul searching—and what I suspected to be some late-night inspection and testing—Jeff chose the woman with the two sons."

"Victoria!" her sister exclaimed. "How can you say such things?"

Victoria was becoming annoyed. "I love you dearly, Caroline, you know that. But you *are* a bit stodgy at times." She hesitated, then blurted out, "Perhaps if you were a bit more expressive with Porter, he might visit your bed more often."

Caroline clasped her mouth as the tears gathered in her eyes. Deep inside, she recognized the truth, but she had never admitted as much, even to herself. Hearing it aloud sounded so vulgar, so judgmental. But Victoria had a habit of seeing the truth, especially in her twin.

Seeing the pain her candor caused, Victoria turned and lay her head on her sister's chest as she slid her arms around her back and squeezed. "I'm sorry, Caroline, I shouldn't have said that. Porter is probably nothing other than the bastard he seems. I always thought of him as arrogant, and I should have said something before."

Caroline sobbed. "I think about being different, about being forward like you. I just can't express my feelings as you do. I know you're right, but that doesn't help." She stroked her sister's hair. She always had forgiven Victoria easily. "If only I could be as expressive with him as I am with you."

Victoria sighed but could think of nothing appropriate to say. Both women knew enough about men. They had sneaked enough looks at their father's medical books to know more than most females learned about men in a lifetime, at least about their physical attributes. But such knowledge was little help in understanding emotions, in comprehending desires. Victoria knew what stimulated her senses when dealing with men, and she had reasoned that the same principles applied in reverse. Such analysis had eluded her sister. Victoria had become one person, and Caroline another, even if they were twins.

"You've always been bold enough for both of us," Caroline admonished as she sought to regain her self-respect. "But it doesn't matter now. I've lost Porter, and that's that. I just don't know what to do about it—if there's anything that *can* be done about it."

Victoria lifted herself and, placing her elbows on the bed, she rested her chin on her interlocking fingers. "Jeff is quite a stud, you know."

Caroline laughed. "You're impossible, Victoria."

"Well, he is. His wife—her name is Molly, and wife isn't exactly the right term, as there was no preacher or anything like that—anyway, she expanded the family by two in the four years since. She gave birth to the second just before we left. And the clubfooted girl has increased my wealth by two little girls. Jeff ignores comments about the possible origin of these two, but I know he's the father. Anyway, two good cotton crops provided the added capital needed to expand our farm from less than a hundred to nearly four hundred acres." She thought for a moment. "That doesn't reach the proportion of being a plantation, but it's more than a farm down in Alabama."

"I envy you, Victoria," Caroline said wistfully. "I'd give anything for a chance to begin again. I truly believe that Porter is taking his affections to other beds. I have no proof, but there are signs. I should have suspected it before we married, but I pushed it from my mind. I knew he was smitten with Bee Alexander, but she's such a flirt. All the men look at her swishing rear end with one eye and their wives with the other." She looked at her sister and smiled. "I haven't talked like this in over four years, Victoria. It feels so good to be able to talk about it."

Victoria leaned over and kissed her sister on the forehead. "We'll have a whole month to talk. That's what I'm here for." Victoria rolled onto her side and flung her legs over the side of the bed. "But now we have to see to Jefferson. He's had nothing to eat since sunup."

CHAPTER 2

Caroline had grown accustomed to silence in the house, so her senses reacted quickly to abnormal occurrences. Victoria's arrival, however, had eased her mind somewhat, so she wasn't alarmed. The creaking, measured sound of cautious footsteps entered Caroline's consciousness slowly, then faded with her return to slumber. Had it been a dream? Was Victoria walking about? She raised her head from her pillow. Straining her ears to recapture the sound she now was positive she had heard, she peered into the darkness. The bedsprings creaked from her movement. Silence. In the adjacent room she heard her sister moan and then turn in her sleep. Caroline relaxed and let her head drop.

Creak. There, she heard it again. Although only half-awake, she was certain that someone had entered the house. "Who's there?" she asked tentatively. "Is someone there?"

She flinched at the immediate, solid rush of footsteps.

"Grab her, Mo," shouted a voice in the dark. A shadow rushed through the doorway.

A hand clamped over her mouth just as she started swinging her legs over the side of the bed. She tried to scream, but the muffled sound emerged as no more than a squeak.

"I got her, Albert. She's a soft one, she is."

"Don't let her get away, Mo."

"She ain't goin' nowhere, Albert. Strike a match."

A flicker of light lifted the darkness. Then a scream broke the temporary silence.

"There's someone else here, Mo. The judge didn't say nothin' about nobody else bein' here." The match flickered out as the man rushed to the adjoining room. Caroline heard a brief struggle.

"Aarrgghh! The bitch bit me, Mo, but I got her now." The small night table toppled to the floor, followed immediately by the sound of breaking glass as the pitcher shattered against the wall. "Mo, you still there?"

"Where'n the hell else would I be, Albert? Ya got her?"

"Yeah, but she's a fighter." He dragged the struggling woman into the larger room. "Bitch! Stop that kickin' or I'm gonna smack you one." Victoria pulled an arm free and swung. The blow caught her assailant on the ear. "That's it," he snarled, then cracked his hand sharply against the side of Victoria's face. She crumpled to the floor.

Caroline struggled, but the man holding her had no trouble overpowering her. Mo jerked hard on her arms, now clasped together behind her back, and forced her face into the pillow. She gasped for breath. "Settle down, lady, or I'll give ya what the other one just got." Caroline stopped struggling.

Another light flickered dimly. "I'll get that lamp," Albert said, holding a match. "You watch the one on the floor." A yellow light illuminated the room. "There, that's better." He swaggered back toward Victoria, who was still stunned from the blow. He placed a knee on her chest. "I told you ta stop your strugglin'," he said. He looked at the woman on the floor. "Which one is which?" Albert asked.

Mo pulled Caroline to a sitting position. "Beats me." He shifted his gaze back and forth between them. "My God, Albert, they look just alike." He hesitated a moment. "They're twins!"

Albert looked first at one woman, then at the other. "Well, so they is." A perverted grin appeared on his face. "Let's have some fun, Mo. There ain't no hurry, is there?"

"Maybe later," Mo replied. "First, let's find out what's goin' on here." He glared at Caroline. "Which one of you is the judge's woman?"

Caroline bit her lip. My God, she thought, Porter sent them! They're going to kill us. She screamed and was rewarded with a hard slap across her face.

Mo shook a filthy finger at her. "Do that again, bitch, and I'll gag ya good."

Caroline began to sob as she rubbed her throbbing cheek.

Mo grabbed the hem of her nightgown and pulled. Caroline's hand instinctively jerked downward in a feeble attempt to push her gown down, but the man's grip on her wrist held her arm in check.

"Well, lookee here. If that ain't the nicest li'l ol' ass I ever seen."
He delivered another sharp whack with his free hand.

"Can I look at this un's ass, Mo?"

"Why not, Albert. Maybe that'll teach 'em who's boss."

Albert jerked Victoria's arms. "Roll over, bitch, an' let's see all of
ya." She yielded to the pain. "Well, if'n you ain't somethin'. It's beyond
me why the judge wants ta rid himself a somethin' like this. Or *are*
ya the judge's woman?" He brought his face close to hers. "Well, is
you the judge's woman, or ain't ya?"

"Let my sister go," Caroline screamed. *"I'm* Judge Wade's wife.
You don't have to hurt her."

Mo turned toward the sounds behind him. Albert struggled to hold
Victoria down while he pulled up her gown. "Yessir. That's prime
woman," he said as he pulled the gown over her head. "Prime indeed."
He crawled on top of his helpless victim.

"Albert, ya dumb son of a bitch," Mo said, laughing. "Ya got ta
take off your pants 'fore ya poke her."

Albert responded with an insane sort of laugh. "Ya think so, Mo?
Can I poke her?"

Victoria kicked with both legs and Albert rolled to the floor.

"I'd tie her down first, Albert—'fore she kicks your balls off."

Albert rose to his feet as Victoria pushed her gown from her face.
She gritted her teeth and glared as she lowered her hand to cover the
blond tuft of hair between her legs.

"Well, if'n you ain't a nasty one," Albert said, placing his foot on
her stomach.

Her face misshapen with pain, Victoria clenched her teeth tightly
and struggled to pull the leg away from her abdomen. He lifted his
foot a few inches, then drove it downward. She screamed.

"Do ya see any rope I can use ta tie—" Albert never finished the
sentence. Sticking from his lower back were the manure-streaked tips
of a four-pronged pitchfork. The handle vibrated behind him from the
force of the blow. His eyes opened wide with shock as his hands reached
behind trying to clutch the handle. A trickle of blood flowed from the
corner of his lips. He looked at Mo as his mouth gaped in horrified
bewilderment.

In a fluid motion, Mo jumped to the floor and turned. Before he
could brace himself, a black fist crashed into his nose. He toppled
backward, his head crashing against the log wall.

With one hand clenching the handle of the pitchfork, Albert wobbled right, then left, then staggered two steps backward. Finally, staring over his shoulder at the source of his agony, he sank slowly to his knees. He turned his head slowly toward Mo. "Mo, help me," he gurgled pleadingly. "It hurts a lot, Mo. Help me."

The black man grabbed the handle and pushed.

"Aarrgghh," Albert screamed in agony. "God have mercy." The force of the black man's shove drove the prongs through Albert's abdomen and pinned him face first in a half-kneeling position against the wall. With a terrified glare of disbelief in his eyes, Albert looked back at his antagonist. "The judge didn't say nothin' 'bout anyone bein' here 'cept his woman." Then his head dropped. The downward pressure of his limp body pulled the prongs free of the wall and he crumpled to the floor. Blood spurted on the planks and flowed down a crack. With his eyes clamped tight, a moan escaped through his clenched teeth as he clutched at the spikes sticking from his blood-stained shirt. Shrieking in agony, he drew his legs into a fetal position. Waves of pain surged through his quivering frame and his legs twitched involuntarily.

"You's done hurt Miss Victoria," Jefferson said coldly. "I don't allow that, y'hear? I don't allow that." As if to emphasize the point, he kicked the end of the handle.

Albert screamed, as did Caroline, her hand snapping to her mouth at the shocking sight of the spurting blood. She desperately wanted to yell for the black man to stop, but the words stuck in her throat. She looked at Victoria, still writhing and moaning from the kick to her stomach. The baby, Caroline thought. My God! the baby. She jumped to the floor. Kneeling beside her sister, Caroline cradled Victoria's head in her arms. "Let me help you to the bed," she crooned. "Everything will be all right. Everything will be all right." She began to sob as she crouched and grasped Victoria under the arms. Caroline half dragged, half carried her sister across the room before lifting her high enough to roll her limp frame onto the bed. Then Caroline felt a tightening grip on her ankle. She screamed as she looked down just in time to see a dirty brown pant leg fly by. The force of Jeff's kick drove Mo tumbling into the wall. The immediate second blow connected with the bleeding man's chin. He crumpled in a heap in the corner.

Mo shook his head and moaned. The first dim light of morning gleamed through the cracks in the barn door. As his consciousness returned,

Mo instinctively pulled against his restraint. The coarse rope scraped against his wrists. He blinked. "Ya goddamn nigger," he yelled, "I'll kill ya for this. When the judge gets through with ya, you'll beg me ta kill ya." A foot crashed into his groin.

"Don't hurt him too bad, Jeff," Caroline said from the shadows, "at least not until he tells me exactly what brought him here." Something in her experience had transformed her. The distressed, forlorn expression, so common to her in recent months, had given way to a hard, spiteful, determined look. Mo's eyes opened wide at the sight of the large butcher knife she gripped in the hand at her side.

"Now just put that knife away, lady." He scooted as far as the rope allowed. "Ya let me go, an' I'll just be on my way." He nodded and forced a distorted, reassuring smile.

Caroline smiled back as she lifted the knife outward, the blade sparkling as it moved through a narrow beam of sunlight.

"Didn't ya hear me?" Mo pleaded, his eyes fixed on the blade. "I'll forgive ya if ya'll just let me go. I won't say nothin' 'bout your killin' Albert." He laughed nervously. "Shit. He weren't much no how."

The knife sliced swiftly toward Mo's throat. He crashed his head against the wall trying to escape the sharp point. Caroline pressed it against his throat. "Who sent you?" she asked coldly. "I demand to hear you say the name."

"N-no one sent me," he stuttered. "We was just lookin' for money an' somethin' ta eat."

She let the knife drop a few inches. "Jeff, did you finish digging that hole out in the pasture?" Her icy glare remained fixed on Mo's throat.

"I sho' did, Miss Caroline."

"Is Albert in the hole, Jeff?"

"He is. Ya said ya didn't want his carcass stinkin' up the place."

"Good. Now you take Mo here and put him in the hole, too. Then cover them both up. Pack the dirt down good with the shovel."

Mo's eyes opened wider. "Ya can't bury a man alive," he said with alarm, shaking his head. "No. 'Course ya wouldn't do nothin' like that."

"Tie him up good, Jeff. I don't want him kicking the dirt around. Place the sod back on top like I told you. I don't want anyone finding the vermin."

Mo pulled at the rope. It cut deeper into his wrist.

Jeff loosened the end of the rope from around a hook in the wall and let Mo fall to the ground. He wound the rope tightly around the prostrate man's legs, then bound his hands behind his back. "He ain't goin' ta do no kickin', Miss Caroline." Jeff pulled Mo's head back and the two men looked into each other's eyes. Jeff smiled. "No, Miss Caroline, he won't do no kickin'."

"Godallmighty, ya can't do this!" Mo screamed. "No one buries a man alive. It ain't human."

"And killing women?" Caroline said as she knelt beside him. "I suppose you call that human?"

"It weren't our idea. We was headin' for prison for theavin'. The judge told us he'd let us go if'n we'd do him a favor."

"The judge? What judge?"

Mo hesitated.

"What goddamn judge?" she yelled as she brought the knife to his throat. Caroline seldom cursed, especially in the presence of a man. But the words added a sense of fierceness to her demand, or so she thought.

"Your husband," Mo said immediately. "He said ya'd be here alone, and there wouldn't be no trouble. We could just keep on goin', he said, once the job was finished. He said ta take anythin' we wanted from the house. Make it look like robbery, he said." Mo began to whimper. "It weren't s'posed ta be like this." He looked at her pleadingly. "Don't kill me, ma'am."

"Do you write?" she asked.

He looked surprised. "My mama taught me some," he replied. "Why?"

"Keep him secure, Jeff, while I fetch a pen and paper." She left the barn. "Pull him up," she said on her return, "and untie his hands."

Jeff followed her directions.

Caroline handed Mo the tablet and pen. She held the bottle of ink. "Now, Mo, you write. Write it all down from the beginning. Don't leave anything out. Mention Judge Wade by name. Write what he told you and what you did. Don't worry about spelling."

He looked defiantly at her. Got to stand up to this woman, he appeared to be thinking.

"It's this, or cold dirt in your face."

That reminded Mo of the simplicity of the matter. Who did he fear most—this coldhearted woman with a knife, or the judge? She was here, speaking words that sent shivers of terror down his spine. The judge wasn't. In view of the circumstances, the choice was simple. He began to write.

Caroline read what he wrote as the pen moved laboriously across the paper. She asked questions and instructed him to elaborate on important points. The sun was well up by the time he finished the two-page confession. She read it aloud and nodded. "Now sign it," she commanded, "and date it." He hastily scribbled his name and the date. "Jeff, bind him again, and pull him up against the wall. Pull him up so his feet are off the ground, then tie his feet down firm with another rope. I don't want him kicking free. Tie a rope around his neck and fasten it to the rafter, just in case he kicks free. I'm going in to see to Victoria." She reached out and grasped Jeff's stout arm and smiled. "When you're finished, you come into the house and have breakfast." She pointed to the straw in the loft. "There will be fresh eggs up there. Bring them when you finish securing this wretched creature."

Caroline dipped a cloth in a pan of water before walking softly to the bedroom. Victoria lay quietly in the bed, her arms at her side. She had awakened, but she just stared at the ceiling. It's my time to be strong, Caroline thought. "How do you feel, honey?" Caroline asked softly. She sat on the edge of the bed and looked sympathetically into her sister's blue eyes.

"Better," Victoria replied in a weak voice supported by a faint nod. "My stomach still hurts some, but it's getting better." She rolled carefully onto her side and looked at her sister. "Porter really does hate you," she said, as if now accepting it for the first time.

"That doesn't matter. You rest now." She placed a wet cloth on her sister's forehead. "If you need me, call. I'll be fixing breakfast for Jeff." She rose, then turned toward her sister. "Victoria," she said. "I want Jeff." She hesitated. "I'll pay for him and his family. You'll have money enough to buy ten good, strong field hands for what I'll give you."

Victoria said nothing at first, just closed her eyes. Her tongue slid across her lips. "We'll talk about it later. May I have some water, please? I'm so dry."

Caroline marched briskly to the kitchen. Her sister had fallen asleep by the time she returned, so she set the glass on the lamp table and tiptoed from the room.

Caroline and Jefferson ate their breakfast in silence. For some unexplainable reason, she was famished. Usually, she ate sparingly. The depression had killed her hunger these last several months. But the depression was gone. In its place she felt many emotions: anger at what her husband had sent those men to do; concern for her sister; a heightened fear of being alone in this isolated place; even delight at being alive. For the first time in more than a year she felt vital, alive, ready to take charge of her life. She felt an exhilarating sense of freedom. She knew she had to plan, but in the end she intended to have her freedom again. Porter faced a terrible risk if she disclosed what she now knew about him. An annulment was only a matter of time. She expected him, of course, to emerge as the offended one. A wife who refused to sleep with her husband was the worst sort of woman. That's what she expected him to assert; the law permitted few other grounds for annulment. What people thought was unimportant to her now. For months she had yearned to leave this place; where she settled no longer mattered. Perhaps Pennsylvania. There was nothing to keep her from going to the farm north of Gettysburg. No one knew her there. If her cousin continued to operate the farm, everyone would benefit.

But first she had to send for a doctor. Victoria needed attention. "Jeff, when you finish your breakfast, take the wagon back to town. And take the other horse with you. There's a doctor in town. His name is Kettle, Dr. Robert Kettle. Tell him Victoria is here and is ill. He'll come. He worked as my father's assistant. Can you remember that?"

Jeff nodded. "Kettle, Dr. Kettle. I'll remember, Miss Caroline."

She patted his cheek. "I know you will. Just hurry, Jeff. Miss Victoria needs his help."

Jeff stuffed the remaining bacon strips into his mouth. "I'll hurry," he said with a nod. "You watch out for that man in the barn. Don't go near him."

"I appreciate your concern, Jeff," she said, forming a wicked sort of smile, just like Victoria's, "but he has more to fear from me than I do from him. Now you go. And Jeff, don't tell anyone about what happened here. That includes the doctor."

Jeff nodded, then hitched up his trousers and walked out the door. Caroline returned to her sister's side.

Late afternoon had arrived before Caroline heard the buggy coming down the road. She rushed to the front porch to see the doctor's buggy moving toward her. Jeff rode out in front.

"What happened?" Dr. Kettle asked as he pulled up on the reins.

"Victoria's in the house. I think she is with child. She received a blow to the stomach. She's very sick." Her tone was firm, an expression of concern to be sure, but a stalwart bearing that had never quite risen to the surface before. "I'll fix some supper while you examine her."

Caroline sipped at the ladle as the doctor entered the kitchen. "She's a very sick woman, Caroline. What happened? It might help to know."

"She was kicked in the stomach. Not so hard, under normal conditions, but conditions aren't normal, are they, Robert?"

"No," he replied as he pulled up a chair. "According to what she told me, I agree with you that she probably is pregnant. One thing is certain, though, she can't be moved. The best thing right now is bed rest. If she's pregnant, she may have a difficult time. Any more trauma may cause a miscarriage."

"She's welcome to stay right where she is, until the baby comes if necessary. I'll send word to her husband."

"That might be best." He sat limply in the chair. "That does smell good, Caroline. I missed lunch."

Caroline smiled. "Some stew and apple pie will solve that. You'll stay here tonight, of course."

"If it's agreeable with you. I told my wife where I'd be. She knows how far it is out here." He sipped at the glass of milk Caroline handed him. "Why do you remain out here alone, Caroline? It's dangerous for a young woman to be this isolated."

She resisted the urge to respond.

"Is that Negro hers?" Kettle asked.

"Yes. He's her bodyguard, so to speak. He traveled with her from Alabama."

"A slave, I assume."

"No. He'll stay here when she leaves." That remained to be settled. "He'll work the farm and I'll pay him fair wages."

The doctor departed early the next morning. Victoria slept most of the day. She seemed more alert when she awoke in late afternoon. Near sundown, Caroline heard another wagon coming down the road. Without looking, she knew it was Porter coming to check on the result of his treachery. He endured uncertainty poorly. She had anticipated his arrival, actually expecting him to arrive earlier.

"Caroline," Porter Wade shouted as he entered the door.

She pressed against the bedroom wall and bit her lip.

"Caroline, are you here?"

Let the bastard think I'm dead for another moment, she thought.

He turned the corner to the bedroom. The smile faded from his lips. Caroline glared at him, the hate in her eyes penetrating his soul. Porter stopped short. The surprise of seeing her alive caused a temporary, immobilizing shock. He looked about the room, then at the parlor and kitchen. No sign of a struggle, he thought. He looked at the bed. And what is Victoria doing here? Something had gone wrong; exactly what was not evident. Perhaps the two men had simply taken their freedom and run. His harsh, threatening demeanor returned. "Why didn't you answer, damn you?"

"I'm concerned about Victoria," she replied coldly, changing the subject. "She has been injured."

"What happened?" he asked, feigning surprise.

"A man kicked her."

He almost hated to ask the question. "What man? I don't see any man."

Just then, at Caroline's prior instruction, Jeff entered the back door.

"Is that him?" Porter yelled, pointing. "What is that nigger doing here?"

"That *nigger* saved my life, Porter, and *he's* not the man who kicked Victoria. The man who kicked her is dead." She turned and walked to her sister's side. "Another man is tied up out in the barn."

"Then you're all right?" he said as he stepped toward her. He tried to take her in his arms, but she pulled away.

"Please, Porter," she said in disgust. "It's far too late for that. That bastard in the barn told me everything." She wanted to pound on her husband, to express her outrage in some lasting, physical way. But then he would win again as he assumed control with his restrained, calculating words. She had to sound cold, more calculating than he. He had to believe how serious she was. He had no experience in dealing with her assertiveness. No one stood up to him anymore. His power had grown too great; his influence reached too far.

Porter's features hardened. "What do you mean?"

"Don't you act surprised," she said with measured words, her brow furrowed in controlled anger. "He told me that you hired him and his partner to kill me. Obviously, they expected to find me alone. They thought it would be so easy, but it wasn't."

Porter looked menacingly at his wife; then his features softened to mock surprise, then to an expression of being wronged. "How dare you think that of me," he replied indignantly. "I'm a man of the law."

She motioned. "Come with me, Porter. Victoria needs her rest." She walked into the kitchen, and Porter followed. Jeff stood at the parlor window looking out. "You think you *are* the law, Porter," she said firmly, "and that's precisely why you expected no trouble in getting away with this." The full impact of her observation caused a momentary jolt. He really believed he was the law! But if that provided his strength, his armor, it also accentuated his weakness. A man clings to power until the last. Porter always calculated the risk of any action before taking it, this she knew. The least of his traits was impulsiveness.

Caroline knew the danger in telling what she knew. She expected him to seriously consider finishing the task his hirelings had botched. But Jeff's presence complicated matters. Killing Jeff would be difficult. Despite his status, the Negro seemed dedicated to his mistress. Caroline expected Porter to consider that before acting. She knew enough about him to know that the more complicated the situation seemed, the more simple the solution he would finally choose. At his core, she knew, he really was a shallow man, with equally shallow intellect. His stern, pious exterior, his controlled demeanor, served only to mask the real Porter Wade. If he was pushed, and pushed hard, she expected him to do what she demanded, if for no other reason than to protect his reputation.

"I don't know what you're talking about," he said emphatically. His voice had a condescending quality made more menacing by an arrogant, chilling glare in his eyes. "You must have gone crazy in your depression." His eyes lit up at the thought. Ever since learning that his wife was alive, he had been struggling to build in his own mind a plausible defense. Now, all of the feigned reactions he had tried vanished as he managed to regain control of his sense of perspective. "You *have* been depressed, you know." He laughed as his confidence grew. "Others have said as much." He shook a finger at her. "I've heard them say it. Crazy people think strange things, do strange things. I see it all the time in my courtroom." He hesitated so as to give the threat time to sink in before he made his final jab. "They even take their own lives when their melancholy overpowers them."

"And people, even judges, who try to kill their wives go to prison." Keep him off balance, she thought. "I doubt you have the will to deal with that, Porter. Think about it," she exclaimed exuberantly, "being locked in with all those men you have sent to prison." She forced a laugh. "You'd be lucky to last a week." Her expression hardened. "I want an annulment, Porter. I want this farm, this house, and everything in it. And I want two thousand dollars in gold. You keep everything else, including your reputation. If not, everyone will know."

"It's the word of a deranged woman against a judge," he sneered. "What chance is there they'll believe you?"

"There's the man in the barn," she answered confidently.

"He's a criminal," Porter replied in an attempt to dismiss the threat. "Who'll believe him? Besides, at the sight of me he'll say nothing." He laughed, but his attempt to sound confident seemed without the normal self-assuredness. "No, Caroline, you have no proof. The law demands proof."

At first she saw the logic in his statement. But a moment's hesitation and her hard-gained initiative would fade. A bluff was better than silence. "Proof, Porter! That's your domain—proving things. All *I* have to do is create the suspicion, set people to talking. *You* must remain above suspicion." She moved briskly to the dresser and opened a drawer. She removed a writing tablet and thrust it in his direction, but kept a tight grip on it. "He wrote it all down, Porter. Unfortunately for you, the man in the barn is less stupid than he looks. Jeff, there, killed the stupid one."

Porter shifted his weight menacingly toward her. Jeff's movement kept the distance constant. Porter relaxed, then his shoulders slumped. She was right. It was common knowledge that he had set the two men free. That was just enough to give the accusations credibility and discredit his defense.

"Victoria's slave is very strong, Porter. He drove a pitchfork all the way through the dead man. Pinned him to the wall. God, what a ghastly sight!" She pointed. "Look at the blood on the bedroom floor if you don't believe me." Her confidence surged as she spoke of the graphic details. She felt intense satisfaction at seeing Porter at her mercy. Lord knows he has had me at his mercy for long enough, she thought.

"If you kill me, Porter, then you must also kill Victoria—and Jeff. You'll need to take care of him first, though. He has this odd, protective urge where his mistress is concerned. His word may have no impact in court, but no one will believe that Victoria is crazy. She'll have a noose around your neck an hour after the trial begins. A hundred people come to mind who'll dance at the thought of your gasping for breath at the end of a rope."

She placed the writing tablet on the counter. "Say whatever you want about me. Say I'm barren. Say that I refused to give you children. It no longer matters. I plan to leave as soon as Victoria is well enough to travel." After hesitating for a moment, she added: "There's also Dr.

Kettle. I summoned him yesterday and he spent the night. He wanted to know what happened, as you might expect." She withheld the fact that she had told the doctor only the barest essentials. She left Porter free to draw his own conclusions.

Porter's shoulders sagged. "What about the man in the barn?" he asked.

"Once this is settled he goes free—or you may kill him if you want. Do you have the guts to do that, Porter—kill a man in cold blood?" She sneered as she shook her head. "I doubt it. You couldn't even kill a woman. That would have been so much easier, you know. Nothing prevented you from saying that a stranger did it. No one would have doubted you. Poor Porter, the grieving widower who lost his wife to robbers. How bad you must have felt for leaving me here all alone. Everyone would have felt so sorry for you as the guilt and regrets poured out." She thought for a moment, then turned and looked at the writing pad. "On second thought, I want you to write something at the end of that man's statement. I want you to say you agree with everything he wrote, that every word is true."

"You're crazy if you think I'll do that."

"You'll do it, Porter—think of the alternative if you don't. I'll give you the confession, once the annulment is confirmed. I have more to gain with you free than if you go to prison in disgrace." She retrieved the tablet and handed it to him. "Jeff will stand by you while you write it down. Just write that the statement is true and accurate, sign your name, and date it. Then you're free to leave. Send word when the papers are in order and the deed has been signed over to me. I'll see that this confession reaches you after all is settled."

It had all been too much. The surprise of finding Caroline alive had overwhelmed him, knocked him off stride. She had never let the advantage slip away, even when he challenged her sanity. She had had the time to plan each move, each response, to look into his mind and anticipate his responses. He had grown accustomed to a meek, sniveling female. He now faced a woman radically transformed from the one he had grown to despise. He suddenly felt attracted to her, but such thoughts were ridiculous, he knew. Something in her bearing conveyed resolve, a belief that she had all the power. He had to settle this now, before she changed her mind. Besides, what choice did he have? He stood no physical chance at all against the Negro. Such a man could kill another without conscience, he believed. He, on the other hand, was civilized. Only in desperation had he devised his plan. It was obvious to anyone who cared to look that Caroline was not a proper wife for a man of destiny. He needed someone more refined, more befitting his lofty station. In his eyes that provided the moral justification. But he suspected that others would think more harshly of the act.

He looked at her and shuddered. Signing such a statement placed his life and reputation in the hands of a woman who now loathed him. Would she decide, upon reflection, that she hated him enough to give up the farm and money for the satisfaction of sending him to prison? He had no way of knowing. He was unsure of anything this woman might do now.

He snatched the writing pad, flipped open the cover, and read the statement. He had misjudged Mo. More flickered behind those dull eyes than had been evident. It appeared to be a totally condemning confession, and Porter's name had been included six times. The bizarre nature of the act ruled out any possibility of fabrication, at least by Mo. People were certain to see a more conniving force behind the act. Yes, he had to sign—and hope.

Caroline handed him a pen and set the bottle of ink on the table. He placed the tablet on the table and sighed as he let his body settle into the chair. Was he thinking rationally? He felt so vulnerable, more than ever before in his life. He dipped the pen and began to write the postscript confirming the truth of the statement, then he signed it. He blew on the last line before handing the tablet to his wife.

She read his statement. Such a beautiful hand, she thought, and such cruel words. She nodded. "Now, Porter, get out of my sight. I know you'll find a way to resolve this matter without further involving me. Just send someone with the legal papers. I never want to see you again."

Porter clenched his fists and sighed, then lifted his weary frame from the chair. "May I take something to eat?" he asked.

"Take whatever you want, then go. I packed your things in a cloth sack in your room. There will be no need for you to return."

CHAPTER 3

....

From the diary of Caroline Wade:

August 6, 1838
A full week has passed since the dreadful events of July 30. Doctor Kettle came by on his rounds to-day and spent thirty minutes examining Victoria. He smiled as he left her room, and the expression elicited a faint shriek of joy from me. The danger is passed, but he recommends against her traveling any great distance before the baby arrives. Going back to Alabama is out of the question! I am delighted that she must remain here for the next eight months or more. I doubt she shares my enthusiasm, but she will do nothing to endanger the child; she wants this child as much as life itself.
After Dr. Kettle attended to business, he handed me a package wrapped in brown butcher paper. It contained two legal documents and a letter. The first document I examined was the order of annulment that became effective upon my signature. My temper was at the boiling point by the time I finished reading it. As expected, I had to agree that I had never "properly" consummated our marriage, as evidenced by my inability to give Porter a child. The bastard! It was he who refused to consider children. Oh well. My anger passed, and I signed it with delight.
The second document was the deed to this land and house. In addition, there was a small leather pouch stuffed full of double eagle coins. A hundred to be exact. The letter explained everything, and also demanded the document that must by now be a source of great anguish for Porter. Porter mentioned nothing of

the man still trussed securely to the barn wall. I suppose I'll free him with a warning to depart the state before Porter sends the law after him.

I gave Dr. Kettle one of the coins. He appeared momentarily shocked, but he soon recovered. He promised to be by every other week, but I'm to send word if problems arise. I wrapped and bound the confession in the same brown paper and gave it to Dr. Kettle to deliver to Porter. Then I forced him to swear on pain of Hell never to reveal what I was about to tell him. I told him everything. He demanded that I make my story known. I think he might have killed Porter had the bastard been here. In the end, however, he agreed to honor his pledge.

It is over.

And I am free! My freedom can be no more lonely than my marriage was. But my departure will be delayed. I am needed. It feels so good to be needed again. Spring will be soon enough. But that I could join Victoria in preparation for my own blessed event. Alas, it is not to be.

January 1, 1839

Doctor Kettle made the long trip out to-day. He is concerned. Victoria has been confined to bed for three weeks but has less energy each day. Doctor Kettle fears that when the time comes it will take too long to fetch him. I have agreed to wrap Victoria warmly and transport her to our house in town. Jeff left with the doctor to cut firewood and start the fire. As soon as he returns we will be leaving this place—forever. There will be no tears from me. I will have to leave my bed. Will it be here if I send someone for it in the spring? It's only a bed. Victoria's welfare is all I live for.

Doctor Kettle is convinced that Victoria will have twins—or triplets. She is so LARGE. This only adds to the worry. Will she survive a difficult delivery? Doctor Kettle ignored my question when I put it to him. He sounded just like Father. I'm a doctor, not God, he used to say. Still, when Father believed there was minimum danger, he said so.

There has been a bright spot. Victoria agreed that Jefferson could stay here when she leaves. She will direct his woman to come to Illinois and bring her children. I will tell Jefferson later, when I find the right moment.

January 4, 1839

We arrived at our house in Harrisburg late this afternoon. Victoria suffered greatly from the cold and unending bumping of the wagon. Jeff did as much as possible to make the ride smooth, but the snow hid the ruts, and the ground was so frozen the road might as well have been solid rock. Fortunately, Jeff had chopped the wood and lit the stove. The house was still quite warm.

Now we must wait. Victoria is so large that walking more than a few steps is impossible. I fear for her life. She is so pale and weak; just eating takes all her strength. Getting up to respond to nature's call is nearly impossible. Doctor Kettle says the babies will come in about two months. I think sooner.

....

Caroline stumbled in the dark toward the sound of her sister's moans. "Victoria, are you all right?" She squeezed her ailing sister's hand. "Your hand is so cold."

"No," Victoria responded weakly. "I am not all right. I think it's time. Send for Dr. Kettle."

Victoria's scream shattered the darkness as Caroline frantically shook Jefferson from a deep sleep. "Jefferson, wake up. Miss Victoria is ready to give birth. Run and fetch the doctor. Tell him to hurry."

Jeff rubbed his eyes.

Letting a Negro sleep in the house with two white women had set tongues to wagging. Porter Wade had done nothing to ease their plight. Instead he had slandered them at every opportunity. The malicious extent of the gossip had reached Caroline's ears only a week earlier. Doctor Kettle informed her what people were saying—fear that the baby might be black caused Victoria to delay her return to her husband. Caroline kept the rumor to herself.

"I'll hurry right along, Miss Caroline." Jefferson pulled on his boots and fastened his suspenders. A cold wind howled through the opening as he unlatched the door and disappeared into the night.

"They's in the bedroom," Jeff said as he slammed the door upon returning. Caroline moved toward them.

"How long between pains?" Dr. Kettle asked as he removed his coat.

"They're close, Doctor," Caroline replied, wringing out a cloth in the small bowl she carried. "Barely over a minute, I'd guess."

The doctor blew on his hands. "Well, let me have a look." He placed his bag on the bed. "Fetch some water."

"Right away, Doctor." Caroline rushed to the kitchen.

Doctor Kettle pulled back the comforter. A large, wet circle confirmed that Victoria's water had broken. He lifted her nightshirt. Victoria flinched at the touch of his cold hand. "It won't be long," he said softly.

"Is there anything I can do, Robert?" Caroline asked. She knew what to expect. She had assisted in several deliveries during the two years before her father's death. But nothing such as this. This was her twin sister, and she had never assisted with the delivery of twins.

"A prayer won't hurt. Bring some clean rags."

Caroline rushed to the linen closet and withdrew a sheet. Victoria screamed and Caroline ran back to her side.

"It's about time," the doctor said. He looked with concern at the thrashing pregnant woman. "Do you hear me, Victoria?"

She nodded.

"Press down with the next pain," he instructed. "I know it will be difficult, but you have to help."

Victoria's breathing grew rapid and shallow, her skin turned even more ashen, and her eyes glazed from the pain. Beads of sweat sprinkled her forehead. She screamed as the pain became more intense.

"Push, Victoria," the doctor directed. The crown of a small head protruded slowly through the opening. "Push hard."

She strained; the blood drained from her face. The baby's head slid out, and with it a rush of thin red liquid showered the doctor's hands. "Soak a cloth in the water and hand it to me," he said to Caroline. "Wring it out first."

Caroline did as instructed. "Is she all right?" Caroline asked, concern furrowing her brow.

"We must take it one step at a time, Caroline. Here comes the baby." He hooked a finger under each of the infant's tiny arms. "It's a boy." He hesitated. "He looks perfect." He snipped and tied the umbilical cord before handing the child to Caroline.

Her worried frown changed to a smile as she cradled the squirming, blood-covered infant. It began to cry. "He's beautiful," she said, "but so tiny."

"Small size is common with twins," said the doctor. The baby yelled louder. "He certainly has good lungs," Dr. Kettle added with a smile.

"That's a good sign. Multiple-birth babies often have breathing problems."

Thirty minutes passed before the birth of the second child. A third emerged ten minutes later. Caroline noticed the doctor's concerned expression as the third infant's head poked into view. "Is there a problem?" she asked.

"It's too soon to say," Dr. Kettle replied. "Let's wait until you clean him up." The second child, a girl, had no apparent problems. The third, a male, smaller than the other two infants, had a purple birthmark that ran from the top of his head to behind the right ear. The dark patch had an irregular shape, bulging to a width of two inches at the middle, then fading to normal skin color at the hairline. The baby remained quiet at first, but alert. Doctor Kettle swatted the infant's rump and it began to cry. He released a long sigh. "That's it, young man," he said as he smiled at the new mother. "Two boys and a girl. Triplets. That's a first for me."

"For me, too," Victoria replied weakly. Her pallid lips formed a faint smile.

"You'll need to stay in bed for a while," the doctor said. "You should be fine in a week."

"I have three babies to care for," Victoria whispered.

"Caroline will do just fine until you're up and about. We'll have to talk when you've had some rest."

Victoria nodded faintly, then turned her head sideways and drifted into sleep.

Caroline placed the second male between the two infants already lying at the foot of the bed. "Aren't they beautiful, Robert. Will the birthmark be a problem?"

"Not for him," he said firmly, "but I can't speak for others. You know how people are about these things." He motioned for Caroline to follow him into the parlor. "The birthmark isn't what bothers me," he said in a whisper. "Her having three infants to feed and care for is the real concern. Your sister is very weak. Full recovery will be slow. I doubt she'll be able to provide enough nourishment for three infants. In fact, I'm certain of it."

"What are you suggesting, Doctor?"

"I'm suggesting your sister may be able to feed two infants, but if she tries to feed three, all will be in danger. Those infants are quite small. Their survival depends on proper nourishment."

Caroline appeared puzzled. "What choice is there?" She thought for a moment, trying to interpret the comment. "My God. Are you suggesting she consider giving away one of her children?"

"Hardly." He pressed tobacco into his pipe and lit it. "I know a woman just across the county line. She's very poor and has no man. Her new baby died a few days back. She still has milk."

"Oh, Robert, I doubt Victoria will agree to that."

"She has no choice." He returned to the bedroom and packed his bag. "That's all there is to do for now. I'll be back in the afternoon to discuss the wet nurse. Your job is to convince her it's the best thing to do. Keep her warm and try to give her some liquid when she wakes up."

Caroline nodded, but only in recognition that the doctor had stopped talking. What will Victoria think, she wondered, when told she must give one of her new babies to a stranger, however temporary the arrangement may be. For the present, consideration of the alternatives must wait. Victoria lacked the energy even to care for herself. Her taking care of the triplets remained out of the question for at least several days. "What do I do?" Caroline asked the doctor.

"What do you do, Caroline? You take care of the infants. Keep them warm and out of drafts. Place a few drops of lukewarm water on their lips to keep them moist. When Victoria regains her strength—she'll probably be up to it by evening—have her try to feed them to start the milk flowing. What milk she provides will be enough to sustain them for the present. If there's any change, such as breathing problems, send for me immediately." Caroline appeared bewildered. "Are you going to help me with this?" the doctor asked.

She had felt herself slipping ever since the moment her sister cried out in the darkness. The hesitation, the uncertainty, the willingness to let fear grip her mind—it all had returned with its debilitating dominance over her life. She had never felt such pride as when she confronted her husband and forced him to bend to her will. She knew she had the strength—that deeply instilled ability to respond to a crisis—but that had been eight months ago, and only once. Then, a more powerful emotion—hate—had pushed fear aside. Now that exhilaration had faded from her consciousness. She had no idea where to find it again.

Was love a powerful enough emotion? Lying before her, illuminated by the dim light of the lamp, were the only people who gave her life meaning. But life had settled down to a dull routine, and now depression and fear filled the void left by faded courage. The old temptation, to do nothing rather than to fail, struggled to overpower her resistance. Yet her sister needed her, now more than ever. And what about the three helpless, squirming infants? They needed her most of all. If courage had prevailed once, then perhaps again, but in a different form—this time to help someone besides herself.

The small female infant began to cry. Caroline smiled to herself as she lifted the squirming ball of flesh. The child's wailing stopped as she began to suck with the instinctive sense that nourishment was near.

Caroline sighed, then faintly nodded. "Leave us, Robert," she said. "We'll be fine."

The doctor squeezed her shoulder lightly, retrieved his bag, and left the house.

"Jeff," Caroline said loudly as she heard the door close, "there's a chill in the house. Put some more wood in the stove."

"Yas'm, Missy Caroline, it does seem a mite chilled in here."

Caroline had little time to think about her apprehension. If one of the infants stopped crying, another began. Victoria woke up at about noon, but her senses persisted in a fog. "Caroline," she said with a wavering voice as her mind cleared.

"Finally awake, huh," Caroline replied cheerfully. "Be there in a moment." She entered the room balancing a small tray with a bowl and a glass of milk. The smell of broth increased Victoria's alertness. She inhaled deeply. "That smells good," she said.

"It's time to eat, big sister," Caroline said firmly. It had been years since she had referred to Victoria that way. The term hardly applied but, in truth, Victoria always acted the part. "You're eating for four now."

"Four?" She seemed genuinely surprised.

"Don't you remember. You gave birth to triplets. A beautiful girl and two handsome boys."

"I remember two," Victoria replied. "I remember nothing about a third."

"Well, if you'll raise yourself a bit, you'll see the living, wiggling proof." Caroline placed the tray on the dresser.

Victoria pushed against her elbows and lifted her head. There, at the foot of the bed, hemmed in by three chairs pressed against the mattress, lay the three squirming infants. Her face lit up the room. "They're so small," she said. She looked for a moment. "Oh, Caroline, hand me one."

Caroline lifted the middle infant and laid him beside the new mother. Victoria's smile faded. "There's something wrong with its head," she said.

"It's nothing to be worried about," Caroline said with a shrug. "Robert says the birthmark won't even be noticeable when his dark hair grows out." He hadn't said so, but she had concluded as much for herself.

Victoria looked at the child, then at her sister. "You don't understand. Henry will never accept it as his own." Tears rolled down her cheek as she examined the child. "A neighbor had a child with a large birthmark on its back. Henry said it was cursed by the devil and should have its head crushed on a rock."

Caroline placed her hands on her hips. "Well, it seems to me, Victoria Thornton, that we married ourselves a strange pair of men. How is it possible for anyone to say such a thing about a baby?"

Victoria let her head sink back to the pillow, then she wiped away a tear with her sleeve. "He's a good man, Caroline. Things are just different in the South. People have some strange ideas down there."

"Strange hardly seems the word for it. But be that as it may, you have a more immediate problem."

Anxiety filled Victoria's eyes.

"Robert says you'll be unable to feed all three children." She tried to sound casual. "He says there's a woman in the next county whose baby died. He thinks you must consider a wet nurse."

"I could never do that!" Victoria exclaimed. "How could I give my child to a stranger?"

"That's what I told him you'd say," Caroline replied. She lifted the naked infant. "See how small he is? I doubt he weighs four pounds. If he's to have any chance at all, he must receive nourishment, as much as the others." She looked sternly at her sister. "After all, Victoria, you don't have three teats."

Victoria laughed. "Don't say things like that. Laughing makes me hurt."

"Milk is milk, Victoria," Caroline said, placing the child in the cradle of Victoria's arm. "We can bring the woman here to live with us. She has no husband."

Victoria closed her eyes. "The thought of my baby nursing at another woman's breast . . ." She covered her eyes with her free arm. "Why is this happening to me?"

"Oh, stop your sniveling. I'd give anything for a child, and you have three."

Victoria lifted her arm from her eyes and looked at her sister. Caroline had seen that look before, many times. She knew that her sister's mind was churning, pondering some great design for the world. What was she thinking?

"How long did Robert say it would be before I can travel?" Victoria asked.

"He didn't say. He says you'll be up and around in a few days." Time enough later for the details. She hesitated. "What are you thinking, Victoria?"

"Oh, nothing important," Victoria replied.

"Well, big sister, no broth for you until you tell me."

Victoria turned and looked at the dark spot on the infant's head. "You won't hate me, will you?"

"Hate you? For heaven's sake, what could you say to make me hate you?"

"I want you to take this child for your own." She said it so fast the words flowed together.

Caroline's mouth gaped. "My God, Victoria! What could possess you to give up one of these babies?"

"I told you what Henry said. I know him. He'll never accept this child. He will hate him. I'd rather die than endure that."

Caroline walked listlessly to the window. She pulled her arms across her breasts as she stared at the stark winter landscape. Her nose twitched as she sniffed. She looked at her sister, then back out at the frozen landscape. Flakes of snow swirled in the wind. Her thoughts ran wild. She wanted a child more than anything in life. Who will ever know, after all, that the child isn't mine? she thought. She planned to leave here, leave the state, as soon as Victoria was strong enough to travel home. It wasn't as though having a baby raised possibility of scandal. Her marriage provided legitimacy. Besides, having a baby, after what Porter had recorded in the annulment document, provided a wry, ironic twist. She turned again to her sister. "I think you must have a fever, Victoria. Otherwise, you'd never suggest such a thing."

"It's the only way, Caroline," she insisted. "Think about it for a moment. If the child looks like me, he'll also look like you. Only Robert knows. Once we leave this place, who'll ever find out?"

"Jeff knows," Caroline said.

"Jeff will die before revealing my secret. But that doesn't matter. He'll be staying with you. My husband will never know. And there's another side to this: I can't stay here until the baby is weaned. Henry's last letter said he expects me home as soon as I'm strong enough to travel. The wet nurse can stay with you."

Caroline slid a chair to the head of the bed; then she returned to the dresser and picked up the bowl of soup. She sat by her sister's side, filled the spoon with broth, and blew on it. "Here, try this." She extended the spoon full of broth. Victoria sipped the liquid into her mouth. They repeated the process until the bowl was empty, then Caroline set it on the floor. She leaned close to her sister. "Victoria, you know how much I want a baby. If I agree to this I'll never give him up, even if you demand I do it."

"I know," Victoria replied with a smile. "It's that knowledge that sustains me."

CHAPTER 4

· · · · · · · · · · · · · ·

From the diary of Caroline Wade:

May 6, 1839

Jessy, Victoria's husband's younger brother, arrived yesterday. Henry sent him to fetch Victoria home to Alabama. As a precaution, Mary, the wet nurse, has moved in with Dr. Kettle until they leave. The babies have thrived. I love Samuel so. I feel as if he really is mine. All we have told Mary is that she will continue to nurse the baby until I take him to his mother. She seems to accept this. She is a dull creature. Robert has sworn to keep our secret.

I plan to leave for Pennsylvania as soon as possible. Victoria leaves for Alabama tomorrow. She is as good as new. It seems impossible that she could leave her son behind, but she seems content with the decision. She even refers to him as "your son." The birthmark is still there, but it seems to have faded a bit. I suppose that's my imagination, but it really doesn't matter. No one will ever know, once his hair grows out. I am so happy, yet I am sad for Victoria. I know I must never travel to Alabama with Samuel. Samuel and Simon look exactly alike. That they are twin brothers is obvious. Does this mean I will never see Victoria again? I pray to God that I am wrong, but Pennsylvania is so far away.

Jeff is back in high stride. As Victoria instructed, Henry sent Jeff's woman and children. Jeff never complained once about being away from them. Being a slave takes the vigor from people, unless they are provoked. Within minutes of her arrival, they sneaked off to the barn together. I intend to free them, legally, as soon as Victoria departs. I hope they will stay with me, but I have sworn to let them decide. Slavery is a curse on this land. Victoria and I will forever disagree on that point. Somehow, in some way, this blight must end. I fear I will die before that day. Perhaps my son will live to see it end. It is my solemn vow to raise him to hate that cursed institution.

July 1, 1839

I concluded the sale of the farm today. It brought more than expected—$2,400—and that, added to my half of the sale price of the house, provides me with nearly $12,000 with which to begin my new life in Pennsylvania. I am a dunce when it comes to money matters, but I understand it is a fair-sized fortune.

Samuel is thriving, so I have decided to leave for Pennsylvania next week. With an infant to care for, I expect the journey to be long. Darling—that is what Mary, the wet nurse, insists I call her now—will go with me for passage and $300. It seems little enough to pay for her lifesaving sustenance for Samuel, but it is all she asks. I suppose that seems a fortune to her. She must fend for herself once Samuel is weaned. She's a strange one. I read her a story about a girl named Judy. Judy's mother always called her Darling Judy. Mary liked the sound of it, so it's Darling now. I have tried to teach her to read, but it seems beyond her. I gave her the book. She keeps it under her pillow at night.

September 12, 1839

I think I shall never set foot in a stage again! The baby was sick for most of the journey. We had to delay our trip twice along the way to rest, but we finally arrived in Gettysburg at noon today. Two of the stage lines refused to transport Jefferson and his family, so we had to travel by wagon part of the way in order to make connections. After a day or so of rest, I shall rent a buggy for the trip to the farm. I wrote Cousin Joseph to expect us, but who can guess if the letter ever arrived. Samuel is crying. I must go.

December 8, 1839

Darling Tuttle took her leave of us today. I wonder if she will make it to Boston, where she says she is going to make her fortune.

I gave her the $300 last week. She borrowed my buggy for a trip to Gettysburg the next day and indulged herself on a shopping spree. Half the money is already spent. The town is small. How she found enough places there to spend that much money is beyond me. She will, however, be the best-dressed pauper in Boston.

I fear I have done something stupid. An old friend of Cousin Joseph's rode by the farm two weeks ago on his way to Philadelphia. The man, Francis Rodman, has this idea for mass producing shoes—says he knows how to make thirty pairs a day—but that he lacks enough money to buy all of the equipment. He had no idea I had any money, and seemed genuinely amazed when I offered to finance the equipment for a third share of the business. I only hope I will see some of my $3,000 again. He is off to Philadelphia to order the equipment from England and establish the business. He seems honest and bright enough.

The house is nearly finished. The first of the furniture arrived this morning. I will be out of these cramped quarters by Christmas. Jefferson is a good carpenter. In fact, I haven't found much he can't do, except read. I shall work on that this winter. I am down to less than $8,000 now, but the farm is large enough to support us all if properly managed. Cousin Joseph seems less than capable, so I have assumed the responsibility of managing the farm myself.

Life has promise.

July 18, 1845

I received my first profit from the shoe factory today: $1,840. These first five years, my partner, Francis, and I have agreed that he should take enough money to support himself and his family and put the profits back into expanding the business. Since I have taken nothing, my share is now up to 43 percent. A profit of $1,840 for the first six months of this year is more than I expected. If the business continues to prosper, I shall have my investment back, with a small profit, by the end of the year. Francis reports that the business is worth more than $20,000 now. There are more orders than we have the capacity to fill. It seems I was wise to trust this man.

September 9, 1850

The Chicago factory goes into production next month. It required everything we scraped together, but we now have the most mod-

ern shoe factory in the country. It never occurred to me that so many people needed shoes. Last year we turned down an offer of $100,000 for the Philadelphia factory, and it's a good thing. We sold a 40 percent share for $140,000 in March. I own 60 percent of the Chicago factory. That, combined with my remaining 30 percent share in the Philadelphia factory and the farm, increases my net worth to more than $200,000. I'm down to less than $2,000 in the bank, but now that I own all of the farm I feel secure enough.

Jefferson owns more than two hundred acres, but he refuses to leave me. He virtually runs the whole operation now that I have to travel so much looking after the shoe business. Samuel is forever telling me that Jefferson says this and Jefferson says that.

October 15, 1860

Today, a great sadness entered our lives. Jefferson died from some illness that the doctor never quite identified. Jeff was such a help to me over the years. He ran the farm, supervising six white hands, for the past twelve years. The patches of land I gave him as bonuses over the years amounted to more than two hundred acres, and he purchased more than four hundred more, so Molly has security. She will stay on—I couldn't make do without her. All of her children except Washington have grown up and left, so I am her family. Washington will stay on to help with the farm. I shall miss Jefferson.

War cries grow more shrill each day. With Samuel in his last year at West Point, I cannot help but hope that all this talk of war is just that, but I fear otherwise. There is no point of compromise. Southern senators are adamant on the issue of slave state expansion, and the South knows that curtailing slavery in the West means the beginning of the end of slavery everywhere. The rumor is that if Mr. Lincoln is elected president, most Southern states will leave the Union. As much as I hate the thought of war, I'd vote for Mr. Lincoln if I could.

I still haven't decided if I'll go to Alabama to visit Victoria. I cannot delay making a decision past tomorrow.

October 16, 1860

I can't believe it! I received the financial statement to-day. The combined value of our holdings in the four shoe factories is more than $800,000, and I own 51 percent. Production reached six thousand pairs a day last month, but the profit margin on each pair is down. The country is growing so fast with all the immigrants coming over. Francis says we could sell ten thousand pairs a day if we had the capacity. He thinks we should expand.

I feel better. I sent Darling a bank draft for $1,000 this morning. I have felt so ashamed ever since I learned that she was working in the Boston factory. I know a seamstress's salary, and her with five children to support!

I'm going to Alabama!

PART TWO

....

Days of Thunder and Fire

CHAPTER 5

....

As she stepped from the train to the platform, Caroline Wade's senses rebelled. Despite the hot, muggy air, a chill ran down her spine.

Everywhere she looked, well-dressed white people stood talking and laughing. They might as well have been at a park picnic on a lazy Sunday afternoon in Philadelphia. But their gaity seemed so out of place within the larger, more perverse image, the part that ripped at her soul.

Black servants responded mechanically to the slightest gesture, many at a trot, always with unwavering obedience. The poorly dressed white men mostly sat, some whittling, some complaining about the weather, but generally doing nothing. At the corner of the station house, two white boys of about seven poked sticks at a terrified Negro boy who looked twice their age. Near the station door, a teenaged white girl, dressed in an expensive hooped dress and ruffled bonnet, scolded a wrinkled, white-haired old Negress for dropping one of three pieces of luggage she struggled to bear. Just beyond the platform a young Negro dressed in nothing but a grimy pair of trousers stood next to a small tree. A thick steel ring held in place by a crude lock circled his neck. A heavy chain had been riveted to the back of the ring. The absent owner had looped the chain around the tree and fastened it with another lock through a link near its point of origin.

Caroline had felt her uneasiness building since crossing the border into Alabama. A sense of shameful perversion filled the air. Everything in combination generated a sense of foreboding. At each stop along the way to Birmingham, when she had left the train to stretch her legs, the feeling grew stronger. Now the worst of what she had imagined took form as she strained to assimilate the essence of this hostile society, a society that seemed dedicated to no other task so much as straining against civilized decency.

But there was more. Once she let her mind move beyond the initial shock, she realized that everyone but her seemed at peace with the corruption, or at least accepted the gnarled wickedness of one element of society exercising total supremacy over another. The evidence appeared everywhere, tightly woven into the societal fabric, confirmed by every expression and gesture.

Only after prolonged vacillation had she decided to travel all this way from Gettysburg. With the rhetoric of war dominating every conversation, her friends had advised her to stay home. Still, if war was coming, she had concluded, it might soon become impossible to correspond with Victoria. She even allowed herself to consider the ironic possibility that her sister might become a foreigner, so to speak, if Southern threats progressed to armed conflict. During the long, uncomfortable ride south, she had spent many hours wondering what had occurred in her nation that death should become preferable to compromise. Now, standing on the platform, she at last realized that she had discovered at least part of the answer.

More than twenty years had passed since the sisters said their last, sad good-bye. Caroline ached to hold Victoria again, to talk with her in an effort to bridge the gap of time that had launched them in such dissimilar directions. There had been letters, many of them, but the secret they shared kept them from ever mentioning the event that bound them with an intensity rivaling their special origin. There remained the ever-present risk of Henry Thornton discovering the terrible truth that his wife had given one of his children—one of his sons—to her twin sister.

The journey south had spanned five long days. Caroline had arrived in Richmond to discover that her connecting train had departed an hour earlier. A forty-hour layover followed. Although a patchwork of railroads now crisscrossed the nation tying east to west, moving from north to south posed a difficult challenge. The train stopped at every backwater town along the way. A variety of equipment failures further extended the delay.

Bad weather, or rather the lack of it, finally persuaded her to risk the journey. Earlier, following a late September snow, she had concluded that the journey would be too stressful. Then, a mild and dry

Indian summer prompted reconsideration. Even more than the mild weather, however, a letter from Samuel had ended the wavering. He wrote that discourse among his classmates grew more strident each day. Some Southern cadets openly expressed a willingness to leave the Academy, even before graduation, if Abraham Lincoln prevailed in the November election. If Caroline intended to make the journey, she knew she must act soon, before winter came, before war engulfed the nation.

At 5:00 P.M. on October 18, 1860, she made the long step onto the broad, brick platform. Before she could retrieve her luggage, three ladies glared and edged away from her, as if sensing her enmity. Until that moment she had spoken not a word.

Is something wrong with me? she asked herself. She examined her attire and brushed a finger across her teeth. Several wrinkles, perhaps, but acceptable after hours of travel. A fourth lady walked up to a man exiting the train. He, too, had suffered the agony of the past two days of foul-smelling air and numbing fatigue.

"Have you heard?" the woman asked the man whom Caroline presumed to be her husband.

"Heard what?" he asked in a grumbling tone.

"About what happened in Boston on the anniversary of the raid of that devil John Brown," she replied fretfully.

"No," he said, but his interest seemed elevated a notch. "We've hardly been off this damnable train since leaving Richmond two days ago."

"There was marching in the streets, singing Brown's praises and calling on all slaves to rise up and kill their masters. If you ask me, Col. Robert E. Lee should have marched north from Harper's Ferry and cleaned the abolitionists out of Boston, too."

Only the most secluded hermit had never heard of John Brown and his infamous raid on Harper's Ferry just over a year before. Fewer people knew of Col. Robert E. Lee, the army officer who captured Brown. Caroline remembered Samuel mentioning the colonel in a letter. The cadets considered him to be the best soldier in the army. Brown's fame had derived from less noble accomplishments. His rampage in Kansas, in the wake of the Lawrence raid, had been front-page news a few years back. Brown had hacked five men to death, and in the wake of his crime "Bleeding Kansas" had become the catalyst for the growing discord between North and South.

The man turned and glared at Caroline. "You're from up north, aren't you?" She had simply mentioned in passing, when they had met briefly at the water bucket, her preference for the cooler climate in Pennsylvania.

She hesitated. She was unaccustomed to being confronted by strange men, especially in a manner so openly hostile. Several other people standing nearby reacted to the sharp tone of the question by stopping to listen. She felt like an enemy in their midst. "I have come down from Gettysburg, Pennsylvania," she replied softly, "to visit my sister, Victoria Thornton. Do you know her?"

The tension seemed to ease. The woman carefully examined Caroline's features. The others whispered among themselves.

"Senator Henry Thornton's wife?" asked the man.

The reference surprised Caroline. Victoria had never mentioned Henry's being a senator. She knew hardly anything about Henry Thornton. Victoria wrote of him only in passing, mostly when his activities involved her directly. But how many Henry Thorntons could there be? "The same," Caroline replied.

"I've been in Victoria's company several times," the woman replied. Caroline concluded the woman intended that the haughty expression added something to the acknowledgment, but exactly what eluded her. "Come to think of it, you do look just like her. A bit skinnier, but otherwise just the same."

Caroline smiled. "We're twins."

"Well," said the man, "it seems to me that she should choose her kin with more care. Let's go, Martha." He snatched his bag and ushered the woman toward the station house.

Caroline felt totally alone in a hostile land. Never had she experienced such rudeness, and for nothing other than where she lived! What would they think if they knew her views on slavery? She resisted the impulse to buy a ticket and return home. She had come so far. Where is Victoria? she thought. She answered my telegram saying she planned to meet me on the platform. Caroline looked around. A hundred people were moving about, but none she recognized. She glanced toward the sun. Dusk was less than an hour away. Standing here drawing attention to herself was ridiculous. But Victoria might never find me if I leave, she thought. She struggled to lift the three pieces of luggage the porter placed beside her, then walked to the ticket window.

"Pardon me," she said.

"Ya'll is from up north," he said.

Caroline flinched. She felt as though a mark on her forehead revealed her source.

"It's your accent," he said. "Ya have a Northern accent." He returned to his task of checking names on a list.

"Pardon me," she said, this time with more force. The man looked up. "I seem to have been forgotten. My sister, Victoria Thornton—have you heard of her?—seems to have been delayed. I expected her to meet me here. Has there been a message, perhaps?"

"No message," he replied.

"Then may I leave a message?"

"If you like."

"Is there a hotel near here?"

"Down the street behind the station house, three blocks on the right."

"If my sister or anyone else should ask about me, will you reply that I am at that hotel?"

"Ya'll got a name?"

"Caroline Wade. Mrs. Thornton is my twin sister. We are identical."

"Name's all I need to know. I'll tell her where ya'll are, if she happens to ask."

Southern hospitality, indeed! Caroline thought disgustedly. She walked to the far side of the station house and gasped at what she saw next. A wagon rolled briskly down the road. Chained behind it, one end of the chain fastened to a hook on the tailgate, were five Negroes. Steel rings, hardly large enough to fit around a man's neck without choking him, linked the men to the chain at five-foot intervals. The men had to trot to keep pace, but with measured tempo lest they stumble over each other's feet. They coughed as they tried to shield their breathing from the dust kicked up by the wagon.

The man at the end of the chain had a pant leg torn away at the hip. Caroline gasped again at the sight of a raw, bloody gash extending down his leg. She wanted to cry out, to protest this abomination. She let her luggage drop as an image flashed through her mind. She imagined Jefferson being dragged that way. An uncontrollable anguish welled up within her. "Stop!" she yelled as she ran into the street. "For God's sake, stop."

The driver appeared startled by the vehemence of the onrushing woman. He pulled on the reins. "Whoa, horse." He jerked on the brake handle. The wagon wheels locked.

Caroline ran to the wounded black man. He attempted to back away as she approached, but the chain restricted his movement. She knelt and touched his leg. "My God!" she exclaimed. "It's cut nearly to the bone."

"What in Sam hell ya'll doin' lady?" yelled the driver. "Ya'll get away from my niggers."

"This is a man," she screamed in reply. "You'll kill him making him run like that." A small stream of blood stained the dirt.

The driver jumped to the ground. "So what?" he said as he approached her. "He's my property to do with as I like."

Caroline lifted her dress. She pulled the top petticoat to her teeth and bit the hem to make a small tear; then she ripped the fringe off all the way around. Holding an end in place, she layered the cloth around the slave's leg several times before tying it off at the ankle. The white cloth immediately turned red from the oozing blood. As she finished, the driver leaned down and grabbed her shoulder. She instinctively swung her right hand upward. The blow made forceful contact with the side of his face. Startled by the suddenness of the attack, the man recoiled. She rose and hit him again with her left hand. "How dare you touch me!" she exclaimed defiantly.

"Caroline?"

Caroline turned to the sound. Victoria ran toward her.

"What are you doing?" Victoria cried out.

"I only meant to tend this man's wound—no less than people in Pennsylvania would do for a stray dog—when this man accosted me."

"You mustn't do that," Victoria said.

"As God is my witness," Caroline replied, "I can do nothing else."

"Does this woman belong to ya'll?" the driver asked Victoria.

Caroline's wrath exploded as she struck the man again. "I belong to no one, you bastard." He staggered back. She kicked at him, but he had moved beyond reach.

"Caroline, stop it!" Victoria admonished. "This isn't Pennsylvania."

"This is America," Caroline screamed in her sister's face.

"Yankee bitch!" the driver spat at his antagonist. "Someone needs to take a whip to your backside and teach ya'll some manners."

Henry Thornton had approached unnoticed. He moved between the visibly angry driver and his distraught sister-in-law. "Take your property, sir, and be on your way."

"Who in hell are ya'll to tell me what to do?" the driver demanded.

"My name is Henry Thornton, sir, Sen. Henry Thornton."

The driver slumped and backed away. "I didn't recognize ya'll, Senator," he said, poking a grimy finger at Caroline, "but that Yankee bitch tried to make a fool of me in front of my nigras."

"You must forgive her, sir," Thornton said softly. "She lacks understanding of our ways."

"Forgive me!" Caroline screeched defiantly. "I want no forgiveness from this wretched man. If I hadn't intervened, his cruel neglect might have killed this poor Negro."

Thornton turned. His eyes expressed sternness more than anger. "He may do worse than that, Caroline, if you persist with this infernal railing."

Caroline glared at her sister's husband but held her tongue. She intuitively sensed that more was at work here than she understood, more than she ever hoped to understand. She turned to the cowering slave. His piercing black eyes stared back defiantly. She wanted to protect him, had to protect him. A man capable of placing a chain around another man's neck was capable of unspeakable debauchery. What had Henry said? He may do worse than that! The words and images of *Uncle Tom's Cabin* flashed through her mind. She knew immediately what Henry had meant. Once the driver has the Negro alone, she thought, he'll have his way with him, and I doubt there's a soul here who will lift a hand to stop him. Worse, she sensed, others might actually expect it, just to keep relationships in perspective. There had been two centuries of stern conditioning, conditioning that instructed everyone in how to behave. She had the sense of being the only actor on the stage who had no idea of the role everyone expected of her.

Caroline's business instincts suddenly took hold. "What is this man worth?" she demanded of the driver.

The man scoffed. "He ain't for sale, lady."

"I asked his worth, you idiot, not if he was for sale."

"A thousand dollars," he replied quickly.

"I'll give you $1,400. Yes or no?"

A bewildered expression replaced his defiance. Caroline had captured his attention. Property was property. It was poor business to let emotions interfere with commerce. "Fifteen hundred," he said. "In gold."

"Done. I'll have it wired tomorrow."

"No deal, lady. Pay up now or I'm on my way home."

"Will you accept payment from me?" the senator asked.

"Ya'll got $1,500 in gold on ya?" the driver asked.

"I'll have it here in thirty minutes. Leave the wagon and your slaves here and go have a drink." Thornton tossed a coin to the driver and motioned to a man standing several feet away. The man approached and Thornton spoke to him softly. The man nodded, then ran down the street. "He's going to the bank now," Thornton said. "You'll have your money when he returns."

"The bank is closed," said the driver.

"Not to me, sir. Now go have your drink."

The driver studied the senator for a moment, then the woman. "He may be worth more'n $1,500," he said. "Maybe $2,000, now that I think on it."

By this time, a crowd had gathered. A man with a badge pinned on his pocket and a straw sticking from his mouth stood to one side. Thornton motioned to the officer, who moved slowly across the dusty road. Thornton took him aside and the two men talked.

The officer nodded several times, then approached the driver. "Do you have papers on these nigras?" he asked.

"Not with me," the driver replied.

"Do you know the penalty for selling a slave when ownership is in question?"

"Wait a minute, now," replied the driver. "That boy was born to my family some seventeen years ago."

The officer looked at Thornton, and the senator nodded faintly. "Well, if you don't have the papers, I s'pose I'll just have to confiscate your property."

The driver reviewed his options. "A man has a right to haggle," he said politely. He looked at the senator. "What with his bad leg an' all, I'll take $1,400—like the lady suggested. Deal?"

The officer turned toward Thornton. A nod sealed the transaction. "Cut him loose," said the officer.

The driver reached in his pocket and withdrew a key. He moved to the slave and yanked at the steel ring. The black man fell to his knees. The driver bent down and removed the lock. "I'll be at the Corner Stone Bar," he said, looking up at Thornton. "I'll write up a bill of sale. I'll send the papers later. I'll give ya the bill when I get the money."

Thornton ignored him and turned to the slave. "Come along, boy," Thornton said. "This lady is your mistress now."

"That's it?" Caroline asked. "A man changes hands, just like that?"

"Just like that," Thornton replied. "Victoria, take your sister to the buggy before we have a riot. With this Brown thing, who knows what will happen. Feelings are still running high. Where is your luggage, Caroline?"

Caroline pointed.

Victoria took her sister's arm, but Caroline pulled away. She looked at her twin with hard, condemning eyes but said nothing—for the moment.

"I swear, little sister," Victoria said as she moved briskly toward the buggy, "you can't buy every slave you see." She thought of Jefferson, but in the end she had given Jeff to Caroline in grateful appreciation for the months of care provided to her. Caroline had paid a fair price for Molly and the youngsters.

Henry Thornton moved with the easy grace of a plantation owner, or at least as Caroline had imagined they moved. He walked less with a swagger than with the movement of a man accustomed to being listened to. His stout, six-foot frame left no doubt that he did, or had done, his share of hard work. Although now over fifty, his deeply tanned but only slightly lined face made him appear ten years younger. Caroline chastised herself for the stirring she felt as she watched him climb into the carriage. She knew that he owned more than two hundred slaves, a fact that, at first thought, diminished him in her view. But he had handled her problem with gracious, soft-spoken firmness. She respected him for that. His obvious intelligence troubled her most. How could such a man be motivated by a backwardness compelling him to reject a person for nothing more than a birthmark? Had Victoria so completely misjudged him, or had his attitudes matured in the intervening twenty years?

The slave purchased by Henry Thornton rode behind them on a horse rented from the livery. Caroline turned to see if he was experiencing any difficulty. He rode proudly beside the man Thornton had sent to the bank for the money. Caroline smiled. She had every intention of refunding the purchase price. She saw nothing to prevent her from taking the slave back to her farm. She intended to provide a good wage if he elected to stay. She wondered if he might have a limp. What could have caused such a cruel wound? she asked herself.

As the moon set, the cloudy night sky turned completely black. It provided an eerie backdrop for the brightly lit mansion shining in the distance. Caroline had remained sullen since beginning the hour-long journey from Birmingham. But the more she thought about the event in the street, the more shame she felt for blaming Henry or Victoria. The time had arrived to make peace. "Henry," she said as the buggy turned the corner to the long, private road running toward the lights, "I want to thank you for your assistance. I don't know what I would have done if you hadn't come along."

"You're a willful woman, Caroline Wade," he replied softly, "but I expected no less. After all, the woman I married is equally head-strong—and I hear that twins are the same no matter the time or distance that separates them." He sighed. "I love Victoria, so I expect I'll have to love you, too."

Caroline felt the glow of a blush spread over her cheeks. "Those are the most gracious words I've heard in years, Henry Thornton. If I was twenty years younger, I'd swoon."

Victoria laughed. "You better be careful what you say to the senator, little sister. He has an eye for a pretty woman."

"I might consider that comment flattering," Caroline replied, "if it was anything other than a self-serving compliment, considering we look exactly alike." She turned and hugged her sister. "I made this long trip just to do that, and it has been too long delayed." Victoria hugged her in return.

The buggy pulled to a stop next to the porch steps. Caroline was awed by the massive plantation house, although the term "house" consigned too bland a description to the place. A tall Negro dressed in white shirt, red vest, and tailored black pants ran down and grasped the reins. "Did the train come late, Master Henry?" he asked.

"No," Thornton said as he stepped down. "We had a delay in town. Caroom, will you do me a favor? That young boy on the horse has a wounded leg. It will need some stitches and salve. Take him to Miss Rivers and have her sew him up. Give him some whiskey to ease his suffering." He hesitated. "And Caroom, no more than three fingers for yourself."

The tall Negro smiled. "Can I use Harvey's fingers, Master Henry? He has big hands."

Thornton patted the man's shoulder. "When he's fixed up, clean him up and bring him to the house. Fetch him some fresh pants from the storehouse." Thornton helped Caroline from the carriage, then his wife.

Caroom nodded and motioned for the injured boy to follow as he led the carriage horses down a narrow graveled road leading to the barn.

CHAPTER 6

· · · · · · · · · · · · · · ·

Victoria walked quietly to the balcony, which was guarded by broad French doors. A chill filled the morning air. She leaned against the door frame and crossed her arms as she looked at her sister's back. She sighed, then she smiled. Caroline looked over her shoulder and returned the smile. Victoria joined her at the rail. "What are you thinking?" she asked.

Caroline drew a long breath, then let it out slowly. "I was thinking how beautiful it is here. I have never seen a place such as this before. I've seen mansions in Boston and Philadelphia, where the bankers and railroad barons live, but nothing as pristine and grand as this. You must be very wealthy, Victoria."

"Perhaps," she said. "I never think much about it. I suspect that Tom had to borrow the money for Henry to purchase the boy in town yesterday."

"How is that possible?" Caroline asked. "This plantation is worth a fortune."

"I suppose it is. But life down here is different. We have to feed more than two hundred people each day. Twenty-three of our slaves do nothing but take care of this place. The price of a pound of cotton may drop by half in a matter of weeks, but expenses go on. This is an agrarian society, Caroline, and everything depends on the worth of what we grow. We are completely at the mercy of Northern businessmen and English shippers. That's why people here hate the Yankees and foreigners so."

"That's absurd, Victoria." She swept her hand in a half circle. "Look at this place. No one I know up north lives in such luxury." That was untrue. She had met men living in mansions in Boston and Philadelphia. Some owned businesses, and some had need for shoes in large quantities. One such businessman, after falling on hard times, had offered his mansion for sale. The asking price had been $60,000, but she assumed that the eventual purchase price would be much less. She thought about buying it for herself, but only for a moment. The farm was her home. She had raised her son there. It was where he had roamed freely and learned proper values from a former slave.

Victoria pointed at a man working in the garden. "See that man? He cost $1,200. It costs more than $300 each year just to keep him alive and well. That's nearly as much as a laborer up north earns in a year. And that man has a woman and three children. The value of her services is perhaps half of his, and the children provide no return at all. All things considered, we probably lose money on that unit."

"That unit! You truly think of them as property, don't you, Victoria?"

"They are, Caroline. That's a fact of life in the South. It's an abomination, but there is no way to escape it. We are their slaves as much as they are ours. We simply live better."

Caroline's emotions flared. "You'd have a difficult time convincing that poor soul I purchased yesterday that anyone is his slave."

Victoria ignored her sister's emotional remark. "I can't explain it. I'm not sure I understand it myself. All I know is, without the Negro, the South will wither and die in five years. We have forgotten how to take care of ourselves. The slaves do everything. They plant and harvest the crops, care for the children, cook the food, tend the livestock, repair what is broken—everything. We don't even teach them how to do these tasks anymore. Each generation of slaves teaches the next."

"So what is your place in all of this?"

"Simple," Victoria replied. "We supply the fear. We never let them forget that we have the power to kill them for an offense no worse than talking back. In return, they don't talk back. All I know for certain is that we are more dependent on them than they are on us." The subject bored her. She possessed no words to adequately explain it. It was the way things were! She had grown to accept it, as one accepts a mole on one's face. Cut off the mole and an unsightly scar replaces it. That described slavery. It was bad, but the alternative was worse. She turned toward her sister. "How is Samuel?" she asked, changing the subject.

Caroline smiled. "Fine," she said affectionately. "He graduates from West Point in the spring. He's in the top quarter of his class. He hopes to be an artillery officer."

Caroline turned away. Tears were running down Victoria's cheeks, and Caroline sensed their cause. A mother never gives up a son, she thought, even in death. But to give up a living son must leave a terrible guilt. In more than twenty years, in all the letters Victoria had written, she had never asked about Samuel except in the most prosaic way, as befitted a distant aunt. "Victoria, there's going to be a war."

Victoria sighed. "I know." She walked to the far end of the balcony, turned, and leaned against the rail. "Samuel will graduate from West Point and Simon will graduate from VMI. They'll be such proud soldiers." Her voice quivered as her hand went to her mouth to hold in the emotion. The effort failed, and she began to sob. "They'll lead men into battle. They'll fight each other as mortal enemies. One, or most likely both, will die—and neither of us possesses the power to stop it." Victoria looked longingly across the distance into her sister's soft blue eyes. Her sadness pulled the tears from Caroline's soul. Victoria extended her arms and Caroline ran to her. They locked in an embrace as the tears streamed down.

"I must go to town," Henry Thornton said as he pushed away from the breakfast table. "We need supplies, and there's a planter's luncheon at noon."

Caroline set her cup in the saucer. "Victoria, may I have a piece of paper and a pen?"

Victoria nodded to a servant.

Caroline wrote a message, then passed it to her brother-in-law. "If you will, Henry, please take this to the telegraph office and have it sent to my bank. They'll wire the money for the boy."

Victoria looked at Henry, than at Caroline. "What will you do with a slave?"

"Take him back to Gettysburg with me, of course." Sadness clouded her expression. "I didn't tell you, Victoria. Jefferson died a short time ago. I need someone to help me on the farm."

"And what if the boy runs away as soon as you get him there?"

"Then he'll have to make his own way, I guess. But at least no one will ever chain him to a wagon again." She tried to maintain her poise, but she could feel her rage, just below the surface, growing with each word.

Thornton folded the message before placing it in his coat pocket. "I'll be home by dark. Tom has his instructions for the day's labor, so you ladies have nothing to concern you other than to catch up on old times."

Caroline rose and looked at her host. "I wish to go with you, Henry," she said impulsively.

"For what reason?" Thornton asked, surprised.

"I want to see the town. I must try to understand what goes on down here." She lifted her chin an inch. "I want to understand why we will be killing each other before long. Is that so strange?"

Thornton sprang to his feet. "Victoria, tell your sister she'll be unwelcome in town."

"I don't need an interpreter, Henry Thornton. I need an explanation that provides some form of understanding." Caroline looked at Victoria. "Since no one seems able to put it into words that make sense, I must try to figure it out for myself. Now, will you take me with you, or must I walk?"

Victoria yearned for the passive sister she had enjoyed during her youth, but still, she admired her. She remembered when Caroline confronted Porter and forced him to set her free from a disastrous marriage. He had beaten her down for years, yet she rose up in a moment of crisis and forced him to bend to her will. Although feeling ill at the time, Victoria had overheard every word. Caroline's meticulous planning and forceful confrontation with Porter had saved their lives that day. Those events had given Caroline self-confidence and a sense of independence.

Victoria knew enough about her sister to know that she had every intention of going to town, with or without Henry's assistance. She smiled and looked at her husband as she brought the napkin to her lips.

"Peas in a pod," he said as he walked to the coat tree. "Bring a wrap, if you must come with me. There's a touch of fall in the air today."

Victoria glanced at Caroline and flicked her head. Caroline moved at the signal, confirming that the matter had been settled in her favor.

"All of this is our land," Thornton said as they glided along the road, the sound of the wheels muffled by fallen leaves, "all the way to the river. Counting the pastureland—we raise all of our own meat—there are more than three thousand acres. It has required a lifetime of sacrifice to acquire it. The original farm, where we built the house fifteen years ago, is hardly sufficient for the slave quarters and all the other activities that support the plantation."

"Why do you call it Christina?" Caroline asked.

"My mother's name was Christina. She raised me in poverty. I think she would have liked it here."

Under different circumstances Caroline would have thought of Henry as a loving, caring man. Reared in humble surroundings, he had educated himself and acquired a fortune in land and property. She knew that Victoria had shared in the effort and sacrifice, at least in the early years of the marriage. Yet what Caroline had learned about Henry during this brief visit served only to confirm her image of a master of a large plantation, a man who conducted his life with careful, reasoned deliberation. But what about the part of him that Victoria had described? Caroline had more interest in what she failed to observe, for she saw nothing of the weakness in character necessary to justify abandoning a son because of some silly superstition. Then, too, she recognized a third dimension in him, a dimension manifest in the nature of his property that made suspect everything that seemed good and decent. Her mind grappled with the perplexity of this complex man. Perhaps acquiring an understanding of life in the South meant learning to understand men such as Henry Thornton. She had to try.

She yearned to grasp the reason why her son, Henry's son, might be expected to die in the process of subduing this culture totally, of ripping it asunder. Would Henry be so eager to defend his domain if he knew what it might cost? Would he give it all up for a son he had never seen, never even knew existed? Even thinking about the question increased the risk of uttering unguarded words. Finding an answer, however, might become imperative if she expected to preserve her sanity. The answers to her questions would reveal the truth about Henry Thornton.

Life had been a trial for Caroline Wade during the previous twenty years. Her life as a widow—she had added that lie to her other sins—had been difficult, but being alone had forced her to be self-reliant. The trip to Pennsylvania, in the late summer of 1839, had been only the beginning. It had taken nearly every cent she possessed to expand the farm and invest in the fledgling shoe manufacturing business. She had built a modest house in the woods behind the main house. In time, she built an identical house for Jeff and his growing family.

There had been suitors—several of them—but for one reason or another, nothing serious had evolved.

Her cousin and his family had continued to live in the main house until his death in 1846. His wife had stayed on, rearing the children still in the home and working for Caroline. Caroline, with Jefferson's assistance, had managed the farm with the help of hired laborers. She had endured drought and flood, but she had persevered. In 1851, she had squeezed enough profit from the shoe business to purchase her sister's share in the farm. With that, she had sole ownership of more than fifteen hundred acres of prime Pennsylvania farmland, but she still lived in the small, four-room house in the woods. Following her cousin's death, Jefferson and his family had moved into the large house.

Under Jefferson's tutelage, Samuel had worked the farm as a laborer until he departed for West Point at the age of seventeen. She had insisted, since the boy turned five, that he attend school. He had mastered the classics by thirteen, taught himself calculus at fifteen, and spoke French and German so well that even foreigners thought him an immigrant. But he never exhibited any interest in shoes. He had grown up thinking of Negroes as equals—except for Jefferson. Samuel always thought of the big black man as his superior and mentor, and frequently as father. It seemed natural to give something in return, so Samuel taught Jefferson to cipher. With this new skill, added to Caroline's teaching him to read, the Negro gradually assumed the management of the farm. This relationship between Jefferson and her son, because of its impact on her son's life, frightened her more than she cared to admit. If it came to it, when it came to it, she expected no man to be more fiercely committed than Samuel to the abolition of slavery.

Now she found herself struggling to understand something that seemed beyond understanding. The wickedness of slavery had broken the will of an entire race. That undoubtedly had been the plan, but its accomplishment had only added to the depth of the evil. Victoria had discovered the absurd irony of it all: The Negro had become the strength of the South, if not its essence. The Negro dictated the pace of labor, and the pace was slow. Jefferson had exhibited this quality when Caroline first saw him sitting on the wagon seat almost afraid to move except on command.

As Thornton and she moved along the road, Caroline studied the workers in the fields. They seemed to work at moving as slowly as possible, as though limiting their labor was a form of defiance for the humiliation the system forced them to endure. She had observed boys of six weed a row with more resolve, yet no one seemed concerned. White overseers, limiting their own efforts to an occasional flip of the head to expel a stream of tobacco juice, sat limply on horses as they watched their charges. The process seemed the same as when she had witnessed guards watching white prisoners working along the Pennsylvania roads. The Southern men of property had a dilemma: They could either accept the Negroes' lethargic efforts and trust in them to be enough to support their fine style of living, or beat them and get nothing from them. It crossed her mind that Jefferson, on his last sick day on earth, exhibited enough fortitude to pick more cotton than these slaves.

Caroline heard the noise even before its source became evident. A large crowd had gathered in the street. A man in a long-tailed coat and top hat stood on the back of a wagon. He said a few venomous words and the people responded with a cheer. A few more words followed, then another cheer. On it continued. "What's happening?" Caroline asked.

"You seem obsessed with understanding the South, Caroline. This is your first lesson. John Brown's raid in '59 put fear in these people's minds. They are afraid their slaves will revolt and murder them in their sleep. They've been trying to reassure themselves for the past year by talking of disunion."

"Well, perhaps if they kept quiet, the Negroes might never learn about it. I understand it's against the law to teach them to read."

"You are naive, Caroline. The average slave understood the meaning of what happened before most whites."

Caroline smiled. Hope remains, she thought, however remote.

Thornton stopped the buggy in front of the telegraph office. He tied the reins before assisting Caroline to the road. "I'll send the message. I'll be back."

"No hurry. I'll just watch and listen."

"We must rebel," said the man on the wagon. The crowd cheered. "We must take command of the arsenals and drive the Yankees from our land." Again they cheered. "The South Carolina legislature plans to meet the day following the election. If Lincoln is elected, the belief is that South Carolina will secede before that wretched man takes office." The cheers were even louder than before. "My Alabama brothers and sisters, if South Carolina leaves the Union, will we do less?"

"No," the people screamed in unison.

"There is talk of taking the arsenals and driving the Yankees from our land. When the call comes, will you stand with your state?"

"Yes," they chanted. "Yes, yes, yes." They broke into a loud cheer.

The man extended a bony finger toward the gathering. "Let no man lead you astray. What the South stands for is right and good. States' rights are our birthright. No government in Washington has a right to control our property." He waved his arms. "Look at those poor black souls. Could they survive without us?"

"Never," the people responded. A hundred or more slaves stood passively at the fringes. Caroline heard no cheers from them. Equally passive, a young Federal captain stood on the boardwalk across the street. I wonder what he thinks of this? Caroline mused.

"Are you satisfied?" Thornton asked. "Are you beginning to understand the South?"

"I understand you are living a fool's dream, Henry. Are you going to fight a war with confiscated rifles from a few scattered arsenals?"

"Don't misjudge the resourcefulness of these people, Caroline. Ours is a cause more than two hundred years in the making. If need be, every Southern man will defend it with his life. If Lincoln is elected, there will be an army of a hundred thousand within a month."

"And the North will send an army of a million to conquer you."

"Then we will raise a million to drive you from our land. We have no other choice. Otherwise, the South will die."

"And none too soon, Henry Thornton. None too soon. You get your supplies and go to your meeting. I'll be fine."

He looked at her sternly. "Caroline, you keep your views to yourself. There are people over there who would hang a Yankee woman and invite the sheriff to hold the rope." He placed his hands firmly on her shoulders. "Do you understand me?"

She dismissed him with a wave, her attention riveted on the crowd. "I'll be fine. Go."

"Be here at three," he said. "I'll have finished my business by then."

She nodded, then walked toward the crowd.

She examined the faces as she listened to the words. There was a sense of joyful excitement in their sparkling eyes, even the children's. The speaker talked of states' rights, but the listeners were thinking of slavery and how to preserve it. Lincoln had said he believed slavery was wrong, but he had also said that he intended doing nothing

to end it where it existed in the South. He had also said that it must
be prevented from expanding westward, and there he departed from
anything Southern. If Southern political control eroded, or if Northern neutrality moved toward intolerance, there existed no power on
earth to keep a man in chains with so many people opposing it, even
if those people had never seen a slave.

Now Caroline knew the crux of the problem. The South had de-
fended slavery as a right, even as a necessity, sanctioned by God. The
Negro, after all, had no status as a man. Everyone here knew it. The
Negroes' ignorant, passively plodding ways confirmed the truth in this
belief. Every Southern state had passed laws to secularize what di-
vine providence already had affirmed. Preposterous, she thought.

A Boston paper had estimated that slaves constituted half the wealth
of the South. The figure seemed high by most estimates, but it accented
the difficulty. It was irrational to expect a people to yield a substantial portion of their wealth without a fight. The speech and the yelling were rhetoric, but that made the commitment no less real. The
underlying economic issue had no less importance than that which had,
some nine generations before, driven their forefathers to wage war against
the most powerful nation in the world. Caroline Wade understood
economics. Would she give up half of her farm or a factory without
a fight? Never! Not without being dragged kicking and screaming from
the portion they tried to seize.

Now she knew with certainty. There will be war, she thought solemnly. The time is near.

Caroline sat silently as the others finished eating. She had resigned
herself to sad acceptance of what loomed ahead for her country and
herself. She had traveled south for two reasons. One had been to see
her sister again, perhaps for the last time. That possibility seemed more
real than before. The other reason had been to see for herself what
promised to destroy her family, to place her son in harm's way. What
she had envisioned had increased her fears enormously. Now she saw
that those fears were justified. As she touched the napkin to her lips,
the shock of her neglect hit her. "Victoria, I feel like such a fool. I
have been here for more than a day and have never asked about Nancy
Caroline. Is she gone?"

"Yes," said Victoria. "She's in New York. She met a young man
while in school. He asked her to come for a visit. I think it's serious,

but there's so much to overcome. He's from Chicago and works in a branch of his father's bank. He's a nice enough man, I suppose, but so worldly."

"And so Northern," Caroline replied without restraint. "When will she return?" Caroline saw her sister chewing on her comment, and it obviously had a bitter taste. More than she had realized had pushed them apart during the past twenty years. Was it possible to ever recapture the closeness of their youth? No, she realized. Nothing stays the same, including sisters—even twin sisters. Only their secret bound them together now, and even that pulled at her soul. She felt that Henry had a right to know, but if she told him, what then? If she had the power to stop a war, she would speak the truth without a moment's hesitation. But that was absurd. If she remained here, however, the subject might surface anyway. Every conversation, every expression, seemed tinged with subdued hostility—sometimes less than subdued. Coming here had been a terrible mistake.

"She's scheduled to arrive at noon on Friday," Victoria replied, "or so she said in her telegram." Her restraint crumbled as she flung a fork across the room. "Damn you, Caroline. Must everything become a wedge to drive us farther apart? Must you think of me as the enemy? I still believe in God. I love my children. Am I so wicked? Why must you antagonize me so?"

"Because, sister," Caroline exploded, "you have abandoned the values taught to us by our father! This gulf between us is *your* creation. What you have chosen to defend will kill our sons, and that is beyond forgiveness." She rose with such force that her chair crashed over backward. "Would you think better of me if I said that killing them is acceptable?" She had wished so desperately to say "your sons," but one avoids killing love so willingly. Even now, in her wrath, the hostility faded at the sight of the anguish in her sister's tear-filled eyes. Caroline realized that the bitter reality of her accusation more than strained Victoria's affection for her; Caroline doubted she had intended less. Her anguish had grown too intense. She had to lash out at someone, to find someone to blame.

Flesh had enduring strength, but words, when spoken with sufficient force, had the power to rip it apart. Caroline clasped the top of her head and stomped her foot in frustration. "Oh!" she exclaimed. "Why do I let this bother me so. It's tied up in Jefferson somehow. Samuel would have died for that old Negro. Jefferson represented father and brother in Samuel's youthful, trusting heart. I made certain of that. I had a dozen opportunities to marry again, but I was so afraid after my experience with Porter. Because of that fear, I denied my son a father. But he had a father, Victoria, or should have had."

Victoria pleaded with her eyes. The words must remain unspoken. The secret must remain hidden.

Caroline made a last desperate grasp at restraint. "And I denied him that," she said as she slumped forward, letting her head droop. "*I* denied him that."

Victoria began to sob. She extended a hand toward her anguished sister.

Caroline gasped for breath as she ran across the room. She fell to her knees and buried her face in her sister's dress.

Victoria leaned over and extended her arms down Caroline's spine. "Go, Caroline, before we destroy each other," she whispered.

Caroline lifted her head. She thought for a moment, then she nodded, tears dropping from her chin. Both understood the bitter truth. If Caroline stayed, they were certain to destroy each other. Emotions powered actions, and now only distance offered any hope of easing their pain. The feelings that had driven them apart had grown too intense. Now, the right of it had to be determined by God—and the death and suffering of uncounted soldiers. But neither of them knew that now. War's horror remained an abstraction. They conceived the horror of it only in the narrow context of their sons. Even that exceeded comprehension with any true sense of reality.

From the diary of Caroline Wade:

October 23, 1860
Impossible things sometimes happen. This afternoon I was waiting for my train in the Washington station when I heard a young woman say "Mother." I didn't react at first; then I heard her call out again from just in front of me. I looked up from my paper into the eyes of a beautiful young lady looking down at me. "Mother, what are you doing here?" she asked. Victoria had described Nancy Caroline many times as the girl grew up, so I had a sense of what she might look like, but I think I'd have recognized her anyway. She looked so like Samuel.

"Nancy Caroline?" I asked.

*"Of course, it's me, Mother," she said. "What are you doing here?"
Only then did I realize she had confused me with Victoria.*

*I rose and smiled. "I'm not your mother, Nancy Caroline," I
replied. "I'm your Aunt Caroline, your mother's sister; you are
my namesake." Her eyes lit up and we embraced. She was on her
way home to Birmingham. We talked for more than an hour, until
she had to catch her train. She expressed so much excitement and
prattled on so that I had difficulty getting in a word. She told me
all about her trip to New York City; then she announced her intention to marry her young banker if he agreed to come to Alabama next summer for the wedding. In her excitement, she forgot to mention his name. I felt both joy and sadness as I watched
her innocent exuberance. She possessed no understanding of what
she faced, and I lacked the heart to tell her. I know her bright
hopes will crumble when she tells Victoria of her plans.*

*Everything seems so peaceful as I look at the flickering lights
rush by, but I feel so sad. It incenses me that Toby—that's the
name of the injured slave I've brought with me to help on the farm—
has to ride in the baggage compartment.*

CHAPTER 7

· · · · · · · · · · · · · · ·

From the diary of Caroline Wade:

May 5, 1861
It has happened. War. Fort Sumter fell three weeks ago. I received a message yesterday saying that West Point officials have advanced graduation for Samuel and many of his classmates to tomorrow. Samuel wants me there, and I will make it if the train gets through in time. The papers report that most Southern states are calling their cadets to come home to take up arms in defense of the Confederacy. I fear that friends and classmates will be killing each other before the first snows blanket this divided land.

Regiments are forming in every state. Young men—boys actually—talk of whipping the rebels and returning home in time for the harvest. I think not. The boys in town marched with sticks as the train pulled out of the station. The ragged, disorganized lines of marchers would have made me laugh if their ineptitude did not so sadly forecast their fate. The thought that my son's safety depends on such men brings tears to my eyes.

Everything now depends on what the border states do. If Virginia secedes, I fear we will lose the war before it hardly begins. God help us all.

· ·

The gray lines of cadets stepped out to the roll of fifty drums. Their ranks had been thinned by the departure of several of their Southern classmates prior to graduation, cadets who had resigned before graduation

in response to the call from Southern states to come home. The proud
young men who remained, almost defiant in their bearing, moved in
a gray wave across the green field. How grand they looked! Caroline
Wade felt a shiver run down her spine. She had arrived barely an hour
before the ceremony and had been able to catch only a brief glimpse
of her son as the ranks formed for the parade. She waved as she took
her position with the reviewing party, but Samuel gave no indication
of having seen her.

When Caroline arrived, she discovered that she was among the honored
guests. She was the mother of the graduating cadet with the fewest
demerits over the five long, grueling years of training—a distinction
Samuel shared with Robert E. Lee, who only a few weeks before had
sadly chosen to follow his home state of Virginia in rebellion. She
beamed when the superintendent bowed stiffly and kissed her hand,
expressing the thought that if all mothers raised their sons so well,
the army was certain to win the war by summer. She declined to tell
him that much of the young man's rearing had been accomplished under
the direction of a former slave who had been like a father to him. She
wondered what horrors were foretold by the emerging certainty that
many of these young men would be committed to killing their countrymen by summer.

All sat silently as the parading cadets marched down the far side
of the plain to take up positions for the graduation ceremony. It was
a calm, balmy day, and the flags hung limply as the color bearers
approached the reviewing party. A stiff breeze arose just as everyone
stood. The red, white, and blue banner trimmed with wide gold braid
lifted and fluttered in the sudden gust. Another chill ran down Caroline's
spine as she drew herself erect. Never before had she felt so proud.

"Regiment—halt!" shouted the First Captain as the formation reached
the center of the plain in front of the reviewing party. Caroline's eyes
met her son's as he looked at the crowd from his position at the left
end of the front rank of cadets. His face remained stern and proper,
but she smiled. So many fine young men, she thought. Soon they will
be marching off to war with no shield other than their honor. Her lips
quivered and tears rolled down her cheeks.

With a sharp succession of commands, appropriate honors were
rendered to the reviewing party. After salutes had been exchanged,
the First Captain bellowed with authority, "Sound the order to advance."

"Graduating class," the adjutant shouted, "by files from the left, forward—march."

With that, graduating cadets marched in single file to the left flank of the reviewing party. When they were in place the First Captain marched stiffly to a position squarely in front of the superintendent.

"Sir, the regiment is formed!" The cadet's saber snapped to the vertical and he brought his hand holding the blade up in front of his face in salute. The superintendent returned it briskly. The wind died as the First Captain did an about-face. "Regiment," he commanded, pausing for the company commanders to echo their preparatory commands from left to right, "Parade—rest." Then the First Captain turned and moved briskly to his own place at the right end of the ranks of proud cadets soon to receive diplomas and commissions in the Union army.

Caroline Wade heard only isolated phrases from the speech that followed. The superintendent talked of duty, honor, and country, and of the stern test that lay ahead. He spoke of the difficult trial facing the nation, of the coming challenge to the courage and fortitude of these dedicated young men. He spoke with circumspection about the outcome of the war. He saw no sense in provoking those of Southern heritage still within the ranks. Caroline clapped politely, as did the others, but her thoughts were on the meaning of the ceremony, on what she expected to follow as the sounds of the fond farewells faded. She looked at the young men, their proud, boyish faces shaded by the black leather bills of their tall shakos, and wondered how many would be alive a year hence. Will Samuel be among the living? she thought with detachment. Please, God, make it so, she prayed.

The First Captain rose, moved to his position in front of the superintendent, and saluted again. He did another about-face and commanded the members of the graduating class to execute a right face and advance in single file to receive their diplomas.

Henry Algernon Du Pont, the top-ranked cadet, stepped off briskly, leading his classmates forward.

When the last of them had returned to his seat, the First Captain moved smartly to where his successor stood waiting, and saluted. "The field is yours, sir," he announced. "Pass in review."

The new First Captain returned the salute, followed it with a crisp about-face, then moved to his position at the head of the Corps. Pro-

gressing with the precision of a finely tuned machine, the orders sounded
and the cadets paraded by. Most of the young men in the ranks that
day were destined to experience the harsh realities of combat before
the war ended—on both warring sides. Many would die or suffer horrible
wounds, but of course they gave no thought to that on this glorious
day. In their minds, war promised only excitement and glory, for they
shared the common bond of a sense of immortality. Forgotten truths
about war's horrors would have to be learned anew by members of
their generation. The oldest among them had been little more than an
infant at the time of the Mexican War, the youngest not yet a gleam
in his father's eye. But the superintendent knew well the forces that
Fort Sumter had unleashed. He had been barely older than these young
men when he marched south into Mexico to depose a despot. Now
the army planned to march south again, but the nation sternly rejected
the idea that it was taking up arms against a foreign power, at least
so far as President Lincoln defined the task.

As the graduating cadets concluded their commissioning oaths, the
superintendent announced solemnly, "By the authority vested in me
by the president and Congress of the United States, I commission you
as officers in the United States Army with the rank of second lieutenant."

A loud cheer erupted as the graduating cadets flung their shakos
into the air. Men and women, boys and girls, rushed to congratulate
them. Younger cadets, upon their dismissal, would later clamor for
position, eager to be the first to receive a salute from the newly com-
missioned officers. Parties would continue into the early morning hours,
and a few of the new lieutenants planned to take marriage vows before heading off to battle. It was the sunset of the time for celebra-
tion, the last peaceful respite before the dawning of war. Beneath it
all, on everyone's mind but expressed only in ambiguous metaphors,
was the knowledge that the time for the frivolity of youth was fast
slipping away.

"Let me look at you," Caroline Wade said as she placed her hands
on her son's stout arms. Tears glistened in her eyes.

"Don't cry, Mother," Samuel said.

"That is what mothers do when they are so proud of their sons."
The tears overflowed. "I thought you knew that by now." She sniffed
and brought her handkerchief to her eyes.

Lieutenant Wade looked over his shoulder. "Mother, there's some-one I want you to meet. I've written of him many times." He took her arm and led her to a young man surrounded by a crowd of well-wishing family and friends. "Mother, this is William Healy. He's from Chicago." Young Healy smiled and bowed. "And this is his father, David senior."

David Healy bowed in response to Caroline's curtsy.

Caroline smiled. Her thoughts wandered as Samuel told her how he and Bill had decided to accept field artillery postings. He explained that the engineers were the elite of the army and that both he and Bill had been offered assignments in that branch. But, he added, promo-tions were slower in that branch during time of war, even though only the best and brightest were chosen to serve as engineers. The artil-lery promised action, however, and five of the fourteen cadets offered postings by the engineers had opted to join young Wade and Healy.

As the rest of his classmates celebrated, Emerson Pollard and four other Southern officers sat alone in their rooms writing out resigna-tions for their just-earned commissions.

Caroline started at the sound of David Healy clearing his throat. "Excuse me, Mrs. Wade, but would you join us for supper?" Healy asked with a smile.

"I don't wish to intrude," she replied with demure, downcast eyes. A faint blush colored her cheeks. He is such a handsome man, she thought. Where is Mrs. Healy? she wondered. "I'm sure you and your wife will want some time with your son."

The senior Healy forced a smile. "There is no Mrs. Healy. She passed on, in the winter of '49."

"Oh. I'm sorry. I didn't mean—"

"Please, join us, Mrs. Wade. Otherwise, I fear we will have no supper. I have learned during the past two days that neither of these two young men moves without the other."

"Well, if you insist, it will be my pleasure to join you."

"Good," he said as he looked admiringly at her bright, smiling face. "Former cadets and their guests are dining in the hotel. I have a train to catch, so I will be able to stay only a short time." He extended his arm and she touched her fingers softly to his hand.

"We'll meet you there, Father," said the younger Healy. The two young men ran ahead.

"Samuel tells me you are a graduate also," Caroline said, looking at the elder Healy.

"Yes. Class of '35. It was a grand experience for an adventuresome if somewhat naive young man, but my deeper interests ran to finance. I resigned from the army when my father became ill and required my assistance. And my wife felt uncomfortable as an army wife." Caroline noticed his distant expression. "I wish now I had stayed in the service."

They walked slowly across the lawn, talking quietly of the pomp and excitement of the recent ceremony. Caroline lied again, telling Healy of her long standing as a widow. They spoke briefly of lost love, but mostly they just chatted about the uncertainty of war and of the shared concern for their sons. Fathers are the same as mothers, she concluded, except in their perspective. Caroline described her farm, speaking with pride of having built her small domain by herself. She never mentioned the shoe business. Most men considered the harsh, sometimes cruel, world of business too crude for the gentler sex. She wanted to keep the conversation light and unspoiled by prejudice. Besides, Healy seemed impressed enough with her enterprising efforts with the farm; then they arrived at the hall.

"Mother, you sit here, next to Mr. Healy," Samuel said. "Bill and I have matters to discuss."

The elder Healy held a chair for his guest. "I failed to ask. Is Samuel your only son?"

"Yes," Caroline replied as she spread her napkin. "And may I assume, since you are a senior, that you have another son?"

"Yes, and a daughter. David junior works in one of my East Coast banks. Ellen, my daughter, is at school in Boston. Both planned to be here, but with the movement of troops and supplies, transportation is in such confusion." He looked at her as he sipped on his coffee. "Will you be returning to Gettysburg?"

"Tomorrow," she replied. "With Samuel leaving for Washington there's nothing to hold me here."

Hearing was difficult what with the hubbub of excitement that filled the large building, so conversation remained subdued. Caroline watched her son, so far as it was possible to do without being obvious. She had seen him only sparingly during the past several years, and she expected to see him less in the years to come. Once she said a silent prayer for his safety and offered a silent thank-you for her sister's gift. Sons grow up and leave their mothers, she knew, but in her mind he remained a young boy listening intently to a former slave who explained why things were done this way or that. Samuel never doubted a word of the Negro's teaching. The young man wrote that he had cried for an hour upon learning of Jefferson's death. Samuel had been on a field exercise at the time, and he learned of his mentor's passing more than a week after the funeral. Caroline was even more grateful now for Jefferson's stern teaching. Her son's preparations were as complete as possible, if ever it was possible to prepare a young man to face death.

The sound of a chair scraping on the stone floor interrupted Caroline's reverie.

David Healy rose from the table. "Well, Mrs. Wade," he said with a slight bow, "I must take my leave. My train leaves in an hour."

Caroline smiled as she touched her napkin to her lips. "Have a safe trip, Mr. Healy. Thank you so much for inviting me to dine with you."

"My pleasure, Mrs. Wade. And please, call me David."

She nodded and smiled again.

"Take care, son," Healy said, gripping his son's shoulder. "Remember what I told you. History belongs to the survivors and the brave. Strive to be both."

Young Lieutenant Healy rose and wrapped his arms about his father; then, as if remembering his newly acquired station, he pulled away and stood at attention. "Sir," he said, "I am responsible for such bravery as may be my good fortune to display. But my survival is in the hands of God."

David Healy's lips quivered as he forced a smile; then he nodded as his hands grasped his son's. He backed away, turned, and, for a moment, stood stiff and still as he squeezed his eyes shut. Only Caroline saw the solitary tear roll down his cheek; then he walked briskly toward the door.

Many tears were shed that night, some in an emotional outpouring as mothers felt their sons slip away, others in darkest solitude, when fathers could no longer restrain them.

From the diary of Caroline Wade:

May 7, 1861

I feel as if I'm riding along these tracks back into the past, and that I have watched my son stride forth into the boiling cauldron.

History will surely pass me by. I will grow old on my Pennsylva-
nia farm, and I will read about great battles and the swirling motion
of change in our battered nation. My thoughts are on the words
of Henry Thornton. What was it he said? "We will raise a mil-
lion to drive you from our land." Such defiance! Such resolve! How
is it possible for Samuel to stand against such commitment, against
such hate? How can anyone?

There they are again, those peaceful farmhouses sliding by, houses
filled with people going about the labors of their lives largely un-
suspecting of what is building about them. There are sons and
husbands and brothers living in those houses. Before this war is
through with us, many will be placing rifles to their shoulders and
doing everything within their power to kill their countrymen. How
many will find their final rest before it ends? Will we be better
for the effort? God help me, but I think we will.

There are so many churning thoughts pushing to break free from
my mind, but I can write no more.

Chapter 8

• • • • • • • • • • • • • •

"Gentlemen," said the colonel, "we believe that the enemy is poised to strike. Our forces are less prepared than I'd prefer, but General Jackson says we will go forward at dawn." The colonel stood staring down at a crude map of the Manassas area. "We will be outnumbered, but if we take the defensive, we should be able to stand firm."

Lieutenant Simon Thornton stood in the shadows of the crowded tent. He watched and listened intently as the colonel outlined the battle plan. Occasionally, Thornton shook his head, but he kept his counsel to himself. No one was interested in the views of a lowly staff lieutenant. He had to find another way.

"The war has been progressing poorly," the colonel said in conclusion. "McClellan has kicked us around with ease in western Virginia. It's a stalemate out west in Missouri. What we do here tomorrow will either give our people the courage to fight on or destroy their will to persevere. I know you will do your duty. That is all."

The officers saluted and filed from the tent.

Stretching as far as the horizon, both east and west, were the countless fires of twenty-five thousand scared but eager Confederate soldiers. No more than a handful had ever fired a shot in anger. Lieutenant Thornton ranked among the majority that evening of July 20, 1861. Many of the men carried rifles brought with them from such varied places as Tallahassee and Atlanta. Many of their weapons were smoothbore muskets with an accurate range of less than a hundred yards. A shiny new black holster holding a new Colt revolver hung from Lieutenant Thornton's hip. His father had acquired the gift with difficulty, ironically having requested it from a Chicago business correspondent who traded in cotton.

Despite his lack of experience, the young lieutenant had confidence. Superbly trained and disciplined at VMI, he lacked nothing but the knowledge of his own will to stand when the first shots rang out. After that, he expected to be all right.

As the last man filed from the conference, Lieutenant Thornton went to his tent and penned a brief message. "Colonel," he wrote. "I over-heard a casual suggestion. I thought it might be beneficial. The sug-gestion was, what if someone posts a regiment in the woods east of our main force? Then we will be in position to push forward with a surprise counterattack if the enemy threatens our main line." He added no signature, just walked back to the colonel's tent and placed the scrap of paper on the map table. Then he returned to his own tent.

Sleep eluded Thornton. The anticipation of battle weighed heavily on his mind. Hardly one brief thought concluded before a dozen more rushed forward to replace it. He experienced difficulty imagining what he had never experienced. Although he had smelled the pungent odor of gunsmoke many times before, it was mainly in the act of shooting at stationary targets. In simulation, when he had practiced firing without loaded shot at a moving target, he always had the sense of firing behind or over or under the target. Concentration had been difficult. How much more difficult will it be, he thought, if the target is a man with a rifle? As thoughts that already had run their course began to return, his eyelids sagged. His next thought was of the annoying disturbance of a shrill, vibrating, distant noise. He sprang to his feet as the crisp notes of the bugle sounded more distinct.

Thornton pulled on his boots and rushed to the colonel's tent. He considered himself fortunate in his assignment to a regimental staff. He had been offered his choice of assignments, or almost. General Beauregard had offered him the choice of a variety of assignments in recognition of his having been the First Captain during his last year at VMI. Thornton had thought long and hard about asking for a field assignment. By then, however, he had become acquainted with some of the political appointees assigned to command companies and regi-ments. Most knew less about tactics than a corporal. Prudence coun-seled him to bide his time; he shared none of the commonly expressed illusions of the war ending soon. There would be ample command opportunity later.

Thornton looked at the map table. The note he'd left on it during the night had been removed. He lowered his eyes to the worn, packed earth. It wasn't there, either. The colonel must have found it. Had he read it? Or had he, thinking it nothing other than a scrap of paper, stuck it in the fire to light his cigar? He let the matter slip from his mind. The sun began to rise. The smell of bacon and corn bread filled the air. He walked to the open fire, where a private cooked breakfast.

"It's a good day for a fight, sir," said the private.

"As good as any," Thornton replied. He lifted a piece of bacon from the pan with a stick and poked it into his mouth. "Hot," he said as he attempted to hold the searing meat away from the sides of his mouth.

"Imagine that," said the private. "Lieutenants," he added under his breath, shaking his head.

"Lieutenant Thornton."

Thornton turned. The colonel stood at the entrance of the tent. "Yes, sir?"

"Come here for a moment," said the colonel as he turned and entered the tent. "Lieutenant, General Jackson has altered the disposition of our troops. He has ordered me to move the regiment to the woods east of the main line. Colonel Canby will send several companies from his reserve regiment to take our place in the line. He will hold the remainder of his men in reserve. A battery of guns will be moved from the left flank to the right flank to anchor the gap. Here are the orders. Please deliver them to the company commanders immediately."

Thornton smiled faintly, saluted, then left the tent. The colonel must have shown the note to General Jackson, he mused. "Sergeant, have my horse saddled."

"Yes, sir. Private, saddle the lieutenant's horse."

The main battle line had formed a half mile north, over the rise. Thornton rode at a trot. As he approached, he heard, beyond the main line, the scattered fire of pickets testing each other's resolve. Union forces were drawing closer, but there remained time before any opposing battle line advanced. Nothing more occurred during the half hour required to distribute the orders. Thornton watched as the men formed up and marched toward the woods. Now we are ready, Thornton thought. He rode back to headquarters. The colonel had ordered their tents struck by the time he returned. Men scrambled to pack the wagons and prepare the teams of horses.

"We're moving into the woods," said a major with a swish of his hand. "Mount up."

Thornton fell in behind the colonel.

"Is everything in order?" the colonel asked Thornton.

"I waited until the companies were in motion, sir. They are in place by now."

"Very well." The colonel spurred his horse to a canter.

Lieutenant Thornton stood over the colonel. The colonel gritted his teeth to hold back the scream. Blood streaks covered his face and hands.

"The leg must be removed, Colonel," said the surgeon. "The bone is shattered above the knee. You'll bleed to death if I don't operate now."

"The war has barely begun," he said, "and I'm out of it." The colonel screamed as a medical orderly began cutting away the trouser leg. "Goddamnit, Sergeant."

"Sorry, sir."

Except for Lieutenant Thornton's quick action, the wound would have been worse. Thornton had been standing only a few feet from the colonel when he observed a partially spent solid shot from a six-pounder kicking up dust as it skipped along the ground. A quick calculation had convinced him that it would slam into the colonel's chest. At the last moment, Thornton pushed him, and the shot slammed into the colonel's outstretched leg instead of his chest. Just now, the colonel doubted that the result was a blessing.

"Is this Colonel Baker's headquarters?" said a voice from the shadows.

"Yes, sir, General Jackson," someone answered. "The colonel is wounded, sir. He's in the hospital tent."

Jackson entered the tent. He hesitated as he examined the colonel's condition. "Looks like you need some minor repairs, Colonel."

Baker strained to lift himself on his elbows. He grimaced at the sight of his shattered leg. The jagged end of the femur protruded more than an inch beyond torn muscle. He sucked in a deep breath to clear his mind of pain. "I'm afraid my war is over, General."

"Nonsense, Colonel. Before this war has ended, men with limbs missing will be leading divisions into battle. You produced a brilliant victory today, Colonel. The whole command might have crumbled if your flank had given way. The men took heart and rallied when your regiment came yelling out of those woods. That was brilliant, Colonel. Brilliant."

"Thank you, General. I hear we won."

"Indeed we did. McDowell is probably preparing his resignation by now. Well, you get some rest. I couldn't let the day pass without commending you for a superb performance."

Colonel Baker looked toward Thornton. The lieutenant stood at attention, his eyes straight ahead.

"General."

"Yes, Colonel."

"I must mention something, sir. There may be no time later." He knew the risk involved in amputation. He strained to point with a shaky finger. "It was Lieutenant Thornton's idea to place the regiment in the woods."

"This young officer?"

"Yes, sir."

The general patted Thornton on the shoulder and smiled. He turned and walked to the entrance, then he turned again and examined the young lieutenant's face. "Haven't I seen you someplace before, Lieutenant?"

"Yes, sir," Thornton replied. "I was in your philosophy class at VMI, sir. I was also in the ranks when you led the Corps to John Brown's hanging. I was First Captain this year and took a commission just last month."

"From classwork to tactical planning in only a month! It's a fast-moving war, Lieutenant."

"It appears so, sir."

The general and the surgeon whispered briefly, then the general smiled encouragingly at the colonel and walked out into the night.

Even with his leg removed in an attempt to contain the bleeding, the colonel died before morning. They were learning the grim lessons of war anew, but, for the time being, the information remained largely useless. When men propel steel and lead at each other, flesh must yield. Still, events demanded that they keep coming in ever greater numbers, pressed shoulder to shoulder in mile-long lines, until one side or the other cried out for it to end. Midsummer had arrived. Except where battles raged or where the armies marched, crops grew green and lush in the fields. Not even the leaders fully understood, at this early point in the war, but one hard reality rose above all else: There remained no wistful hope of being home in time for the harvest.

*   *   *

"We almost had 'em, General," said the aide. "I don't understand what happened."

"We got whipped, Captain. That's what happened." The general sat limply in the saddle as he watched the stragglers file by in the moonlight. There were hundreds of them, thousands, all heading north. Most had lost their rifles along the way or thrown them away so they could run faster. Few signs of organization remained. The army had disappeared, disorganized rabble emerging in its place. Slightly wounded men held up men with worse wounds. None even glanced at the general or his aide.

"But the men just ran! They just turned and ran." The captain pointed. "You there, Sergeant. This is your general. Don't you salute generals?"

"Bum to the generals," the sergeant replied.

The aide stood erect in his stirrups. "Goddamn you, Sergeant, I'll—"

"Leave him alone, Captain," the general said. "Leave him be." The general pulled at the reins and started the horse walking north. The captain followed.

All night men straggled toward Washington. The march continued into the day. Men dropped from exhaustion or loss of blood. Sometimes an ambulance driver stopped to check, and sometimes they drove on by. It was every man for himself. They had suffered devastating defeat, and the distress of it pressed on every man's mind. What had begun in the bright morning glitter as innocent anticipation of glory had ended with fear and panic in the late afternoon haze. The full scope of the defeat would emerge later, marked less by the loss of men's lives—for few men died compared to later battles—than by the damage to reputations and the realization that death and chaos were the rewards for overconfidence and lack of training.

Late that morning the lead elements of the long retreat staggered into the outskirts of the Union capital.

Just south of the battered bridge leading into the city, a cannon battery stood inertly in a meadow adjacent to the road. Along the way, half the horses had died outright or collapsed from injury. Now the survivors had lost the strength to pull any farther. The major formerly in command was somewhere, probably dying in one of the hastily constructed field hospitals that had materialized along the line of retreat. His arm, blown away when a shell exploded a caisson, lay someplace on a trampled, deserted field. The captain had disappeared in the same explosion.

In command by then, no less demoralized than the thousands who ran by, was Lt. Samuel Wade. The pomp and confidence so recently enjoyed on the plain at West Point seemed a million years in the past. Only by the barest chance had he held his ground when the enemy had charged his position. Somewhere deep inside he found the courage, or, more likely, the pride born of years of training, to stand in the face of impending doom. "Keep firing," he had screamed above the clamor of the battle raging all around. "Cover the retreat." Enough of the men had stood with him to load and fire, and the barrage of canister and solid shot they laid down had blunted the attack.

A major rode up to the rickety bridge, jarred partially loose from its foundation by the retreating army's heavy rolling stock. "Is this Battery B?" he asked. A pole with a small V-shaped red flag lay across one of the guns.

Wade pulled himself to attention. "Yes, sir, I'm Lieutenant Wade, sir, the battery commander."

"Who was in command when this battery held off that last rebel attack?"

"I was, sir." Am I in trouble? he asked himself. "All the other officers were out of action by then."

"Lieutenant, you are to report to headquarters as soon as possible."

"What about the guns, sir?"

"They'll be fine where they are, Lieutenant."

Wade began to move, then stopped. "Where is headquarters, sir?"

"About a mile up this road toward the city. Do you have a horse?"

Wade thought for a moment before pointing to the horses used to pull the guns. "Only these, sir."

The major wheeled and rode toward a bedraggled captain leading a balky gray mare. "I need your animal, Captain," the major snapped. "You may retrieve him at headquarters in a couple of hours." The major snatched the reins and turned without waiting for a reply.

"Here, use this horse, Lieutenant, then leave him at headquarters." The major rode off.

Wade thought it proper to say something to the men, but nothing came to mind. The sergeant, his face black with soot, looked at him through bloodshot eyes. "Secure the battery," Wade said finally. After a final look around the clearing, he lifted himself into the saddle and rode north.

*   *   *

"Lieutenant Wade, sir, reporting as ordered." His attempt to come to attention failed and he labored to present a limp salute.

The colonel standing in front of the tent examined Wade sternly as he, too, feigned a salute. Are we asked to win the war with this? he thought. "State your business," he said.

"I command Battery B, 4th Artillery," Wade replied. "A major told me to report here."

The colonel turned and entered the tent. Shortly, a brigadier general lifted the flap. "Come in, Lieutenant. Sergeant, hold this officer's horse."

Wade stepped into the dimly lit tent.

"Take a seat, Lieutenant. What is your name?" the general asked.

"Samuel Wade, sir."

"West Point?"

"Yes, sir. Class of '61."

The general nodded. He had an eye for such things. "I'll be brief, Lieutenant. Courage was in short supply out there yesterday. You may have noticed that the whole army ran."

"Yes, sir. I watched most of it go by."

"So I hear." The general struck a match and lit a cigar stub. "What may lack clarity, Lieutenant, is that this will be a long war. If no one knew that before yesterday, the realization will hit them after they've had time to study this tragedy. What we need now, more than anything, is officers with initiative and courage. Your actions may have prevented thousands of men from being killed or captured."

New energy surged through Wade's frame. "I did what I was trained to do, General."

"Well, most of the men in this army failed by a damned sight to do just that. That includes most of the officer corps. I'm recommending you for a commendation and promoting you to captain. Report back to me tomorrow afternoon at two. That is all."

Lieutenant Wade saluted before he turned and stepped into the darkness. The brief surge of energy that surfaced back in the tent had drained his last reserves. His shoulders slumped. He stood motionless for a moment before pressing his cap firmly on his head. To the north, Washington's lights sparkled in the night. To his front, the seemingly endless procession of defeated men continued to limp along the road. There were no sounds other than the shuffling of feet and the clatter of wagons—and the occasional groan of a wounded man as someone touched a nerve. The defeat had been absolute—utterly complete.

What makes me different from any of them? Wade asked himself. No answer came to mind. Until this moment he had never considered the possibility that he was a hero. Duty and honor, he thought. I performed my duty, nothing more.

He looked longingly at the horse tied to a nearby tree. Its owner remained somewhere out along the road. Wade's pulsating brain and aching muscles resisted even the thought of walking back to the battery for his belongings. He patted the animal's haunches before leaning against the tree. He was asleep before his rump slid to the ground.

CHAPTER 9

• • • • • • • • • • • • • • •

Caroline Wade turned toward the sound of hoofbeats on the hard-packed road. Small bursts of dust popped into the air with each surging kick of the horse's hooves. Soldiers were a common sight by then, so she paid the single blue-clad rider no particular attention. She continued to hang the clothes on the line.

"Excuse me, ma'am."

She turned with a start. Before her, hat in hand, dust covering his rumpled blue uniform, stood a young Federal major.

He bowed slightly, then carefully squared his hat back on his head. "I'm looking for a"—he examined a sheet of paper—"C. Wade. I'd appreciate it, ma'am, if you'd be so kind as to direct me to him."

Caroline pushed her bonnet back as she wiped her brow with her sleeve. The weather was hot, and she had been washing since dawn. She shaded her eyes as she looked into the blinding sun. Nearly noon, she thought. "I'm Mrs. Caroline Wade," she replied.

Obviously, she misunderstood me, the soldier thought. "My instructions are to contact your husband, Mrs. Wade."

"That may be difficult, Major. I have no husband. He died many years ago. But I'm C. Wade."

"C. Wade of Rodman and Wade, the shoe manufacturing firm?"

"The same. May I help you, Major? As you can see, I'm very busy."

"I had expected, ma'am—I don't know what I expected." The young officer appeared flustered, unsure of his next action.

"Well, it's me you're looking for, young man." She turned and draped a dripping cotton dress over the line. "Please state your business, sir."

"May I trouble you for a drink of water, Mrs. Wade?"

Caroline pulled her bonnet back in place and walked impassively toward the house. "Come in, Major, before you have sunstroke."

The officer slapped his coat. A cloud of dust boiled into the air around him before settling to the ground. He rushed forward to open the door, but arrived too late.

"Will you settle for a glass of cool lemonade?" she asked. He smiled as she filled the glass. He drank it down without taking a breath. "Another?" He smiled again.

"Major Courtney," he said between gulps. "I'm with the Quartermaster's Department, ma'am."

"It's a terrible thing, Major Courtney, what happened at Bull Run. It's difficult to think of our army being routed so completely. The papers report nearly a thousand men dead." Caroline's anxiety rose as she spoke of the event now two weeks past. She had sensed Samuel's involvement but had heard nothing. No news was good news, or so she hoped. She forced it from her mind.

"Yes, terrible," he replied, "but I fear it's only the beginning." He examined her as he sipped the refreshing liquid.

"Major, I have this feeling that you are disturbed by my appearance."

He let his eyes drop. "Oh, no, ma'am. It's just that I was told that you were the owner of four shoe factories, one of them the largest in the nation. I never expected to find the owner of such an empire hanging clothes on a line."

She smiled. "I assure you, Major, my business is no empire. Strange as it may seem, even factory owners sometimes have to wash their clothes."

"I—I—yes, ma'am. I suppose they do."

Caroline pulled out one of the kitchen chairs and seated herself on the edge. She leaned back and set her feet widely apart to allow the air to circulate around her legs. She fanned her face with a newspaper. The soft cotton dress settled limply between her thighs. The soldier seemed transfixed by her unladylike pose.

She smiled faintly. The power of imagination, she thought. She leaned forward, cocking her head slightly, and his line of sight shifted to meet hers. "You want to talk about my shoes, Major?"

He blinked, then snapped to attention. "Yes, I do. That is, the army does. I represent the Quartermaster's Department."

"You said that, Major. Please, pull out a chair and relax."

He made a quivering sort of smile, then the stern military demeanor returned. He turned the chair outward and lowered himself onto it. "We—the army has it in mind to contract with your firm to manufacture shoes for soldiers."

"We manufacture shoes for a living, Major. What is your proposition?" He seemed startled by her choice of words. Clearly his mind is someplace other than on shoes, Caroline thought.

"It's more of a request than a—a proposition, ma'am. Procurement officers will be meeting with contractors in Philadelphia next week. I've been directed to extend an invitation, if you're interested."

"Oh, I'm interested, Major. Who are these procurement officers?"

"I'm unsure, ma'am. I'm just delivering the message. The meeting will be at the Hampton Hotel next Monday at nine in the morning." He reached inside his jacket and withdrew an envelope. "I'm instructed to give you this authorization for travel—at government expense, of course—if you wish to be present." He handed her the envelope.

She withdrew the contents and read quickly. "Very well, Major. I will be there. Is that all?"

He rose and bowed. "That is all, Mrs. Wade."

"Are you married, Major?"

"No, ma'am. Why do you ask?"

She smiled. "Nothing, Major. It just seems you're in need of some female attention."

A crimson glow spread over his face. Caroline laughed. "I'm sorry, Major. I didn't mean to embarrass you—or perhaps I did. I'm old enough to be your mother, Major."

"Not *my* mother, Mrs. Wade," he replied emphatically. "I'm the last of nine children."

Caroline rose, then reached out and touched his cheek. She looked into his eyes and smiled. So young, she thought. "Have a safe journey, Major."

"Yes, ma'am, and thank you. I regret if I have offended you, Mrs. Wade."

"No offense taken, Major," she said truthfully. "To the contrary."

The major turned and walked briskly out the door.

Caroline walked to the front of the house. The major rode a short distance, then he turned the horse and looked back. She waved through the window. The major saluted before he wheeled and rode off at a gallop. She smiled at the thought of the young officer looking at her with wanton eyes. More than ten years had passed since she had savored such a look. It made her feel like a woman again. There's more to life than farming and shoes, she thought. She looked at the calendar hanging on the wall. Thursday. She had preparations to make if she intended to be in Philadelphia by Monday.

Caroline Wade stepped into the hotel lobby. A bellhop nearby smiled in recognition and bowed slightly. "It's nice to see you again, Mrs. Wade." She had stayed here many times over the years.

"It's nice to see you again, James. The meeting here, is it in the Falcon Room?"

"It must be, Mrs. Wade. Some mighty important-looking men have been arriving the last hour."

She smiled, entered the hotel, and walked across the lobby toward the massive double doors. She pushed down on the brass handle and entered the room. The air reeked of smoke. All conversation stopped. Several of the men present looked impassively at her face, then let their eyes drift down and back up again. "Good morning, gentlemen," Caroline said firmly.

"Pardon me, ma'am," said a tall bearded man with an eagle on each shoulder, "but I believe you have the wrong room." He expressed no doubt with his tone.

"Are you from the army Quartermaster's Department, Colonel?"

"I am."

"Then I have the correct room, sir."

"Mrs. Wade?" inquired a voice from the back of the gathering.

She cocked her head to the side and squinted to see through the smoke. "Mr. Healy?" She smiled. "Is that you, sir?"

"It is, indeed, Mrs. Wade. I'm delighted to see you, ma'am." He pushed his way through the crowd. "Whatever brings you to Philadelphia?" He extended his hand.

She touched his fingers and curtsied slightly. "Shoes, Mr. Healy. I'm here to discuss shoes. That is, if this is the meeting called to discuss army procurements"—she studied the men—"as I believe it to be."

"That is our business, Mrs. Wade," Healy replied, "in one form or another."

She seemed more to glide than to walk across the room. Caroline extended her hand to the colonel, and he grasped it gently, still unsure of the error of his former assessment. "I'm Caroline Wade, Colonel, of Rodman and Wade Manufacturing. I received an invitation to attend this meeting to discuss a contract for shoes." A faint murmur ran through the room.

"I beg your pardon, Mrs. Wade. I was unaware you were a woman—or, should I say, that a woman was among those invited." He studied a list of names. "Is Rodman a woman also? I see the name is Francis Rodman."

"No." She smiled. "I'd expect his seven children would be offended at the suggestion." The others laughed.

"Perhaps we should have invited Mr. Rodman," the colonel said sternly, obviously ill at ease even at the thought of discussing business with a woman.

"I think not, sir. *I'm* the controlling partner in the business. You will deal with me or no one," she said, allowing a note of stern firmness to creep into her voice.

The colonel seemed shocked by her assertive tone. "I meant no offense, Mrs. Wade."

"Tea, Mrs. Wade?"

Caroline turned. Healy stood behind her. "Thank you, sir. I believe I will." She took the saucer and cup. "Am I the last to arrive, Colonel?"

"I believe you are, Mrs. Wade," said the flustered officer, obviously relieved by the interruption. He turned to the men standing behind him. "If you will follow me into the next room, gentlemen—and Mrs. Wade—we will proceed."

"Begging your pardon, Colonel, but I am unacquainted with these gentlemen—except Mr. Healy, of course."

"My apologies, ma'am. May I introduce you?"

"Please."

The meeting lasted all morning and into the afternoon. Over lunch, Caroline became the object of attention, as each man in turn directed inconsequential comments in her direction. With all of this, the discussion never shifted to shoes. Accepting a woman as an equal in business dealings was a difficult transition, especially for the colonel. He had discussed cotton for uniforms, leather for hat bills, tin for cups and plates, and brass for buttons, but he never quite got around to shoes.

Caroline had felt ignored before, and the feeling gnawed at her. She realized she had to assert herself if she wanted to be heard. Finally, as the conversation shifted to lighter subjects, she pushed back her chair and rose abruptly. Conversation stopped, then everyone rose. She sat down again. They all followed suit. Then she quickly rose again. Once more the men sprang to their feet. By this time, perplexity began to show.

"Please, gentlemen, be seated." One by one, they settled into their chairs. Caroline remained standing. When the last was in his chair, she leaned forward and placed her palms on the table. She turned her head and looked toward the head of the table. "Colonel, you have discussed everything except the price of goat's milk here today, and, of course, the price of shoes. I have come to the conclusion that, since I am the only shoe manufacturer present, you have decided that our soldiers have no need for shoes. Am I correct?" She stared into the colonel's eyes.

The colonel shifted uneasily in his chair. "No, ma'am, we have great need for shoes—many shoes, in fact."

"Well, Mr. Smith here has brass to sell. Are you going to have him make brass shoes for your army?"

The colonel sat impassively rigid as Caroline expressed her displeasure. Women were unsuited for business, of that he was certain. Or was it that men were unsuited to the type of women who engaged in business? Since men ran the world, as he thought they should, the difference seemed of no importance.

"Hmmm. I suppose not," she added. "Well, Mr. Bigelow's cloth will make poor shoes—except, perhaps, for those in the Quartermaster's Department." Don't go too far, Caroline, she thought. "Mr. Garner has leather to sell, but I don't think he knows how to turn his leather into shoes." She looked at Garner. He shook his head briskly. "Just as I thought. It seems, Colonel, you are well on your way to supplying your army, but only from the ankles up. Please, let me know if you decide you need shoes." She reached forward and lifted her cup. She took a sip, replaced the china, then began walking toward the door. She stopped and turned when she reached the exit. "Colonel, I believe your commanding officer is Brig. Gen. Montgomery Meigs. I shall write to the general and inform him that you had no interest in discussing shoes for his army." She opened the door. "What will he think, do you suppose?"

"You *know* General Meigs?" the colonel asked.

"I know *of* him, Colonel. He was an engineer officer and tried to recruit my son before he took command of the Quartermaster's Department. Good day, gentlemen." The door swung shut behind her. She walked slowly to the large doors guarding the main entrance to the ballroom.

"Mrs. Wade."

She stopped but resisted turning.

"Mrs. Wade," said the colonel with a sigh. "Please accept my apology. You have shoes, and I have need of shoes."

She turned with a swish, nodded slightly, lifted her skirt a few inches, and walked briskly back toward the meeting room.

"Gentlemen," she said as she returned to her chair. They all rose. As she bent gracefully to take her seat, her eyes caught those of Mr. Healy, seated at the far end of the large oval table. His lips formed an appreciative grin as he nodded. She acknowledged the gesture with a wink, then she turned toward the colonel and waited.

"Mrs. Wade, please, Mrs. Wade."

Caroline recognized the voice of David Healy, Sr. She turned. "May I be of service, Mr. Healy?"

"Please, call me David."

She nodded. "All right, David."

"Might I have a word with you?"

"It has been a long day, Mr. Healy, and I have an urgent need to put my feet up."

"Then may I escort you to your room?"

"If you please, sir."

He moved briskly toward her. "Mrs. Wade, I must confess, I consider that the most extraordinary exchange I have ever witnessed."

"Whatever are you talking about, David?" she replied in feigned amazement.

"The way you backed that pompous ass into a corner. It was a thing of rare beauty."

"Just business, David, nothing more than business."

"Yes, but *such* business. I do believe I saw him look at that eagle on his shoulder when you walked from the room." He laughed. "I think he must have imagined it turning into a captain's bars."

"About what he deserves," she said.

"Caroline—may I call you Caroline?"

"Of course, David, if you prefer. This is my room." She handed him the key. He fumbled in the effort to insert it into the hole.

"If I might be so bold—"

"Yes?"

"Will you have dinner with me this evening?"

She entered the room and turned. "I'd be delighted, David."

"Seven, then?"

"Seven it will be." She shut the door, took a deep breath, and allowed her back to drift slowly toward the door. She smiled. I feel like a schoolgirl, she thought. He's so very handsome.

It was after ten as Healy walked her to her room. "I noticed you said nothing during the meeting today," she said, "but I saw you taking notes. May I ask the reason for your presence?"

"Money," he replied.

"Money?"

"Yes, money. My banks, and those of Mr. Honeywell, will be financing much of the activity discussed today. I will meet with each of those gentlemen you met today privately over the next several days. Do you know that the government is spending more than $2 million each day to finance the war—and it has hardly started?"

"I had no idea."

"I assume you will need financing. May I accompany you into your room? We can leave the door open."

She handed him the key. He opened the door and they entered the spacious suite. A large basket of fruit sat in the middle of a table. A bouquet of roses protruded stiffly from a large crystal vase on the dresser.

Healy moved his head slowly as he examined the large room. "Well, Caroline, you travel in style. The government certainly doesn't provide enough money to pay for this."

"This is *my* room," she replied. "I stay here often when I'm in the city on business. Please, be seated. I must get into something more comfortable. I'm a farm girl, you know. Taffeta dresses are not my usual garb." She opened her bag and withdrew a cotton dress. Moving behind the dressing screen, she began unhooking her dress. "You said something about money."

"Yes, I did. May I be of service in that regard?"

"I don't see how. I've never borrowed a cent for anything. It takes away my independence. I pay as I go."

"But the colonel talked of fifty thousand pairs of shoes. It must cost a fortune to buy the raw materials for such a number."

"To be exact, about $32,000—including the laces. But that is of no concern. My factories have the capacity to produce that many shoes in less than a week. I doubt that materials will be a problem. The design of the molds will be the main concern. The colonel seems to want to avoid having to fit all of those shoes to individual feet. Producing a design that has the necessary flexibility of a few general sizes may be a small problem. I'll let my partner worry about that. He handles the manufacturing end. I handle sales."

"But you live on that farm in Gettysburg, or have you moved?"

"No, I have people who represent me. It's no more difficult for them to travel to Gettysburg than for me to travel here, or wherever I need to be represented. I usually handle only the main accounts in person." She stepped from behind the screen. "There, I feel much better. May I offer you a glass of sherry? Or do you prefer whiskey?"

"Whiskey, if you please."

She handed him the glass, then pulled two easy chairs together facing each other. She sat in one and lifted her feet to the other. She leaned her head against the back of the chair and pulled the pin holding her hair in place, letting it flow down the back of the chair. She closed her eyes and sighed.

"You are a beautiful woman, Mrs. Wade."

She opened her eyes and looked at him. "Why, thank you, Mr. Healy."

"A remarkable, beautiful woman."

"Two compliments in so short a time." She hesitated, feeling a desperate urge to say something about her earlier behavior. He had expressed admiration for her forcefulness, but had he really meant it? If she had been a man, the subject most likely never would have been mentioned. "I have had to be resourceful, David. A woman without resources, whatever may be required at the time, is at the mercy of a man's world. You saw an example of that today."

"Yes, but I must confess, with the possible exception of the colonel, no one was more surprised than I when you walked out that door."

"Yes, well, that was business, and I know a few things about doing business, as I'm sure is also true of you." There was a stern, almost uncompromising tone to her words. It was a side of her that always seemed to emerge when she immersed herself in the lofty world of business and finance. It had all become a game, she knew, but a game that one had to play. At first she had forced it, but in time it just happened, as natural as opening a door. Now she fought against the inclination. The tone always altered the look in a man's eyes, as if the message was a shove to the chest. She had seen another look in David's eyes as she stepped from behind the screen, revealing herself pure and simple in her cotton dress—as she had intended. It was the same look she'd seen in Major Courtney's eyes. She had rejected that look then. Now, rejection was the furthermost thought from her mind. She smiled warmly. It was up to him.

"Do you mind if I pour myself another drink?" he asked.

"Help yourself." She handed him her glass. "I'll have another brandy, if you please." As she heard the clink of glass against glass, she let her eyelids drift downward. Shortly, she felt the coolness of the glass against her face. Her mouth opened slightly as she slowly lifted her hand to take the drink. Her hand touched his fingers, curled firmly about the glass. She let the touch linger. He moved his hand slowly along her cheek. A soft sound rose from her throat. She quivered as his hand drifted toward her shoulder.

"Caroline," he said softly.

"Yes," she replied.

"The last thing in the world I want to do is offend you, but I want to hold you, to feel your warmth against me."

She opened her eyes and looked into his. "You do?" She paused. "Then do it, David." Her eyes closed again. She sensed him moving into a kneeling position beside the chair, and she lowered her head toward him. He had discarded the glasses. His hands grasped her face as his lips brushed against hers. Then he pressed his face forward as he pulled her shoulders around and toward him. Without ever thinking to move, they joined in a passionate embrace.

Caroline lay limp on the rug, naked as at the moment of birth. She had never in her life felt such contentment. Her lover's outstretched hand cupped her left breast. Every so often, he squeezed slightly. She moaned softly with each contraction of his fingers. "What will you think of me in the morning?" she asked.

"I will think of how I want you when night comes," he replied, without opening his eyes.

She rolled on her side and rested her head in her upturned hand. "And what of when you are discussing your business throughout the day?"

His brow furrowed. "Must you remind me?" He propped his head on his hand and looked into her eyes. "I haven't been a monk, Caroline Wade."

"Certain things need attending to, Mr. Healy." She thought only to let him guess at her own indiscretions.

He leaned forward and kissed her softly.

She rolled him back and pressed her breasts against his chest. She sighed. "Thank you," she said, "for not thinking too harshly of me for my behavior at the meeting today."

"What possessed you to say such a thing?" he asked with a laugh.

"Oh, it has happened before, more than you might guess. I suppose you've noticed, I'm unmarried. No doubt what I do for a living in part explains the reason for that."

"Hmmm," he replied with a smile as he wrapped his arms around her warm back.

They lay silent and contented, each savoring the closeness of the other. For the first time in many years Caroline drifted into sleep with a smile on her lips.

The sun had barely risen when she awoke. She heard a paper boy barking from the street. "Stonewall Jackson raids the Shenandoah," his voice echoed along the deserted street. "Union forces abandon Harper's Ferry. A thousand captured and the remainder routed."

For one brief, enchanted evening, she had allowed herself a measure of peace and a blissful moment of respite from the war, but now it had returned with all its fury. Had Samuel been at Harper's Ferry? She had no way of knowing. She kissed Healy on the tip of his nose. He groaned softly as he lifted his hand and let his fingers sift through her dangling, silky hair. "It's morning," she whispered.

CHAPTER 10

· · · · · · · · · · · · · ·

A blue mist drifted a few feet above the pockmarked battlefield. Scattered about were a hundred or more grotesque shapes of former human beings now lying inert in the wholly unnatural poses sculpted by death. Across the field flowed a slow-moving stream, its once brown water now stained blood red by the rigid, floating forms. Miraculously, the wooden bridge that spanned the ribbon of water still stood. Six months earlier, the price of a bale of cotton would have purchased every splintery board. War increases the value of everything, except life. This morning, gallons of blood had been spilled in the desperate effort to take possession of the nearly collapsed object. Now, with a stalemate achieved, the soldiers had time to dwell on the suffering the common objective had caused.

Occasionally, a form on the field acquired new life and rose, as had Lazarus; then it staggered mechanically into the unmoving air, the bottom half clearly visible, the top half wavering ghostlike in the pungent gunpowder smoke that drifted lazily under a blazing sun.

Without warning, a sharp crack shattered the eerie silence. Before the sound faded, the risen figure had spun and fallen to the ground, frozen again, this time forever, in the pose dictated by the moment of passing. The direction of the sound of the gunshot offered the only reality, with the blue-clad forms struck down from the south, and the gray-clad forms from the north.

Taking its cue from the intermittent silence, a rabbit, its ears fully extended to trap the slightest sound, its nose twitching to suck in the faintest smell of danger, hopped cautiously from a bush, then it moved a few quick jumps into the open. The illusion of safety conferred by the silence proved fatal. On its fourth hop, while still suspended in the air, two more sharp cracks, one moving north to south, the other reversed, converged on the small animal. The hare exploded in every direction at once.

"My bullet hit him first," shouted a man from the southern fringe of the field.

"The hell, you say," echoed another voice, this one from a Yankee picket guarding the approach to the bridge.

"Goddamn ya, Yank, that hare is mine," the first man replied.

A moment of silence followed.

"So it be, Reb. Now all ya need to do is come out'n your hole an' fetch him." A villainous laughter drifted toward Southern ears; then silence.

"Ya'll got any tobacco, Yank?"

"Not since a week ago last Sunday, Reb."

"Tell ya'll what I'll do, Yank. I'll crawl out an' fetch the rabbit. I'll leave a pack of tobacco in its place. Then ya'll crawl out an' get the tobacco. Then I'll have breakfast an' ya'll will have a smoke."

The span of silence between each exchange grew longer.

"How do I know ya won't shoot me, Reb, when I crawl out to get the pouch?"

"Southern honor, Yank."

The boiling sun's rays glistened on the drifting blue smoke. It swirled gently in a momentary gust of breeze.

"Ya ever hear the tale of the scorpion an' the beaver, Reb?"

"Can't say I ever did, Yank."

"This scorpion wanted to get to the other side of the river, but he couldn't swim. Nearby was a beaver, an' the scorpion said: 'Ya know how to swim, beaver, but I can't. Can I hitch a ride on your back to the other side?' The beaver thought that 'un over for a moment before replying: 'How do I know ya won't sting me while I'm takin' ya across?' 'My honor, beaver,' replied the scorpion. 'Besides, I'd drown if'n I killed ya in the middle of that river.'

"That sounds logical, thought the beaver, so he invited the scorpion to climb on. The scorpion settled in as the beaver began to swim. Halfway across, the scorpion stung the beaver. Just before the beaver died, he asked the scorpion: 'Why'd ya do that? Now we'll both die.' 'I changed my mind,' said the scorpion. 'Besides, whoever heard of a scorpion with honor?' Then the beaver sank below the surface an' they both drowned."

A dying horse reared its head. The sound it made was akin to mocking laughter. The mare tried to rise, kicked a couple of times, then flopped dead on the field.

"How 'bout if'n we crawl out together?" the Reb finally answered.

"How 'bout if ya bring me the tobacco," replied the Yank, "an' pick up the rabbit on the way back?"

Nothing developed from the conversation. Although still early in the war, the last semblance of trust had eroded, if ever there had been any. It was, after all, the lack of trust that had lit the fuzes of the cannon that sent shells crashing down on Fort Sumter.

"Sergeant," said a second Southerner's voice, "you're a fool to even think of trusting a damn Yankee."

"I know, Lieutenant Thornton," replied the sergeant, "but I ain't had nothin' to eat since yesterday noon."

The company commander moved in a crouch along the Southern line. "Men," he said as he passed among them, "we have to take that bridge. Load your rifles and fix bayonets. We're going across."

"I never developed a taste for rabbit noway," said the sergeant resignedly, "but I'll be damned if it's human to die on an empty stomach."

From the edge of the woods, the boom of a dozen cannon gave the signal to charge. Three rounds fired from each gun; then the men rose from the ground and moved cautiously across the field. The long line moved in a vee, the outer edges converging on the point. The only way at the enemy was across the bridge. The men on the far side of the field held their fire.

"Hit the ground," Lieutenant Thornton yelled. His men dropped just as a sheet of whistling lead sprayed over their heads barely four feet above the ground. To the right and left, men screamed and crumpled. All of Thornton's men escaped injury. The men who remained standing wavered, then collectively staggered backward from the blow. "Go get 'em, men," yelled Thornton, "before they have time to reload." The soldiers around him sprang to their feet and ran headlong toward the bridge. Hesitantly, the others followed in a crouch, then at a run. A sharp dip in the terrain protected the crouching men from the second volley; then, with gleaming bayonets protruding to their front, they charged into the open toward the Union position. Lieutenant Thornton led the assault, followed closely by a corporal carrying the regimental colors. A piercing, bloodcurdling yell arose as the gray-clad soldiers leaped upon the enemy and began to hack and club with their muskets or anything solid that came to hand. The lieutenant fired his new Colt revolver first right, then left—just in time to stop men poised to end his life with lead or steel.

It ended in less than ten minutes. Gray-clad soldiers herded the men in blue—those still alive or with manageable wounds—into a large knot in a rain-soaked gully. Long, hollow rods of steel, most of them empty, since there had not been time to reload, were aimed at the blue caps on their captives' heads. Had they only known, a dedicated rush by the Union prisoners, who outnumbered the Confederates rounding them up, would have overpowered their captors in a moment. No one wanted to purchase the freedom of the others with his own life, however, so they cowered in the ditch.

Mixed among the captured, his face blackened by powder residue from the four cannon he had commanded, crouched Capt. Samuel Wade. After the shame subsided sufficiently to permit him to lift his head, he looked up. He flinched at the sight of familiar features. The dirty, blood-streaked face might as well have been his own.

"You men squat down and put your hands on your head," commanded the rebel lieutenant. The familiar sound of the voice startled Wade as much as the features. "Watch 'em, men. If anyone moves, shoot him dead." The lieutenant turned and moved toward the approaching general. His movement carried him out of sight but left him within sound of the men huddled in the gully.

"That was a brilliant charge, Lieutenant Thornton," said the general. "But why did you have your men hit the ground just before that first volley?"

"Because we were a hundred and fifty yards from their line, General," replied Thornton.

The general appeared puzzled. "A hundred and fifty yards, Lieutenant?"

"Yes, sir. They seem to wait until we're about that close before they fire the first volley. It takes them about twenty seconds to reload, and I figured we could cross the bridge in that time."

"I see." Very unconventional, thought the general, almost cowardly, but never mind that. No point arguing with success, especially since most of the credit accrued to the general. The ultimate art of war, the ability to survive, always requires learning anew. Time permits some the opportunity to learn, others not. Thornton had bought the time by having himself assigned as a staff officer when the war began. He had watched and learned at Manassas. The experience sufficed when added to what he had learned in five years of military school.

In a more innocent time, when war was all chivalry and grace and the soldier functioned as a mere pawn with no purpose other than to protect the king, the innovative tactic would have served no purpose other than fatal delay. The smoothbore muskets used then, the type still carried by most Confederate soldiers, had no better than a one-in-four chance of hitting a target at 150 yards. But that distance was nearly point-blank for the rifled muskets used by virtually all the Union soldiers.

"The Yanks shot your captain," said the general.

Thornton nodded. "I saw him go down with the first volley, sir."

"Well, your company needs a new captain," the general said. "That will be you, Captain Thornton."

The new captain saluted.

"Round up those prisoners," the general said, "and turn them over to the provost marshal. Well done, Captain."

"Thank you, sir." Thornton saluted again.

Captain Wade and his fellow prisoners moved south, out of the war, or so most of them had concluded. Wade had other plans. Curiosity had taken command of his reason. Who was that young officer who had appeared as a reflection without a mirror? He had to unravel the secret. "Major," said Wade to the man in front of him, "we'll be stopping for a rest in about ten minutes. If the terrain is favorable, I mean to make a break for it."

"Don't be a fool, Captain. They'll shoot you down for sure."

"Perhaps, Major, but it's a soldier's duty to try to escape. I'm going."

The major shook his head. Foolhardy idiot, he thought.

"It sure will help if you could make some sort of diversion," Wade said a moment later.

"If possible, Captain, but no promises."

"Yes, sir," Wade replied.

Once away from the front, it was standard procedure in both armies to rest for five minutes or so each hour. Each step carried them farther away from the sounds of battle raging anew beyond the northern horizon. They were in Virginia, after all. Since the war started, few Yankee soldiers had penetrated this far south. Most of the rebel soldiers had their rifles slung over their shoulders. The first act upon stopping would be to light up the pipes and pump smoke into their lungs to mask the hunger. The best opportunity to escape seemed likely to be as soon as they stopped. The road wound through a dense pine forest. In another hour, Wade had heard one of the guards say, he expected the column to pass into the open. Now or never, he thought.

"Five minutes," said the provost captain. "You prisoners, sit shoulder to shoulder. Smoke if you got the fixin's."

The men lowered themselves to the ground. Erosion and the wheels of slow-moving wagons had, over the years, worn down the road. The side of the road rose about eighteen inches above the base. Beyond the road, stagnant water flowed slowly through a shallow ditch. Just beyond that, no more than a few paces, rose the edge of the forest.

"I'm going to roll over backward into the ditch," Wade said in a whisper. "It'd sure help if you'd close ranks and fill my hole when I go."

The major nodded, as did the man to Wade's left.

"On the count of three. One, two—" Wade rolled backward into the ditch. The shifting line of men closed the gap. He hesitated for a moment, then rolled toward the trees. Hidden by the bushes at the edge of the forest, he slithered along the ground for twenty feet, moving ever deeper into the woods. Then, rolling to a stop behind a fallen tree, he hugged the ground and waited.

"Everybody up," said the provost captain. "Let's move."

Ten minutes passed before Wade felt it was safe to stir. He raised his head for a cautious look and saw no one. Chirping birds made the only sound.

The war had been in progress for more than a year. General McClellan just plodded along, trying to come up on Richmond's south side by way of the York-James peninsula. Captain Wade had seen little action since the battle at Bull Run, and now, on the morning of his return to the fight, he had lost his battery and suffered the humiliation of being captured. Such a catastrophic series of events normally would have dominated the thoughts of any man. Not Sam Wade. He had become obsessed by thoughts of the man who, except for the color of the uniform he wore, might as well have been himself. What had the general called him? Thorben. No. He strained to jar the thought loose. Thornton! Lieutenant Thornton!

From the same event, which had ended in disgrace for Wade, the man received a promotion to captain for his efforts in causing that disgrace. For a brief moment, Wade had admired the man as he led his soldiers across that bridge toward almost certain death. But the order to fire the second volley had been given at precisely the wrong moment, as the rebels descended into the depression on the north side of the bridge. It had taken them too long to reload for the third volley. The gray-clad soldiers had piled into the trenches almost without resistance. Only his battery had dulled the charge, but there had been no time to load with canister or to depress the angle of fire to stop the final assault. The Rebs had overrun his guns and captured him and his men. No. That wasn't true. They were the major's men. The major had overall command of the guns, but that offered small consolation. Capture was capture—the only result he expected anyone to remember.

"My God," he said aloud. The words sounded dully against the dense growth. "Aunt Victoria. Her name is Thornton." He had never seen his aunt, not even in a picture. Taking pictures was a recent, expensive innovation. But he knew her to be his mother's twin. Twins are the same, he thought, so why not their sons, too? His mother had spoken only infrequently about her sister. They had gone their separate ways with only a fragile link maintained by infrequent letters. His mother never read to him the replies to her own letters. The family lived in another country, or so it seemed. He had not learned, until long after the event, that his mother had gone to Alabama in the fall of 1860 to visit his Aunt Victoria. He did know, however, that his cousin had attended the Virginia Military Institute—a sort of secondhand West Point in Wade's opinion. Still, the lieutenant had acquitted himself well.

Wade's curiosity turned to anger at the thought of his capture. Then the feeling of disgrace returned, this time even more agonizing than it had been initially. Resolve soon replaced the sense of disgrace, however. He had to complete the journey back to Union lines. He now knew his cousin's unit, the 2d Alabama. The regimental color bearer had planted the banner in the ground just in front of his guns. The humiliation of it all!

The sun was low in the sky. Light faded fast in the dense growth, which stretched endlessly in every direction. Armies avoided such entanglements, so he felt safe for the time being. Night was the best time to move, although it meant having to move more slowly. He headed north. At first, the setting sun lighted his way, followed by the dim glow of such light from the half-moon that penetrated through the branches. When it became totally dark he had to stop.

At first light in the morning he continued moving north. He thought he heard the distant sound of thunder, then realized it was only the sound of the large guns that McClellan had ordered pulled through the swamps. At least he knew he had been heading in the right direction. At times, he became unsure. He had no compass. The sun's movement offered the only clue.

Late evening had arrived before he detected the first signs of human life. Ahead, he heard the muffled voices of people talking. Gray or blue? he wondered. He crept closer. The conversation seemed normal enough, but the accents suggested caution. He waited for the sun to set. The smell of cooking nearly drove him crazy. Almost thirty-six hours had passed since his last few bites of food. Only now did he realize the hunger he felt. He crawled forward to the edge of the clearing. Most of the men were languishing around the smoldering fires. To the right, in the shadows, a young officer leaned against a tree smoking a pipe. Wade crawled in that direction. In the distance, some soldiers were singing, and the young officer hummed along.

Wade examined the surrounding area. He estimated it was thirty feet to the nearest fire, which had dwindled to coals. He saw no one looking in his direction. Picking up a stout stick, he rose cautiously and moved to the backside of the tree. He gripped the stick tightly and, reaching around the narrow tree trunk, pressed the stick hard against the man's neck, clutching the other end as it touched flesh. The man squirmed, but there was hardly any sound; then he went limp. Wade took no chances. He continued to press the man's neck against the tree.

When he finally relaxed the pressure, the man slumped to the ground. Wade grabbed a limp arm and pulled the body into the shadows. They were nearly the same size, Wade concluded, so he stripped off the gray uniform and pulled it on over his own. He retrieved the pipe that the man had dropped and sucked vigorously on it. A spark sprang to life, followed by a bright glow. He moved casually into the opening. His immediate objective was to move as far from the surrounding fires as possible before anyone missed the officer. He pulled the brim of the hat low over his eyes and began moving north again.

"Halt. Who goes there?" said a voice from the shadows.

Wade halted. He cocked his head to examine the insignia of rank on the collar. "Captain Thornton," he replied in a normal voice. "At ease, sentry."

"Yes, sir," the sentry replied as he stepped into the dim light shining from a crescent moon. "You the same Cap'n Thornton what led that charge yesterday mornin'?" he asked.

"That's me, all right," said Wade, attempting to talk with an accent. But it didn't sound very authentic, even to himself. The sentry faded back into the shadows. Wade continued to walk, then he turned. "Sentry, you wouldn't know where the 2d Alabama might be, would you? They seem to have moved while I was at General Lee's headquarters."

"Last I heard, they was maybe a mile north of here, up by the river."

"Much obliged, soldier."

"Yes, sir."

Up by the river? That must be the James, he thought. He had traveled too far west. The Union lines were at least three miles, maybe more, back to the east—unless they had advanced during the past two days. Still, he had to see for himself.

Wade moved along the twisting road past several units of camping soldiers. With each inquiry, he moved closer to his objective. "Corporal, is that the 2d Alabama up there?"

" 'Twas when the sun done set," the corporal replied.

I never could master this language, Wade thought with a smile. "Thank you, Corporal." He stepped in a puddle of water. He reached down and dipped his fingers in the mud, then streaked it across his face to hide his features.

"Where might I find Captain Thornton?" Wade asked the first soldier he encountered in the next camp.

"Down yonder by that second tent," the private replied, pointing, "only he's a major now."

In time of battle, promotions apparently came quickly in the Southern army, Wade thought.

The back of the tent faced the trees. Wade worked his way into the woods and moved slowly toward it. A lantern hung on the front pole. Two officers sat on folding canvas chairs near the opening. Both had their backs to Wade. He listened. The one on the left spoke with a voice he'd heard the morning before. It sounded like his own voice, or as he imagined it sounded to others. He had to be sure.

Wade worked his way past the tent and stepped out of the woods twenty paces beyond. He relit his pipe before moving into the open. A small bank of clouds slid across the sliver of moon. He moved casually down the path some fifteen feet in front of the tent where the two officers sat talking. "My God, I was right," Wade muttered softly under his breath. He looks exactly like me, he thought. Wade seemed mesmerized by the realization that he had a twin, or as near to one as seemed remotely possible.

The sight of a soldier standing statuesque in the middle of the path, with no apparent mission in mind, was certain to capture the attention of one of the officers. Still, Wade's mind seemed incapable of acting with the caution required in his present circumstance. His attention remained riveted on the man. The other officer leaned forward in an effort to identify the stationary figure looking in his direction. It was too dark to see.

"Are you looking for someone, sir?" the officer asked. It was too dark to make out the rank insignia, but the uniform was plainly an officer's.

Wade's face twitched as he realized the jeopardy he courted. "I thought I saw somethin' in the woods," he replied in a gruff voice. "Must'a been mistaken." He saluted and turned his back.

"Just a minute," sounded the voice from behind.

Wade froze, then concluded that prudence dictated moving, even if it raised suspicion.

"Just a minute, there," the voice said again, this time from closer range.

He had to do something. Wade turned. There, only five feet away, stood the man with the mirror image. Just as the blood and dirt had failed to conceal his look-alike's features the day before, his own efforts at disguise also had failed. Thornton stepped back with a start as he looked into reflections of his own eyes. Wade took advantage of Thornton's momentary paralysis and bolted for the woods.

Wade looked over his shoulder as he ran. Although Thornton stood mesmerized, the other officer reacted quickly. Wade saw the pistol being drawn from its holster. He drove his legs with all the energy his weary mind commanded.

"Halt, or I'll fire," the officer shouted.

The resonating sound of danger that followed sent an electric charge through the camp. Everywhere, all at once, men were running in the direction of the warning shot. Wade had only one option, to run. Capture meant certain execution. The rebel uniform offered a single conclusion: He was a spy. Just as he reached the woods a bullet snarled past his ear. Wade heard the dull plunk of the round as it peeled away the bark of the tree in front of him. Now he had a chance, but running through the woods at full speed was nearly as hazardous as running in the open. He heard more cracks, this time with deeper sounds, as Minié balls crashed through the foliage all around him. He had to assume his eventual capture. Wade lifted his hat and let it sail away. He unbuttoned his tunic on the run, slipped his arms out of the sleeves, and let it fall to the ground. He hopped on one leg as he pulled the other leg free from the trousers, then repeated the process. Now, at least, he was not a spy, or he expected that proving so would be more difficult if they captured him.

His right arm crashed into a tree. The force of the blow spun him completely around, but somehow he maintained his balance. What good is running? he thought. For all I know, I'm simply running toward another enemy camp. But his West Point training had conditioned him never to quit until all hope had evaporated. So he ran, dodging the shadows of trees, some only by throwing himself at the last moment to one side or the other. With it all, the energy drained slowly from his mind. Instinct kept him going, more than fear, more than training, more than reason. A faint ray of hope entered his mind. They can't move any faster than I, he reasoned, and I have less to be cautious about. But a man has only so much luck, and what happened from here on depended on chance more than reason or self-discipline. Besides, he suspected, he had used up all his luck traveling twenty miles through enemy lines. So instinct drove him forward. If it failed him, capture or death was certain to follow.

Wade broke into the open and saw lights flickering in the distance. Friend or enemy? He had no way of knowing. He heard a crack, then a sound like an angry bee as the bullet zipped by his ear. He had no doubt what awaited him if he so much as stumbled. The bullet meant for him kept going. A distant lantern exploded as the bullet passed through the camp.

"Night attack," echoed a distant voice. Lights went out all through the camp that drew closer with every stride. Then a frightening thought entered in his mind: Those must be the Federal lines. They'll think I'm a rebel. If the rebels don't kill me, my own people will. The next instant confirmed his fear. A Minié passed by going in the other direction, then another and another. He dove headlong into a nearby bush, gasping for breath. Adrenaline had powered him this far, but no reserve remained. With a last desperate effort, his muscles revolted. His legs ached from the pain. His right calf began to knot. Careful to hug the ground, he bent at the waist and vigorously rubbed the aching muscle. As he rubbed, he strained in the darkness to look back from whence he had come. His pursuers had stopped, then turned back as the return fire thumped into the tree line. Wade looked the other way. Nothing moved in the clearing, although he could make out a line of Union troops kneeling along its edge. He had taken refuge in a no-man's-land. Both sides were trying to snuff out his life.

"I surrender," he yelled as he looked to the north. "I'm Samuel Wade, a Union captain."

"If'n that's so," came the reply, "why're ya surrenderin'?"

"Don't shoot. Please," Wade pleaded. "I'm going to crawl forward." He forced his arms to move, then his legs. The Union lines were two hundred yards beyond, perhaps more. It was a long way to crawl.

"Who are you?" a man yelled.

"Captain Wade of the 4th Artillery. Rebs captured me yesterday morning, but I escaped."

"Move forward to a hundred yards, then show yourself."

Wade thought of the beaver and the scorpion. If someone shot him, it would be unfortunate, but of no more concern than any other of an infinite number of accidents of war. "I'll crawl in, if you don't mind. Someone might act carelessly."

The tall grass felt damp and clammy. No, it seemed more wet than damp, as did the ground. He had entered a swamp that had largely dried up from lack of rain. That explained the tall grass. The moon drifted below the horizon. He saw nothing to his front except the distant shadows of the Union camp perched on a ridge and silhouetted by the fires. That's dumb, he thought as he slithered toward the lights, his training reasserting itself. "I'm coming in. Don't shoot." He removed his coat. "I'm going to lift my coat into the air to identify my position. Don't shoot."

Men rushed toward him and he stopped moving. Even in the darkness, he saw the bayonet-tipped rifles pointing down, about a dozen altogether. "Don't shoot, damnit! I'm a Federal officer."

A shadow bent down to within a few inches of his face. "How have things been, Samuel?"

In all of that chaos, a familiar voice. "Bill? Bill Healy?"

"I thought I recognized your voice, Samuel."

"You almost killed a good West Point man," Wade replied. He extended his arms and grasped his friend's shoulders. "Is there anything to eat in camp?"

Healy rose. "At ease, men. I know this man. He and I were roommates at the Academy." The soldiers lowered their rifles.

"Easy, Captain," said the colonel, "or we'll have to charge you extra for the rations."

"Sorry, sir, but I haven't eaten in two days."

"How in the hell did you ever get captured?" Healy asked.

Wade swallowed a mouthful of bread before taking a sip of brandy supplied by the colonel. "The battalion was overrun yesterday morning at the start of the battle. We were being taken south and I rolled into a ditch. Except for a few hours' sleep in a wooded area last night, I've been on the move ever since."

"How did you get through their lines?" asked the colonel. "There are fifty thousand enemy soldiers between there and here."

"I hid in the woods where possible, sir. Then I killed a Reb officer and put on his uniform. Then I walked about three miles through their camps."

"I'll be goddamned. The general will want to talk to you."

Wade told his story to the general, then to the general's general. How many men had he seen? What regiments did he pass through? What supply problems did he observe? Did they have plenty to eat? How was morale? On and on the questioning continued.

"I can't think of anything else, General," Wade said finally. "I was more interested in blending in than in looking at their supply situation or counting them. I remember at least a dozen regiments, and many more were scattered through the woods. It seemed to me they hadn't a care in the world. Right now my thoughts are rather fuzzy."

"Very well, Captain. Get some sleep, and we'll talk in the morning."

The general officers talked in a whisper. Twice they looked at him and shook their heads. He had decided against telling them the whole story, the reason for his near capture at the end. It seemed farfetched, even to him. Why should they believe it? Besides, if he did tell them, they might suspect *he* was the Confederate, sent into the Federal camp to spy on them! That's what he would have thought had circumstances been reversed. He finished his dinner and poured another three fingers of brandy.

"Captain Healy," the senior general said, "take this officer and find him a cot."

"Yes, sir. Come along, Samuel."

"One more thing, Captain Wade. I want a full written report on this matter by noon tomorrow."

"Sir?"

"Everything, Captain, from beginning to end, down to the last detail. That's all."

As Wade saluted and left the tent, the Seven Days' campaign, yet unnamed at this early stage, was drawing to the close of its second day. Was the information provided by Captain Wade of any value? He had no way of knowing, and didn't much care at the moment. His muscles ached too much. Even the endurance of a youth with West Point training had limits.

Chapter 11

• • • • • • • • • • • • • • • •

Spacious but crudely constructed wooden buildings had sprung up all about the fringes of Washington. There were quartermaster storehouses, open-ended stables beyond counting, quarters for staff officers and common soldiers, and office buildings of all sorts. The city teemed with men who served vital functions but who never expected to fire a shot or be fired on in anger. These temporary structures were freezing cold in winter and stiflingly hot in summer, and the men who worked in them complained incessantly about the privation they had to endure.

In one of the largest of these buildings, a regiment of men routinely but reluctantly performed a variety of clerical tasks. They compiled and coordinated the voluminous information flowing in from battlefields of major and minor consequence. There were casualty reports, leave records, intelligence reports, pay records, hospital reports detailing the status of the wounded and sick, and on and on. The bureaucratization of modern warfare had begun.

Most of the men working here were content to suffer the inconveniences, for in return they avoided the danger represented by a more active part in the war. But Maj. Jason Thompson wanted none of this. He repeatedly sought field assignments to "get into the war," as he described it—but without success. He was a brilliant young man, tall and self-assured, with a demeanor that almost commanded a salute, even without the military uniform. Brilliant young men made their superiors look better than their own efforts revealed, so his thoughts of glory had to wait.

Colonel Michael Eckert, a man holding a position far beyond his capabilities, was Major Thompson's immediate superior. One of his subordinates appropriately described Eckert as "a man with the insight of a rock." The next man up the command chain was Gen. Cadwalader Washburn, a man of modest skills and sufficient political acumen to recognize the benefits that accrued from having a man such as Major Thompson around.

General Washburn had a brother, a congressman from Illinois, named Elihu. In every sense of the word, Congressman Washburn was a consummate politician. He never forgot a name or an event. He most especially remembered events that might someday come back to haunt someone besides himself, if only the right circumstances developed to justify the haunting.

As with so many bright young men whose circumstances of birth placed them in the Midwest as the country was growing during its first half century, the congressman had found himself denied the opportunities for the type of rigorous, formal education designed to propel an ambitious individual into the rarefied circles of power. So, as with his sometimes friend and infrequent confidant, Abraham Lincoln, Washburn had educated himself and, as had Mr. Lincoln, he became a lawyer. In his youth, Washburn had immersed himself in every form of legal document. There weren't that many in the 1830s. Illinois had a sparse population at the time. Enterprising men of means, thinking that the essence of the law existed in what men had the ability to hide, preferred to settle their affairs beyond the prying eyes of men such as Elihu Washburn. It seemed natural that, in time, such a man would acquire enough support—or fertilize enough fear—to ascend to at least a modest level of importance.

Congressman Washburn had instructed his brother to bring to his attention any report that seemed in the least unusual, and all reports that had a link to his home state. Most especially, he was interested in reports that met both criteria, a condition that, so far, had proved largely illusive.

One day, in the late summer of 1862, Major Thompson sat reading through the mountain of reports that had piled up following the first great campaign of the war. Some weeks before, General McClellan had withdrawn his troops from the James peninsula. It seemed to many that the only lasting result of the disappointing adventure there had been the enrichment of those in the paper business. At least the major thought so. His mind had grown numb from scanning the brief abstracts of the reports—more than a hundred on this day alone. Time for one more, he thought, then it's off to freshen up for the monthly officers' ball. Anticipation of that event had diverted his attention during the day, for he had a date with an important young lady, the daughter of a prominent Chicago banker. Thompson read the last report, the one on the bottom of the pile, then hurried off to the nearby officers' quarters before picking up his date.

"You look lovely this evening, Miss Healy," the major said as he handed her a bouquet of flowers.

"Why, thank you, Major Thompson," she replied with a demure smile. "And have you had a good day?"

The expression on his face revealed more than the reply. "About like any other, I suppose. I'm in the middle of the greatest event in our country's history, and I might as well be stationed at the furthermost outpost in the western territories." He had said more than he intended in that last brief expression. In a social forum, one had an obligation to avoid expressing professional discontentment. "But there is time. Shall we go?"

He helped her into the carriage and they rode off into the night.

During the orchestra recess, the young major and his lady strolled on the lawn. He felt uncomfortable in the presence of such a beautiful young woman. His conversation was stilted at best. She had recently concluded her schooling at one of those highbrow northeastern schools for ladies. She had become, as he viewed it, a victim of the haughty air instilled by such training. He had first met her nearly six years before when she was a girl of sixteen, back when her spirit flowed freely and her views on worldly matters were no more evident than the corset that hugged her bosom. Their fathers had been briefly associated in a business deal. Their offspring had met at some social engagement, the purpose of which had long since been forgotten. In truth, Thompson had attended the engagement at the request of David Healy, Jr., whom he had met during their recent freshman year at Yale. The young men's relationship had been only casual at the time. Thompson thought of it as friendly now, but less than close. As far as he could recall, Ellen Healy had become a different person, but then so had he. He conceded that as being part of the problem.

"How is your father?" he asked.

"He's fine. He's planning to marry again, but the engagement has not been formally announced. Hadn't you heard?"

"No. I suppose congratulations are in order." Even in the dim light he could see in her dark, sparkling eyes that she had guarded enthusiasm for a relationship that promised to remove her from the center of her father's life.

"I suppose he is as entitled as anyone to his share of happiness." Although the words conveyed concern, the flippant tone was unmistakably self-centered. "Mother has been gone so long. I hardly remember her."

"And who is the lady of his interest?"

"A Mrs. Caroline Wade. She has something to do with shoes. They met at my brother's graduation from West Point. Mrs. Wade's son roomed with my brother at the Academy. She has been a widow for many years, so I suppose it is all right."

Wade. A modestly common name, but it jogged something in his memory. What it was eluded him. They strolled for a while. The conversation grew easier as her formal training gave way to her more deeply rooted Midwestern breeding. In time, they returned to the dance.

It was nearly 1:00 A.M. when Thompson stopped the buggy in front of the elegant old house that the senior Healy maintained for his frequent business trips to the capital city. Business was good for a man with the means to invest.

"It has been a lovely evening, Miss Healy." Thompson helped her from the carriage and briefly clasped her gloved hand. "May I call again?"

"If you wish, Major Thompson. We plan to be in the city for a few weeks." By turning her head and lifting her chin slightly, she signaled permission for a brief kiss. He complied, touching his lips properly to her cheek, followed by a smile and bow. He centered his hat and walked down the steps as the ever more appealing Miss Healy closed the door behind her.

The weather had turned oppressively hot, and Thompson found the thought of returning to the officers' quarters filled with snoring men especially bothersome. He turned the buggy and headed the mare in the direction of the documents warehouse, where he worked. He seldom did that on a Sunday, and never this late at night. Something kept spinning through his thoughts. He was unsure of what he was looking for, so he started at the top of the pile of reports he had examined during the day.

"My God, do you suppose?" The words popped out without his really thinking. He penned a note and fastened it to the document. He walked to the general's office and placed it on the desk, then returned to his own small corner of the war.

"Major, I realize you are ambitious, but don't you think this is carrying dedication a bit too far?"

Thompson lifted his groggy head from the desk. "General?"

"It's eight o'clock on a Sunday morning, Major. What are you doing here?"

Thompson rubbed his eyes. His mouth felt as if a herd of horses had spent the night on parade. "I must have fallen asleep." Then he remembered. "General, I placed a document on your desk. I suggest you take a few minutes and read it. It might be something."

"Very well." The general walked to his office.

The general was more conventional than his older brother, the politician. As with so many bright but poor young men, he had had few choices to make in his youth. The law, the military, or the ministry were the principal paths to success open to him. His agnostic tendencies had eliminated one, and his brother had chosen the law. So he had applied to West Point, the most direct route to a good, if narrow, formal education for a youth with no money of his own. He had participated in the war with Mexico, then resigned his commission with the intention of making his fortune in business. He had experienced some success, but nothing spectacular. That was about to change.

"Major, come here." The command echoed through the vast, noiseless space. Thompson rushed to the office door. "When did you first see this?" General Washburn asked without looking up.

"Yesterday, sir."

"Why did you fail to mention it then?"

"It was late, sir, and you had already left for the day."

"I see." His lips moved as he read the summary again. "I want you here for a meeting at two this afternoon. Go to your quarters now and freshen up. We'll be meeting with my brother this afternoon."

"Yes, sir. Anything else, sir?"

"Later, Major."

"Well, what do you think, Elihu?" General Washburn asked his brother.

The congressman did not reply. He turned back to the front page of the report and began to read again, nodding frequently as he read. As he concluded reading through it again, he smiled and leaned back in his chair. "How many reports do you review each day?" he asked, looking at Thompson.

"As many as a hundred some days, sir. It's a tedious job."

"Yes," the congressman said, "but uncovering this obviously points out its importance. It required considerable insight to see anything in this, young man." He leaned forward and crossed his arms on his desk. He smiled to himself as the potential began to emerge in his mind. Still, it was best to be certain. "Let's talk about this, to make sure we're not on some wild goose chase. This Wade feller, he's the son of Caroline Wade, is that right?"

"Yes, Congressman, as best I can determine," Thompson replied. "According to the young lady I am seeing, her father—David Healy, Sr.—is about to marry Mrs. Wade."

"It will be the marriage of the year, Major. This is no ordinary woman. She's wealthy, self-made in every respect, a woman who, when she speaks, people listen to—even a congressman now and again. And she is well known to have represented herself to be a widow." He knew better. He smiled as he made a faint, satisfying noise. He remembered reading about the incident, so many years before. At the time it had seemed more titillating than important. One just never knows, he thought. What were the facts? "It's all coming back to me," he said. Judge Porter Wade, the congressman recalled, had been a southern Illinois circuit judge back in the '30s and now was chief justice of the Illinois Supreme Court—an all-around son of a bitch if ever there was one. His marriage to a Caroline Wade was annulled back in '38 or '39. The judge claimed the marriage was never consummated. He smiled again. Incredible! he thought. So how did she become pregnant? He paused, rose from his chair, and walked to the door and closed it. "Are you sure this is her son?" he asked, looking at Thompson.

"Confirmed, sir. I checked his records myself."

"And we know she is about to marry one of the most prominent men in Illinois, a man from my district, a man who helped me get elected." The congressman walked to the window. With his hands clasped behind his back he stood silent for a minute or more before turning.

"Something is missing," he continued. "I don't know what it is, but there's more here than meets the eye." The congressman walked to where Thompson was sitting and placed his hand on the young major's shoulder. "Cadwalader, can you spare this young officer for a week or so?"

"What do you have in mind, Elihu?"

*   *   *

Other than the capitol building, the Supreme Court building was the largest structure in the Illinois capital. The offices of the justices were isolated along a secure corridor on the top floor, out of the way of cocked ears eager to overhear some indiscretion that might portend a legal advantage. The men who worked here, men at the pinnacle of power in the state, were unaccustomed to any but the most deferential of treatment. The absence of that respect now resulted in the raised voices presently shattering the normal tranquillity of the place.

"How dare you barge in here and question me like that, Major! Do you know who I am?"

"Precisely, Your Honor, or else I'd have no reason to be here. This is a matter of national security. My inquiry is at the behest of the War Department, authorized and directed by Secretary Stanton himself."

"That gives you no right to question me on a personal matter, as though I were a common criminal."

"No disrespect intended, sir, but there are certain matters that must be examined."

"Who is your superior, Major?"

"General Washburn, sir, Gen. Cadwalader Washburn."

"And did *he* send you?" the judge asked, his voice slightly softer.

"Yes and no, sir. The formal request originated with Congressman Washburn, the general's brother."

The chief justice's features hardened. He knew Congressman Washburn well, although he liked him less than smallpox. Unlike most men who rose to power as a result of *whom* they knew, the congressman had acquired his power because of w*hat* he knew, and what he knew could ruin the chief justice. We should bury the past, thought the chief justice. Am I never to be permitted to put this matter behind me? "Ask your questions, Major."

"As I asked before, Mr. Chief Justice, do you have any children?"

"Certainly. I have two children, by my recently deceased wife."

"And what are their names?"

"Frederick is the older, born in '42; Maggie is the younger, born in '45."

"Are there no others?"

"I resent the implication of that question, Major."

"You were married twice, sir, am I correct?"

The chief justice hesitated. He must avoid lying, but it seemed permissible to hang his answer on a strict interpretation of the law. "No, I was never married before."

The major leaned to his right, covered his mouth, and whispered in the ear of the lieutenant colonel seated beside him. The officer, never altering the fixed, formal expression he had assumed since entering the office, nodded. He was a lawyer whose only purpose at this meeting was to advise the major on legal matters. The major did all the talking.

The major straightened himself in his chair. "I beg your pardon, Mr. Chief Justice. Let me rephrase the question. Did you have a marriage annulled prior to your marriage to the late Mrs. Wade?"

Porter Wade saw no way around that question. Be brief, he thought, and offer nothing beyond the facts. "I did."

"Were you married to a Caroline Wade?"

"I was."

"And, sir, did that marriage produce any children?"

"Most certainly not, Major. A marriage cannot be annulled if there are children. It's the law."

"What provided the legal basis for the annulment?"

"That is none of your business, Major."

"Mr. Chief Justice, if you resist confiding in me, I have the authority to summon you to Washington."

"I'd consider that to be highly irregular, Major." It couldn't hurt to call the major's bluff, the pompous son of a bitch. Wade crossed his arms and held firm. This man had no power to make him answer.

The major whispered to the lawyer again. The colonel rose and walked briskly from the room. "I regret the inability of settling this in private, Mr. Chief Justice. That had been my intent."

"Where is he going?" asked the chief justice.

"To summon the provost marshal, sir. It shouldn't take long. His office is just across the street."

"For what reason?"

"To assign an escort for you, sir, to take you to Washington."

"That's impossible! I have cases to review. This is an outrage!"

"Yes, sir, I suppose it is."

The chief justice glared at Thompson. How dare he confront the chief legal officer of the state of Illinois—the home state of the president of the United States, for God's sake!—in this manner. Outrage was too lame a word for this affront. He studied the major's face. No emotion at all; no sign of wavering, Wade thought. Military men had a duty to perform, and when they had the support of such men as Congressman Washburn and the secretary of war, was it reasonable to expect them to waver in that duty? He undoubtedly fears his superiors more than me, thought Wade.

"Ask your question again, Major."

"What reason did you give for the annulment, sir?"

"Incompatibility." He hesitated. Better to get this over with before the others returned. His gaze wandered to the ceiling. "Failure to consummate the marriage."

The major looked disbelievingly at Wade. No consummation during three years of marriage? Impossible! Although he knew the answer to the next question, Thompson yielded to the urge to hold the chief justice's feet to the fire. "How long were you married, sir?"

"By God, Major—" The chief justice fidgeted in his chair. "About three years."

"I see," replied Thompson. He wrote down every answer, although no prepared question existed in this instance.

"How long did the first Mrs. Wade remain in this area before she departed?"

"Perhaps a year," the judge replied. "She went back East. Pennsylvania, I believe. Yes. I believe she left in the summer of '39, right after her sister went home."

Her sister? That was new information. Thompson knew when and where Mrs. Wade had gone at the time, but he knew nothing about a sister.

"About a year, you say. And was she pregnant during any of that time?"

"I saw her from a distance on several occasions. She never appeared pregnant, although her sister was."

"Her sister was pregnant?"

"Yes, her identical twin sister. She came to visit during the summer of '38—about the time the annulment was approved—and she became ill. She remained until after the babies were born."

"Babies, plural?"

"Yes. It was quite an event. There were three I believe, two boys and a girl." He had volunteered too much. "I never paid much attention."

It seemed that the congressman lacked all the facts. Nothing about an identical twin sister had surfaced during the investigation, much less that the sister had given birth to triplets. The record stated only that Mrs. Wade had a sister, and a brother who had died during the 1830s in some sort of accident. "If they were identical twins, how did you know her sister was the pregnant one?"

"Major, however unsatisfactory our relationship might have been, I lived with Caroline for three years."

I hope I never experience legal troubles in Illinois, the major thought. "I'm sorry, sir, but I have to ask."

"Get it over with please, Major."

"Just two more questions, sir. What is the twin sister's name?"

"Victoria Thornton."

"And where might I find her?"

"In Alabama, Major, somewhere around Birmingham." Wade smiled cynically. "I suggest you go visit her, Major."

Thompson seemed distracted. Thornton! That confirmed his suspicions. It was the name of the look-alike rebel officer Wade had mentioned in his report. Wade doesn't know it, Thompson thought excitedly, but he has a twin brother in the South! Fighting to conceal his agitation, Thompson left the office and walked down the stairs. The lieutenant colonel was waiting in the lobby. "I received all the information that is required, Colonel, and more," Thompson said.

The lawyer smiled. "So it won't be necessary to contact the provost marshal after all?"

Thompson nodded. The major, it seemed, had better poker skills than the chief justice. The president had no need for new enemies at this time, especially powerful Illinois enemies. Thompson's instructions had been precise: Tread softly with the chief justice. Those were Lincoln's personal orders. But the major had larger fish to fry than the chief justice of a backwater frontier state. He had an idea, which he had planted and nurtured in General Washburn's mind. Wherever it led, he meant to see it through to the end. Most assuredly, he thought, it will lead to action.

CHAPTER 12

• • • • • • • • • • • • • •

Rarely before had Chicago seen such an event. The city had only recently begun to assert itself as a regional center of commerce. What most people who visited the city remembered, however, were the rows upon rows of noisy establishments along the lakefront where, for a dollar or two, depending on his taste, a man could have a quart of whiskey and a woman for the night. The commercial center remained small. A man with reasons to avoid dealing in the open felt comfortable in such a setting. David Healy, Sr., was such a man.

It was not that his practices were illegal; they had been legal before the war, and still were, if one had the correct papers. But money was money, whatever its source, even if it had its origin in Southern cotton. There was a war going on, and hardly any cotton grew in the North, this at a time when the demand had never been greater. True, one could purchase the commodity from England, but that meant a roundabout journey that did nothing except elevate the price. Most English cotton came from the South, brought over by blockade-busting fast schooners with the sail power to outrun almost any ship in the Federal navy. Was it wise to pay double the price for cotton that came from the same illegal source? Eliminate the middle man was the motto that had sustained his father. One retains such basic values until the last.

Banking was Healy's formal business, but commodities were his passion. The two made for a good marriage, almost as good as the one about to take place in the Grand Hotel. He was about to marry Mrs. Caroline Wade of Gettysburg, Pennsylvania. All things considered, she was the most desirable catch imaginable. Added to that, he adored her passionately. The feeling might even be called love. Only one thing still bothered him. He had almost had to delay the marriage because of her reluctance to come to Chicago. She regularly traveled all over the country, for God's sake. She even owned the majority share of the flagship of her shoe-making enterprise, located right here in Chicago. It had shocked him to learn that she had never even seen the factory, the principal source of her expanding wealth. Only after he had agreed to announce the wedding using her grandmother's maiden name did she agree to proceed. Why would a woman from Gettysburg, Pennsylvania, be reluctant to travel to Chicago, or be so secretive about her name? The reasons remained a mystery.

"It is bad luck to see the bride before the ceremony," Caroline admonished as he stood at the door to the large dressing room.

"Rubbish," Healy replied. "That old tale is the product of fearful women who wanted a good head start in case they decided to skip out."

She smiled. He was a man with both feet planted squarely in the real world—one of the things she liked most about him. "Have the guests all arrived?"

"The place is packed," he replied with a nod. "This is the social event of the decade, you know. I only wish you could have come out earlier. Everyone is eager to meet you." She had arrived only two days before and had spent all the time since preparing for the ceremony. He remained staunchly opposed to the idea of her bridesmaid, for all the good it did him. Caroline had transported a black woman with her, the widow of her former farm manager. In her youth, the woman had been a slave! But Caroline insisted. Her only explanation was her desire to express where she stood on the question of slavery.

"Who has been invited?" she asked as she worked on her veil in the mirror.

"Oh, just about everyone who is anyone in Illinois. There are a couple of supreme court justices, a senator, and three congressmen, among others. I've also invited a number of business associates and, of course, prominent representatives of the military."

"How many in all?"

"About three hundred."

"My God, David! I thought we had planned a small gathering."

"This *is* small. I pared the list down from about a thousand."

From a distance, the sound of squeaky instruments drifted into the room as the orchestra began warming up. Healy walked over and stood behind Caroline. He smiled as he studied her profile in the mirror while the attendants fussed over her dress. "Jesus, you are beautiful."

"For a woman in her mid-forties, you mean."

"For a woman of *any* age. I still don't believe you said yes."

"Oh? I thought you knew. I said yes before you asked. Let me see. Where was that?" A coy smile curved the lines on the sides of her mouth. "Oh, I remember. It was back in Philadelphia when—"

"Caroline, please, this is hardly the time."

She leaned over and kissed his cheek, smiling that mischievous smile that he enjoyed so much. "Please leave. I have things to do."

Caroline's legs shook as she walked down the aisle. She had never thought to have this experience again. There had been suitors before, several of them, but she had always felt that she had been their secondary interest. The first one positively drooled at the idea of getting his hands on her farm. Every conversation moved in that direction before it concluded. The next seemed more interested in a cheap shoe supply for his string of small haberdasheries scattered throughout Philadelphia. She had the feeling that no man wanted her for herself. Money was a curse as well as a blessing. Now she had found a man with more money than she had, or so it seemed. He seldom talked business around her, but she accepted that as his way. He never asked much about her business activities, either. That served just as well. She had never enjoyed business that much. Her principal source of pleasure and accomplishment had always been the farm.

As she moved cautiously down the aisle, she allowed herself to glance this way and that, to take brief looks at the faces looking up at her. Her view of them was better than theirs of her through her mother's veil. She had taken it with her as a souvenir of her past on the long journey to Gettysburg more than twenty years before. She still longed for the beautiful brass bed that had been her single prized possession. Whatever happened to it? she wondered. She walked to her intended's side and looked at him out of the corner of her eye, but kept her head forward. A sense of mild anxiety clouded her thoughts as the minister spoke. She dreaded the reception.

"I do," Healy said at last.

"Please place the ring on the bride's finger," said the minister.

Caroline smiled as he fumbled to find the ring. She had instructed him to keep it on his little finger, but he had forgotten. He finally fished it out of his watch pocket and slipped it on her left hand.

"I now pronounce you man and wife. You may kiss the bride."

Healy lifted the veil and kissed Caroline hard, as hard as he had during that first moment of pure passion between them back in the hotel in Philadelphia.

She smiled as she turned to face the gathering, then she gasped. No! It's impossible, she thought. Not Porter. Did he recognize her? She had changed so much in more than twenty years. She had been just barely twenty-two when last they spoke, a mousy thing with only a moment of assertion in all the time they had known each other. He sat looking down, seemingly unaware of her, as unconcerned as ever. She replaced the veil just as he looked up. He seemed bored by the proceedings, as if being there was a necessary inconvenience. Why was he among the guests? she wondered. Is he so important now? If her new husband had made the cut down to the honored three hundred, he had to be somebody of importance. Does he know my grandmother's maiden name? she thought with a faint gasp. The old woman had died when Caroline was still a small child; she never knew her grandfather. They had lived in Pennsylvania all their lives. She had no memory of ever talking about her grandmother with Porter.

"David, I'm feeling a bit faint," she whispered through a smile as they moved down the aisle. "I must return to my dressing room to gather myself."

"What about the reception?" he asked.

"I'll be out shortly, as soon as I get my breath." She knew now, more than ever, that coming to Chicago had been a mistake. She had avoided the place, the whole state, for half her life. She had never quite admitted the reason, even to herself. Only one thing had forced her to remain away. Fear. She knew a terrible secret about a man, a secret that could ruin both of them if it ever became known, a secret that could destroy the relationship between her son and herself. Could Samuel ever forgive her if he learned that she had denied him a father, a father who wasn't even his? But how could he prove that? He looked enough like her to be her natural son, down to the same dimples on the chin and cheeks when he smiled. He even had the same smile that David liked so much in her. In a sense, he even had her blood.

Her breathing became more labored as she thought about joining the guests, but she had to do it. She expected no one to understand her reluctance at making an appearance. Leave the veil down, she thought. After the ceremony, that might be a bit out of the ordinary, but she was a bit out of the ordinary. She inhaled a series of deep breaths and exhaled them slowly before lifting herself from the loveseat.

"So nice to meet you, Mr. Tucker. And you, Mrs. Tucker. Your dress is lovely," said Caroline.

"Thank you, dear. It's difficult to get good cloth these days, what with the war and all. Don't you agree?"

"I certainly do."

"How long will you be staying in Chicago?" asked another guest as he passed by.

"We're leaving day after tomorrow on the 9:00 P.M. train. David, the darling, has reserved a whole car for the trip. It belongs to Mr. Honeywell, doesn't it, David?"

Healy smiled and nodded.

The reception line moved along. Somewhere in the gathering, waiting to look her squarely in the eye, even if a veiled eye, was Porter Wade, but she had not seen him since cutting the cake. Because of her long delay, the cake cutting had preceded the reception line. Porter had been standing on the far side of the room talking with some men, or rather he did the talking and they listened. He seemed to have no interest in her at all.

The line required an hour to pass, but Porter seemed to have disappeared. The people gathered around as she opened her gift from David: a diamond necklace with a large emerald as the centerpiece. Then he opened her gift to him: a two-carat diamond stickpin for his tie. As announced, they would take the other gifts and open them during the trip back east.

Caroline scanned the crowd. Porter was nowhere in sight. Her fears eased, allowing time to enjoy the moment. If only Samuel could have gotten leave, she thought, the day would be perfect. The telegram he'd sent expressing warm congratulations also informed her that taking leave had been impossible. She had received only two letters from him since summer, but in her letters to him she pretended that his were slow in arriving and she didn't answer his questions. It seemed impossible that he could have encountered his twin brother as he'd described. A satisfactory explanation still eluded her.

After the wedding, Caroline sipped on a glass of champagne as she studied her reflection in the hotel room's window. She kicked off her shoes and placed her feet on the ottoman. I'd give anything for a long drag on a pipe, she thought—a secret habit known only to her son, and he had caught her quite by accident. To avoid the temptation, she had left her only pipe back at the farm.

Her husband pulled up a chair next to hers. "You seem distant, Caroline."

"Tired," she replied with a sigh, "just very tired." She thought for a moment. "David, do you remember that tall man in the black suit and mutton chops, the one sitting on the left about six rows back in the middle."

"As we faced away from the altar, or coming to."

"Coming to."

"Let me see. Ah, yes. That was Judge Wade, chief justice of the Illinois Supreme Court." Surprise showed in his furrowed brow. "Judge Wade, the same last name as yours. Do you know him?"

I knew better than to ask, she thought. "Heavens, no. I didn't know even a dozen of your guests. What makes you think I'd know a Supreme Court justice?"

He shrugged. "Now that I think of it, he didn't come through the reception line. Why do you ask?"

She had no answer, at least none that made sense. She shrugged. "Oh, he just seemed to have a scowl whenever he looked at my bridesmaid. Do you suppose he's prejudiced?"

"You should know, my dear, that there were several scowls on that account. People are less pure than you might think on the issue of the Negro. Quite a few present today had extensive business links with the South before the war started." He neglected to mention that he had been one of those, or that his ties continued.

"Pardon my insensitivity," she said sharply, "but she's my best friend." She turned and looked at him. "I bought her, you know."

His mouth dropped open. "My God, Caroline, never mention that again."

"And why not?" She had grown unaccustomed to taking orders. "I gave her her freedom within the hour. But that all happened more than two decades ago. It's ancient history now."

"Nevertheless."

Caroline smiled and changed the subject. "I thought your daughter looked lovely."

"She is a princess, isn't she."

"Who was that young man with her?"

"A Major Thompson."

"I know that, but what does he do?"

"Something to do with records. He won't talk about it much. I think it's getting serious."

"Well, he'll surely know me if he ever sees me in a crowd."

"Why do you say that?"

"Every time I looked in his direction, I noticed him staring at me. The moment our eyes met he would look away. I felt a bit uneasy."

"Beautiful women do that to men."

"I'm old enough to be his mother, for God's sake!"

"Well, you look pretty good to me—and me with the soul of a twenty-year-old."

She smiled as he leaned forward and kissed her on the cheek.

"Let us go to bed, Mrs. Healy."

"I notice, Mr. Healy, that you refrained from saying let us go to sleep." She lifted an eyebrow.

"A twenty-year-old soul could never think of sleep on a night like this."

Caroline bolted from her sleep with the sound of screeching wheels in her ears, then her head slammed against the headboard. She clutched her head as her husband rolled to the floor. It was still dark, with the barest hint of dawn against the eastern horizon.

"What the hell is happening?" David asked.

"The train has come to an emergency stop," Caroline replied. She lifted the shade as she rubbed her head. Riders in gray uniforms rode beside the train. "Rebels!" she screamed.

The door to the car crashed open. "Well, what do we have here?" said a Confederate sergeant dimly outlined in the opening. "A gentleman and his lady, and in such elegant surroundings."

Healy attempted to rise, but the butt of the sergeant's revolver drove him back to the floor. He moaned, but made no movement. Caroline reached over the side of the bed toward her husband's head. The sergeant kicked her in the side under her outstretched arm. She screamed as she rolled against the far compartment wall, lost her balance, and crashed to the floor. She looked in horror at the sticky red substance on her hand.

"Goddamn you, Sergeant," said a second voice. "I told you to avoid roughing up these people. These are civilians, noncombatants. The papers will have our scalps for this, North and South."

"He resisted, sir."

"And I suppose *she* resisted?" He shoved the sergeant against the compartment wall. "You idiot." The Confederate officer extended his hand. "Sorry, ma'am."

She reached hesitantly for the protection of the outstretched hand.

"Get the lady's nightcoat, Sergeant, and be quick about it."

"Yes, sir." He extended the nightcoat with a defiant gesture.

The officer bowed. "Sorry, ma'am," he said again.

"What do you want, sir?" she asked.

"We received information that you have valuable jewelry in your possession. The South needs hard currency, ma'am, and such jewelry is easily converted to our needs. If you please, ma'am, where is it?"

Caroline hesitated; the sergeant bent down and grabbed her husband's hair. David yelled in pain.

Thank God! she thought, he's alive. "All right," she yelled. "Don't hurt him. It's in the dresser—over there by the wall."

The officer opened the top drawer. "And the diamond pin, ma'am. Where is it?"

"How did you know—"

"Where is it, ma'am? We're in a hurry."

"It's in the bottom drawer."

He opened the drawer and fumbled in the dark. He turned and placed a knee on the bed as he held the jewel next to the window. It sparkled in the soft, morning light. He wrapped the necklace and pin in a handkerchief before stuffing them in his pocket. "Now, ma'am, get dressed. Quickly."

"Why?"

"Don't ask questions," he said threateningly. "Just do it."

She looked past the officer at the sergeant's smiling face.

The officer turned. "Leave the car, Sergeant."

"But, sir."

"Goddamnit, Sergeant. One more word out of you and I'll have you court-martialed. Now move, and bring the horses to the back." He turned. "Get dressed, Mrs. Healy."

He knows my name, Caroline thought. How is that possible? She moved to the small compartment where her clothes hung and withdrew a cotton dress. She pulled it over her head without removing her nightclothes. Sitting on the edge of the bed, she pulled on a pair of cotton stockings, then her shoes. The officer took her arm before she could fasten the hooks. She heard movement on the floor where her husband lay. The officer turned and fired his pistol. The flash blinded her for a moment. The movement ceased. Had the bullet struck him? It remained too dark to see.

"Out the back door, ma'am." Caroline hesitated as she looked at her husband, trying to detect any sign of movement. The officer grabbed her arm and jerked her from the bed, then gave her a sharp push in the small of her back. She stumbled forward, straining to brace herself on the back of a chair. He grabbed her arm again and dragged her toward the door. "Do you know how to ride, Mrs. Healy?"

"I spent most of my life on a farm."

He lifted her under the arms and sat her firmly on the horse. "Take the reins of her horse, Sergeant." The young officer sprang to his white stallion. "Let's ride!" he yelled, and the dozen or so men stationed beside the train began to yell. They rode off into the trees, heading southeast into the dawn. The Kentucky border lay fifty miles beyond, a long ride through enemy territory. They expected to be at least an hour away before the train reached the next station to sound the alarm. When they were safely out of sight of the train, the officer turned his men southwest.

CHAPTER 13

• • • • • • • • • • • • • •

"Majuh," said Capt. Thomas Bottoms, "looks to me like we's got maybe a one-in-four chance of completin' this mission."

Major Thompson drew the pipe smoke deep into his lungs, then blew it out slowly. "That good, huh? I figured they were no better than one in ten."

"If'n ya'll ain't got no more confidence in it than that, why'd ya'll even suggest this operation?"

"Because, Captain, it offers a chance to shorten the war."

"That may be all right for the war, suh, but what about us?"

"What *about* us, Tom? We're soldiers. Soldiers die every day, sometimes quite a few of them."

"I reckon so, but still—"

"Attention!"

"At ease, men." General Washburn removed his hat and slid his ample figure into the desk chair. "Are you prepared, Major Thompson?"

"I believe so, sir."

"All right, let me hear the final plan."

"It's fairly simple, sir. We get in and we get out."

"How good do you think your intelligence is?"

"That's the problem, sir, or one of the problems. All we know is, General Jackson's wing of the army is somewhere in the upper Shenandoah, near Winchester. We will have to travel fifty miles through enemy territory, find a specific tent and a specific man inside that tent, capture him without leaving a trace, and get him back. None of us even knows for sure what he looks like."

The general shook his head. "I still think there has to be an easier way, Major."

"I'm open to suggestions, General."

"Hmmm. What happens if you're captured?"

"That's the easy part, sir. They'll shoot us. We'll be wearing rebel uniforms, so they'll try us as spies. Should take no more than twenty minutes or so."

"You seem rather cavalier about it all, Major."

"Some things it pays to put out of your mind, sir. Knowing what will happen if we're captured may work to our advantage. We'll be more alert, since there's no point in surrendering."

"And what about you men? What do you think?" Washburn asked, fixing his gaze on the rest of the troopers.

The other soldiers looked questioningly at one another. They made no attempt to disguise the anxiety in their eyes. Their silence spoke more eloquently than words.

"Well, come, come, gentlemen," said the general. "What do you think, Captain Bottoms?"

"I done tol' the majuh heah, I think we have a one-in-four chance, suh. He figgers it's one in ten. I can live with my odds, but his're a little long."

"Do you want out?"

"No, suh. I just hope I'm right an' the majuh is wrong."

"Where were you born, Captain?"

"'Possum Lick, Geo'gia, Genrul."

"What in the hell are you doing in the Union army?"

"Well, suh, I really don't wanna be in no army, but since I had ta choose one, I figgered this country's been damn good ta me, all things bein' equal, so I'd like ta keep it together a while longer. 'Sides that, there's slavery."

"What about slavery, Captain?"

"No man's got a right to put a chain 'round another man's neck, don't matter what his color is. They's wrong for doin' that, Genrul."

The general liked the captain. Unpretentious almost to a fault, he seemed as at ease talking to a general as to a private. His relaxed, easy drawl probably caused him trouble at times. A Southern twang drew attention within the Northern army. But his bright smile, with the corners of his mouth upturned and curling slightly inward, immediately eased concern.

Bottoms had entered the army as a private. While advancing under withering fire at Bull Run, he had pulled three wounded men to safety without the slightest regard for himself. With that act, all concern for his loyalty evaporated. The offer of a commission quickly followed his promotion to sergeant. Once, a major who knew nothing of him questioned his loyalty in the presence of several junior officers. "Why is he fighting his friends and neighbors?" the major asked. "How can I trust such a man?"

Bottoms had just smiled. "Down in 'Possum Lick," he said, "wheah I was raised, my family raised pigs. I had this prize sow that produced the best litters in the valley. They was this surly sort'a fella what had the best bottomland ya'll ever seen, an' he took a fancy ta my pig. He decided ta take 'er when I refused ta sell. I pounded on him all the way down the hill ta his property an' kept it up 'cross the fence. It took half a day." He smiled, as if to confirm that he was making a point rather than telling the truth. "He was my neighbor, an' he'd married my sister. But he was wrong ta try an' take somethin' that t'weren't his. The way I figger it, some unscrupulous politicians have gotten control down there an' they're tryin' ta take part of the country. That's wrong."

No one ever questioned Bottoms's loyalty again, at least within earshot of him.

"Anyone else have anything to say?" asked the general.

The major waited before answering. "Well, sir, all of these men were raised in the South and know its language and ways. I have to trust them to take care of me, because everything Southern is foreign to me. Anything else, sir?"

"What's your schedule?" asked the general.

"Four days in, a day to reconnoiter, and five days out. With any luck at all, we'll be back here with the prisoner a week from Sunday. We'll travel out in the open going down, but try to stay invisible on the way back."

"What do you plan to do with the prisoner?"

"Wish you hadn't asked that, sir. We're still working on that part of it."

"One more thing, Major. This mission is strictly unofficial. There are no records and no orders. If you're caught, you're on your own. If you're successful, there will be no official recognition."

"We understand that, sir. All I ask is, if you can't help us, please don't obstruct us."

The general remained noncommittal; he had no authority to promise anything. Officially, this meeting never took place. The war had taken a nasty turn, he thought. Any lingering illusion of chivalry died in a railroad car in southern Illinois. If men and their reputations required sacrificing, well, so be it. The only remaining priority was the preservation of the Union—at any cost.

Now, military business stayed within the military if possible. At the public level, concealing Confederate successes had become common practice. Officials had also covered up the kidnapping of a prominent Gettysburg citizen by Confederate raiders. For two days, military officials had isolated all the passengers at the water-stop hamlet of Newton. Interrogators repeatedly told these tired, bewildered people, first individually, then as a group, that the attack on the train, actually carried out by Confederate John Hunt Morgan's men, had been nothing more than a training exercise to test public reaction to a Confederate invasion. It had to remain secret, they were told. Their government depended on them. In time, all except one came to believe this interpretation of events. Officials also found a solution for that problem. The disbeliever, a young man of nineteen, was on a business trip. The army had become his employer by the time he reached his unexpected destination, and he reluctantly became a private, with orders never to discuss the matter on penalty of treason. He believed that.

Outside a small circle of officers, General Washburn and Major Thompson included, and, of course, the president and Secretary Stanton, as far as anyone knew, Mrs. Healy had departed to parts unknown for an extended honeymoon. Mr. Healy had at first resisted this deception. He had yielded only after receiving word through unofficial channels that the government planned to do nothing to secure his wife's safety if the unfortunate incident became public. They planned for him to surface later, after fully recovering from his painful chest wound, then to make light of her absence by claiming that she had gone to England on an extended shopping trip. At all costs, the administration sought to avoid admitting that rebel soldiers had ridden fifty miles into Illinois and then retreated without so much as a single shot being fired by Federal forces.

Much about the train robbery remained a mystery. Central among the unanswered questions was how the rebels learned about the jewelry and then reached the train in time for the attack. Or had an unknown plan already been in effect, with the robbery simply a cover for that undiscovered motive? But why take a hostage—especially a woman—an action certain to slow their escape? One thin string of clues had emerged during the investigation that had concluded only two days before, and no one had any proof they were related, or even that they meant anything.

On the afternoon of the wedding, someone had sent a telegraph message from Chicago to Danville, Illinois. It read:

PACKAGE TO ARRIVE AT DAWN.

A second message arrived in Harrisburg, from Danville, stating simply:

ARRIVAL TIME AND DESTINATION CONFIRMED.

A third message arrived from Harrisburg in Effingham, north of Harrisburg:

INDIVIDUAL ARRIVING E. DAWN SUNDAY. ACTION IMPERATIVE.

An A. Brown sent the first message. The second, from an unknown sender, went to B. Smith. The third was for a C. Johnson. The names were certain to be aliases. None had been identified. The abduction had taken place thirteen miles southeast of Effingham, Illinois, at a point about as close as possible to the northern Kentucky border—given the scheduled route of the train—and the attack had been just at dawn, forty-seven miles, as the crow flies, from the nearest point on the Kentucky border.

Why had the first message referred to a package but the third to an individual? And why the roundabout route for the series of messages? The potential for delay, especially on a weekend when even official communications were unreliable, seemed risky for a finely timed affair. Identifying the person who sent the first message offered the best chance for unraveling the mystery—but here the final enigma developed: Someone had killed the Chicago telegraph operator, apparently during a robbery while he was on his way home.

A string of coincidences? Perhaps. But General Washburn and Major Thompson thought otherwise. Yet none of this mattered now. The raiders had disappeared, as if the earth had swallowed them up. There were more than enough Southern sympathizers, once the raiders reached Kentucky, to hide them or aid them safely on their way.

A warm breeze blew in the riders' faces as they rode past the last Federal outpost into the enveloping darkness. Six days earlier, the Army of the Potomac and the Army of Northern Virginia had met in a titanic struggle along Antietam Creek outside Sharpsburg, Maryland.

Unofficial word had filtered back to Washington that more than twenty-five thousand Yankee and rebel soldiers were killed, wounded, or missing as the sun set on that terrible day, the bloodiest in American history.

With predictably disastrous results when fighting Gen. Robert E. Lee, Maj. Gen. George McClellan had committed his overwhelming forces piecemeal throughout the day. Whenever conditions turned in the Union's favor, a fresh supply of rebel troops seemed to arrive, always just in time. When conditions were at their worst for the Confederates in midafternoon, Maj. Gen. A. P. Hill's division marched onto the battlefield after a grueling seventeen-mile forced march from Harper's Ferry. The fighting sputtered on for a while, but the serious struggle had ended.

It was not the magnitude of the battle, or the resulting carnage, that concerned Major Thompson. He was looking for the Confederate army, or at least Lt. Gen. Stonewall Jackson's portion of the army, and word had reached Thompson just before he rode out that the Confederate army had retreated southward in the general direction of Winchester.

All of the uncertainty, combined with the joining of the Confederate forces into one cohesive body, elevated the odds against his mission's success. Captain Bottoms cherished the thought that the odds had risen only to the previously unacceptable ten to one. Major Thompson declared that twenty to one seemed more reasonable.

The major commanded the small party, with Bottoms as second in command and the only other member of the group with a reasonably clear understanding of the mission. The other five soldiers, all enlisted men of Southern heritage, knew only the general outline. If Thompson and Bottoms died, or otherwise were unable to proceed, the soldiers' orders were to cancel the mission if the first phase remained unfinished. Assuming the first part of the mission was accomplished, they were to take whatever actions necessary to accomplish it.

As they rode at an easy gallop in a west-southwesterly direction, Bottoms pulled up beside Thompson. "Majuh," he said, "I hate ta raise this question now, but how do we know that the offisuh we're seekin' weren't killed in the battle?"

Thompson turned and looked at his companion, but said nothing.

"Sorry, Majuh, but it seemed like a reasonable question ta me."

The implication of the captain's question defined the main problem: They had more questions than answers. None had had any experience in clandestine activities. The Pinkerton organization had dabbled in skullduggery but with marginal success. The odds against success increased with each new threshold.

They kept moving throughout the night. They munched on hard-tack and pressed biscuits at dawn but kept moving. Only at noon, when the horses and men were feeling the debilitating effects of the long, weary ride, did they pull into a foliage-shrouded gully, tend to the animals, and settle down for some sleep. They had a story ready if a rebel unit passed by: They were a patrol from Stuart's cavalry out looking for supplies and forage. They were dressed for the part, wearing tattered and dirty captured uniforms. None of the parts fit.

Late in the afternoon they encountered the first rebel cavalry patrol, a company sent out from Stuart's cavalry division to see what might be happening in the far rear of the army.

"What unit are you men from?" asked the cavalry captain as Thompson's men walked their horses south.

"The 1st Virginia," Bottoms replied as he chewed on a piece of burned corn bread.

"Where ya headin'?"

"South," Thompson replied.

"That's right," Bottoms added. "We're late with a report for Genrul Jones. Ya'll know how ol' 'Grumble' can get."

The rebel captain nodded. "Good luck," he said as he spurred his horse and wheeled to catch up with his patrol.

The moon set early, so they found another ravine in which to catch a few hours' sleep. They were in the saddle again before dawn. They encountered several rebel units on patrol as the day progressed. In midafternoon, they came upon two stragglers. Thompson ordered his men to dismount and build a fire in a small grove of trees some thirty yards away. The stragglers appeared nervous when they realized there were officers in the area, but acting nervous usually raised suspicion, so they stayed put but kept their distance. The infiltrators boiled some coffee and unsaddled their horses to give them a rest before beginning to fry grits. Drawn by the smell of food, the two stragglers edged closer.

"You got some extra?" asked a private with no shoes.

"Might," said one of Thompson's sergeants. "You got a chaw?"

The two deserters conversed between themselves. "Naw, but Jeb here has some smokin' tobacco."

"Bring it on over," replied the sergeant.

Bottoms stuffed his pipe and propped a foot against a tree. "What unit you men from?"

The two looked at each other. "We're out scoutin'," replied one.

"Didn't ask ya that."

"We're from the Stonewall Brigade, sir, Stonewall Jackson's corps."

"I hear'd you men did some fightin' back up a ways."

"We sho' did, and we give those damn Yankees somethin' to write home 'bout."

"Licked 'em good, huh?" said Bottoms.

The two men wolfed down the grits and coffee.

"Reckon we best be gettin' on our way," said the first, wiping his sleeve across his mouth.

"How far ahead is the army?" asked Bottoms.

"No more'n six or eight miles, I 'spect. Could maybe be nine by now."

"Time to be movin', men," said Thompson as the two stragglers scurried off into the trees. "Saddle up."

"We save a day if we do the job tonight," Bottoms said as they trotted along.

"The same thought occurred to me." Thompson looked at the sun. "Three hours to sunset. If we hurry, we'll have light to look around." He picked up the pace. Within the hour, they were passing the rear units of the army. Men stretched ahead as far as the horizon. Thompson and Bottoms kept moving at a canter past line after line of plodding troops; then they came to the wagons. Signs of the recent battle were everywhere. Wounded men in the wagons moaned with each bump of the transport; others who were still whole dug shallow graves beside the road and deposited the once-flowering youth of the fledgling nation. Thompson led his men onward for an hour before spotting the colors of the 27th Virginia, one of the regiments of the Stonewall Brigade. Although Jackson was now a corps commander, he was fond of his old brigade and usually located his headquarters nearby. The sun had moved low, almost to the horizon. Already, the rebel soldiers were beginning to pull off the road to boil coffee.

Bottoms spotted the headquarters element first. "There's Genrul Jackson hisself up ahead," he said softly.

Thompson nodded. He slowed to a walk and turned the mare's head to the right. The others followed. They paralleled Jackson and his staff until they pulled into a clearing and stopped. Thompson dismounted and led his horse behind some bushes about a hundred yards to the west. "Sergeant, gather some wood. Act as casual as possible."

"Yes, sir. Come help me, Joe," the sergeant said to the corporal.

"Unsaddle the horses, but keep them together," Thompson said softly.

The corporal formed a circle with some rocks, arranged the wood, and lit a fire.

"Gather 'round the fire," Thompson ordered. The others moved casually to form a loose circle. "Listen up. As soon as it's a bit darker, Captain Bottoms and I will move closer to their camp. This is the rough part. We're looking for a Lieutenant Colonel Vincent. He's one of Jackson's staff officers. Since we don't know exactly what he looks like, we have to hunt for him. All we have is a rough verbal description. When we find him, we'll wait until everyone is asleep. Midnight should do. Captain Bottoms will take you, Sergeant Clinton, and you, Corporal Humboldt, and go to the back of the colonel's tent. Once certain that everything is quiet, cut open the tent. Sergeant Clinton will chloroform the colonel. Once you're sure he's unconscious, carry him back here the same way you went in."

"What if someone sees us?" asked Humboldt.

"Act as natural as possible. We have to get in and out without being suspected. We have to make this appear as though the colonel deserted. Otherwise, this will all be for nothing. Captain Bottoms has a forged note to leave on the colonel's cot. It says his new bride was trapped in the North at the start of the war. Sources tell us he has requested leave several times to go get her, but the general won't let him go. The note says he's gone to get her and will return when possible. Hopefully, they won't look too hard for him."

"What about the slit in the tent?" asked Clinton.

"With luck, they'll think he went out that way to avoid being seen. Sergeant Wartburgh, you and Private Matthews will join me. We'll guard the perimeter in case anything goes wrong. Benton, you stay with the horses. Be ready to move at the first sign of trouble. Benton, you ride double with Sergeant Clinton until we find a horse for the colonel. We'll bring the colonel back here, throw him over a horse, and head west. Captain Bottoms will lead the colonel's horse. If we have time, Matthews, you tie the colonel to the saddle. We'll try to circle far enough to get beyond their guards. If they start looking for him, I think they'll conclude he went east, the shortest route back to

Baltimore, where his wife is known to be. We'll travel all night. Getting back will be more difficult than getting in was. We'll look more suspicious with an injured man along. We'll have to keep the colonel knocked out and wrap him in bandages. We'll travel only at night. Camps will be cold on the way back, so don't even think about hot food. Any questions?"

They all shook their heads.

"Feed and rub down the horses, then get some rest."

The major and the captain moved to the right. Thompson crouched behind a bush and dropped his pants. Better to appear to have business if someone is looking. He lifted his binoculars and studied the movement of the men in the command post area. There were two lieutenant colonels, one tall and one short. Reports identified the target as being six feet tall. The tall one went in and out of the northernmost end tent several times. The other spent most of his time around the third tent south of the command tent. Thompson motioned for Bottoms to concentrate on the north tent. He pulled up his pants and sat next to a tree.

The tension grew as they waited. A thousand things could go wrong, any one of which might be fatal. If detected, there wouldn't be a chance in a million of riding through half an army. If captured—well, none of them wanted to think about that. As a last resort, if outright escape became impossible, their orders were to attempt to blend in and wait for an opportunity to slip away one by one.

Who was this rebel colonel with enough importance to risk seven lives to capture him? Only Major Thompson knew the answer to that question. Each man knew exactly what he needed to know, nothing more. Bottoms had strict orders: Abandon the colonel only after exhausting all chance of escape. The others could take off on their own if need be, but each was expected to stick with the captain if worst came to worst. Plans had been examined and reexamined. Had something been forgotten? It always seemed to be. Surely they had overlooked some trivial point. Nothing ever went completely as planned.

The major had expressed his main concern when they were no more than a few miles into their journey. What if the colonel had been wounded or killed at Antietam? What if he had been sent off on some mission and just wasn't here? What if they found an officer who fit the description and he turned out to be the wrong man? Would the mission be a failure if they captured another officer? On and on the questions ran through their minds, each in relation to his own assignment.

One moment it was light, the next dark. Gradually, the men around them began settling in for the night. The staff tents were clearly visible with the lanterns glowing inside. Men moving about cast giant shadows on the canvas. All the staff came together at about nine. Probably a conference to plan the next move, thought Thompson. Or maybe they intended to have a card game. The minutes dragged on, then the hours. All the lights were out by 11:30. An occasional sentry walked by. Most of them were too far off to raise concern. But two made a constant circle around the headquarters area. Why hadn't anyone thought of that? the major asked himself. God, how stupid can we be? The simple things were the easiest to overlook. He timed the route. If the sentries kept an equal distance apart, they had four minutes to get in, get the colonel, and get out. What if someone smelled the chloroform? In the clear night air, the smell seemed certain to radiate a distinctive odor. A hospital tent nearby was too much to expect. Another oversight, perhaps because they had delayed too long deciding upon this part of the plan.

Why hadn't they simulated the capture? That way, the dumb oversights might have emerged. Next time, if there was a next time, they planned to be more rigid in their planning. Were two hundred-to-one odds too optimistic?

"Sergeant Clinton," Thompson whispered.

"Yes, sir?"

"Don't open the chloroform bottle until the last possible moment, and keep your hat over the rag. Don't take any chances on spilling the bottle. Close it before you put the rag over the colonel's nose."

"I thought of that, sir."

Good man, thought the major.

"Captain Bottoms?"

"Yes, suh?"

"Have you noticed the guards?"

"I know, majuh," he whispered. "We have, at best, fo' minutes ta complete the job. We'll go in as close behind the guard as possible, ta give us maximum time. It'll be close."

Another good man. All minds were working. Perhaps they wouldn't overlook anything productive.

Thompson looked at his watch. "Time to go," he whispered. "Stay in the shadows as much as possible. If there's any movement, come back here and we'll try again in a half hour."

The captain, followed by the two enlisted men, rose to a crouch. What had happened to the guard? If he stayed on schedule, he should be coming into sight. Would the two guards be too close to each other now? Nothing to do but wait.

Bottoms withdrew his knife. He had sharpened it to a razor edge. He expected cutting through the tent to be the only easy part.

The guard walked by. Zip. The cut exposed the tent's interior. Two men were in the tent, a colonel and a major. The major snored. He squirmed and coughed as the drifting smell of chloroform entered his nose. A minute had passed. The colonel squirmed. The captain had his knife an inch away from the rebel major's throat. If he opened his eyes, his death would follow in the next second. God, that odor is strong, Bottoms thought.

The colonel squirmed for a moment before going limp. The two enlisted men lifted his inert body and carried him out the back opening. Bottoms placed the note on the cot and moved into the open air. They had completed the task in time. Crouching as low as possible with the heavy load, the enlisted men shuffled toward the trees. The captain followed, then stopped. It's impossible for the guard to miss that smell, he thought. He's sure to be attracted to the cut in the tent and sound the alarm. He had to kill the guards, hide the bodies, and hope no one found them. Men desert all the time, he reasoned. If a colonel, why not two privates when they had the best opportunity? That seemed the only option, sorry as it might be.

The first sentry went down with only a dull gurgle. There remained a chance if the other guard failed to check on the smell when he passed in front of the tent. No such luck. The sentry began to sniff even before reaching the tent. This problem presented a greater risk. Bottoms realized he would be in the open, in full view of other sentries, but he had to take the chance. He grabbed the private's chin and slipped the knife upward through the neck into his brain. Hardly even a gurgle. He dragged the body around the tent and into the bushes.

"Quick thinking back there, Captain," whispered the major. "But we have to take time to dig a shallow hole. Otherwise, they're sure to find them."

Bottoms motioned for two of the men to help dispose of the bodies. They carried them fifty yards into the woods and placed them in a shallow gully. "Push dirt over 'em, cover 'em with leaves, an' there's a chance," said the captain.

The eroded gully banks were soft. At least something was working to their advantage.

Thompson dragged a fallen limb over the grave. "That's good enough. Let's get out of here."

Dawn broke clear and windy. Drying leaves fell from branches that would soon be bare. Early October had arrived, and military activities were settling down to bare essentials. Patrols roamed the countryside during the day, but major military operations were on hold as both armies licked their wounds after the savage fight on Antietam Creek. Although the bulk of the Confederate army had escaped to safety, Lee divided his forces, leaving Jackson in the Shenandoah Valley while Longstreet moved to the vicinity of Culpeper.

Although the roundabout route selected for the abductors' return from their mission sometimes led them away from rather than toward their own lines, they felt certain they had avoided attracting suspicion. It had been less difficult than expected, and the weariness of seven straight days in the saddle had dulled their senses. The objective was Harper's Ferry, twenty miles to the north-northeast up the Appalachian Trail. It seemed unlikely that rebel troops still occupied the place, that Lee would have been so foolish as to station men there to be captured after pulling his army back to Virginia. If the weary group pushed hard, they might possibly reach their objective by dark, even if they had to travel off the main road.

The high-pitched rippling of the rapids, where the Potomac and Shenandoah converged, provided the dominant sound as they rode to within sight of the small town. Darkness came quickly to the small valley. It would have been better to approach the picket lines while light remained. The troops here, assuming they were Union, were certain to remember the rude ejection they'd experienced when Jackson first decided to occupy the place the previous month. More than a thousand of the men from the Union garrison there were now someplace down South in a prison camp.

"It looks peaceful enough," Captain Bottoms said to Major Thompson as he leaned on the front of his saddle. "Do ya think we should go in?"

"I'm sure those are Federal forces," said Thompson. He waited before adding, "The thought of spending another night in rebel country doesn't sit well with me."

"My sentiments, too, suh," replied Bottoms. "Let's go on in."

"All right, but let's take it slow and easy."

They rode at a walk along the ridge on the southern approach to the town. "Shed the Confederate uniforms," Thompson said. "Throw them in the bushes."

A hint of light from the sliver of moon and bright, starry sky shone down on them. It either provided too much light or too little, depending on one's point of view. Major Thompson lagged behind. He checked the ropes binding the rebel colonel, then his gag and blindfold. All secure. "Hold those reins tight, Captain."

"He ain't goin' nowhere, Majuh, not after all we went through ta get 'im."

They rode to the tree line bordering the south edge of a small hillside cemetery. A two-hundred-yard clearing provided an open field of fire. Nothing higher than grass was visible in the faint light. Just beyond had been constructed a barrier of logs, and behind that was a shallow trench. Neither was visible now, but the major had seen them when he had passed through on an early summer assignment. There must be sentries now that it's dark, he thought, although none were visible against the black backdrop of trees.

"I don't like it," said Sergeant Clinton.

The major said nothing as he moved his binoculars from right to left. Nothing, he thought. There are lights through the trees, but I can't see any movement.

"Let's go in, men. Move slow."

They had moved a hundred yards into the open when the first sounds of life ahead reached their ears. "We're coming in," shouted Thompson in reaction to the noise. "Don't shoot. We're Union forces back from patrol. *Don't shoot!*"

Captain Bottoms had snapped almost horizontally backward by the time the sound of the rifle reached them. *Craaaack.* The sound lingered in the damp, heavy air. Thompson looked at his friend as he rotated limply in slow circles about the fulcrum of the saddle. The major reached out to hold him upright, but it was too late. Bottoms leaned to the right, then rolled out of the saddle. He hit the grass with a muffled thud, but felt nothing. He had been dead since before the sound of the rifle reached the others' ears.

Men ran toward them from the north. "Who goes there?" said a loud voice.

"Don't shoot," shouted Thompson, the sound echoing back from the high rock cliff on the far side of the river. "For God's sake, don't shoot!"

As the men ran, the torches bounced ghostlike in the cool night air. As the blue-clad soldiers surrounded the position, their rifle muzzles pointing menacingly at the unidentified soldiers, Thompson dismounted and moved to his friend's side.

A young lieutenant approached. "Who are you?"

"I'm Major Thompson of the Quartermaster's Department in Washington."

Bottoms, his eyes fixed on eternity, had a peaceful expression; there had been no time to react to the horror that confronted him. Oh, how he'd wanted to live, thought the major. No man had spent more time calculating the odds of survival. Yet he never wavered, even at the worst of times. All he wanted was to repay his country for the opportunity it had given him. For that, he had given up his home, his friends, and his family, and ridden north.

"Who fired that shot?" Thompson demanded.

A moment of silence followed. "I did, sir," said a soft, cracking voice from the shadows.

"Come here, soldier." Thompson grabbed the torch from the lieutenant and lowered it toward the dead captain. "What do you see, Private?"

There probably existed no more frightened soldier in all the Union army at that moment. "I—I see a dead man," replied the private.

"Look at his right hand. What do you see?"

"The hand clutches a horse's reins, sir." A hint of surprise joined the fear in his voice.

"Private, this man left Washington more than a week ago. He had orders to hold onto those reins and bring back this prisoner, no matter what happened. Even in death, he holds onto those reins." Thompson clenched his fists, trying to hold in the emotion pushing to burst forth. He had a strong urge to grab the private, to shake him until he screamed understanding of the gravity of the act he had committed. "That's duty, soldier," he said sharply. He lowered his head. "That's duty." The words were barely audible. He lifted the torch. The private's terrified eyes stared into the bright, flickering light, his pupils invisible against the glistening whites of his eyes. Tears were building, but he doubted that crying was the appropriate response. He had become a soldier, after all, and to this very moment, nothing in his life had given him more pride.

The major studied the soft features of the private's smooth face. Hardly a day over seventeen, Thompson thought. His anger subsided and turned into grief. "Remember this, soldier, when *you* are called upon to do your duty. Remember this man lying on the ground. Remember the reins in his hands. Then remember your duty."

The private sank slowly to his knees. He looked at the dead captain; then he lifted his head and looked into the major's eyes. Even though the boy remained silent, the words echoed in Thompson's mind. Forgive me, the private's eyes were saying. Oh, please, God, let him forgive me. Tears ran down his cheek, his mouth hung open, and his hands clutched at his knees. He's so young, Thompson thought.

"I don't blame you as much as I blame myself, soldier. We should have been more cautious approaching the camp in the dark." He intended the comment to ease the private's suffering, but that made the remark no less true. They had made so many mistakes on this mission, and they had endured and survived them all—except the last. They possessed no guidelines, no training procedures; they were at the forefront of an emerging, modern war: total war, war carried out with all means available, at whatever the cost. The good and the brave were most likely to die, for the good did their duty. No man was better or more brave than Captain Bottoms. This was no less true of what he had done than of what he had sacrificed to do it.

The major felt numbing agony at the death of his friend, and vowed to remember.

"No," said the private. "I should have asked who you were before I fired. Those were my orders. I was afraid." The controlled whimper gave way to heaving sobs. "I was afraid."

More men ran in from the dark. "What's going on here?" asked a colonel with drawn pistol.

"A man has been accidentally shot," said the lieutenant.

"Who are you men?" the colonel asked Thompson.

Thompson explained briefly as he bent and closed the captain's eyes. "Colonel, do you have a locomotive here?" he asked finally.

"Yes. Why do you ask?"

"We need it, sir. We have to get to Washington as soon as possible."

"I have no orders authorizing me to release a locomotive, Major. Who do you think you are, asking such a thing?"

No sense trying to explain, even if Thompson's orders permitted, which they did not. "Do you have a notepad and pencil, Colonel?"

The colonel searched his pockets.

"Here, Major," said the lieutenant, holding out a tablet and pencil. Thompson took them from him and wrote:

> OCT. 1, 1862
> MAJ. GEN. C. WASHBURN
> DEP. COMMANDER, SPEC. PROJ.
> SPEC. ENGINEERS
> WASHINGTON ·
> PRIORITY: URGENT
> ARRIVED HARPER'S FERRY SUNSET TO-DAY. CAPT. BOTTOMS DEAD. HAVE PRISONER. NEED OFFICIAL AUTHORIZATION TO REQ. LOCOMOTIVE TO TRANSPORT US TO YOU SOONEST. RESPOND TO COLONEL COMMANDING, H.F.
>
> J. THOMPSON, MAJ.

"Colonel, will you please have this sent by telegraph as soon as possible?"

The colonel read the message. He resisted the idea of some major riding in from the darkness and trying to confiscate his locomotive. One never knew when those gray-clad soldiers might come marching up from the same direction and demand the return of the town so recently recovered. Locomotives provided for faster escape than horse and wagon. "I don't know this General Washburn," he said. "I think I'll just hold onto this message until I get to the bottom of this."

"Oh, I neglected something," Thompson said. "May I have that back for a moment, sir?"

The colonel shrugged and handed him the tablet.

Thompson penciled at the bottom, under his own name:

> CC: SEC. WAR STANTON
> PRES. LINCOLN

He returned the message to the colonel. The president and Secretary Stanton were certain to be surprised when they received their copies. Rumor had it that Lincoln read everything that came into the War Office telegraph room, but Lincoln's name on the message was certain to command special attention, and he would not have the faintest idea what it meant. The secretary, on the other hand, had approved the mission, but he knew few of the details.

The colonel's eyes grew wide as he read the addition. "Lieutenant, I'll take over here. Take this message to the telegraph tent and send it immediately. Wait for the reply, then bring it to me at once."

"Yes, sir." The lieutenant saluted and ran toward camp.

"Sergeant Clinton," said Thompson, "take the captain's body to the train depot. Wrap him in a blanket. We'll return him to Washington for burial."

"Yes, sir." A tear rolled down Clinton's cheek. "Damn! A dumb, scared kid points a rifle and it ends forever."

"Sergeant!"

"Yes, sir?" Why, thought Clinton, is it all right for a major to say something and not a sergeant? Captain Bottoms was my friend, too.

Chapter 14

Confederate Lt. Col. Frank Vincent sat in a corner, his back pressed against the damp, cold stone wall. He had long since lost track of the hour, of day and night, of the day of the week. He had arrived in the dead of night, blindfolded, frightened out of his mind. Someone had untied his hands before pushing him into the barren, windowless stone cell; then the steel door had slammed shut behind him, effectively severing all contact with the human race.

Each day continued the same, or varied only by degree. Twice each day, a fat private opened the door and placed a tray of rancid food on the floor before removing the empty tray from the previous meal. Vincent judged, by the food and the distant sound of reveille, that morning arrived with every other meal. The process progressed at what seemed like twelve-hour intervals, except that every other visit the private replaced the putrid-smelling waste bucket with one that passed for fresh. The private never said a word, even in response to a direct question, although he occasionally permitted himself to glare with bared teeth. Vincent thought of the private as the personification of every man's enemy, the one sent by Satan to instill the sense of hell that awaited each man who failed to pass the trying test of honorable existence.

The process varied only infrequently when a baby-faced corporal performed the chores. He suspected that happened on Sundays, when the fat private was off duty, but Vincent was only guessing.

Once or twice a day, a small steel door in the middle of the larger one slid back. Two dark eyes, always the same, peered through the hole, sometimes for a minute or two, sometimes longer, but the encounter never progressed beyond that. What had he done to deserve such inhumane treatment? Nothing about it passed the test of reasoned analysis. He had gone to sleep one night bone tired and he had regained consciousness to find himself draped over a horse with the feeling that his insides were going to squeeze out his mouth. No one had spoken to him since then. He knew something unfortunate had happened near the end of the journey. Someone apparently was shot and killed. His mind had been only half-clear at the time. Then someone had tossed him into an enclosed car and moved him someplace by train. There had been one stop before he arrived at this place, wherever and whatever it was.

He knew only one thing for sure: He was slowly going crazy. If they intended to shoot him, why did they let him linger? He ran his fingers through his matted whiskers. He had tried several times to crawl away from the smell of the waste bucket, but it always followed him.

He snapped from his stupor at the sound of keys rattling outside the door, then he let his head drop against his left knee, which was pressed against his chest.

Just then, the door squeaked open. A Federal officer stood in the doorway. "How are you doing today, Colonel?" the officer asked politely, as if he really cared.

Vincent forced a smile as alertness returned. Someone had acknowledged his existence! And the voice sounded familiar. Questions rushed through his mind. "I've been better," he replied softly. He felt surprised at discovering he still had a voice.

The Union officer walked the three steps across the room. "Well, we'll change that." He squatted and thrust a lantern in the rebel's face. "I'm appalled at what they've done to you. I apologize." He reached down and grasped the Confederate officer's arm. "Come with me. There's a hot tub waiting and, after that, a large steak. We have to put some meat on your bones."

Vincent lost his balance as he attempted to stand. There had been little reason to walk in the eight-by-eight cell.

"Here, Lieutenant," said the Federal officer to another man waiting outside the cell, "show Colonel Vincent to his new quarters. Give him anything he requests—within reason."

"Yes, sir."

Vincent scrubbed himself, then scrubbed himself again. It felt good to see the pink tint of his skin again. He dried his wilting body and pulled on the warm cotton robe before lifting the cover from the plate.

He ate the well-done steak eagerly, then munched on one of the two apples they had provided.

Shortly, the lieutenant walked in with a pitcher. "Sorry, Colonel, but we don't have anything stronger."

Vincent's eyes sparkled. Beer! During this period in hell he had thought of a glass of beer more than any single thing—except the thought of seeing his wife. He had tried putting thoughts of her out of his mind because of the pain they brought. "How long have I been here?" he asked the lieutenant. The officer smiled but kept his counsel to himself. Apparently the silent treatment remained in force. Vincent felt he could endure anything after drinking the pitcher of beer. He held the glass to the lantern. He swirled the golden liquid for a moment, as if to confirm its genuineness, then guzzled it down without a breath. By the time he finished the second glass, the room began moving slightly— only a little, just enough to distract his thoughts from his physical pains and mental anguish.

The door opened. "Colonel Vincent, I'm Lt. Col. Jason Thompson. How did you like the steak?"

Vincent licked the foam from his upper lip. "Fine, Colonel, but the beer tastes better."

Thompson smiled, enjoying the feeling that came with being addressed by his new rank. "Thought that might be so. How are you feeling?"

Vincent had no interest in gratuitous chatter. "What am I doing here, Colonel?"

"We'll get to that in time."

Vincent studied Thompson. "You were the one who brought me here, weren't you?"

It had been impossible to keep Vincent sedated with the chloroform during the full five days of the return trip. Thompson suspected Vincent had heard more than they wanted. It was important that Vincent trust him. "Yes," he said finally.

"How did you capture me? I remember nothing until I woke up bouncing around on the back of that damnable horse."

"In due time, Colonel. Let's go for a walk and get some circulation back in your legs."

When they returned, a screen stood at the back of the room. "Sit here, Colonel," Thompson said. The chair had its back to the screen. "When did you join the Confederate army, Colonel Vincent?"

After his long isolation, Vincent had a commanding urge to talk to someone, but a distant voice counseled caution. He was, after all, a prisoner of war. Nothing could compel him to say anything beyond basic information that surely they already knew. "I joined in the late spring of '61."

"What rank were you at the time you resigned?"

"Captain, captain of infantry."

"And your wife? How long since you last saw her?"

How did they know about her? "We had just gotten married when I went South. I haven't seen her since. Do you have any word of her?"

"I assume you wish to see her again," Thompson replied without answering the question. Keep Vincent off balance, he thought.

"My God! Is that possible?" He felt the caution slipping.

The questioning continued far into the night. Between the beer—the supply seemed endless—and periodic mentions of his wife, Vincent's resolve to remain discreet weakened, then collapsed completely. The Federal colonel wanted to know the habits of General Jackson's staff officers—who did what, when, and how. He often changed the form of the questions, but covered the central issues repeatedly. Finally, he shifted to the people themselves, their personal habits, their families, their favorite color, their lovers—if they had any—down to the most insignificant detail. What attitudes did they have about the war? What did they think about slavery? Were there any rivalries among the staff? When an answer varied, no matter how slightly, from a previous, forgotten response, they went over it again from several angles. Colonel Thompson never wrote a word, but all the time Vincent heard a faint, rustling activity behind the screen. The more weary Vincent became, the faster the questions came, until he hardly remembered his own name. In eight hours, they paused only twice to attend to body functions.

"Well, Colonel, that's enough for now," said Thompson as the first faint light of dawn shone through the window. The combination of the brew and fatigue had taken its toll. Colonel Vincent let his head drop to the table. "We have a nice room prepared for you. I'll bet clean sheets would feel good about now."

Vincent tried to move, but thought better of it.

"Come with me for a moment, Colonel Vincent."

Vincent sighed. He lifted his head slightly and tried to focus his eyes. No part of the room seemed square anymore.

Thompson led the wobbly Confederate down a stone-walled hall to a room that looked out on a large open area. "Sit here for a moment,

Colonel Vincent." Vincent sat. Thompson went to the only window and drew back the curtain. He waited for a few moments, as if waiting for something in particular. "Come here, Colonel."

Vincent lifted his weary body from the chair and shuffled toward the window.

"Look out there, Colonel."

Vincent shifted his weight and looked out the window. Across the way he saw two soldiers escorting a woman—or were there four soldiers escorting two women? The figures faded in and out of focus. He strained his eyes to see in the still dim light. The figures came closer. His alertness heightened; then he rubbed his eyes and pressed his face against the glass. "My God, Colonel. That's my wife!"

Thompson smiled. "I believe you are correct, Colonel Vincent."

"May I see her?" There was a pleading in his voice and sad eyes.

"Later, Colonel. You need to get some sleep first. This afternoon we'll go over some of the questions again and see how you do."

"Goddamnit, Colonel, how do you expect me to sleep knowing *she* is here?"

"Rest then, Colonel. But you have to be fresh if you are to confirm the information you provided." Thompson took Vincent's arm and led him back to the interrogation room. The screen had been removed. On the table sat a plate containing fried eggs, bacon, and fried grits, a cup half filled with honey, and a large portion of corn bread. Candied fruits filled a small bowl. "Eat it all, Colonel. We want you well when you see your wife again." At the edge of the table, a razor lay next to a porcelain bowl filled with steaming water. A private in a white apron stood by the chair fronting the bowl. "Freshen up a bit, Colonel. The corporal will give you a shave. Your hand may be a bit unsteady. If you do well when we talk again, your wife will be permitted to spend the night with you." Thompson turned and clasped his hands behind his back as he walked from the room. He could only imagine the anticipation reflected in Vincent's eyes.

"Wake up, Colonel Vincent." Colonel Thompson stood looking down.

Vincent rubbed his eyes. The long shadow of the chair informed him it was late afternoon.

"It seems you slept with no difficulty," Thompson observed.

Vincent swung his legs over the side of the bed.

"We have someone we want you to talk to."

"My wife. Is my wife here?"

"Later, Colonel. For now, just keep her in your thoughts." Thompson clapped his hands together. The guard opened the door. Except for the fading light from the setting sun, there was no illumination in the room.

"Get in there, damn you," a voice called from the hall. The guard pushed a man into the room. He wore a soiled and torn Confederate uniform. The rank insignia was that of a major. With hair uncombed and a two-week growth of whiskers, he looked a fright. He had a black eye, as if he had been on the losing end of a fistfight. The man wore only one shoe and had to keep one hand on his trousers to keep them from falling.

Vincent stiffened. "Simon? Is that you? They got *you*, too?"

"Do you know this man?" Thompson asked.

"Of course I do. He's Major Thornton."

"How do you know him?"

"I told you last night. He's on General Jackson's staff. The general hardly ever goes anywhere without Simon—Major Thornton."

"Well, it's obvious they are separated now," Thompson growled.

A private brought in another plate filled with food. "You two go ahead and eat now," Thompson said. "We'll talk later." He flicked his head. The corporal opened the door and left the room as another soldier placed a dimly glowing lantern next to the wall. Thompson followed and shut the door.

"How did they capture you, Simon?" Vincent asked in a whisper. What did it matter if they talked, thought Vincent, so long as they did it quietly? Except for the two of them, the room was empty.

As he shoveled food into his mouth, Thornton told a story that paralleled the colonel's. "Did you get here with the same group that captured me?" Vincent asked when Thornton finished. Thornton said he had no memory of the trip. He remembered being knocked out with chloroform most of the time and professed to have no knowledge of Vincent's capture.

Vincent ate as he questioned Thornton. Thornton seemed disoriented. He would express something, then shake his head and shift to a different subject. Lack of sleep obviously made his thoughts unclear.

"What did you tell them, Simon?"

"I don't remember. After a time, every question seemed the same. I suppose they learned what they wanted."

Vincent questioned the major on the same subjects he had discussed, only he confined his concerns to a narrow range of important issues. New information entered the conversation, information that Vincent had withheld during the previous long night, but information that he knew to be inaccurate in vital respects. But that seemed understandable. The major seemed confused, tired, unable to keep things separated in his mind. Vincent corrected several of the major's statements. His estimate of the casualty count at Sharpsburg, for instance, was incorrect. Thornton overestimated the Confederate losses by nearly three thousand, the equivalent of four whole regiments.

For Vincent, going to sleep had been difficult that morning. Thoughts of seeing his bride, and of Thompson's demands before permitting the visit, had forced him to review in his tired mind everything he had said. If the story changed, if one important detail appeared out of place, they might keep him from her. He had to know what the major told Thompson. If any of their statements conflicted, varied in the slightest respect, he had to decide how to make the two versions conform. Vincent gave scant attention to the personal matters. What use could they make of such information? He had gone into detail on those matters, held back nothing. He had even revealed the general's favorite Bible verses. Trivia. Unimportant trivia.

Thornton slid his hands up the side of his head, pulling his hair between his fingers.

"Simon, I never noticed that black mark on your head before." He cocked his head and looked at the irregular shape.

The major thought for a moment before answering. "I woke up once, and this son of a bitch Sergeant Clinton hit me with a board." He pressed on the area and winced. "It swelled up something awful. I guess there's still blood under the skin."

Vincent nodded.

After more than two hours, the door opened. Two privates entered. They grabbed Thornton by the arms and dragged him from the room.

"Why are you treating him so rough?" Vincent demanded of Thompson as he entered the room.

"He has been very uncooperative. But don't worry, Major Thornton is bound for a prison camp out west. His war is over. We've finished with him, and about finished with you. Your wife is waiting; you can see her after we clarify a few points."

Thoughts of Major Thornton faded from Vincent's mind. Get the answers straight, he thought. Oh, Maggie. I've missed you so much.

David Healy had reached the extent of his patience. His side hurt. The bandage pulled with every move. The doctor had refused to dismiss him from the hospital, so he had just walked out when no one was looking his way. Now he questioned his own wisdom. He groaned as he shifted, trying to find a comfortable position. "Miss, when did you say Congressman Washburn will return?"

"I expected him before now, Mr. Healy. If you had made an appointment . . ."

Healy rose and walked to the window. The capital city was a beehive of activity. Healy thought he knew why the army had so much difficulty defeating the rebels: All the soldiers were in the capital. Standing hurt worse than sitting, so he returned to the chair.

"Don't forget that committee meeting at ten tomorrow," said a voice in the hall.

"And don't *you* forget the reception tonight," sounded the reply.

The door opened. "David Healy," said the congressman. "It's been a long time." The sound of admonishment grated on Healy's sensitive nerves. He had expected a more welcome tone. "Have you been waiting long?"

"An eternity, Elihu. I'm all trussed up and hardly able to move."

"I heard about your—accident. Come in." The congressman shut the door behind them. "You're in no condition to be up and about," he said sternly. "What the hell are you doing here?"

"Do you know what happened?"

"Of course I know. Nothing happens that I don't hear about sooner or later—usually sooner."

"What is the government doing?" Healy demanded

"Can't rightly say for sure. There *is* a war on, you know." The congressman appeared annoyed by his friend's demand.

"Goddamnit, Elihu, they took my wife!" Healy yielded to his anguish. He was unaccustomed to being controlled by events, but this was worse. He had no options at all. His frustration had driven him from the Indiana hospital and compelled him to take the long train ride to Washington.

The congressman's attitude softened. "I know. Sorry I couldn't attend the wedding. It's just too hectic around here."

"Has there been any word?" Healy asked.

"So far as I know, nothing. They escaped into Kentucky. The army lost the trail within ten miles of the abduction. They apparently rode down a stream and exited on a well-traveled road."

"Don't we have any people in position down there to find out?"

"Probably, if they had time to stop scouting and getting information back about enemy movement, and any one of a thousand other important activities. Christ, David, put this into perspective. She has disappeared into what is, for all practical purposes, a foreign country."

Healy lowered his head. He had become irrational, but she *was* his wife. "Is there someone I should talk to?"

"Probably, but I doubt they want to meet with you." He placed his hand on his old friend's shoulder. "David, you're a distraught husband. The government can't trust you to act rationally. You'd recognize that in any other situation."

Healy lowered himself carefully into a chair and placed his face in his hands. He had reached the point of desperation, willing to promise anything in exchange for information. "Elihu, set up a meeting. You owe me that much. I'll behave myself." More than anything, he hated begging. He thought it a sign of weakness.

The congressman nodded. "Perhaps, but this is largely out of my control. I will ask, but that doesn't mean they'll agree."

Healy looked pleadingly at his friend. "Try. Please."

Healy's imploring tone touched the congressman. He *did* owe Healy, more than it was possible to repay. Someone had, many years before, kidnapped the congressman's young daughter and held her for ransom. Healy and two other men had paid the $5,000, but to no avail. The child surfaced three days later in a neighbor's pond with a bullet in her head.

In addition, Healy had greased the way, both with money and arm-twisting, for the congressman's first election. Beyond that, and more important in the long run, Healy had counseled him on who was and was not trustworthy in Washington. The congressman knew Illinois politics, but Washington operated on a different plane. Power here had an illusive, fleeting dimension. Knowing which mundane little men, which men of seeming unimportance, were the power brokers meant the difference between success and defeat on important issues. Here, the congressman had learned, *who* one knew often proved more im-

portant than *what* one knew. One had to know such things to move
ahead. Healy knew, and he shared the information willingly.

"Do you know Willard's Hotel?" Washburn asked.

"Of course."

"Be there at eleven tonight. Go to the dining room and have a drink.
I'll send someone to pick you up."

"Is all this secrecy really necessary?"

The congressman declined to answer. He opened the door.

"Eleven."

Healy nodded.

Healy arrived at Willard's at 10:15. He had tried resting, but the
discomforts of flesh and mind were too intense. His daughter, Ellen,
had attempted to ease his distress, but her effort lacked enthusiasm.
She remained uncertain if she approved of his marriage, and it showed.
Her attitude was more than an irritation to her father. He had no need
for her permission to marry, or to do whatever else he pleased. In the
end he had told her that, and she had run to her room crying. As he
had stood in the foyer putting on his coat, she had stood at the top of
the stairs impassively watching him. He knew she wanted forgiveness,
any kind word, but he was in no mood to forget her insensitivity. Now,
nearing the completion of his third double whiskey, he waited.

"Mr. Healy?"

Healy swayed slightly as he lifted his head. A young man with blond
hair and a bushy mustache stood over him. "I'm Healy."

"Come with me, sir."

Healy fished through his pockets until he pulled out a money clip.
He placed a bill on the table and pushed back his chair. He stumbled
slightly as he tried to rise.

"Is this your coat, sir, on the back of this chair?"

Healy nodded. The young man held out the coat. Healy stabbed twice
before his right arm slipped into the sleeve. "I've been sick," he said
softly.

"Yes, sir." The young man smiled as he assisted Healy with the left
arm.

"Where are we going?" Healy asked.

The man touched Healy's arm and motioned with his head. Healy
followed. An enclosed carriage waited by the curb. The young man

assisted Healy up the step and closed the door. The rocking motion made Healy dizzy. Only after the carriage began moving did he realize that the young man had remained outside. Healy looked out the window. The man rode behind on a horse. Healy pulled his head inside and closed his eyes. He expected a short journey, and he needed to put his thoughts in order.

"Mr. Healy, wake up."

"Are we there?"

"Yes, sir."

Healy looked out the open door. They were in the country, miles south of the city. How long have I been out? he wondered. He leaned on the young man as he stepped from the carriage; then he walked toward a small house barely visible through the trees. The sleep had helped. At least his mind still worked.

Congressman Washburn looked through the window, then opened the door. "My God, David! You smell like a still."

Strange, thought Healy, the congressman is dressed in formal clothes. Then Healy remembered. Someone had said something that afternoon about a reception before the congressman entered his office. "I arrived at Willard's a bit too soon," Healy said, smiling. "It must be the injury. I believe I passed out in the carriage."

Washburn sniffed. "I shouldn't wonder. Are you all right?"

"Let's say I'm better." He entered the small house. The only light twinkled from a short-wicked lantern sitting on a table. The house was cold. There was no fire. "What is this place?"

"We use it to meet in from time to time," Washburn said. "It's out of the way of prying eyes and ears. Have a chair. I believe you know my brother, General Washburn."

"General. How are you doing?"

The general nodded.

"And over here, well, you know him, too."

Healy turned. "Major Thompson?"

"It's Lieutenant Colonel Thompson now, sir. How do you feel? It grieved me when I learned of your experience."

"What are you doing here? Are you involved in this?"

Thompson lowered his eyes.

"And this young man who fetched you," said the congressman, "this is Lieutenant Clinton. Congratulations are in order for him, too. He was recently given a battlefield commission."

Healy extended his hand. "You were very kind, Lieutenant." Clinton smiled as they shook hands. Healy turned to the congressman. "Why have you brought me here?"

"Simple, David. If there is anyone with information about your wife, besides the rebels of course, these are the men."

"Have you found her?" Healy asked excitedly.

"Not exactly," said the general.

"What does that mean?"

"It means we don't know where she is, but we think she's still alive. That's more than we knew this time last night."

"How do you know?"

"We can't say, sir, it's a security matter," said Thompson.

Healy spun toward the colonel. "Security? That's poppycock! We're talking about my wife, a civilian."

"I know, sir. We just can't tell you *how* we know."

Healy sighed. That's something, he thought. He had never allowed himself to think that Caroline might be dead. What point was there in killing a woman? Because she supplied shoes to the army? Nonsense. There were other shoes. "What can you tell me that isn't a secret?"

Thompson rose and walked across the room. A square of white cloth hung on the wall, suspended by two nails. He nodded toward the lieutenant.

Clinton opened the door. He looked around, then shut the door. "All quiet, Colonel."

Thompson pulled off the cloth that covered a map. "This is where they stopped the train," Thompson said as he pointed. "They cut southeast into some trees, then changed direction back to the southwest. They rode down this stream for about three miles before turning south along this road."

Healy strained his eyes in the dim light to follow the path. "They were headed toward Kentucky," observed Healy.

"Yes, but Kentucky was only their first destination. We believe— we *know* now—that they placed your wife on a wagon about—here, at Morrisonville. Other soldiers took charge of her there. There was quite a row. Any number of people watched the confrontation. It became very loud before a major pulled rank on the lieutenant who led the raid on the train. The major and his party continued south with your wife into Tennessee. There they disappeared somewhere near the Alabama border."

"God, I'll never get her back now," Healy said. "How do you know all of this?"

"I'm sorry, sir. I can't tell you."

"So that's it?"

"Mr. Healy."

Healy turned toward General Washburn. "It is our understanding that you still retain, shall we say, business contacts in the South."

"I have the blessing of the government in everything I do," Healy snapped.

"I know that. I signed the exemption order myself. We appreciate everything you've done. You've saved the government a considerable amount of money."

"Who are you people, anyway?" Healy asked with obvious confusion.

"Well, that's difficult to say," replied the general as he lit a cigar. "Originally, we worked in the Quartermaster's Department. Still do, after a fashion. Then we attached ourselves to the Engineers, but we don't engineer much—wouldn't know how to if they asked us. That just gave us direct access to important geographical information. Working through the bureaucracy between departments can be hell. Actually, we deal in information, information of all kinds."

"And that allowed you to get information about my wife?"

"That's right. There's nothing peculiar about this, Mr. Healy. We're all Americans, you know, North and South. They have their people up here, and we have our people down there. You're a part of all of this, in your own way."

Healy rubbed his side. The dulling effect of the alcohol was wearing off. "Do you have a drink?"

"Get Mr. Healy a glass of water, Lieutenant," said the general. "There's a well out back and some glasses in the back room."

"I meant whiskey, General."

"Sorry, no spirits."

"Why did they take my wife?" Healy demanded.

"We don't know for sure, sir," said Thompson. "We don't think it had anything to do with the war, however, except indirectly."

"Does that mean she's safe?"

"No, not exactly. It may mean the opposite."

Healy's brief hope faded. Little of this made sense. They talked in cir-

cles, in riddles. It had nothing to do with the war, and that's more dangerous? What could be more dangerous than war? "So what happens now?"

Thompson took the glass and handed it to Healy. "Nothing, unless—"

"Unless? Unless what?"

The general went to the wall and removed the map. "Unless, Mr.
Healy, we find a way to rely upon your avoiding doing something,
shall we say, stupid." He wrapped the map in a blanket before handing it to Clinton. "You attended West Point, Mr. Healy."

"So?"

"If you were in the military, subject to orders, we might have more
latitude in this matter."

"Oh, no, General. I'm over fifty years old. What could I do in the
army?"

"Age is no concern," replied the general. "Many of our field grade
officers are over fifty, some are even in their sixties."

"I've forgotten everything about the military, General. I was twenty-
six when I resigned my commission."

"Twenty-six and seven months to be exact, and you never forget
what they teach you at West Point, do you Mr. Healy?"

The general had him. What he had learned at the Academy had guided
his whole life—the discipline, the self-control, the meticulous attention to detail, the technical skills, everything. It had guided him like
a beacon through all of his business activities.

"Does this have something to do with getting my wife back?"

"Everything," said Colonel Thompson.

Healy looked apprehensively at the colonel. "Young man, I'm growing
more uncertain by the moment that you're the right man to be seeing
my daughter."

Thompson smiled and nodded. "Yes, sir. I know what you mean."
Seeing was too formal a term. Despite the shaky start, his infatuation
with her had grown with every date. There was no formal announce-
ment—yet—but they had talked of marriage. Not now of course, but
someday, perhaps after the war.

General Washburn walked to an official-looking satchel sitting in
the corner of the room and opened it. He pulled out a small folder
containing some papers. "It took some doing to get this done after working
hours, Mr. Healy, but here it is. This is the authorization to restore
your commission with the rank of lieutenant colonel. Now, sir, if you
will raise your right hand and repeat after me. . . ."

CHAPTER 15

· · · · · · · · · · · · · ·

"How are you doing, Captain Wade?" Thompson asked as he hung his coat on the tree.

"Sir, what am I doing here?"

"You are expected to study these transcripts, Captain. I thought you understood that."

"No, you misunderstood me, sir. What am *I* doing here? I'm an artillery officer, Colonel. I've gone along without complaint up to now. But I need some questions answered."

No one seemed willing to tell Wade what he wanted to know. First, his mother had ignored an inquiry into the identification of the man who looked like him. Now there were no letters at all. There had been no correspondence from her since the letter informing him of the wedding. Because his services as an artillery officer were too important, officials had denied his request for leave. Now this, and it had nothing to do with artillery. That business with the Confederate colonel— what was his name? Vincent? They had told Wade he had performed well, but what had it all been about?

"Captain," Thompson said as he shut the door, "perhaps it's time to tell you what we have in mind. It appears we may have to move earlier than expected. But first, let me ask you a question. What have you concluded so far?"

"This has something to do with the report I filed describing my escape last summer."

"Yes, it all started from that. What else?"

"There's someone who looks similar to me in the rebel army."

"Not similar, Captain, but enough like you to be your double. Colonel Vincent thought you *were* this other person."

"Who *is* this other person, Colonel?"

"*Who* is less important than *what*. He's one of the few people on General Jackson's staff with total freedom of access to information."

"Not good enough, Colonel. I want to know who he is."

"I don't believe that information is vital."

"The situation is clear, Colonel." It really was unclear, but simple deduction led in only one direction. "You plan, in some way, to substitute me for this other person. That's why you've gone to all the trouble to gather information about all the other people on the general's staff. I insist on knowing what I'm getting involved in."

Thompson had expected this. He had told the general of his concern for jeopardizing both the mission and the man by sending him in half blind. But fully informing Captain Wade might complicate matters beyond repair. The plan—the plan that appeared to have the best chance of working—was to substitute Captain Wade and kill Major Thornton, then dispose of the body. Perhaps murder offers a more appropriate description, if murder even applies in war. The man, after all, was an enemy soldier. If obtaining Lee's and Jackson's plans shortened the war by even a day, would not any action be justified? War meant redefining morality. But once Wade knew everything, Thompson expected him to oppose the killing of his brother, to support capture instead. This was what he would demand. This, however, would increase the risk of failure for the already complicated timing where everything would have to work perfectly to have any chance of success. "Wait here, Captain."

Wade waited. He wanted no part of this. He had exhaustive training as a line officer; he was not reluctant about taking his chances in battle. But to be shot as a spy? No. He intended to refuse to do this unless he knew everything, including the identity of the man they expected him to replace. He knew the rules. They had authority to order him to perform only conventional duty.

"Captain," said a corporal, "General Washburn wants you in his office, sir."

Wade followed the corporal. "Captain Wade reporting as ordered, sir."

"Have a seat, Captain." The general sifted through a pile of papers.

"You've had some remarkable military experiences so far, Captain. You're making quite a name for yourself."

"Thank you, sir." He's trying to soften me up, Wade thought.

"So why are you placing your career in jeopardy now?"

"I don't look at it that way, sir. Send me back to my unit. I'll do my duty."

"But your country needs other services from you just now, Captain."

"Then let my country fully explain what is expected, General. I don't think I'm being unreasonable. This isn't a conventional military operation, at least as I understand conventional."

"So what happens if I give you a thorough explanation and you decide you don't want to participate? What is your attitude about that?"

That was more difficult. He was a West Pointer—duty, honor, country. "All I will say, sir, is I have sworn to do my duty for my country. Forcing me to sacrifice my honor exceeds military authority."

Washburn smiled. Good answer, he thought, but how does one define honor in war? Values have unequal weight when the safety of the nation is in jeopardy. "I suppose my only choice is to trust you, Captain. Colonel Thompson, tell the captain what we expect."

"Very well, sir. You have already guessed the essentials of this operation, Captain. We intend to substitute you for a Major Thornton on General Jackson's staff. If you are to be successful, you must become Major Thornton. It will be insufficient just to look like him. Even a minor slip may result in suspicion and, perhaps, your being tried as a spy."

Wade nodded. "As you said, Colonel, I had guessed as much. But who is Major Thornton? Really, I mean. Is he my cousin?"

"We *think* he's your twin brother, Captain."

"Are you saying my mother gave away my brother?"

Thompson and Washburn glanced at each other. They had reached the difficult part. "No, Captain, just the opposite: We think your *real* mother gave *you* away. We believe you were born to Caroline Wade's sister, Victoria Thornton. In fact, we think you were one of triplets, the third child being a girl. We don't know *why* you were separated, but triplets were born to Victoria Thornton, *that* we do know. You were born in Illinois. So far as we have determined, Caroline Wade never had a child. But in late '39, she arrived in Pennsylvania with an infant. She claimed she was a widow. In fact, she had been married to a man named Porter Wade. He annulled the marriage for incompatibility. Records confirm that your mother received a substantial settlement in that arrangement. Mr. Wade is alive and well—and an important person. He's the chief justice of the Illinois Supreme Court."

"Is he my father?"

"No, we're certain of that. The woman you refer to as your aunt evidently discovered her pregnancy shortly after arriving for a visit with her sister—your mother, Mrs. Wade. Something happened—exactly what we can only guess—but she was too ill to return to Alabama until after the children were born. We think your father is Victoria's husband, Henry Thornton, a general in the Confederate army."

"My God!" Wade exclaimed. "How could this have been kept a secret all these years? How confident are you that this is true?"

"Very," said Thompson.

"Tell him everything, Colonel," said Washburn.

"Sir?"

"Tell him everything."

"Captain, how long has it been since you last heard from your mother?"

"More than a month now, sir. I've requested leave to explore the problem. I've heard nothing from her since she married a Mr. Healy."

"How well do you know Mr. Healy?" asked Washburn.

"Only slightly, General. He's my best friend's father. It delighted me to hear of the wedding. He seemed like a very nice man the few times I talked with him."

Thompson stood, hands clasped behind his back, in front of the window looking out. "Mrs. Healy was abducted by rebel forces while on her honeymoon trip following the wedding. Her husband was seriously wounded during the resulting struggle. We think Mrs. Healy is somewhere in Alabama."

"Why was she abducted?" Wade demanded. "Why would anyone want her!"

"That we don't know, not for—" He spun around. "My God."

Washburn turned his swivel chair and looked up at Thompson. The colonel seemed to have lost his train of thought in mid-sentence.

Why didn't I think of this before? thought Thompson. It solves everything. But I have to think about it, look at all the implications. Still, if it worked . . .

"What is it, Colonel?" asked Washburn.

"Sir, I must talk with you in private. Is there anything else, Captain?"

"A hundred questions come to mind, Colonel."

"Write them down. I'll do my best to answer them later. Now, if you will excuse us, please."

Captain Wade rose and saluted. His mind swam in a sea of confusion as he walked from the office. The colonel had told him many facts, some of them startling if not for his emerging suspicions. He remained uncertain whether it made him feel worse learning what the colonel had said, or learning that his true mother had given up her child—he suspected the latter. But what the hell does all of this have to do with Major Thornton? Wade thought. Are they holding something back? They just told me that I have a twin brother in the rebel army and that my mother is not really my mother. What could possibly be more disturbing?

Substituting me for Major Thornton might prove difficult, to be sure, but hardly impossible. They had, after all, gotten Colonel Vincent out. Getting me in is what's going to be difficult. They intend to take Major Thornton—that's it! They mean to kill him. That's why they were reluctant to discuss it with me. They plan to kill my brother. They never said so, but that's the plan. It makes sense militarily: Kill him, dispose of the body, and burn all the bridges, thereby assuring a balance if events later soured. Simple military logic. The only problem is, how does a twin feel about the killing of his other half, or worse, about participating in the killing? That was a troubling thought. Wade felt no anger, or even sadness, but he had to acknowledge some feeling here, a feeling of loss that eluded reasoned analysis.

"Well, Colonel, I'm waiting," said General Washburn.

"Sir, I need time to think. Will you do me a favor, sir?"

"What's that?"

"Promote Captain Wade to major, sir. Immediately. I want him to become used to being addressed as major."

"Consider it done. He will have earned it if he pulls this off."

"Sir, what do you know of the rumors of a winter offensive by General Burnside?"

"Very little. As you know, we've been equipping the army for winter field activity. What the operation involves, or when it will commence, I can't say."

"Find out, sir, as fast as possible. We may have to move with greater speed than I had intended."

"What is this all about, Colonel?"

"I'll give you a full report as soon as I know myself, General. Sir, where is General Lee's army at this time?"

"In the Fredericksburg area, I believe."

"And General Jackson's corps?"

"Still in the Shenandoah Valley."

"Fast rider coming in," yelled the sentry. "Friendly."

The rider pulled on the reins, causing the horse to stumble to its front knees. He slid off, removed his gloves, and swaggered toward the cabin. "Captain Jonas to see the general," he said to the sergeant standing in front of the door with his rifle held firmly across his chest. When the man didn't respond, the captain shoved him aside. The sergeant reacted instinctively, grabbing Jonas's arm as he stepped into the open doorway. Jonas pulled his pistol and stuck it in the sergeant's face. "Keep your goddamn hands off me, Sergeant."

A colonel moved to the doorway. "Colonel," the captain demanded, "I want this sorry excuse for a soldier put under arrest for striking an officer." The colonel stood his ground. The captain tried to move around, bumping the colonel in the process. The colonel grabbed the captain's arm, twisted it behind his back, and shoved him against the wall. Jonas, a stream of blood flowing down his face, broke free, spun, and pointed his pistol. Three enlisted men rushed from the other side of the small log cabin. The colonel, now in a crouch, held his arms high, palms out. He turned and spoke softly to the three men now pointing their weapons at Jonas: "If, by the time I lower my hands, the captain still holds his pistol, kill him." The colonel straightened up slowly, then started to lower his arms. A dull clunk ended the immediate crisis. The pistol thumped to the floor. "Place the captain under arrest," the colonel ordered.

With a defiant look in his eyes, Jonas backed against the wall.

"If the captain resists, shoot him and feed his body to the pigs." Who is this arrogant son of a bitch? the colonel thought. One of Morgan's goddamn irregulars. No discipline at all. Why Mr. Davis puts up with them is the best-kept secret of the war.

One of the soldiers stuck his rifle against the captain's chest. "Move along, Cap'n," said the corporal, "like a good boy."

Jonas turned and started to swing. A rifle butt hit him in the side of the head and he sprawled to the floor.

All the while, the general sat at a table across the room quietly eating biscuits smothered with sausage gravy. He continued eating as the enlisted men tied the captain to a chair.

Jonas shook his head trying to clear his vision. Blood from one wound matted his hair; more blood dripped from his chin. When consciousness fully returned, he pulled at the rope, causing the chair to topple over. A sergeant moved forward to assist him.

"Leave him alone," said the general in a soft, firm voice. "He put himself there, now he can get himself up."

"Colonel Morgan'll hear about this," Jonas said as he strained to pull himself to his knees.

"Unlikely, Captain, unless you've learned to talk with three bullets in your heart." The general patted his mouth with his napkin.

Jonas rose to a half-standing position, then lowered himself to a sitting position.

"Captain," said the general, "is it the habit in Colonel Morgan's command for a captain to seat himself in the presence of a general without being given permission?"

The captain strained at the rope as he rose to a half-squatting, half-standing position.

"You have thirty words in which to state your business, Captain. Count them, Sergeant."

Jonas turned his head and tried to wipe his bloody face on his shoulder. The binding held him too tightly. He spit blood on the floor. "My name is Captain Jonas, from Colonel Morgan's raiders," he said, "here to see Major General Thornton."

"I'm General Thornton."

"You have a prisoner, sir, a Miss Caroline Healy. Colonel Morgan sent me to get—"

"That's thirty, sir," said the sergeant.

"Were you about to say *her*, Captain?"

Jonas nodded.

"You have had a long ride for nothing, Captain. It's not my practice to release detainees held in my department's jurisdiction."

"General, your men took her from Colonel Morgan's men."

"What comes into my department area is mine, Captain—even your colonel if I so choose."

"Begging the General's pardon, but we were in Tennessee at the time."

"Not so, Captain. The town the colonel's men were in straddles the border. They were on the Alabama side."

"That's a technicality, General."

"But it's *my* technicality, Captain, and that's important, don't you think?"

"Sir, if you refuse to give me my prisoner, then shoot me. I won't return without her."

"Very well, Captain. Sergeant, take the captain to the parade ground, select a firing squad, and shoot him."

"General!" exclaimed Jonas.

General Thornton stood and walked from behind the table to where Jonas was struggling against the rope that bound him to the chair. Thornton placed his face next to the captain's. "You struck an enlisted man under my command, Captain. You struck a colonel in the Confederate army. You resisted my orders to submit to arrest. Which offense, Captain, do you suggest I shoot you for? I'm limited to doing it only once."

Jonas sighed, then let his head drop. "I'm tired, sir. I've been riding for three days straight."

"That explains your ill manners, Captain, but says nothing about your ignorance. But I'm a fair man. I'll give you a choice: the firing squad or thirty lashes with a whip."

Jonas gasped as he jerked his head up. "You can't whip me like a nigger, General."

"It appears the captain has chosen the firing squad," Thornton said to the NCO, ignoring Jonas. "Carry out your orders, Sergeant."

"Yes, sir. It'll be a pleasure, sir." The sergeant grabbed the rope and jerked. "Cut this, Corporal. And you, Private," he said over his shoulder, "if he so much as flinches, club him."

After the corporal cut the captain loose from the chair, he tied the obstinate officer's hands again. "Move along, Cap'n," he said, prodding Jonas toward the door.

The squad led Jonas toward the open field bordered by a split-rail fence. The captain struggled as the corporal pulled on the rope. General Thornton followed. Sensing something was about to happen, a crowd of soldiers began moving toward the field. The sergeant tied the captain to a fence post, then walked toward the gathering crowd. He counted off ten men.

"You men, follow me with your rifles," the sergeant ordered. They followed. "Knock the balls from your rifles and lay your weapons on the ground." They complied. "Now, turn your backs." They responded. "Corporal Smith, reload three of those rifles—and be quick about it."

The corporal pulled three cartridges from his cartridge case and quickly loaded them before returning the weapons to the ground. "Loaded, Sergeant."

"You men, turn around and pick up your rifles." The sergeant walked over to where Thornton stood watching and saluted. "General, the firing squad is ready."

Jonas looked at the general in amazement. He refused to accept the fact that Thornton intended to kill him so casually.

With hands behind his back, the general strolled up to the captain. "You men move away. The captain and I have personal matters to discuss." The crowd of men backed out of earshot. "Captain, don't mistake me. I'll walk away if you fail to provide even one satisfactory answer. If that happens, no power on earth will save your life. Do you believe me?"

Jonas nodded sharply.

"Why was Mrs. Healy abducted?"

"Orders, sir. From Colonel Morgan."

"I find it impossible to believe that Colonel Morgan simply pulled this woman off a train without a reason. Do you believe he did that, Captain?"

The captain shook his head.

"Now tell me, why did Colonel Morgan order her abduction?"

Jonas hesitated.

Thornton started to turn away.

"Someone ordered him to, sir."

"*Who*, Captain?"

"Don't know his name, General." He added quickly, "And that's the God's truth."

"What do you know about him?"

"Only that he's a Southern sympathizer with close connections to our government, sir. He's one of the leaders of some organization up North called the Knights of the Golden Circle, I believe."

"What did your colonel plan to do with Mrs. Healy?"

"As I understood it, sir, he planned to have her shot as a spy."

"That's absurd, Captain," Thornton said, feigning surprise.

"The information was, she came south, sir, right before the war started, and that she had come down here to spy. People saw her in Birmingham snooping around a militia armory on the edge of town—and she attacked a man leading some slaves."

Thornton flinched. He remembered the incident well, although he had no knowledge of her snooping around the militia armory. That must have been during the period when I left her on her own, he thought. But at the time, the building was under Federal control. There was no way anyone could make a case for spying. But irregulars made their own rules of war. He had no doubt of their intent to carry out the execution.

Only by accident had he learned of the plan to kidnap his sister-in-law. Some drunken soldiers had bragged about being selected to shoot a Northern woman when Morgan's men got her to town. Since it was in Thornton's military department, the officer who overheard them, recognizing the men as irregulars, had reported the incident. The report reached Thornton barely in time to act. At the time, he had no information on the woman's identity, but he had ordered his men to intercede until he could sort through the facts.

"Captain, if this situation you are in were reversed and Morgan was here in my place, what do you think *he* would do?"

The captain thought for a moment. "He'd have me shot, I suppose."

"I think so too. My men are watching, Captain. If I back down, discipline will go to hell. I'll be accused of showing favoritism to officers. I can't have that. Please, Captain, submit to the whipping."

Jonas's head dropped. He had seen a man after thirty lashes, several men in fact. It had been a common punishment for slaves on his father's plantation. But whip a white man? he thought. My God, that's inhuman. Still, dying was even less appealing. "In my condition, sir, I doubt I'll survive."

"It's a chance, Captain."

Jonas came to attention as best he could in his present condition. "I will accept the lash, sir," he said firmly. His knees buckled slightly and his legs began to shake.

"Turn the captain around, Sergeant, and prepare for a flogging." He spoke softly to the captain. "Captain Jonas, refrain from crying out. It will speak badly for you in front of the men. A man must think of his honor at such times."

The captain peered apprehensively over his shoulder. The sergeant had appointed himself to administer the punishment. There remained no thought of the strokes being moderately administered. The whip cracked in the air. Jonas gritted his teeth in grim anticipation.

Crack! "One."

Crack! "Two."

At the fifteenth lash, Jonas's knees buckled completely, but he bit off a scream and regained his feet. At the twentieth, the captain sank to one knee, the rope cutting into his wrists. Each lash hurt more than the last. He wondered how a man could endure such agony. A brief pause followed. He strained to rise to his feet.

Crack! "Twenty-one."

God was merciful. He remembered no more.

When the punishment had been administered, the general ordered Jonas cut loose. "Carry him to my quarters," Thornton commanded.

Four men carried the captain's limp body into the cabin and laid him on a cot. Twilight had settled in before his head began to clear. Someone had placed grease on the wound, the best treatment available. He shook uncontrollably and his body convulsed with fever. "Water," he pleaded.

A corporal pushed a dipper into a water barrel. He placed it to the captain's lips and turned it upward. Some of the liquid ran into the captain's mouth; most poured on the floor.

"Clear the room," Thornton ordered, "and shut the door." He waited. "Captain, do you hear me?"

Jonas nodded.

"The woman Colonel Morgan ordered abducted is my wife's sister."

The captain squeezed his eyes shut and clenched his fists.

"That's right, Captain, my sister-in-law. She was visiting my family at the time you described to me earlier. I can assure you she is no spy. The woman makes shoes, Captain. Shoes. She apparently does it very well, but she still only makes shoes. Now, I ask you again. What can you tell me about the man who gave Colonel Morgan his orders."

"All I know is he's a judge, General, up in Illinois. Apparently he's very influential with the colonel. Apparently the relationship goes back more than twenty years."

"Yes, well—" Thornton rose and went to the water barrel. He dipped some water and brought it to the captain. Now it made sense. Morgan had sent Jonas on a fool's errand, Thornton thought, making him a simple victim caught in the middle of a personal grudge. Jonas had sought only to do his commander's bidding.

Victoria had told her husband what Porter Wade had done more than twenty years before. Thornton had thought to settle the matter then, by sending someone to dispose of the judge. In time, however, Thornton's anger subsided. His failure to act had been a mistake. Now the war had become personal. He regretted telling the captain of his relationship to the captive, but he had no means to undo it. He did, however, have the power to keep the captain from returning to Morgan. There existed a hellhole of a fort, on an island down in Florida, where half the men had died of cholera. The commander there needed replacements. Whether Jonas knew it or not, his war was over. But someone had to travel north to inform Colonel Morgan of the woman's terrible plight. Another officer would serve that purpose well. Unless Morgan placed no value on his command, not even he would dare to take revenge on a general's personal envoy. Thornton had concluded that the best way to resolve this matter lay in relieving Colonel Morgan of his concern: He should inform this judge that the woman had died from the hardships of her ordeal. As for the possibility of the judge seeking to confirm the story, well, a Northern judge, regardless of his sympathies, might find the journey south too risky.

"General," said the captain.

"Yes?"

"I never cried out, not once."

"I know, Captain. I doubt I could have stood up to it as you did." Thornton thought back to the days of his youth, when he'd first begun expanding his agricultural domain. He had no more than twenty slaves during those first struggling years. Seldom had he whipped his slaves; it was poor economics. Oh, it might have been necessary, now and again, to open the flesh on a man's back, but in truth, the man had less worth after that than the cost of keeping him alive.

In time, Thornton had stopped the practice completely—after his field boss had gotten emotional and killed a prized buck for some minor affront. The practice, however, had a value in stimulating the others. An enterprising farmer had to be practical. Thirty lashes had become, over the years, the standard fare, but Thornton had always thought that too harsh. The world, however, needed cotton now that the blockade had nearly eliminated shipping from Southern ports. He expected business to be good after the war. Some options had to be explored to make his slaves more productive. No doubt about that. Perhaps when the war was over and conditions had returned to normal, he would be more humane. Ten lashes, no more than fifteen, seemed enough. A man still had his wits about him at that point, and had the ability to return to work within a few weeks.

Thornton walked to the doorway. He felt relieved that it had been unnecessary to kill the captain. As he stuffed his pipe, he looked at his chief of staff, Col. Robert Andersen, sitting on a battered old chair and leaning at an angle on its two back legs. The colonel's shoulders rested on the side of the cabin. Thornton watched attentively as Andersen sucked the smoke from his pipe, made a circle with his lips, and blew perfect rings into the still evening air. Thornton had tried to master the art but finally gave it up. Some people simply lacked the knack. It felt warm for an early December night, almost balmy. Wisps of ground fog hung like window drapes in the low spots. Thornton walked into the open and looked up wistfully at the stars. "Lovely night, isn't it, Bob."

"Right peaceful, General," replied the colonel.

"Have you ever been to Tennessee?"

"No, sir. Why?"

"Let's go for a walk, Colonel."

Andersen shifted his position, letting the chair settle slowly on its four legs, then rose and walked out toward Thornton.

"Colonel, I have a mission for you. It should be peaceful around here until spring, so I'll have to get along without you."

"Yes, sir."

"Actually, Colonel, it's a two-part mission. First, I want you to find Colonel Morgan for me. The second part will take you into Illinois. Do you feel up to it?"

"Whatever you say, General."

"Do you have any civilian clothes?" asked Thornton.

"No trouble getting some, General."

"Good."

CHAPTER 16

• • • • • • • • • • • • • • •

The sound of thunder echoed from the distant hills. Fire lit up the night. Major General Ambrose E. Burnside, the latest in a succession of generals called on to command the Army of the Potomac, had ordered his artillery to open up on the quaint little town of Fredericksburg, Virginia. He had eighty thousand men poised to cross the river, if ever the pontoon bridges arrived. He now had only one option: shell the place to soften it for the grand assault that he allowed himself to envision in quiet moments, the event destined to propel him into immortal glory.

The Army of Northern Virginia, under the command of Gen. Robert E. Lee, had established defensive positions across the narrow river valley. Beside Lee, in his tent, were his two favorite corps commanders, Lt. Gen. James "Old Pete" Longstreet and Lt. Gen. Thomas "Stonewall" Jackson. Jackson had a reputation for being a pious, solemn man, an enigma in every respect. One had difficulty determining what guided him most, religion or superstition, or if there were any differences as the general saw them. Jackson seemingly took perverse delight in watching Yankee soldiers pitch forward as one-ounce Minié balls drilled into their flesh. If Jackson liked a man, the man could do no wrong. If he disliked a man, the man's life often resembled a living hell. He liked Maj. Simon Thornton. The general had remembered a chance encounter back at the start of the war. With his dying breath, Thornton's commander had commended Thornton, then a lieutenant, for saving the Confederate flank at Bull Run. Jackson had use for such men, men who at a young, adventurous age were willing to take the initiative and thereby save an army from defeat. He had no trouble believing that. Loss of the battle seemed certain if that flank had crumbled, and

177

with the loss, the Southern cause might have crumbled, even before its first loud birth cry. Such was the fickle nature of war. Jackson gave much weight to such things in his private deliberations.

While delivering a message near Guiney Station a few days before, the general's favorite staff officer suffered a wound when a shell exploded close by. A spent fragment had slammed into the major's head, knocking him from his horse. He still complained of dizziness as a result of the experience, and expressed difficulty at remembering names and details. The experience had left a large, ugly-looking purple bruise on the side of his head. But a good soldier leaves his general only when he has no choice, so the major had ridden back into camp that night with blood-matted hair and suffering from disorientation. He had failed, understandably, to deliver the message. A young lieutenant by the name of Clinton, an unattached scout bringing a message from Richmond, had found the major and helped him find his way back. The major, who appreciated the assistance, had asked if the lieutenant might remain with the army—provided officials in Richmond agreed. Jackson's headquarters issued an order to that effect, then sent it on its way to Richmond with the sergeant who had accompanied Lieutenant Clinton on his mission. The lieutenant was a good man, with a pronounced Southern accent. The general had laughed upon learning that the man hailed from 'Possum Lick, Georgia. He had laughed even harder as the lieutenant told his favorite stories to the staff, relaxed around the evening fires—especially the one about the man who had tried to take the lieutenant's pig. The lieutenant had borrowed the story and the birthplace from an old friend, but he left out that part.

The lieutenant also left out the fact that he had delivered the real Maj. Simon Thornton into the hands of Colonel Thompson, who spirited Thornton back to Union lines and on to Washington for interrogation and subsequent incarceration apart from his fellow Confederates. The knowledge that his brother was safe and would be allowed to live helped relieve Samuel Wade's troubled conscience.

Now Wade, posing as Major Thornton, stood in one corner of the tent. He had to stoop slightly to avoid knocking off his hat against the low, sloping ceiling. Men with gold stars and fancy braid on their collars and sleeves crowded the tent. Body heat provided the only protection against the cold from a brisk winter wind blowing outside. Next to Wade stood a small folding table. The only objects on the table were a tin cup and a metal pail half-filled with water. A large chunk of ice in the pail clanked against its sides whenever anyone bumped the unsteady table.

Wade's left hand rested on the unsnapped, cracking leather flap of his holster. He thought often of the uncomfortable sensation. The people who had conditioned him for this insane project had forgotten to advise him, if they even knew, that the real Major Thornton was left-handed. *This* Major Thornton was right-handed. He had to keep his hand bandaged to feign a wound to explain the difference in his writing and other awkward efforts. His thoughts never wandered from the fact that he was now with the enemy, surrounded by sixty thousand men ready to kill him at the least suspicion. He remained constantly alert for any information that might help keep him alive. Little of it was of a military nature. His greatest fear was of someone he had never heard of, but should know, coming up and saying, "How are you, Simon? Haven't seen you since VMI." He had let his whiskers grow to provide some slight, natural disguise. The beard itched constantly. His gut rumbled unceasingly from the nervous apprehension. At times, he had an insane urge to scream at the top of his voice, "I'm an impostor. Please kill me and get it over with." If only he could chance talking with Lieutenant Clinton more often about his feelings, about his fears. The lieutenant seemed much more at ease in his surroundings, but he could be himself: Southern to the core, except for his hatred of slavery and love for the Union. The lieutenant intended to leave eventually. His main purpose was to act as courier if there arose a need to carry back that one vital piece of information that promised to change the course of the war.

The major's orders made no sense. Standing side by side at the table covered with battle maps were three men with the best military minds in either army. Nothing prevented him from slipping his revolver from its holster and killing all three before anyone reacted, thereby plunging the Confederate command structure into disarray for the foreseeable future. Wade, of course, as a result of a shot from another gun slamming into his skull, would be absent during this transformation. The second best choice, he figured, was to use the six bullets in the cylinder of his revolver to kill the bungling Federal generals. But his orders were clear. He must avoid taking violent action—except as a last resort, and then only if required to protect his own life.

Men began filing from the tent. With the battle plan approved, the conference ended. Except at the northern extremity of the line, the Confederate army commanded the high ground. The plan, therefore, had a strong defensive quality. Federal regiments faced the prospect of attacking across open ground into withering rifle and cannon fire. Disaster appeared certain. If the Federal army tried to attack Lee's lines now, the act would likely rank as one of the war's greatest follies. This seemed evident, even to a lowly major. If Burnside had attacked upon arrival, before Lee had developed such stout defensive positions, there might have been a chance. But the opportunity had passed.

The most ominous obstacle had required no effort at all to construct. At the base of Marye's Heights, directly west of the town, ran a sunken road ground down by a century of wagon traffic. Local people had constructed a four-foot-high stone wall to keep the hillside from washing away. Two infantry divisions crowded onto the eight-foot-wide roadway and along the face of the hill behind. Every five seconds a brigade of two thousand men could unleash a withering hail of lead down the slope at foolish onrushing Federals—if they came that way, which they almost certainly would. The road continued along the base of a high hill, soon to be renamed Lee's Hill by the locals—the general had his command post there, and Lee had placed several batteries of heavy guns along the ridge. The low ground would remain untenable as long as those guns were in position to unleash shot and canister. It seemed to Wade that sending word of what waited here was the best service he had to offer to his country, but he judged it to be a useless gesture. Burnside had a reputation for being both rash and imprudent, as deadly a combination as ever guided an army's commanding general. He had the demeanor of a man certain to conclude that only an all-out effort against the place offered any chance for success. In the end, more, rather than fewer, men were likely to die if a warning reached him.

Wade followed General Jackson to their mounts, pulling up his collar in an effort to ward off the cold.

"Follow me back to headquarters, Major," said Jackson. "I will have several orders to deliver to division commanders."

"Yes, sir," Wade replied.

A day passed before sufficient pontoon bridging material arrived on the east bank of the Rappahannock River. The Federal engineers worked through the night and into the day to span the swift, frosty barrier. Rebel snipers fired down on them from buildings fronting the river. Wade watched as much of the activity as his churning stomach could endure. Finally, General Burnside ordered his large guns to level the structures providing shelter for his men's antagonists. Even this failed, however; the sharpshooters simply scratched out positions in the rubble and continued to harass the bridge builders. Thoroughly annoyed, the petulant Burnside ordered infantry to cross in small boats to clear the far shore. The mission accomplished, the bridges were finally extended to the western shore.

Lee did not offer greater resistance at this point. To have done so would have exposed his men to devastating fire from the Union guns dominating both sides of the river from Stafford Heights. Why not, Lee mused, just sit tight and allow the Federals to assault his well-prepared defensive positions. It seemed the only logical thing to do.

Across the Rappahannock, confusion reigned in the Union command. Although the bulk of the Army of the Potomac was able to cross the river under cover of dense fog on December 12, the extent of the Confederate positions and the size of the force occupying them were unknown. Burnside further complicated matters by issuing ambiguous orders that rendered his concept of how the operation should be conducted about as clear as mud to the commander charged with executing the plan.

All that remained was for the fog to clear on the morning of the thirteenth so the assault could begin.

As the last wisps of fog blew away, a bewildering thought crept into Samuel Wade's mind. Instead of the surge of pride he sensed he should feel at the sight of seemingly endless ranks of blue-uniformed men moving across the low ground toward Prospect Hill in the bright, midmorning light, he felt apprehension. They were suddenly the enemy. If they broke through, they were certain to come directly at the command post where he stood watching. Any of the thirty-odd thousand assault troops would kill him without a second thought. It was damned unreasonable to expect him to want the rebel lines to crumble.

Wade glanced at his watch. It was a little after 10:00 A.M. He raised his field glasses to his eyes and a thrill raced through him. The Union advance was faltering! He swung his glasses to the right and saw Maj. John Pelham's horse artillery battery pouring enfilading fire into the Yankees' flank from the Port Royal road.

"General," Wade screamed above the racket. "The Yankees are on the move!"

Jackson finished pulling on his old Mexican War battle jacket and tugged a visored VMI cap down on his head as he raced from his tent followed by four staff officers. He grabbed Wade's field glasses and looked at the battle unfolding before him. "Major Thornton," the general shouted at Wade, "ride down and tell General Hill it looks like they're threatening his left flank. Tell him I expect him to hold at all hazard."

Wade acknowledged the order, jumped onto his horse, and galloped toward Maj. Gen. A. P. Hill's command post. Lieutenant Clinton was close behind. It seemed that he, too, had made the same mental transformation and now viewed the advancing Federal forces as, if not the enemy, at least something very near akin to it. Wade's horse skidded to a stop in front of Hill's tent. Hill didn't move; he just continued to calmly observe the activity to his division's front.

"General Hill, sir," Wade said breathlessly, "General Jackson thinks your left flank may be threatened. The Yankees on the right are being delayed by Stuart's horse artillery, but the blue-bellied bastards on the left are approaching the railroad through the woods. He said to tell you he expects you to hold at all hazard, sir!"

Hill continued to look to the front, nodding his acknowledgment. Then he barked orders to several staff officers standing nearby. They leaped for their mounts and rode off to deliver the general's instructions to the brigade commanders. As they sped away, a bullet zipped past the ear of Lieutenant Clinton, who was standing behind Wade, and severed the command tent's front post.

"Those boys are serious!" Clinton exclaimed as the tent slowly crumpled to the ground.

Hill finally turned and looked at Wade for the first time. "Well, Major, looks like I've got a bit of a problem on my hands," the general said calmly. "The damn Yankees are trying to get between the two brigades on my left. I've instructed General Gregg to move his brigade into the gap between them." He hesitated for a moment as he brought the field glasses to his eyes for another look. He moved his head from left to right, then lowered the glasses and turned to Wade again. "But that may not be enough. May I borrow your services, sir?"

"I'm at your command, General," Wade replied.

"Find Colonel Walker. Tell him I need his light guns to help bolster my left-flank brigades." Hill appeared thoughtful. Events were unfolding rapidly, yet he maintained an air of quiet calm. "I need help lest they break through between the brigades. If the bastards penetrate my line, it's likely to cause a panic."

Wade sensed the urgency of the situation despite Hill's calm. He slung his leg over the sand-colored stallion's back and rode at a gallop toward the rear in search of Walker's artillery. He was barely out of sight of the crumpled command tent when his horse suddenly tumbled headfirst into the ground, throwing Wade headlong into a shallow ravine. Blood trickled down the side of his face and he wiped it away with his sleeve. He crawled to the top of the gully and spotted Clinton. "Get the general's message to Colonel Walker," Wade yelled. "Here, throw me your revolver."

Clinton tossed Wade the weapon and sped off.

Wade crawled forward and looked at his horse. A bullet had entered the animal's right eye, killing it instantly. He strained to see ahead. He heard plenty of noise but saw nothing other than the shapes of a few wavering trees.

"Keep moving, men," said a voice just beyond the trees. "The colonel wants to know what's ahead."

Wade gripped a revolver in each hand. Only his head and arms protruded above the gully's rim. A shape began to materialize. It wore blue. Wade waited, nervously fingering the trigger of the Colt in his right hand.

"Reb!" the figure screamed as he lowered his rifle and charged.

Wade hesitated, his eyes fixed on the gleaming steel point of the bayonet moving toward him. His emotions were in turmoil. The figure coming toward him appeared to be only a boy, no more than seventeen. Everything moved in slow motion as his thoughts raced. He dodged at the last instant and the soldier stumbled into the gully. Wade turned and pointed the revolver. The boy raised his rifle in an attempt to fire. Fire spewed from the Colt first, and the young soldier slammed against the side of the gully, his piercing dead gaze fixed on the major, the ominous barrel of the rifle, held firmly in a dead hand, pointing at Wade's chest.

"Hank, did ya get him?" The voice seemed to echo from several directions at once.

"Hank didn't make it, soldier," Wade said firmly, "and neither will you if you come forward. Men, prepare to fire at the first sign of their advance. Aim low—at their crotches." That should give them something to think about, he thought.

An eerie silence hung over this minute corner of the war. The Federal soldiers had no way of knowing what confronted them. It could be one man or a regiment. Wade fingered the trigger, waiting, hoping they would retreat. He might kill a couple, perhaps even three or four, but death in this frozen ditch seemed a certainty, with the likely insult to injury his being buried as a Southern hero.

"We have to get back to the colonel," said the voice on the other side of the trees, "and tell him the force facing us here is too strong. Pull back, men." The clank of metal and the slosh of moving feet faded.

Only then did Wade allow his ears to listen for the larger sound beyond. The battle raged to the south and north. A fair share of it was unfolding within his sight. The unceasing thunder of the large guns echoed against the high, west bank of the river. The steady, rolling cracks of rifle fire and the occasional whine of a Minié ball passing too close for comfort sent chills down his spine. The warming gleam of the sun, combined with the fire from the muzzles of a hundred thousand rifles, warmed the air. The landscape along a three-hundred-yard front had become littered with inert blue and gray forms. First, the surging waves of blue moved forward; then men in gray sprang mechanically from their positions and drove them back; then a new blue wave moved forward. On and on it continued, as if some giant but unseen puppeteer pulled on ten thousand strings. The siren call of battle pulled them forward, mindlessly, heroically, toward the abyss of death. Wade had never seen hand-to-hand combat on such a grand scale. Nobody had on this continent. And all the while the staccato rattle of muskets filled the air.

In time, the Union forces began to back away, then they began to run back to the bridges. During the lull, Wade turned and looked into the cold eyes of the young private, his finger frozen a fraction of an inch from the musket's trigger. His expression was more one of surprise than fear. A youth of such vigor thinks he will live forever, Wade realized. For himself, the certainty of life had faded to a wish after seeing so much war. But for the very young, death is an unthinkable event, even in battle. The real fear is of being maimed, of having to spend the rest of one's life denied the joy of holding a woman's flesh in passionate embrace. Men talk of advancing sideways to guard against the unthinkable wound. No such thought troubled the private's mind on this day only twelve days short of Christmas 1862.

A tear slid down Wade's cheek as he looked at the stubble of beard on the private's cheeks revealing the first blush of manhood. My God, Wade thought in his anguish, how did they miss envisioning this possibility when they sent me here?

A rumble rose to his left. The thunder of cannon grew louder, booming across the valley. Walker's artillery. Clinton had found the guns.

A figure rode toward Wade, advancing through the trees. The horse came to a stop at the rim of the gully. "I never expected to see you alive, Major," Clinton said. Then his eyes dropped to the dead private. "Did you do that?"

Wade nodded.

"It was you or him, Major. Looks like he was about ready to shoot. I've kilt maybe fifty of my countrymen. The thought of it haunts every dream."

"Catch," said Wade as he tossed Clinton his revolver. The barrel was still warm.

"You used *my* gun to kill him?" Clinton asked.

Wade nodded again.

"Figures. Climb on, Major. I'll give you a ride back. Looks like your stallion's war has ended, too."

The major stuck his foot in the stirrup and swung up behind the lieutenant. Clinton turned his head and looked Wade in the eyes. "You know, Major, this war's gotten clear out of hand. We probably did as much as anyone, more than most, to seal a Reb victory here today. If that doesn't keep you awake tonight, nothing will. Getup, horse."

Clinton walked the horse up the shallow grade toward the corps command post. General Jackson stood in front of his tent. Officers were coming from every direction to report on the battle's progress. The general would listen and give an order, and the men would mount up and ride away.

Clinton brought the horse to a stop and Wade slid off. He pressed his hand against his head wound as he approached the general. "Sorry for the delay in getting back, General. General Hill had need of my services."

"You've been wounded again, Major." A large knot disfigured the side of Wade's head. "If your head keeps getting in the way of this war, you'll be in bad shape when it's over."

"Yes, sir, it seems so, sir." He staggered from the dizziness.

The general held his arm. "You need some rest, Major. You no longer have a tent. It took a direct hit a while back and just evaporated. Go into my tent and rest."

"If the General doesn't mind."

"The war must move on without you for a while, Major."

Wade stumbled into the tent and collapsed on the cot.

As he rolled on his back and opened his eyes, Wade heard himself moaning. Darkness was coming, and with it the sounds of battle had receded. The top of the tent moved slowly in half circles, first right, then left. A drumlike, pulsing pain pounded inside his skull. He squeezed his eyes shut, then opened them with a start. "General, I'm sorry. I suppose you want your cot back."

"Not a bit of it, son. General Hill just left. He told me quite a story."

"What's that, sir?"

"He said that errand he sent you on was the smartest decision he made all day."

"I didn't do anything, sir. Some damn Yankee shot my horse from under me. Lieutenant Clinton had to deliver the message to Colonel Walker."

"Oh, that was important, but there's more to it than that. It seems that a large gap had formed in our line. You went down right in the middle of it. The Yankees were feeling around in the woods when they came upon you. There were three separate reports of your holding that line against a whole regiment while General Gregg was moving his brigade up. We faced certain defeat if they had come forward."

"Sir, I only drove back a patrol."

"A patrol with an entire regiment less than fifty yards behind it, Major. They shifted left and ran right into one of our strongest positions. They recovered a Yankee's body from the ravine where you were seen. What did you do to drive them back?"

"Nothing much, sir. I just let them know that, if they advanced any farther, my regiment would shoot their balls off."

The general roared with laughter. "You said *that?* You actually said *that?*"

"More or less, sir."

"And what regiment did you plan to use to perform the castration?"

"They didn't *know* I didn't have a regiment, sir. The woods were pretty thick."

"Well, son, that's the damnedest thing I ever heard. If there's one thing I've learned, it's that if a man is going to command a regiment, he needs the rank to give him the authority. Your promotion to lieutenant colonel is official, as of this moment."

"Thank you, sir. What about Lieutenant Clinton?"

"Well, Colonel, he's under your command."

"He will be a fine captain, sir."

"I'll take care of the paperwork tonight. I've had another tent set up, so you keep this one. Get some rest, Colonel." Jackson patted Wade on the shoulder and walked from the tent. "Wait 'til General Lee hears what you said to those Yankees."

"Clinton."

"Here, sir."

"Did you hear?" An unmistakable sign of pride appeared on Wade's face. He smiled as Clinton entered the tent. "You're now a captain. You were right. We're both heroes."

Clinton displayed less enthusiasm. He sat beside the newly promoted lieutenant colonel and patted him on the knee. "Congratulations on your promotion, Colonel, but as for being a hero, I doubt it's proper to take much pride in that. Our action today probably saved five hundred rebels and caused the death of five hundred Federals."

Wade's smile faded, then his features hardened. "My God, Jim," he said in a low voice. "What have I done?"

"You did what they sent you here to do, sir," Clinton replied in a whisper. "You gained the general's confidence so that we could get information to help shorten the war. You can't help doing what you were trained to do."

Wade lowered his throbbing head to his hands. "I forgot, Jim. I actually forgot for a while."

"It's the wound, sir. Head wounds do strange things to a man. War does even stranger things. Don't forget, I'm the one who brought Colonel Walker's artillery up to help close the gap. That's just one more thing to crowd into my nightmares."

CHAPTER 17

•••••••••••••••

Finding Colonel Morgan had been difficult. It had taken Colonel Andersen more than a week. His meeting with Morgan had gone well, all things considered. Morgan expressed regret at the idea of losing a man, but such things happened in war. He had expressed himself more forcefully when he learned that there were no plans to return his prisoner, although he softened somewhat upon hearing that she was dead. The two colonels had eaten a relaxing lunch while discussing the war; then Andersen mounted his horse and continued his journey north. More than a week passed before he crossed the border into southern Illinois.

He sold the horse in a small town two miles from a rail terminal and walked the remaining distance. It had turned cold, as cold as he remembered Maine, but less damp. He bought a ticket for the capital, then waited in a small saloon. He thought it a backwater town. It couldn't have been a greater distance from the war. There seemed no chance of anyone recognizing him.

"Bob, is that you?"

Andersen turned at the sound of his name and recognized an old classmate. The man wore a Union uniform with captain's bars on his shoulders. My God, Andersen thought, out of twenty million people. They had gotten along poorly in school. In fact, they had been as close to being enemies as two sixteen-year-old boys can get without becoming violent. A dozen years had passed since then. How am I to explain being here? Andersen asked himself. Perhaps I can bluff my way out. It's been a long time since we last saw each other. "You must be mistaken, Captain. My name isn't Bob."

"Sure it is. Bob Andersen. Remember me? Gerald Hartley? From the Trenton School for Boys?"

"Sorry. I've never heard of it—or you."

"Wait a minute. Weren't you from Alabama. Yeah, you were from Mobile." His hand eased toward his holster. "What's a good Southern boy like you doing in Illinois? You wouldn't be a Reb now, would you?"

Andersen shoved Hartley over a chair and ran for the door. A shot rang out, then another. The second bullet slammed into Andersen's right shoulder and spun him to the ground. He bounced up and ran behind a building. The sound of footsteps told him he had about ten seconds of freedom remaining if he stayed put. He ducked into a side door and ran upstairs.

"Sergeant, you check behind," shouted Hartley from outside. "I'll check in here." A pistol appeared first, then an arm, and finally the man. The stairs provided the only path. The boards creaked as he took the steps two at a time. A two-shot derringer provided Andersen's only means of defense. He ducked into a room on the second floor, a bedroom, and stood panting against the wall. He felt a warm liquid on his back. His arm felt like lead. He tried to move it but the pain made him wince. He reached toward the bed and grasped a pillow, then he returned to the wall.

The door opened slowly and drifted back against the wall on the other side of the doorway. The pistol came into view. Andersen gripped his small weapon in his limp arm before grabbing the arm coming through the door. He pulled with all his strength. The captain spun to the floor. Andersen dove on him and pressed the pillow to his face. He lacked the strength to hold it in place and keep the man down at the same time. In a last, desperate effort, he raised his leaden arm and pushed the pistol into the pillow. He fired. A dull thump followed the explosion muffled by the pillow. The captain stopped struggling.

Andersen rolled over and grasped his shoulder. Broken, he thought—feels like the bullet hit the collarbone. He felt himself growing faint. He turned Hartley's limp body parallel to the bed and shoved it underneath with his feet. A small rug lay on the floor in front of the door. He placed it over the blood-stained floor. What now? he asked himself. Did anyone hear the shot? He doubted it. But what about the captain? They would probably tear the place apart looking for him—and it wasn't that big of a place.

Andersen staggered into the hall and leaned against the wall. He forced his legs to move toward the window at the end of the hall. He chanced a brief look outside. Seeing no one, he opened the window with his good arm and sat on the ledge. Although it was only the second floor, the drop seemed impossibly long to him in his condition. Think! he said to himself. Don't panic. Easy now. He rolled onto his belly and wriggled out until he hung by his good arm. He hesitated for a moment, then dropped into the alley.

He landed with a thud in the hard-packed dirt and rolled onto his wounded shoulder. God! he thought. The pain. Everything in sight began moving in a slow, wavering circle. He froze. A soldier had turned the corner of the alley and was looking down the narrow passageway between the buildings.

Andersen pressed himself tightly against the wall behind a barrel and held his breath. He heard footsteps start down the alley, then retreat. Bleeding to death seemed certain if he kept moving. If he stopped, however, his pursuers were equally certain to capture him and shoot him as a spy—if not for murdering an army officer.

He got up and edged carefully along the building to the street. He looked right and left, then dashed in a crouch across the open space. The next building was a livery. He crawled to the back, opened the door, and fell inside. On the other side of the large room, the blacksmith was pounding on a wagon rim. He had heard nothing. Andersen grasped a piece of firewood with his good hand and crept toward the smith. With his last remaining strength, he smashed it against the smith's head. The man staggered sideways, then crumpled to the ground. Just before he passed out, Andersen clutched a hooked knife and plunged it into the smith's throat.

It was dark when Andersen regained consciousness. It could have been only minutes or hours. It had been dusk when he had dashed to the livery, and the sun set quickly in the winter. He reached for a rag as he removed his jacket and stuffed the rag into the hole in his shoulder. With a second, longer rag, he fashioned a sling to immobilize his arm. Eventually, he thought, someone will come to check on the smith. In the darkness, he saw the outline of a horse. He tried to lift the saddle but lacked the strength. He climbed the stall's fence and threw his leg over the horse. He grasped the bridle and, leaning forward, inserted the bit in the animal's mouth. He backed the horse from the stall and guided it toward the large double doors. He pushed one door open and walked the horse into the dark street and turned south. In seconds, the darkness closed in around him and he kicked the horse in the flank.

At the far end of town, the train pulled out. Ticket's no good now, he thought, then put it out of his mind as the horse trotted along the side of the road.

Andersen rode all night, sometimes almost falling asleep, sometimes just letting his head rest on the animal's neck as it moved along the road. He had to get as far away from town as possible before they began searching for him. The road appeared well traveled. This reduced the chance of anyone tracking him. Just the same, there was no reason to take chances. He heard a small stream close by, so he led the horse off the road and into the water. The animal splashed along for a mile or more before coming to a bridge, where the road turned east. He exited the stream and began to trot down the road. In the distance, Andersen saw a house, dark as pitch. He slid off the horse and guided it to the barn in back, closing the door behind him as the first light of dawn revealed the horizon. Then he collapsed in some hay.

Andersen awoke with a start. The sun had risen. "Here, chick, chick, chick," a woman's voice said. "Time for breakfast." He flinched as he tried to rise. His injured arm had grown too stiff to move. He forced himself to stand, then walked cautiously to the door and looked out through a crack. A woman of about thirty stood casting grain in the chicken yard. Everything began to spin; then he slumped to the ground. He tried to rise, but his body refused to respond. Darkness enveloped him again.

The dream seemed real. Andersen felt the refreshing flow of water washing over his face, and the thought of water reminded him of his thirst. He opened his eyes. I've seen that face before, he thought. "I'm so hot" was all he could say.

"You have a fever," said the woman. "You're very ill."

"Where am I?" he asked.

"You're in my barn, sir." She lifted his head. "Who are you?"

"Who are *you*?"

"I'm the person who owns this farm. What happened to you?"

The sweet smell of lilac water drifted into his nostrils. "A man tried to rob me." It was the first thought that came to mind.

"You've been shot. I think your collarbone is broken. Can you walk?"

He tried to rise, but a sharp pain shot down his spine. He fell back. "I guess not."

"Let me help you." She placed her arms under his arms. "This may hurt, but I have to get you into the house." She lifted.

"Ahhh."

"I'm sorry, but you can't stay here." She lifted him to a sitting position. "Now try to stand." She placed her arms around his chest as he shifted to a kneeling position. Next she slid her arms down to his waist and pulled.

Andersen staggered as he rose to his knees, then to his feet. He backed against the wall and closed his eyes. A wave of nausea washed over him. He started to fall. The woman pressed her hands against his chest and held him upright.

"Put your good arm around my shoulder. I'll help you to the house."

The short walk seemed an eternity. The woman helped him up the stairs and led him to the bedroom. He sat on the edge of the bed and toppled onto his side.

It's just as well he passed out again, the woman thought. I have to get the bullet out. She had seen a bullet wound before, suffered by her husband in a hunting accident. She had watched the doctor operate. But the doctor had proper tools. She would have to improvise.

She rolled Andersen on his back and removed his coat before tearing away the blood-stained shirt. She took a bottle of whiskey from the kitchen cabinet and poured it over the wound. The stranger groaned. She pressed her finger against the wound and felt the bullet lodged against the bone. She opened the top drawer of her sewing cabinet and withdrew a pair of tweezers. She poured whiskey over the instrument and took a deep breath as she looked at the nasty, swelling hole in the man's back. Small beads of sweat popped out on her forehead. She took a deep breath and expelled it slowly. Finally, she inserted the tweezers and began to probe. "There it is," she said aloud. It had looked so easy when the doctor did it, but the doctor was gone. The army had drafted him. She had to do it.

She spread the tweezers and felt the ends grip the side of the ball. Blood spurted from the hole. She pressed hard and the bullet began to move. The tweezers slipped off, so she repeated the process; the lead ball sucked loose. She placed a compress over the wound and bound it. Nothing remained but to wait. She placed a blanket over him and turned down the lamp. She was unafraid. What could he do?

* * *

"Hello."

The woman walked to the doorway of the bedroom. "Hello. How do you feel?"

"Terrible," Andersen replied. "Where am I?"

"In my bedroom. I brought you in here yesterday morning."

"I had a bullet wound."

"Yes. I removed the bullet. You should be all right with time. Are you ready to talk?"

"About what?"

"About what happened."

He had a vague memory of saying something about that. What had it been? "May I have some water, please?" he asked, his mind racing. He needed time to think.

She went to the kitchen and returned with a glass of water.

He gulped down the liquid. "More," he gasped.

She returned with another glass full. "You had a fever, but you're better now."

"Where am I?" he asked, hoping for a broader response.

"This farm is about seven miles from Harrisburg, Illinois."

"Where is your husband?"

"Dead."

"Oh, I'm sorry."

"People get killed in war. He was killed at Shiloh."

"Do you tend this place all by yourself?"

"No. I managed to get hired hands to help with the fall harvest. I plan to sell the farm in the spring before going back east. Where are you from?"

"Maine," he replied.

"We're sort of out of the way around here. Don't see many strangers."

"I'm just passing through."

"Doing what?"

"I'm on a mission for the army, a secret mission."

Her expression conveyed her skepticism. "For *which* army?"

"Why do you ask that?"

"Union army people came by yesterday evening. Someone shot a Union officer the day before. They were looking for his killer."

He thought for a moment. She will never believe, he thought, that I didn't kill the man. "I killed him," he asserted, "but it's not what it seems." Telling the truth, or at least part of it, seemed the best defense. "We suspect widespread corruption in this military district. Southern cotton has been smuggled across the border. It couldn't happen without military assistance. I had questioned several soldiers and I was about to leave town when this captain shot me. He aimed to shoot me again when I shot him with my derringer." He waited. Had he convinced her? She appeared to be mulling it over.

She sat silently as she looked into his eyes. He seemed honest enough. "Rest now. I'll get you some soup." She returned with a bowl of broth. "Here. This is hot. You need to blow on it. Do you want some help?"

"Just help me sit up."

"More," he said as he sipped the last drops from the bowl.

When he finished the second bowl she sat down beside him. "I don't know whether to believe you."

He looked her in the eyes and smiled. "Then I guess you'll have to turn me in."

"But if you're telling the truth, what then?"

"They'll kill me. They'll take me away from here and shoot me for trying to escape."

She sighed.

A week passed before the numbness left Andersen's shoulder and arm, another before he could move the arm with relative ease. The bullet had only cracked the bone. The sling kept the pressure off as his strength gradually returned. He reluctantly directed his thoughts to his mission. He had started out more than a month before. He had to get to a train.

One evening, three weeks after his arrival, Andersen sat in front of the fireplace smoking a pipe the woman had given him. Her name was Rebecca. He had nearly fallen asleep when he heard her walk across the room. Her hair was wet. As she rubbed it with a towel, she knelt before the fire. He slid from the chair and sat on the rock hearth. She raised her head and looked at him. He placed a finger under her chin before leaning forward to kiss her. She pulled away, continuing to rub the towel on her hair.

"I have to leave," he said.

She looked at him again. "I wondered when you'd say that."

"I won't return."

"I know that." She lowered her eyes. "My husband was about your size. Take whatever clothes you need." She rose and walked to a dresser. She pulled out a drawer. "Here. You'll need this." She handed him the derringer. "You really should take another week to heal. The wound could open up again."

"You never told me your last name," he said.

"Wade," she replied.

He blinked. Wade. He was searching for a man named Wade, but it was a common name in these parts. "Do you know a Judge Wade?"

"I don't know him, but I know who he is. He's kin to my dead husband. My husband was on the black sheep side of the family, you might say." Her features hardened. "My husband hated Judge Wade, or at least the elder Judge Wade. The judge loaned my husband's father some money. When he couldn't pay it back in time, the judge took the family farm. This all happened before we got married. Why do you ask?"

"Oh, nothing. I just ran across his name in my investigation. It's getting late."

"So it is."

Andersen rose and walked to where his jacket hung on a hook. He placed the small pistol in the pocket. He wanted to tell her the truth about his mission. Would she hate him if she knew—or think more of him? He had no way of knowing. Without so much as a questioning expression, she had accepted the lie as truth. His attraction for her had grown, more than he chose to admit. She had treated him with kindness, been so trusting—she was much different than he'd imagined Northern women to be. She was a good woman.

He returned to the fireplace and sat down beside her. "I'm going to kiss you again, Rebecca. I can't leave without doing that. If you want it to end at that, it will." He placed his hand on her neck and pulled her slowly toward him. He kissed her hard on the lips. She responded. As he pulled away slightly she smiled, closed her eyes, and lay back on the rug.

The crackling fire cast a warm glow across the room. Its warmth felt good on his naked body. How long did I sleep? he wondered. He looked at Rebecca's soft, glowing face. Her hair was dry now, her breathing even and slow. As he looked at her stretched out on her side, she rolled onto her back, her small breasts flattening against her chest.

If I stay another day, I'll stay forever, he thought. He rose and put on his clothes. This war asks too much of me, he thought as he slipped on his jacket. He replaced the sling and lifted his arm into the fold. He knelt beside her and kissed her cheek softly. She smiled but remained asleep. He took a shawl from the back of the rocker and spread it over her before walking quietly into the kitchen. He found some paper and wrote, "If I stay longer I will only bring you trouble. Better that I leave now with no questions asked. I love you."

Andersen placed the note on the table and left the house.

Chapter 18

....

David Healy sat on his bunk in the bedroom of the small house south of the city. April was half over. The wound in his side had long since healed, but the bullet remained lodged somewhere deep inside his chest. If he turned just right, he thought he heard it grinding against a rib. He had been idle for months waiting for word on his wife, but nothing more had surfaced. The South had closed in around her, smothering her in some deep black hole beyond the reach of anyone. He felt both trepidation and anticipation at the task confronting him. A relay of employees arrived, one each week, with a report on his business enterprises. He always met them at this house near the city. Colonel Thompson remained unwilling to risk anyone finding out about the mission, or even that Healy was in the army.

He eagerly anticipated the weekly trips. They gave him a few hours with his daughter. But she kept active enough without him. She was always bubbling about this dinner or that ball that she had attended in the company of the dashing Colonel Thompson. Healy resented the colonel's freedom of movement. So far as Miss Healy knew, her father had no association with the colonel except for infrequent army business, affairs in which she had no interest at all. Except for the men associated with Thompson's group, his daughter and his weekly business contacts were the only people Healy saw now. He couldn't help wondering if it hadn't been better being detached from his financial empire. Assets had increased by 13 percent in the past six months, twice the usual growth rate. Only a fool failed to make money in time of war.

Healy looked forward to getting into the open. His clothing lay on the bed next to the carpetbag. Only one item, a revolver, had been placed in the bag. He fingered the train tickets that Colonel Thompson had handed him an hour before. I'm too old for this cloak-and-dagger nonsense, Healy thought. He heard the muted conversation in the parlor, but his attention focused on the uncertainty of the weeks ahead.

"Are you about ready?" asked Thompson as he entered the small room. "The carriage is waiting. Let me help you pack."

"Have all the arrangements been made at the other end?" Healy asked.

"Yes. Horses will be waiting in Nashville. Sorry we couldn't get you closer, but guaranteeing an open line beyond that point is impossible. You'll be on your own getting through Confederate lines. Captain Clinton will meet us at the station."

Shortly after Wade had been sent to the rear for medical treatment, Clinton had staged his own death and worked his way north. Before leaving, however, he had managed to gather detailed information on virtually every brigade in the area. He didn't want to return empty-handed. The high command had been amazed at learning the true strength of the Army of Northern Virginia, a number much lower than previously believed. Clinton's promotion to captain in the Union army followed within a week.

"Don't you think it's risky sending Captain Clinton with me? What if someone recognizes him?"

"That's unlikely," Thompson replied as he placed Healy's belongings in the bag. "There's hardly any link between the eastern and western departments of the Confederate army. He's been eager to get back into action since returning from his last mission. He has a good understanding of their command system and, with his distinct Southern drawl, he will give you more credibility. There, you're packed. We have to leave. It's nearly two hours to the station. If you don't mind, I'll ride with you."

Healy sat silently as the carriage rolled through the sleeping city. An hour remained before dawn. The only people moving about were a few staggering soldiers trying to find their way back to their barracks. The carriage pulled to a stop in the shadows west of the train station.

"I have one more piece of information to pass on to you before you leave," Thompson said. "There's been a slight change in plans. You'll be meeting another person when you reach Ohio."

"And who might that be?" Healy asked.

"A young army officer we recruited. If your end of the mission doesn't work out, he has orders to try something else."

"I don't like this, Colonel. Last-minute changes always complicate matters. Why didn't you tell me this earlier?"

"This plan only surfaced in the last few days. Besides, it really doesn't affect you. He'll just be a companion and will stay out of the way. His cover is that he's your accountant."

"Are you sure he'll know what he's doing?"

"I don't know. You tell me. He's your son."

"David?" It *had* to be David, thought Healy. Bill knew nothing about accounting, or anything else associated with his business.

"That's right."

"He isn't even in the army, for Christ's sake!"

"He is now."

"I won't do it, by God! You can't make me. This is dangerous activity. If you think I'm going to take my own son down there just to get him killed—well, I won't do it."

Thompson smiled and listened patiently as Healy vented his anger. Thompson had anticipated no less. Waiting until the last minute to tell Healy had seemed less risky than having him know in advance and worrying about it. "As you wish, Colonel. It isn't vital that he accompany you. We'll simply send him on his own. That, however, will make his part more dangerous."

"You bastard," said Healy. "When I tell my daughter about this she'll never speak to you again. She adores her brother."

"One problem at a time, Colonel."

"Where is David now?"

"At a training camp outside Cincinnati. You have really neglected that young man's upbringing, Colonel. He didn't even know how to fire a weapon. He's undergoing some crash training at this time."

Healy sat silently as he pondered the alternative. He knew Thompson well enough by now to expect him to carry out his threat. Thompson had a detached, fatalistic view of the war. He believed that everyone had a stake in the outcome, so everyone had to contribute his share. Nothing excluded David junior from this obligation, least of all the pleadings of a concerned father. How had he let himself get drawn into this harebrained scheme? he wondered. And what made David junior's contribution so vital that he alone had to participate in this mission?

"You're a real bastard, Colonel."

"I know. It goes with the job. What's it to be?"

"Will he meet us?"

"He'll meet you at the station when you pull in tomorrow night. I'd have you put a rose in your lapel, but I suppose he'll recognize you."

"That wasn't funny, Colonel."

"Sorry. There's the whistle to begin loading. I assume you're on your way?"

Captain Clinton stepped out of the shadows and walked to the carriage. "Everything's set," he said, and Thompson nodded.

Healy reached for the handle of his bag and opened the carriage door. The three men walked slowly toward the train. They stood silently in the brisk morning air. There remained nothing more worth saying. The whistle blew again. Healy and Clinton stepped up onto the car platform.

Thompson handed Healy a leather bag. "There's a thousand dollars in gold here. It might come in handy if you have to grease some palms. Don't worry about accounting for it. The government trusts you."

Healy opened his bag and dropped in the coins on top of his clothes. "There won't always be a war, Colonel," he said, looking sternly at Thompson. The train lurched, then moved slowly away from the station.

Thompson waved and smiled.

At least they were traveling in comfort. The government had offered coach fare; Healy paid the difference for a compartment. The two men played rummy until Clinton owed Healy $50,000. Clinton complained that it would take two lifetimes to pay the debt, so Healy settled for a dollar. They made good time and arrived in Cincinnati slightly ahead of schedule. As they stepped onto the station platform, Healy spotted David junior, and waved.

"Father," said the younger Healy.

David senior smiled. "Hello, son, it's good to see you." He extended his arms and the two men hugged. "How did you let yourself get pulled into this mess?" asked the elder Healy.

"The history of our nation is wrapped up in this war," replied David junior. "It didn't seem proper for me to sit it out. Besides, it makes more sense for *me* to be in it than it does for *you* to be in it."

"I'm a West Pointer, David."

"That's no answer."

"I suppose you're right." Healy stepped back and admired his son. "Well, I see they made you a lieutenant. You do look dapper." He turned to Clinton. "Son, this is Captain Clinton. He'll be going with us."

Young David saluted, then shook Clinton's extended hand. "A pleasure to meet you, sir. Are you supposed to take care of us?"

"Something like that, Lieutenant," Clinton replied.

"We need to board," said Healy. "The train is scheduled to leave in a few minutes."

The trip south progressed much slower than the first leg of the journey. Much of the track was in disrepair as a result of so much war traffic. Despite the gnawing urgency of his mission, Healy welcomed the time with his son. He had seen so little of David in the last two years. They talked about the war and about the wedding. They talked about their separate lives growing ever more distant. At some point during the journey, Healy even forgave Thompson for bringing his son into the war. Healy realized he had been selfish. So many young men were fighting and dying, and so many sons of the wealthy were buying their way out of the service. He felt pride in the knowledge that David junior wanted to do his part. Still, he thought, it's only natural for a man to want to protect his son.

Late on the second day out of Cincinnati the train stopped at a whistle-stop water station just short of the Tennessee border. Fewer than a dozen people remained on the train by this time. As the train loaded coal and water, two horsemen rode up. One was a Union captain, the other an enlisted man. They talked for a few minutes before the captain jumped to the ground with a small bag and the enlisted man rode off, leading the captain's horse. The officer beat the dust from his uniform and boarded the train.

Shortly, Healy heard a knock on his compartment door. He opened it. "May I help you?" Healy asked.

The captain saluted. "I'm Capt. Josiah Mason, sir. May I come in?"

"I'm expecting no one, Captain," Healy replied.

"I know, sir. There's been a hitch."

"Well then, come in."

"Thank you, sir." The captain removed his gloves and pulled them under his belt. "May I have a glass of water, sir?"

Healy poured the water and handed it to him. "What is this all about, Captain?"

"Sir, the army thinks there's been a leak. We suspect some people will be waiting for you in Nashville. It will be best if you get off before reaching there."

Healy's eyes expressed his concern at this new development. No more than six people even knew of the mission. Now at least one stranger knew. It could be anybody, even a Confederate. "Who sent you, Captain?"

"General Rosecrans, sir. He received a message from a Colonel Thompson."

Healy relaxed. "What do you suggest, Captain?"

"Sir, arrangements have been made for you to leave the train about ten miles north of the city. My orders are to accompany you as far as the Alabama border."

"Not in those clothes, Captain."

"No, sir. I have some civilian clothes in a bag."

Healy looked at Clinton. Clinton shrugged. Neither man liked this change in plans. The result placed their lives in the hands of this stranger, and they had no way to confirm that Thompson had sent him. "What arrangements have been made, Captain?"

"We'll depart at the last water stop on the line, sir. Four horses will be waiting. We are to bypass Nashville and go due south."

"That's it?"

"That's what they told me, sir. I was also instructed to tell you that you have the authority to abort the mission if you think it wise."

"I see. You look tired, Captain. Try to get some rest while I think about this."

"Thank you, sir. I've ridden more than forty miles today."

Healy sat looking out the window of the slow-moving train. He had a true dilemma to consider. He wanted his wife back. It was agonizing for him to even think of turning back when they were so close. But he must also think of his son. The young man was out of his element. He looked at the stranger lying on the bed. He seemed to be asleep. "What do you think, Captain Clinton?"

"I think it's your decision, sir."

"I want your opinion, Captain."

"Well, sir, I spent three months with the Confederate army. I never had a moment when I wasn't looking over my shoulder. By comparison, this is downright relaxing. If I had to make the decision, I'd say let's get your wife, sir—and take whatever comes." He hesitated for a moment. "There *is* an alternative, though."

"What's that?"

Clinton pulled his finger across his neck as he motioned in the stranger's direction.

"That will be embarrassing if he's legitimate."

Clinton shrugged. It was worth suggesting.

Healy turned to David junior. "Son, you never told me your part in this."

"I can't, Father. They told me to expect your insistence on knowing my mission. My orders are to resist every pressure. I am authorized to tell you only that *my* mission is to be canceled if *yours* succeeds. That's all."

That goddamn Thompson doesn't trust anyone, Healy thought. But perhaps it's for the best. If I fail, David might succeed. "That settles it. We'll stick with the plan."

Several hours later Healy shook the sleeping captain. "Time to get up. We're approaching the water stop."

Mason rubbed his eyes. "What time is it, sir?"

"Nearly eight. It's been dark for an hour."

The stranger changed to civilian clothes. When he finished, Healy picked up his bag and walked to the rear of the car. The others followed. He leaned past the end of the car. There were four horses hobbled in the shadows of some trees about fifty feet short of the water tower. Healy stepped off the train as it screeched to a stop. He moved quickly into the shadows. Better to keep our departure a secret, he thought.

The four men cut the hobbles and mounted. Healy noticed how uncomfortable his son looked on a horse. Too late to worry about that now, he thought. He pulled on the reins and headed the horse down a road that angled slightly to the southwest. Mason pulled into the lead when they were out of sight of the train. They had a long ride ahead.

"This is where I leave you, Colonel," Mason said. "I wish I was going with you."

"What is the full extent of your orders, Captain?" Healy asked.

"Just to make it back the best way possible."

"We're a hundred miles into enemy territory. That's a long way to go for a man who speaks with a New York accent." Healy had assumed that Mason was along for the duration. Although their mission had elements of risk, traveling north alone was far more dangerous. Healy had grown fond of the young man. He learned that Mason had run away from an orphanage the day he turned seventeen and joined the army. The war had been in progress less than a week at the time. Now Mason was nineteen and had earned the rank of captain. There were thousands in the army like him, young men who otherwise would have been doomed to struggle through life, never realizing their potential. The war changed all that. As a result of its greatest challenge, the nation was discovering its true strength. Mason had requested the cavalry and worked his way up the enlisted ranks to sergeant. Then, following the death of his lieutenant, he had led a cavalry charge. That got him a commission. He led a charmed life in the months that followed. Before his promotion to captain, he had fought in three major battles and twice as many skirmishes. If Mason could make it this far, perhaps David junior could too, Healy thought.

Mason smiled. "Maybe I should cut my throat, sir, and pretend I can't speak."

"I have a better idea. I think I have the authority to exercise some discretion in this matter. If you're willing, I'll order you to come with us."

"I'm yours to command, Colonel."

"Captain Mason, your orders are to come with us," Healy said with a smile. "Men, from here on we're on a first-name basis. No mention of rank—or personal relationship, David."

"Father," said David, "I will be using an alias. My association to you is to be purely business. To eliminate confusion, my first name will remain David, but call me Hazard—that's the name on my papers."

Appropriate, thought Healy. "Hazard it is." He looked at his watch. "It's two hours before dawn. Let's keep riding."

At first light, the four men stopped at a deserted house next to a small stream. They unsaddled, fed, and watered the horses before stretching out for some sleep.

"You, in there," said a commanding voice, "come out with your hands up."

The four men awoke immediately. Healy moved cautiously to a window and looked out from the side. A dozen or more men had the house surrounded. All wore Confederate gray and carried carbines. Cavalry, he thought. "We mean no harm," Healy said. "We're here on a business trip."

The officer repeated the order. "Come out with your hands up."

Healy turned to the others. "Move into the open, gentlemen. Try to act natural. Remember, we're just civilians here on business." Healy opened the door a crack. "Don't shoot. We're coming out." The four men moved single file into the clearing.

"Hands on your heads!" commanded the officer.

They complied.

Men carrying carbines rushed from the cover of the trees. Two went into the house. The young lieutenant moved more slowly. "Who are you men?" he asked.

"We're on a buying trip, young man," said Healy. "Cotton is our business. We're looking for General Thornton. Do you know where he is?"

"Lookee what we got here, Lieutenant," said a sergeant as he walked out of the house. He held up a handful of gold coins.

"What is it?" asked the lieutenant.

"Gold, sir. Must be a fortune here."

"Let me have that, Sergeant."

"But sir—"

"I said to give it to me, Sergeant, until I determine who these men are."

The sergeant dumped the coins back in the carpetbag and pitched it to the lieutenant.

"Why do you wish to see General Thornton, sir?" asked the officer.

"I understand it's within his power to arrange for us to purchase cotton, Lieutenant."

"We'll see about that. You men there, saddle their horses. You two tie their hands after they're mounted. Sergeant, bring their belongings."

Within minutes the rebels led the four down a narrow dirt road. In less than an hour, the smell of smoke surrounded them. Men were cooking breakfast off in the trees. It appeared to be a large army camp. In a clearing ahead stood a cabin. A command flag fluttered from the roof. A large Confederate flag hung limply from a short pine pole near the corner of the cabin.

"Help them from their mounts, Sergeant, and stand guard over them." The lieutenant entered the cabin. Shortly, a high-ranking officer came to the doorway. He buttoned his tunic, then looked at the prisoners for a moment before turning to speak to the lieutenant, who handed him the carpetbag. The general approached the four captives.

"Who are you men?" asked the general.

"How are you doing, Henry?" Healy asked.

"You have the advantage of me, sir," replied the general.

"We've never met, sir, but I always felt I'd know you anywhere." The two men had long been in the same business—cotton—Healy as a buyer and sometimes speculator, Thornton as the seller, but all of their business activities had been conducted through their agents. They had written each other on several occasions, and their names had jointly appeared on contracts, but they had never met. Even in the twilight period before the dark years of war, men of the North and South had conducted business as though they lived in two countries. "All of our business arrangements have been by correspondence. I'm David Healy, from Chicago."

"You have some proof?" asked Thornton coolly.

"In my pocket, General."

Thornton motioned to the lieutenant, who removed the papers from Healy's coat. Thornton flipped through the papers, then looked up. "Untie these men," he said. He studied the papers more closely, then smiled as he extended his hand. Healy shook it and returned the smile. "I wish to thank you, Mr. Healy, for the Colt you sent me. I purchased it as a gift for my son. I suspect he has made good use of it by now."

"If I had known of its intended use, sir, I doubt I'd have sent it."

Thornton thought for a moment, then nodded. "I suppose not." So this is the man Caroline married, he thought. Strange that I never made the connection. Hell of a coincidence, him being here on business with his wife detained by the South. I wonder how much you know, brother-in-law? "Have you and your men had breakfast?"

"No. If you have something to spare, it will be appreciated."

Thornton nodded to the lieutenant. "And who are these other men?" asked Thornton.

Healy turned. "This young man is David Hazard, my accountant. This is Josiah Mason, and this is James Clinton. Mr. Clinton is sort of my bodyguard." The men nodded at the introductions.

"I assume this is your gold, Mr. Healy?"

"Call me David. I feel like I know you so well, Henry. And yes, that is my gold."

Thornton handed Healy the bag. "Eat, then we'll talk."

*   *   *

"Now," Thornton said as the others sipped at their weak coffee, "what may I do for you?"

"I'm here to purchase cotton, Henry. I have in mind a thousand bales. I might take more if it's within your power to arrange it."

"There's a war on, David. Cotton is in short supply in the South."

"And saltwater is scarce in Florida," Healy replied.

Thornton smiled. "There are people down here who think it is immoral to trade with Yankees."

"War is war, Henry, and business is business. I don't see why one has to interfere with the other. You and I both know how difficult it is to get your cotton out of the South. The blockade has become quite effective. I'm prepared to pay half in gold and half in greenbacks."

"You have such a sum with you?" Thornton asked, already knowing the answer. The $1,000 in gold had been all the money found.

"Of course not, Henry. I have a down payment, that's all."

"But nothing prevents me from keeping that, and also keeping our cotton."

"When word gets back that you took my gold and kept your cotton, I suspect your business will cease entirely."

"And how will word get back?"

"Come now, Henry. There must be twenty cotton brokers who know I'm here. If I don't return, it's unlikely our government will continue to look the other way. In fact, I'm certain of it."

"Excuse me for a moment, gentlemen," said Thornton. He left the cabin for several minutes, then returned. "Let me hear your offer."

The two men talked for nearly two hours. Besides the price, there were other details to consider. Moving a thousand bales of cotton in wartime was no easy task. They were still discussing the details when they heard a knock on the door.

"Come in," Thornton said.

A tall, dark-haired man opened the door and walked in, followed by a middle-aged black man. Classic Southern described the white man's dress: wide-brimmed hat, waistcoat with tails, tight-fitting pants, and highly polished boots. He held a long cigar between his fingers. A looping gold chain led from a clip to a small watch pocket. Obviously, men of property in the South were making do.

"This is Quincy Gibbon, gentlemen. Mr. Gibbon is a plantation owner and cotton dealer."

"Good morning, gentlemen," said Gibbon. "I was informed you are here to purchase cotton."

"Good morning, sir," replied Healy. "You have been well informed."

Gibbon looked at Thornton. Thornton nodded. No words passed between them.

Healy nodded toward his son. "My associate is just preparing a contract," he said. "I trust it will meet with your satisfaction." Young Healy handed him the rough draft.

Gibbon read the paper, nodding several times, then returned it to Healy. "Five cents a pound seems low to me," he said finally. "It will cost you twice that from England."

Healy had anticipated this. "And you will sell it to the English for three. The shippers will make the profit. We'll have our cotton just the same, but you'll lose two cents a pound. My government is willing to buy your cotton, sir, but only to a point. When we take control of the Mississippi we'll get all the cotton we need from Louisiana and Texas."

"That will never happen, sir!" Gibbon said, flaring. "You will never take Vicksburg. Every Southern gentleman will die before that happens."

"Perhaps, Mr. Gibbon, but General Grant seems to be a very persistent man."

"The man is a drunkard and a butcher," Gibbon retorted. "He'll never get close to Vicksburg. When General Johnston is finished with him, he and whoever is left will rot in prison."

Healy suspected that Thornton's nod had sealed the deal. Southern honor, however, might elevate the price. Best to leave politics for later, he thought. "You have my offer, sir. It's what I'm authorized to pay."

"What about transport?"

"You will transport the goods to Nashville. We will unload it there. Everything will be clearly stated to your satisfaction in the contract."

Gibbon read the draft again, this time without the revealing nods. "Five-and-a-half cents," he said finally. "Take it or leave it."

Healy performed a hasty calculation, then leaned back as if thinking about the counteroffer. "Five-and-a-quarter, and you will provide twelve hundred bales. That is my final offer."

Gibbon thought for a moment. Appearing too eager invited difficulty in business. "Done."

"Do you have this much cotton available?" asked Healy.

"Delivery will begin June first with completion by the fifteenth. Is that satisfactory?"

"That will be fine. Mr. Hazard will prepare the final contract." Healy placed the gold on the desk. "This is the down payment, a thousand dollars in gold. I trust this seals the transaction." He rose and extended his hand.

Gibbon turned without accepting the gesture. "My signature will be sufficient, sir. Now, if you will excuse me." He motioned to the black man and they left the cabin.

Healy turned to Thornton. "There *is* one other matter, General Thornton," Healy said with formality.

Here it comes, Thornton thought. "And what is that, sir."

"The matter of a woman you hold captive. I am here to retrieve her."

Thornton offered no facial expression. "I have no idea what you are talking about, Mr. Healy."

"Yes, you do, General. Of that, I am certain. I speak of the former Mrs. Caroline Wade. Her last name is now Healy. She is my wife, sir, and I mean to take her back with me."

"That will be impossible, sir. Even if I were to agree that I know what you are talking about, the act of spying is dealt with harshly in the South."

"My wife is no spy, sir. She's a business woman with no thought of politics."

"She is a dedicated abolitionist, sir. She has spoken openly on the matter several times."

"Then you may count me as a spy, sir, for I think slavery is an abomination. The same applies to virtually everyone in the North."

"This matter is more complicated than that, Mr. Healy. I lack the authority to discuss details with you. The matters of cotton and Mrs. Wade are unrelated."

"May I see her, then, to assure myself that she is in good health?"

"You have my word on her good health, sir, and seeing her is impossible. My government is in control of this matter. It is out of my hands."

"May I inquire about her location?"

Thornton thought for a moment. "All I am empowered to tell you is that she is with her sister. That closes this matter, sir." He slid the gold toward Healy. "If you are unsatisfied, sir, take your gold and go. I will provide you with safe escort."

Healy looked at his son. The young man seemed uninterested in the conversation as he worked on the final contract. I have no other cards to play, Healy thought. What is David's part in all of this, or is his assignment totally unrelated? "Very well, General, I suppose I will have to rely on your word."

David junior handed his father the two sheets of paper. "Here is the final draft of the contract, Mr. Healy. If everything is as agreed, I will prepare copies for signature; then I will be on my way."

On his way? Where? Healy struggled to maintain his composure. He had always expected, in the end, to be a part of his son's mission. Apparently not. His mind wandered away from the words. He had to begin over several times. When he finished reading, he handed the final draft to Thornton.

"Very good, young man," Thornton said. "I believe everything is addressed." He looked at Healy. "That is, provided this other matter is disposed of."

Healy did not reply at first. Obtaining Caroline's release would remain his obsession until he knew she was safe in Gettysburg again with him by her side. "If it is acceptable, General, I will stay for a few days to inspect the cotton to make sure it meets government standards. Mr. Hazard and Mr. Mason will head back to Nashville to prepare for the shipment's delivery."

Thornton shrugged.

Young Healy and Mason rode off during the night. David watched them slip from under their blankets and fade into the darkness. He had to choose between being proud or terrified. He chose the former. Something had happened to David junior on the trip. Besides learning to appear modestly comfortable on a horse, his command of himself seemed to change. He had always been good at business affairs, but there his expertise ended. He and his brother were very different. Bill had always been the outgoing one, self-assured and athletic, always with something to say. David junior had reserve and polish and felt more at ease at a reception or a business meeting. The elder Healy had long since accepted that the world provided room enough for both young men. He accepted them as they were. That now worried him. David junior had no place in this war, except perhaps behind a desk in some large building in Washington. He was more like Colonel Thompson.

* * *

"Where are you going?" Mason asked his new friend.

"To save my father's new wife," he replied. "She's an important woman, Joe. She makes shoes for the army."

"Shoes?"

"Yes, shoes. The government wants her rescued, and I mean to do it."

"Where will we find her?"

"If General Thornton told the truth, on a plantation north of Birmingham. We should reach there by late tomorrow afternoon. Let me do the talking if we're stopped."

Little has changed, young Healy thought. He had traveled South twice before the war on business trips. The warm Southern breezes were a contrast to the chilling winds in Illinois. It was only late April, but black men worked in the fields without shirts. There was, however, a noticeable absence of white men. The smaller farms lay fallow or women and children tended them. There were only two economic conditions: garish wealth and grinding poverty. He expected land to be cheap here after the war. A man with a few dollars and the willingness to invest them might make a fortune. He made a mental note. There seemed to be no fear this far south. Hardly anyone paid any attention to them, not even the few soldiers they saw. The war had yet to reach this far into the heartland of the South.

"Will you direct me to the Thornton plantation?" young Healy asked a woman hoeing small sprouts of corn.

She wiped the sweat from her brow and leaned on the instrument. "Go to the next crossroads and turn east. I reckon it might be ten miles or so," she said.

"Thank you, ma'am. Do you think we might have some of your water."

"Help yourself." She returned to her chores.

"Let's walk the horses for a while," Healy said. "I don't want to arrive before dark."

"What are we going to do when we get there, David?"

"I'm still thinking about that. My orders are to find my stepmother and get her safely back north. I'm open to suggestions."

Mason may have been young, but hardly a fool. "That's it? Pick her up and head north across four hundred miles of enemy territory, with the militia of two states combing every bush and holler for us?" He shook his head. "That's a fine plan, that is," he added stingingly.

"You're the one who wanted to come along. My orders were to proceed alone."

"*My* orders, from *your* father, were to accompany *you*. It just never occurred to me that you didn't know what you were doing. Have you thought about this? What if she isn't at this plantation?"

"Then we find out where she is and go get her."

"Oh, I see. I suppose that is phase two of this detailed plan."

Healy led his horse to a small stream near the side of the road. Mason followed. "Joe," Healy said, "you've been on your own most of your life. I've always been protected, told what to do and when to do it. I'm sure my father believes I'm on a fool's errand. That may be so, but I intend to do it or die trying. Either help me or leave me alone."

"Don't get angry," Mason replied. "This just takes some getting used to. Perhaps this is best. Any plan is sure to blow up in our faces. This way we won't be disappointed. There's something to be said for that."

Healy smiled and Mason grinned back. "Let's get moving."

They reached the tree-lined road leading to the plantation at dusk. They stood behind a large tree and examined the surroundings. The house appeared somewhat run-down. The stalks of last season's flowers drooped in what must have been, before the war, well-tended beds. Now every effort had to go into the field. In the distance, near a crumbling barn, a woman sat on a one-legged stool milking a cow. Another, older, woman sat on the porch shelling corn. To the right, a line of slaves walked slowly toward the shacks that lined a side road. Darkness was near, but there were no lights in the large house. "You stay here," Healy said. "I'm going to the right to see who that is milking the cow." He crouched and ran from tree to tree. The last daylight had nearly faded away when he crept close enough to see the young woman. He moved cautiously along the edge of the barn until he stood no more than thirty feet from the woman.

"Nancy Caroline," he said in a loud whisper.

The woman looked up, then turned her head from right to left. "Who's there?" she asked.

"Over here. Come over by the barn."

She rose and moved cautiously into the shadows. "Who is it?" she asked again.

"David. David Healy."

"David!" she exclaimed. "My God. What are *you* doing here?"

"Shhhhhh. Don't talk so loud." Her gleaming smile sparkled, even in the dark.

She patted her hair, then ran toward him.

He embraced her and kissed her hard on the lips. "I never thought I'd see you again," he said, stepping back. "It's been so long, I wasn't sure I'd remember what you looked like." He kissed her again as they pressed close to each other, her back to the wall, her arms tight around his neck. All the pent-up passion rushed forth. Two years had passed since he had seen her last, in early April of '61. They had made love during that visit to New York. Since the wedding was only three months away, or so they thought, it seemed only a small sin. The event had progressed awkwardly. Neither had seemed to know what to do. But nature had a way with such things, and visions of that hour had dominated his thoughts since. She seemed so happy afterward, he remembered, as if she had discovered this delicious secret that no one else knew. After a while, when modesty returned, they had dressed and everything returned to normal. Now Healy often thought of that as the last night of real life. She had boarded the train the next afternoon for the trip back to Birmingham. The war began less than a week later.

"How did you get here?" she asked.

"I rode a horse."

She smiled shyly. "You silly, foolish boy. They'll shoot you if they find you here."

"Then I shall have to keep anyone from finding me. How is your mother?"

"Lonely and tired. Life has been difficult since the war began."

How best to deal with the next question presented a problem. She must surely suspect that my being here has something to do with Caroline. "Is anyone else here?"

"No. Father is off fighting the war someplace. He came home about three months ago. We haven't heard from Simon since early December. We received word that he had been wounded at Fredericksburg, but nothing since. He's with General Lee's army someplace." She let her shoulders slump. "Oh, David, this awful war has been a terrible mistake. I don't see how survival is possible. A third of our slaves have been taken for war duty. The others don't get enough to eat to sustain them for their labor. If we lose the Mississippi, I fear it will be all over."

He had to try a more direct approach. "I'm sure you are aware that my father and Caroline were married. I met her only once. We don't have much information, but she has disappeared. Have you heard from her?"

"She stayed here for a while, until a month ago. One day some soldiers came and escorted her away. I don't know where she is now. She has written a couple of times. Did you know that they kidnapped her? The war has come to that, David. My mother protested, but it did no good."

This altered everything. If she had been taken into military custody, what chance had he of finding her or of moving her through enemy lines if he did find her? He wanted only to forget the war, to lead Nancy Caroline into the barn and express his undying love for her. "Come with me," he said pleadingly. "I'll get another horse, and we'll go west, away from the war."

"You must be crazy! My mother will never approve."

"Don't ask her. Let's just go, now."

She pulled away. "No. That's impossible. It'd be no different than running away with the enemy."

"So it has come to that. Now I'm the enemy."

She flung her arms around his neck. "No. You know I didn't mean that. Oh, I don't know what I mean. It's just the times." She relaxed and stepped back. She placed her hands on his shoulders and looked him in the eyes. "But I'm a Southern lady, David, and you are a Northern gentleman. We can't change that. We were infatuated with each other for a while—maybe it was love, I don't know—but that time has passed and we must put it out of our minds. Mother made me see that it could never work. We're from different worlds."

"You planned to call off the wedding?" he asked.

"No. At least not at the time. But everything has changed."

There remained only one option. He had to act, to do something rash, before someone heard them. "Is there a wagon in the barn?"

"Yes. Why do you ask?"

Healy gritted his teeth, made a fist, and hit her hard on the chin. He grabbed her before she fell and lowered her gently to the ground. Moving in the shadows, he headed into the barn. Once inside, he lit a match and found a lantern. He attached the two scrawny horses to the wagon and threw some hay and several horse blankets into the bed. He pulled a long strand of rope from a hook and picked up a dirty shirt from the ground. He led the horses to the side of the barn, then bound and gagged Nancy Caroline. He still loved her, despite her harsh words, but personal feelings had to be suspended. He placed her in the wagon and covered her with hay before leading the horses into the darkness.

"Nancy Caroline," said a woman's voice, "where are you? We need the milk for supper."

Desperate to escape before Victoria found the bucket full of milk and began looking for her daughter, Healy moved faster. In time, she was certain to become aware that the wagon was missing. He began to envision his own death, with his body dangling from a tall tree along some lonely road after they captured him. These people were expert hunters, he knew.

"Bring the horses, Joe," Healy said as he approached the place where Mason waited. "I have her in the wagon. We have to move fast before they realize she's missing." Better to delay for the time being telling him who *she* is, he thought. He flipped the reins. These are poor-looking horses, he thought. We'll need to make a trade before long. He whipped the animals to a run.

Chapter 19

· · · · · · · · · · · · · · · ·

Major Samuel Wade, alias Lt. Col. Simon Thornton, had recovered from his wounds. He had even begun thinking of himself as a Thornton, which he was, in fact, if Thompson's version of his origin was true. The head wound had been more serious than first thought. The doctor diagnosed it as a small fracture and sent him to Richmond to recover. On the way, he suffered an even worse affliction. Scouts had reported a regiment-sized Union cavalry patrol in the area, deep behind Confederate lines. At the sound of firing in its rear, the ambulance train commander ordered the wagons to a gallop. As the wagons entered a wooded area, the lead elements of the Federal cavalry struck from ambush. Stuart's cavalry came up shortly, but not until after the wagon transporting Wade had lost a wheel and overturned. The wagon rolled over him, breaking his left arm in two places. Dizziness from the head wound persisted, and the simple but painful fractures had healed slowly. Winter had passed and spring was in full bloom when the doctor released him for duty.

While Wade had been in the hospital, General Burnside tried to turn Lee's flank by marching his army north along the east bank of the Rappahannock. Unfortunately, the ground had thawed and the Army of the Potomac bogged down in what was already being referred to sarcastically as the "Mud March." Lee's men watched gleefully from the heights overlooking Fredericksburg as the Yankees flailed in the mud before giving up and returning to their positions opposite the Confederate lines. The two armies remained there for the rest of the winter.

As Wade approached Fredericksburg on the Richmond road, he noticed frenzied activity in the Confederate camp. A warm southerly breeze blew through the trees as he galloped along the damp lane. It had rained the night before and the clinging mud tired the horse, so Wade dismounted and led the animal. It was the first opportunity he'd had to study the men. What he saw appalled him. Food and forage had obviously been scarce during the winter. Most of the horses appeared malnourished, but the men looked worse. Hardly a man in sight had a regulation uniform hanging from his gaunt frame. At least half of them were without shoes. Many still wore rags wrapped around their feet. Conditions would have been even worse if it hadn't been for their mid-December thrashing of Burnside's army. The mounds of Yankee bodies piled in front of their positions had provided a ready supply of footwear for many of the rebels.

How do they endure? Wade thought as he tramped through the mud on that late April morning. But he knew the answer. They were veterans now, almost to a man. One of them was worth three of the green troops who had fought at Bull Run nearly two years before. They showed no sign of quitting, not even of being the least bit discouraged. Back in the hospital, the men who had been brought in expressed eagerness to return to their units as soon as possible. As Wade moved along, a mind-numbing reality began to emerge: With proper leadership and modest success in providing supplies, these men will fight forever. The only realistic option is to kill them, kill them all! They would have to drain the South's manpower to the dregs.

Wade spotted a soldier headed rapidly in the opposite direction and waved. "What's the hubbub all about?" Wade inquired. "I'm just back from the hospital and I'm looking for General Jackson's headquarters. I'm assigned to his staff."

"I'm on my way to find General Longstreet now, sir," said the private. "Stuart's cavalry found out that Hooker's men are moving north. General Longstreet's corps has been on a foraging mission. I'm to tell the general that he is to prepare to move his corps back as soon as possible."

Hooker? Wade thought. So Hooker's in command now? Just as well. Burnside had been a disaster. "Fightin' Joe" was sure to do better. He thanked the private and continued up the road until he found General Jackson's command post. It was buzzing with activity. Wade dismounted and entered Jackson's tent.

"Colonel Thornton reporting for duty," he said, saluting the grim-faced corps commander, who stood studying a map on the camp table.

Jackson turned and smiled. "You're just in time, Colonel. We have reports that as many as three Yankee corps are moving in the Wilderness area north of Chancellorsville. That means the blue-bellied bastards have managed to sneak across the Rapidan." Jackson paused and grasped Wade's arms, shaking him gently. "It's good to have you back, Simon. You seem fit."

"I'm all healed up, sir," said Wade. "My arm isn't as strong as it was, but if I'd stayed in that hospital a moment longer I'd have gotten too fat to mount a horse."

Jackson laughed. "We'll take care of that in short order, Colonel."

"Is Captain Clinton around, sir?" Wade asked.

The smile on Jackson's face faded. "I'm sorry, Simon, but the damned Yankees appear to have killed him. He led a patrol that was ambushed. Eight of his men were killed in the opening volley. The rest rode back without him. One of the men said he saw Clinton's horse go down. We never found his body. Scavengers were unusually active. The bodies we found were a mess. We assumed they dragged him into the trees."

Captain Clinton eaten by dogs? thought Wade. My God, now I'm alone!

Jackson reached out and patted Wade's shoulder. "I'm sorry, son. I know what he meant to you."

"Yes, sir," said Wade, tears welling up in his eyes. "What do you want me to do, sir?"

"Stay close at hand. We're getting ready to attack. I think Hooker's move into the Wilderness is a feint, an effort to lure us out of our trenches, then he'll attack our rear with the forces he's got here. General Lee told me he'll approve an attack if I think it can be successful. I'm going out now on a reconnaissance, then meeting with him later this evening to discuss our next step. I want you to come with me."

So typical of Jackson, thought Wade. He knew that the general chaffed at the thought of defensive action—hated the idea of digging in. After watching the Yankees' December debacle, Jackson still favored an attack. Wade just nodded. It began to rain lightly as he followed Jackson out of the tent.

*   *   *

The moon was out when they rode up to General Lee's headquarters. The commander of the Army of Northern Virginia was standing outside his tent.

"Good evening, General," said Lee. Jackson dismounted and shook Lee's proffered hand. "Well, Thomas, what do you think?"

"I think, sir, that an attack here would be inexpedient," replied Jackson.

Lee nodded. "I agree. Despite the large number of men they have here, I think the main effort will come from upstream. I think these forces were meant to fix us while Hooker maneuvers on our flank. General Anderson's division is already in position south of Chancellorsville. I want you to leave General Early's division here and move with all haste to join forces with General Anderson. Dividing the army in the face of the enemy is risky, but it's a gamble I'm willing to take. I'm convinced they won't try to take these heights again."

Jackson nodded. "We'll move before morning, sir." He turned to Wade, who stood holding their mounts. "Simon, go back to headquarters and pass the word that I want all of the corps except General Early's division on the road and ready to move by 3:00 A.M. Then get some sleep. You can stay in my tent. I'll be along shortly."

Wade was awed by the flurry of activity that his arrival at Jackson's headquarters generated. He was even more awed by Lee's orders. To divide his army in the face of superior forces and move with the enemy to his front and flanks invited disaster. Even if everything evolved as planned and Jackson's corps linked up with Anderson's division before Hooker attacked, the Federals would still outnumber them three to two—and they would not have the advantage of prepared positions on high ground.

The two armies were destined to clash. Both commanding generals had made decisions that sent the blue- and gray-clad soldiers moving toward inevitable confrontation. Hooker and Lee were the main characters. What they thought of each other would play more of a part in the eventual outcome than the effectiveness of the soldiers in the field. It would come down to who blinked first. Samuel Wade recalled that he had detected not a glimmer of doubt in Lee's eyes as he discussed his plans with Jackson. As for the corps commander, Wade thought, Jackson seemed created for battle. He seemingly ignored the details that drove other men to despair. His eyes were always looking at the horizon, fixed on some distant, hoped-for outcome, the destiny *he* envisioned—not what his opponent sought to impose. Jackson would fight, never losing hope of victory, until the moment of his death. Although he was the enemy, the man commanded Wade's respect.

Wade had learned much about the Army of Northern Virginia—enough to justify, at any time, his return to Washington. He knew the true strength of every division and the condition of the men. He had experienced the Confederate medical system and had lived, even thrived, on their meager rations. Most of all, he had observed their generals—but his observations were useless. To know a man, one has to know both what and how he thinks. The what eventually becomes evident through the army's movements. The how remained a mystery. Lee obviously was the thinker. His thoughts moved through complex problems as effortlessly as water from an artesian well flowing to the surface of some deeply hidden reservoir: clear, pure, without any flaws at all. Jackson, in contrast, was the highly tempered spring: capable of absorbing any blow and contracting; ready to strike back at the least provocation with a devastating recoil.

Wade's thoughts continued to drift as fatigue washed over him. Finally, he slept.

He awoke with a start at the touch of a hand on his shoulder.

"Wake up, Colonel Thornton," said Jackson's aide-de-camp. "General Jackson is waiting for you out on the road."

"What time is it?" Wade asked groggily.

"It's almost three. Come on, sir. I've got your horse ready. The lead units are already moving."

"All right, all right," Wade mumbled. "I'm up."

He sat up, swinging his legs over the edge of the cot. After pulling on his boots he stood and stretched, then buttoned his coat.

Outside, Wade found Jackson sitting on Little Sorrel. The general was wearing his Mexican War battle jacket, and his VMI cap's visor was tugged down over his brow. He was sucking furiously on a lemon, an act that Jackson said settled his "dyspeptic" stomach, as he watched the columns march by in the darkness.

"Good morning, sir," said Wade. The general must expect a fight when we get where we're going, he thought.

"Colonel," said Jackson with a nod. He wiped his sleeve across his mouth and spat. "Mount up. Let's head for General Anderson's headquarters."

The first light of day was filtering through the woods around them when they heard the gunfire to their front. By eight they were with General Anderson. Four miles ahead, beyond Anderson's line, was the intersection of the Old Turnpike and the Plank Road, the place known as Chancellorsville.

Wade listened as the two generals discussed the situation. Jackson was alert and anxious to fight, even though he'd hardly slept the night before.

"We've got to get at Hooker while he's still in these damnable woods and can't see his hand in front of his face," said Jackson. "I'll have McLaws move on the Turnpike and I want your division to come with us on the Plank Road. We'll see how much fight there is in old 'Fightin' Joe.'"

Just then, a courier from Stuart's cavalry rode up.

"General Stuart sends his regards, sir," said the sergeant. "He said to tell you he made it around General Hooker's flank and saw no sign of their cavalry. He stands ready to protect your flank. He said to tell you he'll help all he can when the ball begins."

Jackson smiled. "Well, he won't have long to wait. Go back and tell him we're on the move."

"May God grant us victory," said the cavalryman.

"Here," said Jackson, handing the sergeant a folded note, "give this to General Stuart. And don't worry, I trust God will grant us a great victory. Now stay closed on Chancellorsville!"

The courier saluted and rode off in the direction from which he'd come.

In the hours that followed, the Federals kept falling back. Wade couldn't believe it. Perhaps it was Jackson's audacity. Perhaps they believed they were outnumbered—that thought had been General McClellan's undoing on the Peninsula and at Antietam Creek. Perhaps they were just tired and didn't have their hearts in it. Whatever the case, Jackson's badly outnumbered forces moved steadily through the thick woods.

Wade stayed with Jackson as he rode up and down the lines on Little

Sorrel, directing the battle. They finally found Jeb Stuart on a small crested hill.

"General Jackson, sir," shouted Stuart, waving. "It's good to see you! We've got the blue-bellies on the run."

"Indeed we do, Jeb," said Jackson. He pulled up next to Stuart, leaned over Little Sorrel's neck, and playfully prodded the cavalry commander's arm. "Now, how can I get behind them? What roads have you found in this godforsaken mess?"

Stuart pointed out those he knew of, but the woods were so thick that Jackson could only vaguely comprehend what Stuart was indicating.

"Damnit, sir!" Jackson exclaimed in frustration. "The Yankees are in these woods and I aim to find their positions and get around them. If you can't show me the way, Providence will! Simon," he said over his shoulder, "let's go!"

Jackson and Wade rode back down the Plank Road until they saw A. P. Hill. Hill wore his trademark red flannel shirt and was loudly exhorting his men to move forward. The sounds of battle carried through the forest to their front. The two generals exchanged excited greetings and rode in the direction of the gunfire. They soon found General Heth's division stalled by determined Federal troops. Farther along the line they found General McLaws, who told Jackson that, given the lateness of the afternoon and the determined resistance he had encountered, he had ordered his men to erect hasty defensive positions.

Jackson nodded his approval. "Colonel Thornton, I must know Hooker's strength and disposition. Let's go back."

They wheeled their horses and headed back to the Plank Road, where they soon encountered an excited Confederate officer galloping toward them.

"General Jackson, sir!" shouted the officer. "You must come with me. I think what you'll see will be very interesting."

Without waiting for a reply, the officer—a captain—reined in his mount, wheeled, and sped off in the direction from which he'd come. Jackson looked at Wade and shrugged. "Let's go, Simon," he said as he spurred Little Sorrel forward.

They followed the captain off the road onto a narrow trail that led to the top of a hill. When they reached the crest they dismounted.

"There," said the captain, pointing.

Jackson pulled out his field glasses and scanned the terrain to their front. "Damn! Look at them, Simon," said Jackson, passing the glasses to Wade.

The colonel took the field glasses and saw three Union battle lines behind heavy earthworks. "Captain," said Jackson, "you stay here. Come on, Colonel, I've got to find General Lee."

The men mounted their horses and raced back to the Plank Road.

They reached Lee at about 8:00 P.M. Following the usual amenities, the two generals talked in private. Finally, prompted by occasional sniper fire, the two generals walked from the Plank Road into the nearby trees. They stood for a moment before sitting on two facing logs. Fearing that if he sat down he might never rise, Wade stood by his general's side.

"What do you think they mean to do?" asked Jackson.

"I can't understand why they pulled back today," replied Lee. "They appear to be going on the defensive."

"By tomorrow we'll be strong enough to attack their center, which I've located here," said Jackson, pointing at the map lying on the ground between them. "Provided, of course, we find a weak spot."

"Perhaps," replied Lee, "but I'm not sure." His thoughts drifted. Finally, he pointed to the map with a stick. "What if we found a means of getting around them, over there to their right?"

"I've considered that, General," said Jackson, "but I didn't see any roads in that area. Besides, if we march across their front, they'll see our movement."

"Perhaps, but still . . ."

Wade glanced at the map. Lee's suggestion seemed impossible. The name Wilderness best described the bramble-covered landscape. The trees were as thick as wheat in a bottomland field. A rabbit could scarcely hop a straight line more than a few feet. Lee's suggestion would require marching the army for miles to accomplish its objective.

"Rider coming, General Lee," announced a sentry. "It's General Stuart, sir."

Stuart swung from his horse, walked over to the campfire, and poured a cup of sweet potato coffee. "General Lee," he said, "my scouts report that the Union right flank is hanging in thin air. If you could get a force around there, you could do a lot of damage."

Lee had a barely perceptible smile. He straightened up and placed his hands on his knees. "What will it require to get our men there, General Stuart?"

"Well, sir, the roads are terrible in this area. Movement can't be out in the open. The men in the Federal balloons will be able to spot us for sure."

"Find out for me, General."

"Yes, sir." Stuart mounted and rode west.

"What do you think, General Jackson?"

"I think I must have my men on the move by four in the morning, sir." He rose and stretched. "If I'm going, I have plans to make."

"Then make them, General. You will attack their right flank and Stuart will protect yours."

The generals rose from the logs. Lee bid Jackson good night, placed his saddle on the ground, and soon fell sound asleep.

Jackson wandered to the edge of the fire's light, deep in thought. After a while he turned to Wade. "Colonel Thornton," Jackson said finally, "find Chaplain Lacy."

"Sir?" said Wade, surprised at the strange request.

"Fetch me the chaplain. I want to speak with him."

Wade rode off into the darkness toward headquarters. Only a hint of a moon gleamed through the closely packed trees. After riding about a mile, he approached a sentry. "Do you know where Chaplain Lacy is?"

"Yes, sir." He pointed. "He should be down that trail."

Wade rode on, then spoke to a soldier leaning against a tree. The soldier pointed to some tents pitched by a small stream. Wade found the chaplain and told him that General Jackson wanted him.

The chaplain's face lit up. *He must want me to pray over some battle plan,* he thought.

"I found Chaplain Lacy, General," said Wade, as the two men rode back into camp. Both officers dismounted.

"Chaplain," said Jackson, "it's my understanding that you once served as pastor at a church in this area."

"Yes, General. Wilderness Church."

"How well do you know the roads here?"

"Fairly well, I'd say, General, although it has been some years."

"I want you to do some scouting for me tonight. Here is what I want." Jackson outlined his intentions. Basically, he wanted a safe route around the Federal flank, out of sight of the balloons. The chaplain had orders to find that route and report back soon, preferably before dawn. "Colonel Thornton will accompany you," Jackson added.

"Very well, sir."

The difficulty was in finding anything in the junglelike darkness, even the road they traveled by. A man might wander off into the trees and disappear forever. Many years before, the area had been a forest of towering oaks; then settlers had cleared the large trees to try their luck at farming. But the soil had worn thin and the fallen acorns of untold thousands of oaks littered the ground. As soon as axmen cut down a tree and the light reached the ground, ten new saplings sprang up. Soon, all thoughts of farming had faded. The farmers abandoned the place and left it to grow into a scrub forest covering more than a hundred square miles. Branches were so thick and entangled that hardly 5 percent of the sunlight that struck the top of the canopy reached the ground less than fifteen feet below.

It was in this Wilderness, as people now called it, that the two officers searched for a path along which to move an army. The search required most of the night. Wade detected no advantage in obtaining the information. The route to the western flank stretched a dozen miles long. Avoiding detection in daylight seemed impossible. The plan suggested nothing to him so much as folly. He resisted expressing this at 4:20 in the morning after he shook General Jackson from his sleep.

"We found a route, General. It's roundabout, but it might work."

"Do you think you'll be able to find it again and lead the army to the objective?"

"You'll have to ask Chaplain Lacy, sir. He's more familiar with the area."

Jackson looked at the chaplain. Lacy nodded.

By this time, Lee had awakened. "Why aren't you on your way, Thomas?" Lee asked.

"I've been waiting for a scouting report on the roads, sir. My scouts just reported back." Jackson spread his map in the early morning light. "Show us the route you found, Colonel."

Wade traced the route with his finger as Lacy looked over their shoulders.

"Is that about it, Chaplain?" Wade inquired, seeking confirmation.

"That's it, Colonel. It's about twelve miles or so. The road is narrow, but it's there."

"How many men will you take?" Lee asked Jackson.

"The whole corps, sir."

Lee looked at him in bewilderment. "The whole corps? What will you leave me to hold Hooker's army?" The question had a rhetorical ring. If the entire corps left, Lee would stand alone to fend off Hooker's eighty thousand or more troops.

"Two divisions, sir. I'll take all but two divisions."

Lee pondered the alternatives. Less than fifteen thousand against eighty thousand were poor odds. He saw a slim chance, but only if Hooker remained on the defensive. There were few facts to guide Lee's private deliberation. Hooker almost certainly realized that he outnumbered the enemy troops on his front. Yet, knowing this, he had halted his attack and dug in the day before. The late evening reports had been of frantic activity to make those defenses stronger. Had "Fightin' Joe" Hooker lost his nerve? The fate of the Confederate army hung on the answer.

What is Lee thinking? Wade wondered. Dividing an inferior force in the face of the enemy defied all military logic. He had done it once, now he proposed doing it again! Even a halfhearted attack by Hooker would drive Lee's men back to Richmond. Worse, Jackson's force faced being cut off, with no hope of escape. What was Lee thinking about?

"Well, go on then," Lee said with a nod. Lee had always taken desperate gambles, waging all—the lives of his men, the hopes of his fledgling nation—on little more than his own insight into the thoughts of men who most likely knew less of what they would do than did Lee. There was no alternative. He had never led troops into a battle with anything approaching even odds. But, more than anything, he knew Jackson. If Lee had the nerve to endure the long wait, Jackson would fulfill his appointed task.

Wade shook his head. What Jackson is about to attempt is impossible! he thought. Thirty thousand troops needed to march all day, virtually without rest, and attack a superior force—all before nightfall. Why did Lee trust this man so completely? A terrible thought entered Wade's mind. Although any chance of success seemed remote, one fact stood out above all others: If Jackson made it happen, he had evolved into a menace beyond calculation. If so, the Federal high command was wrong in believing that disposing of the Confederate generals would be a mistake or offer no real advantage. These two men, while sitting on crumbling logs, had hatched a plan more daring than any written in any West Point textbook. Missing were even glimmers of concern in their eyes, let alone the desperation that justifiably should have been there. There had been no discussion at all of what to do if the inevitable disaster came crashing down on their heads. When Jackson expressed that he saw no problem with taking his whole corps, Wade thought of a dozen questions to ask, a hundred reasons to conclude that the effort had no chance for success. And Lee said he should go on. Go on!

The morning burned away as Jackson scurried about in the effort to organize his troops. Wade and the other staff officers were in a frenzy, carrying messages and returning with the responses. Only the jostling of his horse kept Wade awake. The lead column began moving at 8:00 A.M., with others following as the morning wore on. Wade took heart when he heard that the lead element had broken out into an unexpected clearing and was spotted by a Federal battery before it could slip back into the woods. Surely someone has alerted Hooker by now, Wade thought. When all he heard was a few scattered booms from the Federal guns, it became evident to Wade that the pieces were falling in place for the disaster he had predicted, if only to himself.

It was just past four in the afternoon when a staff officer rode up to Jackson. "General," he said calmly, "please come with me." The general and his escort rode up the road for about a quarter of a mile. The messenger pointed off the road toward a hill. "Up there, General, but be quiet."

They rode to near the top of the hill before dismounting, then crouched as they approached some bushes at the crest. Jackson spread the bushes apart and looked down the hill. A broad smile appeared amid his massive growth of whiskers. "By the grace of God," he said in a whisper, "there they are."

Wade parted the bushes in front of him. Down the small hill and across a clearing were hundreds of men in blue. With their weapons neatly stacked, they were building fires in relaxed preparation for the evening meal. The air was warm, with only a slight breeze blowing from the south. They were close enough to hear the sounds of their laughter and boisterous talking. The smell of woodsmoke and coffee excited Wade's olfactory nerves. Only now did he realize the extent of his hunger.

Jackson turned and examined the terrain in the direction from which he had come, then turned back toward the enemy, moving his field glasses slowly from south to north. The heavily wooded area offered minimum opportunity for maneuvering. The ridge tapered off gently on either side of the knob where they now stood, providing ample cover for the secret gathering of an army.

The general withdrew a small notebook and began to write orders. One by one, he sent his staff officers rushing off to bring the lead regiments into place. Within minutes the lead column moved through the trees; then the units turned alternately north and south along the near side of the ridge. For an hour, brigade after brigade of troops filed quietly into position. Even before the last of the assault element arrived, the Union soldiers were cooking their evening meal. They were totally oblivious to the mass of men gathering a quarter of a mile away with nothing on their minds but to make this the Yankees' last meal. Jackson stood at the midpoint of this gathering, directing traffic, this regiment to the north, that one to the south, until the battle line stretched for a mile in either direction.

Wade considered mounting his horse and charging down the hill to warn the Union troops. Then he reconsidered. He realized the absurdity of riding forward inviting death. He would appear to them as a Confederate officer obviously gone mad. Before listening to anything he had to say, they most likely would shoot him from his horse. They might remain on alert for a while, maybe even post a few extra guards, but nothing much would result. If they did take him prisoner, no matter how carefully he tried to put it into words, the magnitude of the force now facing them would come as an overwhelming surprise. No. If he had suicide in mind, the desperate act had to offer the promise of producing better results.

Shortly after five, Jackson turned to General Rodes, the commander of the lead division. "Are you ready, General Rodes?" he asked.

"Yes, sir."

"You may go forward, then."

To the Union forces, the first indication of the approaching devastation appeared with the panicked rush of forest creatures across the clearing. Wade watched in disgust as the Federals laughed and threw rocks at the darting animals. A few took potshots at the terrified creatures, no doubt expecting to supplement the freshly butchered beef already cooking on the fires.

But the real danger, from an infinitely more cunning and treacherous animal, lurked just out of sight. The time for merriment was past. With a bloodcurdling yell, the surging gray line crashed into the open and rushed forward in a pulverizing mass. For a moment, paralyzed in a disbelieving stupor, Union soldiers watched in bewilderment; then they broke and ran. Few bothered to take the time to grab a rifle as they scampered in terror into the woods. Everywhere, all along a two-mile front, the same panic resulted. To the south, the Confederate line overlapped the dismayed Federals. The rebels gobbled up whole Union companies; then, often leaving only a dozen or so men to guard five times as many, they herded their captives into tight knots for transport to prison camps. Many of the blue-clad soldiers who escaped being shot or driven through by bayonets melted into the trees. Whatever there had been of the army in them had disappeared with that first thought of running. Now it was becoming every man for himself, not because they were cowards, but because their generals had given them a calling beyond mortal endurance.

From his secluded perch on the hill Wade watched in disbelief. He wanted to cry, but angrily forced back the tears. How had it been possible for the Union high command to be so careless? he silently raged. Placing the men here, with their flank exposed to attack, represented a blunder of criminal proportions. He turned and looked at Jackson. The general stood serenely in his element, smiling, his hands behind his back, casually slapping the back of one hand against the palm of the other. Beaming with satisfaction, he relished the carnage unleashed below. This is the man who brought the Union army to ruin, Wade thought. The onrushing Confederate soldiers were nothing more than his instruments of destruction. The general, a genius of military tactics, made it happen. It had been, from beginning to end, the most daring of gambles, a venture without reasonable chance of success. Lee, to be sure, had developed the plan. But Jackson, by projecting his iron will and his unflinching determination to bring the god of battle crashing down on the unsuspecting Federals, had *made* it happen.

Within minutes, the Union positions were overrun. Already, Jackson's thoughts were someplace out beyond that near horizon. "Colonel," Jackson said to Wade, "send an order to bring up the reserves. We will press the attack after dark."

Wade hesitated.

"Do it, Colonel, do it *now!*"

Wade ran the short distance to his horse, then he careened down the hill. Glancing briefly over his shoulder, he saw Jackson sidestepping casually down the hill toward Little Sorrel.

The man *must* be killed, Wade thought, or we will lose the war. For the first time since the moment they met, Wade saw Jackson as the enemy. The last, best service Wade could provide for his country was to prevent such a humiliation as this from occurring again.

"General Hill," Wade said, "General Jackson's compliments. He wishes you to bring the reserves forward to press a night attack." The moon will be full tonight, Wade thought, and visibility will be good if the sky remains clear. The survival of the Army of the Potomac depended on a whim of nature, or a calculated plot by a single man. The bottom rim of the sun had already slid below the treetops, with darkness less than an hour away, even sooner within the dense growth of the Wilderness, when Wade wheeled and rode off to find Jackson.

Now Wade saw the whole plan, the part that had remained unspoken in the brief period of planning between Lee and Jackson. Most of Hooker's army had moved south and east of Jackson's wild-eyed soldiers. If the Confederates pressed the attack successfully along the Plank Road, then turned eastward along the Turnpike, Hooker's soldiers would be clamped in a vise. By now the Confederate forces around Fredericksburg should have joined Lee's meager force holding the front. For all Wade knew, Lee had ordered Longstreet's entire corps to join in the final onslaught. With that, despite still being outnumbered, the Confederate forces, aided by Union panic and surprise, had the capability to overwhelm Hooker's weakest points with concentrated strength. Already, the last stages of the plan were in motion. Everything depended on Jackson's success at keeping his attack moving after dark, an action intended to disrupt every element of the Union defensive plan. Bold beyond imagination, Wade thought, but just the brazen action required if the South is to survive.

Wade caught up with Jackson shortly after eight that evening.

"Colonel," Jackson said, "I thought you had gotten lost."

"Sorry, sir. It took longer than I expected to find General Hill."

"Did he come forward as ordered?"

"Yes, sir, but the Federals were running so fast I doubt he caught up with them."

Jackson smiled. He had it in mind to keep them running. Jackson rode up to where the staff cooks were preparing a meal. None of the staff officers had eaten since early morning. "Eat quickly, men," he said. "I want to ride ahead and see to the advance."

Wade grabbed two biscuits and dipped them in melted lard, then in a bowl of molasses. He ate eagerly between gulps of weak coffee.

Jackson checked his watch as the men ate. Wade saw in Jackson's anxiety that even this brief stop delayed action too much. "Let's go," Jackson said, stuffing a biscuit into his coat pocket. A half-dozen cavalry mounted and led the way; another half dozen followed, making about twenty staff and escorts. Even with a full moon, the visibility had become poor beneath the trees. In a few minutes, when the moon sank below the tree line, there would be no light at all.

"General," said Wade, "it's dangerous out here in the darkness ahead of our line."

"It's dangerous everywhere, Simon." Jackson paused. "The danger is over here, though. Go back and tell A. P. Hill to press on! I'll be right behind you."

"Yes, sir." Wade spurred his horse and disappeared into the darkness. He had ridden about six hundred yards when he was challenged. Wade halted, then pulled his horse into the trees. The men reacted nervously. "Don't shoot," he said in a loud whisper. "I'm with General Jackson's staff." He moved forward at a walk. "Who's in command here?" he asked.

"The colonel is just over there," said an officer, pointing. Near total darkness closed about them as a broad cloud bank covered the moon.

"Colonel," Wade said in a whisper, "you'd best be on the alert. There's a troop of Union cavalry coming up the road behind me. They should be approaching at any moment."

The colonel nodded and rushed forward. "Be on the alert, men. Enemy approaching." The men scrambled for cover.

The dull thump of hooves against the packed road gave the first warning. "Don't shoot until I give the order," said the colonel in a loud whisper. The thumps grew closer. "Hold it, men, hold it." The shadowy men on horseback were just about even with them. "Give it to 'em!" yelled the colonel. Sparkles of stabbing lights lit up the trees.

"Cease firing! Cease firing!" yelled someone on horseback. "You're shooting your own troops." The firing slackened.

"Don't be fooled," Wade shouted. "They'll get away. For God's sake, let 'em have it."

The whole line fired into the panicky group of riders. Within seconds, most of the men had been knocked from their saddles. At first, Jackson escaped the pummeling. His horse bolted into the underbrush on the far side of the road. When the first volley ended, he turned Little Sorrel back toward the road, reaching it just as Wade ordered the second fusillade.

"Goddamn you!" shouted a survivor. "We're your own men—General Jackson's staff and escort."

The firing stopped and Wade faded into the trees.

"Come quickly," someone shouted. "General Jackson has been hit."

Wade listened from the shadows. In the still night, with the sound held close to the ground by the dense growth above, every word sounded audibly.

"Let me help you, General. Where are you hit?"

"Wild fire, that," Jackson said. "You had better help me down. My arm is broken."

The first bullet had shattered Jackson's left arm just below the shoulder. The second, less-serious contact, had been in the lower arm. A third bullet had passed through his right hand. None of the wounds was mortal, but blood spurted from a severed artery in the general's upper arm. His strength faded as the blood soaked the ground.

"Get a stretcher!" someone screamed in panic. "The general is bleeding to death. Get the surgeon, for God's sake!"

Wade heard nothing more as he wheeled his horse and moved slowly into the dense, clinging growth. He rode casually through two rebel camps as he continued moving south.

"Better be on the alert, Colonel," said a lieutenant in the second camp. "Those are Yankees just ahead."

"Thank you, Lieutenant. I'll be careful." Useful information, Wade thought. He rode up to a clearing a few hundred yards ahead. On the other side rose a small hill. A row of heavy cannon was barely silhouetted against the horizon. The guns' muzzles faced north. They must be Union, Wade thought. A dark thought suddenly crossed his mind. He remembered Colonel Thompson talking with his men about the accident that resulted in Captain Bottoms's death. They shoot first and ask questions later, Thompson had said. Wade thought it ironic to have survived so long in the enemy's midst only to have his own men kill him at the moment of escape.

"Who's out there?" Wade shouted. He observed a scurry of activity as men scooted across the horizon; no one replied.

"Which side are you?" he yelled.

"Who wants to know?" said an inquisitive soul in a deep, hollow voice.

"Colonel Thornton, Col. Simon Thornton, of General Jackson's staff."

"Which Jackson?" There were numerous men named Jackson on both sides.

"Stonewall," he replied.

"Colonel, we've taken about all we intend to take from your men today. Now skedaddle—and make it fast."

They're Union, Wade thought. "Hold your fire. I'm alone. I'm coming across." He added as an afterthought, "I'm wounded."

A brief pause followed. "Come slow, Colonel. There are two hundred rifles pointed at you."

Goddamn, thought Wade. They just told me they have no more than a regiment here. How will we ever win this war? "I'm moving into the clearing. Stay calm, men. Keep your fingers away from those triggers." Leaning low behind the animal's neck, he moved his horse at a walk. The horse snorted, then stopped to munch a mouthful of grass. He pushed a spur gently against the animal's side. Slowly, the horse crossed the clearing before beginning an angling stride up the hill.

A few yards from the top several men rushed from the shadows with rifles leveled. "Climb down, Colonel. Take it slow."

Wade slid from the saddle.

"Where are you wounded, Colonel?"

"I'm not," he replied. "I figured you'd be reluctant to shoot a wounded man." He strained to see in the darkness. Nothing but residual light from the moon lit the top of the hill. Wade counted at least three batteries of large guns dug in behind abutments. "I must speak to your commander at once. Take me to him, Sergeant."

"This will come as a surprise to you, sir, but I don't take orders from Reb colonels." The sergeant removed the pistol from Wade's holster, then pulled his saber from its scabbard. "Bring him along, men." Two privates grasped Wade's arms and led him over the crest of the hill. "Colonel, this man insists on speaking with you."

"You must be crazy," said the Union colonel, "riding alone out there in the darkness. You are a prisoner, sir."

"Are you in command here, Colonel?" Wade asked.

"I am, sir."

"Do you have any coffee on the fire, Colonel? I have something to tell you."

The colonel nodded. Two enlisted men led Wade to the fire. He sat next to the smoldering embers. "Do you have anything to eat? I haven't eaten much since morning." The biscuits hardly counted. The colonel nodded again.

"All we got is some bread and cold bacon," said a corporal in a white apron.

"That will do fine," said Wade. "Please, Colonel, join me by the fire." Wade spent the next ten minutes outlining the past five months. The colonel showed no emotion during the long recitation. Wade stopped when he reached the part about crossing the clearing.

The colonel leaned forward and looked into Wade's eyes. "You must think I'm crazy if you think I'd believe a tale like that."

"May I take off my boot?" Wade asked.

The colonel nodded.

Wade pulled off his right boot and held it over the embers. Within seconds, drops of wax began sizzling in the flames. He picked up a small stick and poked at a hole on the front of the heel. A small, folded piece of paper popped to the ground. He handed it to the colonel.

"What's this?" asked the colonel.

"Please read it, sir."

The colonel unfolded the paper and read. "Who is this General Washburn?"

"He's deputy commander of the Quartermaster's Department in Washington."

"Anyone could have written this, Major Wade."

Wade thought for a moment. "You must have someone here who knows the general's handwriting. His name is on most quartermaster requisitions."

The Union colonel considered the response. "Anyone could have forged this, Major." He returned the note.

Wade stuck it in his pocket. He thought a moment before asking, "Do you have anyone here who attended West Point in the last few years?"

The colonel nodded. "I believe we do." He rose and spoke in a whisper to the sergeant. The sergeant disappeared into the night. He returned shortly.

"You wish to see me, Colonel?" a young major asked.

"Yes, Major. Do you know this man?"

The major moved to the other side of the fire. He squatted and peered at Wade's face. "Sam? Is that you, Sam?"

"How has the war been treating you, Bill?"

"Oh, satisfactory I suppose." Healy smiled. "Congratulations, Sam. I see you made lieutenant colonel, although it's in the wrong army."

Wade laughed. "It's a long story, Bill." He rose and clasped his old roommate's arms. "God, it's good to see you, old friend."

A third of a continent away, the moon hung full above the horizon. Colonel Robert Andersen stood in the shadows of an alley. He rubbed his shoulder. It had never quite healed.

More than four months had passed since his departure from General Thornton's headquarters in northern Alabama. By now the assumption must be that he had failed in his mission. More than once he had considered turning around and riding back to the security of the southern Illinois farmhouse. The love of a fine woman gives a man a strong reason to live, but a soldier has his duty.

Nothing had gone as planned since the meeting with Colonel Morgan. First, the Yankee captain had recognized him, then wounded him when he'd tried to escape. Then there had been the delay while he recovered from the wound. Perhaps worst of all, emotion had diverted him from his mission. Against his better judgment he had left the seclusion of the farmhouse haven before completing his recovery. Then, fearful of being recognized again, he had decided to make his way to Springfield along back roads rather than risk detection on some train. Near his destination, his horse had bolted and thrown him in a ditch. He had landed on his shoulder and reopened the wound. Infection followed and he had spent another month secluded in a hotel waiting for it to heal.

Delay followed delay. By the time Andersen reached Springfield, the judge was out of town attending to court business in Peoria, then in Chicago. Then there had been the period of surveillance. If there was to be any hope of escape, he had to complete the mission in a way that would eliminate, or at least reduce, suspicion of a conspiracy. He had now completed the surveillance.

The judge proved to be a secretive man, undoubtedly a common characteristic for a man who played both ends against the middle. Important officials knew his politics to be a little tilted, if not downright askew. He had spoken out against the war long before such talk became fashionable. But law was law, and politics were politics, and by fostering the illusion that his eye remained fixed on the law, Judge Wade had shielded himself from public criticism. Eyebrows had lifted a notch when he persuaded his colleagues on the bench to declare a mistrial in the case of a man who, in a fit of anger, shot a Lincoln supporter. Some key witnesses had disappeared in the interim. The man eventually went free. But there remained the judge's close association with a former congressman by the name of Vallandigham, a Democrat known to be the leader of the Copperheads, the organization most opposed to the war, if not outright supportive of the South.

Still, appointments to the Supreme Court were for life. Raised eyebrows and questionable associations were hardly grounds to impeach a judge.

But Judge Wade had made one critical mistake, a mistake beyond his ability to explain in certain quarters. He had directed the kidnapping and planned execution of a prominent businesswoman. In his attempt to justify the act he had impeached the integrity of a Confederate general who, unfortunately for the judge, possessed the power to redress his own grievances. All things considered, the judge had become a liability— to both sides. Since impeachment was not a viable option, counteracting his imprudent tendencies demanded direct action.

The judge met each Wednesday night with some of his more radical associates. The meeting usually lasted until nine or after, and they never held consecutive meetings in the same place. Uncovering the pattern had been a long process of elimination. It would have been easier for Andersen to walk boldly into the judge's chambers and solve the problem swiftly, but the act had to suggest that people, important people, had concluded that enough was enough. So Andersen had planned and plotted. Now he waited—waited to act at a place and in a way that would make it convenient for enraged officials to deduce that politics had motivated the act.

Two men stood at the rowhouse doorway and chatted. One of them looked like Judge Wade, but in the dark it was difficult to know for sure. When the conversation concluded, one of the men turned west. The other turned east toward Andersen's alley. Andersen withdrew a half-filled bottle of whiskey and waited. The whiskey had no other purpose than to add another piece to the puzzle that Andersen hoped to leave behind. The figure moved down the sidewalk toward the alley. He walked close to the building. As the man crossed the alley opening, Andersen moved behind him. "Judge Wade?"

The man turned. "Yes?"

Andersen raised his arm. The small derringer was hardly visible in the dark. There was an explosion and sparks flew from the barrel.

The judge clutched at his chest before staggering backward, then leaned against the wall. "Why?" he asked.

"Wars should remain impersonal, Judge." The second bullet, fired from two feet away, entered the judge's forehead just above the nose. Andersen opened the bottle of whiskey and poured it over the body. Then he removed the judge's wallet and sprinkled the contents on the street. Another part of the puzzle. Andersen stood looking at the body for a moment. He turned and ran down the alley when he heard the clatter of approaching footsteps, dropping the whiskey bottle as he ran. In the distance, he heard the shrill sound of a policeman's whistle.

At the alley's dark exit he ran into a trash can and tumbled forward. He lost his grip on the pistol. It disappeared into the darkness.

"There he is," someone shouted from behind, "in the alley." Andersen heard the distant sound of wagon wheels bouncing noisily on the cobblestone street.

Andersen turned to his right and ran down the street. In his planning, he had hoped to avoid suspicion by walking calmly when he emerged into the open, so he had tied his horse a block away in another alley. Now the idea seemed perilously stupid, perhaps even fatal. He angled across the street. Light from the full moon bathed his route. He crossed to the other side and, endeavoring to hide himself in the shadows, ran as close to the building as possible. He turned into the alley, yanked at the horse's reins, and flung himself into the saddle.

"Where did he go?" a man cried out.

"He must have gone down an alley," yelled another. "Spread out. Don't let him get away."

The horse's hooves will give me away, Andersen thought. He spurred the horse anyway.

"There he goes," a man shouted. "He has a horse!" The sound of his voice echoed down the alley.

Andersen dashed across the next street, into the next alley, and on to the next street. The distance between him and his pursuers had stretched to more than a block. He had a few seconds to think. To his right, a stairway led to a level below the street. He rode the horse to the next alley and jumped off. He slapped the horse's rump and sent it galloping down the alley, then turned and ran back across the street and down the stairway. He tried the door. It opened. Just as the wagon rolled into the street barely forty feet away, he stepped inside. He eased the door shut and drew a deep breath.

Andersen turned at the sound of footsteps. He started to speak. A blinding flash lit the room as both barrels of a shotgun exploded. The double-aught pellets caught him full in the face. No one would recognize him this time.

CHAPTER 20

· · · · · · · · · · · · · · ·

A provost major approached tentatively and saluted. "General Lee, sir, I'm Major Pleble. I have someone here you must speak to."

Lee looked up from the maps spread haphazardly before him. "I'm quite busy, Major. Can't it wait?"

"No, sir, I think you should speak to him."

Lee sighed. Depression had enveloped him. The message had reached him less than an hour before that his chief lieutenant, Lt. Gen. Stonewall Jackson, had been seriously wounded and barely clung to life at a field hospital. In Lee's mind, the cost of the recent victory had been too severe. Still, hope remained. Although surgeons had removed Jackson's arm, it was his brain that made him important. Lee prayed for Jackson's survival. "What is it, then?"

"General, this is Colonel Vincent, formerly of General Jackson's staff. We had listed the colonel as a deserter last November, but it appears that something much more distressing occurred. I think you need to hear him out, sir."

"Come in, Colonel." Was such a matter worth interrupting a commanding general's planning for the critical phase of a battle? "I seem to remember this matter."

"Yes, sir. Union infiltrators abducted me shortly after the Sharpsburg battle, back around the first of October."

"*Abducted,* Colonel?"

"Yes, sir." Vincent told Lee the story of his capture and interrogation, and about his conversation with Major Thornton. Lee listened attentively without changing expression.

"This Major Thornton you talked to while you were a prisoner," said Lee, "are you sure he was an impostor?"

"I didn't think so at the time, General, but the more I thought about the conversation, the more I realized I was being asked questions rather than simply carrying on a conversation with this man. I was exhausted, General. I had been in isolation for weeks. I was just so pleased to see someone I knew." He lowered his head. "I said too much, General. I'm sorry, sir."

Lee rose and placed a hand on Vincent's shoulder. "It's all right, son. You couldn't have known. Tell me, Colonel, how do you come to be here?"

"I escaped, sir. Guards put me on a boat with about three hundred other prisoners. The guards were careless. I slipped into the water when their backs were turned and swam to shore, where I stole some clothes. Then I made my way cross-country. I was on the move, mostly at night, for more than three weeks. I finally made it to one of our encampments in the Shenandoah. They sent me to Richmond—that happened four days ago—then here. Sir, if you catch up with him, you'll recognize him by a large birthmark."

"Birthmark?"

Vincent nodded. "Yes, sir. It's on the side of his head. It's larger than your fist, sir. It's the first thing you see when you look at him."

"Sir," said the provost officer, "do you know what this means?"

"I do, Major," Lee replied. "It would appear one of General Jackson's staff officers is a spy. You must find this impostor and bring him to me."

"I'll do the best I can, sir."

"Start with General Jackson's staff, Major, although I suspect Thornton will have departed by now." Lee lowered his head and sighed. "I suspect he has accomplished his mission and is trying to make it back to Union lines, if he has not made it there already."

The Union's big guns began pounding rebel positions at eleven that night. The bombardment continued for three hours. Major Wade had reported the location of the rebel encampments along the Turnpike and in the woods to the south. Following that, the colonel commanding the batteries asked for and received permission to open fire. During the bombardment the Confederate army suffered another major loss. General A. P. Hill was wounded by shell fragments. Although he was in less serious condition than Jackson, medics still carried Hill from the field on a stretcher.

There were, however, more urgent concerns within the Confederate high command. The big guns would seriously disrupt future battle plans if they remained operational. With this in mind, a regiment of rebel cavalry, followed by two brigades of infantry, charged across a field and up a hill, the same path taken by Wade. Dawn was near. Only the distance of the crossing averted complete surprise.

Under other conditions, provosts would have shuttled a man of Major Wade's importance to the rear for more thorough questioning. But with less than three hours' sleep in the previous forty-eight hours, Wade had requested time for some much needed rest. Following the frantic activity necessary to conduct the bombardment, the soldiers on the hill had availed themselves of the opportunity to get some sleep themselves in the few hours remaining before dawn. As events developed, Wade was still sleeping next to the fire when the rebel forces boiled from the woods.

Major Wade, an expertly trained artilleryman, had a strong call to battle. Driven by conditioning bordering on instinct, he had rushed forward to replace a wounded battery commander just before the first line of gray-clad soldiers reached the crest of the hill. The Union soldiers' efforts to defend themselves were futile from the outset. If men were willing to suffer the punishment of cannon shells bursting in their ranks, they would succeed in such an assault. These angry, screaming Confederates were willing.

Some of the Federal troops rushed headlong down the back side of the hill, there to disappear into the trees. The majority, however, died or surrendered to members of a force three times their number. The onslaught ended almost before it began. Major Wade, dressed in a new Union lieutenant's jacket and torn, soiled Confederate trousers, counted himself among the captured. His uniform was a combination certain to attract attention, especially since he had been in the process of directing fire when a rebel private jammed a bayonet two inches into his thigh.

"Shall I send a messenger instructing them to send a detachment to take charge of these prisoners?" Maj. Calvin Jennings asked his superior, Lt. Col. Emerson Pollard.

"Yes, Major," said Pollard, "but we will escort them until the provosts meet us."

The major spoke to a staff officer, who immediately dispatched a rider. Pollard gathered the prisoners together and posted his men about the perimeter; then he marched them down the side of the hill toward the rear, so far as the rear was definable in this battle where rear and front frequently occupied the same space at a given time.

Lee's blocking force of fifteen thousand still held the southern edge of the battlefield. More gathered from distant parts as the morning wore on. The majority of the Union forces had entrenched themselves along a cup-shaped line. They faced south, east, and west. The Union cup had two handles at the outset, with the troops dug in at the bottom of the cup, closest to Lee's blocking force. Troops stationed along the sides of the cup faced east and west, to ward off any flank attacks. General Meade's corps made up the east handle of the cup. General Howard's corps had formed the west handle, but Jackson's surprise attack had dislodged this handle. Howard's men were now intermingled with other units, or they found themselves in isolated pockets cut off by rebel forces to the north and south. The mixing of the soldiers, Union and Confederate, had by now become so complete that it was difficult to say for sure what was front and rear.

Rifles began cracking off to the right as Pollard and his men led their prisoners through the thick undergrowth. The rattling sound moved closer, much as a wave rising to a crest; then the noise jumped the gap and began clattering off to the left. Pollard ordered the prisoners taken into a clearing at the base of a small ridge. He then rode to the crest in an effort to locate the source of the noise. Within minutes, there developed a sustained racket as the battle resumed in earnest. Although the sound of battle came from every direction, nothing was visible from the ridge except the tops of the budding trees that spread endlessly toward the circular horizon. Only the slowly rising smoke offered evidence of the raging conflict.

The provost guards finally joined Pollard's regiment in the clearing at the base of the hill. "We had considerable difficulty finding you, Colonel," said the provost captain, saluting. "All hell is breaking loose again."

"I hear it, Captain," Pollard replied, "but seeing anything in this infernal growth is impossible." He pointed to the prisoners. "Search them, Captain. We didn't take the time. We'll wait until you finish. With the sound of battle rising, I think we had better accompany you until you are clear."

The captain saluted. His men quickly searched each of the prisoners for weapons; then they emptied their pockets and checked identification. Plans were, following the search, to move the prisoners south of Lee's main force for final processing, and from there to march them to Richmond or other confinement sites. In time, some would be exchanged for Confederate prisoners held in the North.

"There are men in need of medical attention," Wade said to Pollard as the detailed search continued.

"In due time, Lieutenant," Pollard replied.

"My rank is major, Colonel. I have this—"

"I said in due time." Pollard seemed temporarily distracted by the officer's inconsistent dress, as well as the man wearing it. He had familiar features, but his identity eluded Pollard for the present. "Sergeant, separate this man from the others." The contents of the prisoners' garments received no particular attention. The searchers confiscated money and other valuables as the spoils of war and threw personal items into blankets held at their four corners by pairs of soldiers. "I also want to examine his possessions," Pollard said as an afterthought.

"Yes, sir." The sergeant pushed on Wade's shoulder, causing him to fall to his knees. The sergeant pulled Wade to a standing position before handing the confiscated items to Pollard. "Get along with you, Yank. Over by that tree."

Pollard waited patiently as the guards completed the search. As their comrades carried out the operation, other men with leveled rifles stood at three-pace intervals around the perimeter. While he waited, Pollard unfolded a paper the sergeant had handed him. He had to look closely to read the finely scripted print:

Please be advised that the bearer of this document is Major Samuel Wade, USA. Major Wade has been on secret assignment as an observer, from within, of Confederate operations. His orders are to abandon his assignment only if convinced that his own life is in immediate danger or if detected by the enemy. The purpose of this document is to secure his safety if circumstances compel him to surrender or otherwise expose his identity to Federal authority in the field.

Resp.
Brig. Gen. Cadwalader Washburn,
Commanding
Special Engineers.

Pollard read the note quickly; then he read it again, this time more carefully. A strange correspondence, he thought. What does it mean?

Wade sat preoccupied with the pain in his leg. He seemed unaware of the colonel's attention to the note, or anything else going on around him. As blood continued to seep from the wound, his eyes grew heavy from shock. As the guards organized the prisoners for the march to the rear, Wade struggled to lift himself to a standing position. Halfway up, a wave of nausea rolled over him; then he slumped to the ground. Wade attempted to speak, but the jumbled sounds made no sense. He passed out.

Wade regained consciousness with the bright sun shining in his eyes. Although his leg still hurt, the nausea had passed and the bleeding had stopped. Two Union prisoners carried him on a makeshift stretcher.

"You feeling better?" asked the rear bearer.

"I believe I am, Corporal," Wade replied. "Thank you."

"We've been walkin' in circles, Major. Every place we turn there're more Union troops. The battle's all around us. I ain't sure who's catchin' the worst of it."

"Keep quiet, up there," said a Confederate sergeant. "Keep moving."

Muskets opened fire to the left. "Everyone down," said Pollard. "You prisoners, put your hands on your heads." The clattering sound, accompanied by a rushing movement in the underbrush, moved closer. A rebel soldier stumbled through the trees, then another, then a dozen more. Pollard grabbed a soldier as he attempted to scamper by. "What's going on over there?" Pollard asked.

The soldier looked anxiously over his shoulder. "Let go, Colonel. Thar's a whole Yank regiment comin' through them woods. They'll be here any second."

Pollard loosened his grip and the soldier ran off. He was useless without a rifle. "Prisoners, face down on the ground. *Now!*" Pollard hollered to the guards: "If any prisoner moves, shoot him."

"Colonel," said a sergeant, "don't you think we'd better get out of here?"

"I won't give up these prisoners," Pollard said defiantly. "Prepare to make a stand."

More rebel soldiers approached. The retreat was rapidly turning into a rout. The colonel drew his pistol. "Get your bayonets up," he yelled. "Prepare to stop these running men." The guards formed a kneeling line behind the prisoners. "You men there, stop," yelled Pollard. He grabbed an officer. "Captain, tell your men to stop, or we will receive them on our bayonets."

The captain was no less wild-eyed than the retreating enlisted men. "They'll simply overrun us, sir."

Pollard swung the captain around to face his retreating soldiers. "Tell them to stop, I said. Form a line with my men."

The captain looked at the guards standing anxiously firm. His fear subsided. "Form ranks," he yelled above the din. Most kept running, stumbling, and falling as they tried to thread their way through and around the carpet of prisoners blocking the way. A few stopped, then a few more. A stout defensive line began to form. "Prepare to give fire."

The order came too late. A volley rolled through the trees. Men began to fall. The first to go down, shot through the throat just above the shoulder, was Pollard. A nicked artery spurted blood into the air. The dark liquid arched and splattered on Wade's face and neck. Wade shifted his position and squinted at the colonel, who was trying to stem the flow with his own hand. Blood oozed through his fingers and flowed onto the dried leaves. Pollard tried to call for help, but no sound followed; then his eyes rolled back in his head as his bloody hand dropped limply to the ground.

Wade inserted his finger in the wound and found the artery. He pressed firmly. The bleeding slowed to a trickle. Pollard moaned.

Both from behind and in front, the musket fire continued its staccato roll. Several of the prisoners began to crawl through the underbrush; others followed. A few screamed as bullets ricocheted from the trees and slammed into their backs and legs.

"You're killing your own men," one of the prisoners shouted. "For God's sake, quit firing!" But the firing continued.

"Take 'em, men," someone yelled from the concealment of the trees. The Union soldiers crashed through the brambles, hesitated for a moment, then rushed the defenders. None ran. The two forces met with a powerful clash of bayonets, gun butts, and flailing sabers. Wade covered Pollard with his own body and continued pressing against the wound. In contrast to the conflict raging all about, this had become his personal battle, a compelling, overwhelming urge to save this man's life in the midst of all the dying. He had spent too much time with the rebel forces. He had trouble seeing them as the enemy. Even so, he reached out, grasped Pollard's revolver, and pulled it under his chest as the words *duty, honor, country* echoed in his thoughts.

"Sam," a man screamed from a few feet away, "we have to get out of here." It was Bill Healy.

"You go, Bill," Wade hollered back. "I'll try to catch up."

"I'll help you," Healy replied. He knew of Wade's wound.

"Get the hell out of here, Bill. If I don't escape, send word to General Washburn that I'm still alive."

Healy hesitated for a moment, nodded, then rose to a crouch and rushed headlong into the dense growth.

Men screamed and hacked and fired as the close-quarters battle raged. Few of the prisoners remained. Those who did were either wounded or dead. Instinct compelled Wade to rise to his knees, to stumble off in the attempt to save his own life. Another instinct, this one less primitive, commanded him to remain.

Some color returned to Pollard's face. His eyes opened to narrow slits. He licked his lips and soundlessly pleaded for water. A Confederate soldier, his head split open with part of his brain exposed, sprawled forward and pinned Wade to Pollard. Wade rolled the dead man to the side, then looked at Pollard. With apparent understanding of his desperate plight, Pollard's eyes pleaded for Wade to remain. Even a minute of relaxed pressure on the artery meant death.

From the midst of the flailing and stabbing men, a rebel soldier appeared, his rifle raised, his bayonet gleaming, a mixture of fear and rage in his wide-eyed stare. Blood flowed from a gash in his scalp. One arm hung limply at his side, the broken blade of an officer's saber still quivering in the muscle. He stared at Wade for a moment, as if confused by the contrasting parts of his uniform. Then, apparently having resolved the conflict and now committing himself to killing the blue half, the soldier let out a rebel yell and lunged forward. Wade lifted Pollard's revolver and shot the man in the face, killing him instantly.

Several shots, these more distant, rang out. The immediate struggle subsided as both blue- and gray-clad soldiers reacted to approaching uncertainty. Then, as if on command, the Federals began running. Holding their fire to avoid killing their own, a rebel regiment crashed through the trees. The battle ended with the same suddenness as it began. More than a hundred soldiers from both sides lay among the trees. Many of them remained locked in death's final embrace. Some were dying, others were only disabled.

"Are you wounded, sir?" a Confederate officer asked Wade.

"Don't concern yourself with me, Captain," Wade replied. "Do you have a surgeon with your regiment? This man needs immediate medical attention."

"We do, sir," the captain replied. "I'll find him."

A medic approached first. He knelt and visually examined the wound. The colonel's pale, ghostlike appearance indicated the need for immediate action. "Maintain the pressure," said the aidman. "The surgeon is on his way."

Wade nodded as the surgeon arrived.

The doctor examined Pollard. "He has lost much blood," he said to the medic. "I want you to slip your finger into the wound and relieve the lieutenant, Corporal." With the transfer completed, Wade relaxed.

The infantry captain watched the procedure for a moment, then shifted his attention to Wade. "Are you a Yankee?" he asked.

"I am, sir. I'm a prisoner."

"Why did you remain while the other prisoners ran?"

Wade smiled. "Two reasons, Captain: I have a hole in my leg where a soldier stuck his bayonet, and I saw no way to carry this man to safety if I tried to run."

"He *is* your enemy, Lieutenant."

"Major."

"Sir?"

"I'm a Union major. I only borrowed these clothes." Better to keep the situation confusing, Wade thought.

"I see," the captain replied. His attention shifted to the operation in progress. "Will he recover, Doctor?"

"Unless he has lost too much blood," said the surgeon. "Only time will tell. Corporal, clamp the artery with your thumb and finger while I suture it. Be quick, now." He worked swiftly. "There," he said. "You can dress the wound now, Corporal. There are others in need of attention. Keep him quiet, or the bleeding will begin again." He turned to Wade. "You saved this man's life, sir. A noble act. A noble, compassionate act."

The sun had set before medical personnel carried Wade to the relative safety of a field hospital. A thousand or more groaning men carpeted an acre or more. The gruesome sounds of bone saws and screaming men shattered the cool, evening air. Many already had died from lack of attention; many more were certain to breathe their last before the next sunrise. A medic ripped open Wade's pants, examined his wound, then slapped on a fresh dressing before moving to the next man in line. Wade closed his eyes and tried vainly to shut out the sounds of agony.

"Is this the man, Major Pleble?" The words seemed to drift into his ears from a far-off place. Wade opened his eyes, then let them close.

A new day had arrived. Wade's first sense was of the absence of gunfire. Perhaps the battle is over, he thought. I wonder who won? Then he knew. There remained little sign of the frantic activity that had pervaded this place the night before. If Confederate forces still held the ground, it meant that the Union army had retreated. Wade opened his eyes again. Everything was blurred. A crusty mat of mucus pulled at his lashes. A giant of a man, his features sparkling in the glistening sun, stood over him looking down. Wade shaded his eyes with his arm.

"It may be." The man spoke with a degree of uncertainty. "The man Colonel Pollard spoke of has a large, dark birthmark on his scalp. This agrees with Colonel Vincent's description." He leaned closer. "I believe this is him. Get up, sir."

"This man is unable to walk," said the physician. "It will be several days before he recovers sufficiently to travel on his own."

"The man will walk, by God, or I'll shoot him where he lies. He is responsible for the shooting of General Jackson."

"That may be, Major, but, I tell you, he cannot walk. It will be murder if you shoot him in his condition."

"No more so than what he did. He undoubtedly revealed our position and caused the shelling that killed so many of our men." The major pondered his dilemma. "If he's unable to walk, I'll have him carried. That's the best I'll offer. But one way or another, I'm taking this bastard with me."

The doctor nodded.

A soldier chained Wade's legs together and two other men carried him to a wagon. One guard sat at his head, another at the tailgate. Four cavalrymen rode behind. The wagon moved south, then east, then south again. The journey lasted for more than an hour. Wade knew now that they knew, or strongly suspected, his identity. The logical conclusion was that he would be shot as a spy. The wagon rolled to a stop at General Lee's headquarters.

"Lift the bastard out," said a man beside the wagon. "Don't bother being gentle with him." A soldier grasped the end of the stretcher and jerked as the inside guard reached for the other end. "Bring him over here and lift him to his feet." The two enlisted men grasped Wade under the arms and jerked him to a standing position. "Is this the man?"

An officer looked at him. It was Maj. Phineas Croft of General Jackson's staff.

"This is the Yankee bastard, all right." The major shoved his face close to Wade's. "How could you do it, you son of a bitch?" Croft spat in Wade's face and glared at him before angrily stomping away.

Wade lowered his eyes. He had resisted his assignment from the start. Spying was not war, he had told Colonel Thompson, or at least not the type of war West Point had trained him to fight. Spying was for shady characters men in cheap suits. It was war he had witnessed the day before, where men met in pitched battle and killed each other until one side had suffered enough. That he understood. That he could explain. If death resulted, at least it was an honorable death. But to be tied to a post and shot! Where was the honor in that?

And what of Colonel Pollard, the man whom he had saved? Wade had been suffering too much, had been too distracted by the pain, to direct much attention to a Confederate officer, but the man's name stuck in his mind. Even while he held his finger to the artery, there had been too much bedlam to dwell on his identity. But now he suddenly remembered. The man with thick whiskers covering a scarred face had been Emerson Pollard, a West Point classmate, the First Captain of his graduating class. Had the man betrayed him? Did Wade have any right to condemn him if he had? Nothing made sense. Wade's leg ached so much that he simply passed beyond caring about the future.

The wagon bounced along the soggy, deeply rutted road. Rain fell steadily—it had rained for two days without letup—and the large drops splashed in Major Wade's face. Soon, the sun would rise. He had a sense of what awaited him, but no one had told him that the time had arrived. He had lived in dread of this day, the day when he expected them to tie him blindfolded to a post and send him into oblivion. He had lost track of time. He had concluded that it must be near the end of June. Why had they waited so long? More than a month had passed since the trial. They had clarified the charge, but only with considerable difficulty. He had no quarrel with the charge—or the punishment:

They had sentenced him to death for spying. General Washburn's note provided the deciding piece of evidence. Colonel Pollard had argued for leniency. The crime, however, had been judged too grave. After all, Stonewall Jackson was dead. It had been a difficult death. The Confederacy mourned as it had never mourned before during its short life. The irony remained that the general's name never surfaced during the trial. As far as anyone knew, the general's death had been nothing more than a tragic accident, a circumstance of war. But everyone at the trial knew the cause of the tragedy, even if the words remained unspoken.

Where were they taking him? Wade wondered. Probably to Richmond, he thought, where the press would witness the execution of a spy and report the event to the Northern papers—anything to undermine the war effort there.

The sun made a feeble attempt to break through the low-hanging clouds, then the rain began again. Shortly, another wagon pulled in behind. It had been waiting at a crossroads intersection. It had a cover. Probably the firing squad, Wade thought. A large contingent of cavalry pulled in behind the second wagon; then half of the cavalry peeled out and rode to the front. The attention being given to his execution surprised him.

The rain slowed to a drizzle, then stopped. Soon they were traveling under the high canopy of large oak trees that lined the road. There was a dispiriting eeriness in the slow, swirling motion of the fog that hung a few feet above the ground. A good day to die, Wade thought. A perfect setting.

"Company," said an echoing voice, "halt."

Now he heard no sound at all. All the riders sat stiff and still on their mounts. Even the sedate horses seemed to sense the awful gravity of the moment as they stood motionless while the fog rolled over them.

"Party approaching," a man's voice echoed from far out in front. "Bring the prisoner forward."

"Major Wade," said a captain in formal dress, "if you please."

Wade looked to his right. An eerie figure stood all alone at parade rest in the fog. It was impossible to underestimate his importance. The man was dressed in a stiffly pressed gray uniform with the gold braid and stars of a major general. A wide gold sash girded his waist before dropping from the bold knot and seeming to flow into his leg. A long, gleaming sword hung at his other side, adding to the iridescent quality that seemed to defy the drabness that surrounded the figure. When the faint light caught it just right, the sword appeared to twinkle like a candle on a clear night. The general's identity was a mystery to Wade.

It appears I won't see Richmond after all, Wade thought. He slid to the end of the wagon. Water dripped from his bare head. The wound in his leg had healed, but a slight limp remained. A corporal kneeled and unlocked the leg irons, the first time they had been removed since the trial.

General Henry Thornton stared at Wade through the mist. The resemblance *is* incredible, he thought. If I didn't know better, I'd swear he was my own son.

Arranging the prisoner exchange had been difficult. General Lee, stricken with grief over the loss of Jackson, had adamantly demanded that Wade be executed for his perceived perfidy. A personal audience with Lee was denied Thornton. Lee wrote to say that his thoughts on the matter were in the court-martial record and there was nothing further to be said.

Thornton had finally been able to get the ear of Confederate president Jefferson Davis and was able to convince him that Morgan's kidnapping of Thornton's sister-in-law was as blatant a violation of the laws of war as young Wade's actions had been. Under the circumstances, Thornton argued, exchanging Wade and his mother for Thornton's son and daughter was both politically expedient and humane. With Davis's blessing, Thornton had then contacted David Healy, Sr., and begun the process that brought them all together this morning.

"Follow me, Major," the captain said. He motioned to someone behind.

Wade froze at the sound of a commotion coming from the rear of the covered wagon parked behind his own. A pair of rebel soldiers finally came into view, supporting a haggard woman in a pale blue cotton dress.

"Mother? Is that you, Mother?" Wade gasped. Caroline Wade-Healy appeared so wan and worn that he hardly recognized her.

She nodded and smiled weakly.

"Be silent!" snapped the captain. "Now follow me."

After about twenty paces the captain stopped. "Wait here," he told Wade, then stepped out of view.

In the distance, barely visible through the fog, stood another line of cavalry, a wagon, and more cavalry. The men wore blue uniforms. A Union officer walked slowly down the middle of the lane in which Samuel and Caroline stood. Behind him came another man, then a woman. The second man wore gray, the woman a simple green cotton dress. Like Major Wade, the man in gray wore no hat.

The party halted about fifty yards from where Samuel and Caroline waited. The Union officer spoke to the Confederate, then stepped behind his two charges.

"Prisoners," said a voice from behind Wade, "walk forward."

Wade began to walk. His mother followed close behind. The four—two men and two women—met in the middle, in a no-man's-land of their own. They stopped again. The two men looked into each other's eyes, eyes that reflected the identity of the other. Everything about them was the same, except that one wore blue and the other wore gray—and one had a large birthmark on his dripping head. Something passed between them, something neither would ever be able to explain. Each, in turn, tried to speak, but the words remained unspoken. Wade thought for a moment to reach out, to touch this extension of himself, but his arm resisted the command.

Wade's eyes shifted to the young woman. There was something familiar about her, too, but he had no memory of her face. She looks so unhappy, he thought, as though her last great illusion of a hoped-for love had drifted away into the fog.

"Hello, Nancy Caroline," said Wade's mother.

"Aunt Caroline," the young woman replied dryly.

"Move along," said a voice behind Wade.

Wade flinched, as if jarred from a spell, then moved slowly ahead. His mother stood for a moment, looking into her nephew's clear blue eyes. She smiled, and the young man responded in kind. Judging by her looks, the woman could be his mother. But Simon Thornton knew better, even without his sister's cool response. Nevertheless, he reached out and hugged Caroline. She hugged him back.

"May God keep you," she said as she stepped back and their eyes met. "May God keep and protect the three of you."

He nodded faintly, then began to walk away.

Caroline watched as he faded into the fog; then she turned and looked at her son. It had been wrong to separate them, she thought, so very wrong.

Another figure moved through the mist. She did not recognize him at first, dressed so splendidly in his Union colonel's uniform. More than eight months had passed since that night on the train. She had long since accepted his death. But there he was, straight and tall, smiling at her. Her eyes lit up. David Healy, Sr., extended his arms and Caroline ran toward them.

Events had acquired a dark balance, twisted and gnarled though it might be, and no one thought it would endure. Evil had been done, all in the name of war, and no one ever was the same following such experiences. A short distance from this spot, Lee had pulled his army together following the bloodletting at Chancellorsville. Now he had his men on the move again. "Fightin' Joe" Hooker had been found out: His pugilistic reputation exceeded his will to persevere, an altogether unsatisfactory tendency for a commanding general entrusted with the responsibility of saving a nation. His superiors in Washington were, even now, working to induce Hooker's resignation. His subordinate, Maj. Gen. George G. Meade—whose men had formed the right handle of Hooker's cup-shaped line in the Wilderness—was about to become the new commander of the Army of the Potomac.

General Lee, emboldened by his recent success, was already leading his army north, away from his beloved Virginia homeland, in a bold effort to bring the pain and destructive misery of war to the Northern population. Something had to be done to pull men and resources away from Grant's army now holding Vicksburg in siege. Hardly anyone remembered that Lee had done poorly on his last venture into Yankee territory—only General McClellan's famous "slows," as Lincoln called his lack of aggressiveness, had saved Lee at Antietam. Furthermore, whatever happened now, his able lieutenant, Stonewall Jackson, would play no part in the proceedings. Meade's only alternative, once he took command, was to follow Lee, to stay between the Gray Fox and Washington. Neither general knew the other's location, which served just as well. The time of their first meeting as opposing army commanders was to be a cataclysmic rendezvous with destiny. It is doubtful that either would have proceeded had he known what was coming.

Caroline Wade-Healy would have shuddered if she had known where the armies were heading. Never in her most desperate thoughts would she have guessed. But fate weaves dark, ironic tapestries in war. Rumor had spread among the Southern soldiers that there were shoes stored in a warehouse along their path. They meant to get at those shoes if there existed the slightest possibility. Coincidence settled the issue, for the place where those shoes were stored, a sleepy little town in the middle of the Pennsylvania countryside, was also the point of convergence for five important roads and several lesser ones. Lee inevitably would recognize the importance of those roads, both to deny their use to Meade and to keep them open for his own use, so the town's importance gradually merged in the minds of everyone in the two armies. In just over a week, the collective minds of an agonizing nation would also merge there—at Gettysburg.

PART THREE

Gettysburg

CHAPTER 21

● ● ● ● ● ● ● ● ● ● ● ● ● ● ●

From the diary of Caroline Wade-Healy:

June 28, 1863

*I am writing this in the train station as I await the dawn train.
I will arrive at Gettysburg by evening. I yearn for the tranquillity of that lovely place.*

*Oh, the terrible things I have experienced. I anguished over the
fate of both nations when the war started. No more. I hate the
Confederacy and everything it stands for. Its utter destruction is
all I pray for, what I look forward to with glee.*

*Dear David is so happy now that I have returned. We dedicated
much of the night to consummating our marriage vows again when
we reached Washington—just in case—and he left at sunrise without
a wink of sleep. He said he was willing to request more leave, but
I told him I was a big girl and could make my own way back to
Gettysburg. I sensed the tension in him, although he said nothing. Something is about to happen, I feel it. Whatever it is, David
wants to be a part of it. I remember him saying, that first day we
met, how he wished he had remained in the army.*

*I dared not express the humiliation I suffered at the hands of
my captors. I hate Henry Thornton. He never came to see me once,
to ask how I was doing, yet I know he controlled my fate for those
many months. He left me to wither in a damp cave, to be raped
and defiled by those awful men. The time I spent at the plantation was better only by degree. At first, I blamed Victoria for her
husband's actions. I realize now that was unfair, but at the time . . . I*

do suffer for Victoria. The thought of her loving that terrible man turns my stomach.

The Union has lost so many qualified officers. David is now a full colonel and commanding a brigade in Hooker's army. He will abandon all caution if he learns of what happened to me. I fear this war will consume him the same way it is devouring our nation. God, please protect my family.

....

"Major Wade reporting as ordered, sir," said Samuel Wade as he stepped into Col. Jason Thompson's office at the War Department. The time was eleven in the morning, June 28.

Thompson stood and smiled as he extended his hand. "Nice to have you back among the living, Sam."

Wade shook the colonel's hand and nodded. "Nice to be back, sir. For a while there I doubted I'd live to see the next Christmas. By the way, those eagles look good on you. Congratulations on the promotion."

"Thanks," Thompson said as he moved from behind the desk. "Have a chair, Sam." Thompson pulled up a chair for himself. "Have the physicians checked you over?"

"Just left the hospital, Colonel. I'm down about fifteen pounds, but it's nothing to worry about. The doctor thinks I may have worms. He gave me some medicine for that. Otherwise, I'm fully fit."

"Are you ready for duty or do you need some rest?"

Wade hesitated before replying. "I've rested in prison for the past two months, sir." He hesitated again. He realized the risk in war, even enjoyed it at times, but being foolhardy seldom brought reward. "Sir, they'll shoot me on the spot if they catch me behind their lines again. They don't like me much since General Jackson's death."

Thompson smiled. "I understand your apprehension. No, I doubt we'll be sending you on a similar mission. I think we can find something more traditional."

"Then I'm ready for an assignment, sir."

"I've read your report, Colonel," said Thompson. "It's a remarkable document."

"Uh, that's major, sir."

"Wrong, Sam. You've been promoted to lieutenant colonel." He clapped his hand on Wade's shoulder. "Congratulations."

Wade smiled broadly. "Thank you, sir. Now I hold the same rank in both armies."

"Which brings up another small matter, Colonel. I've taken the liberty of censoring a segment of your report. That section about your holding the line against one of our regiments at Fredericksburg—well, let's just say it might be somewhat embarrassing to the high command."

"You directed that I tell everything, sir."

"So I did, and I appreciate your candor. That part enhances the credibility of everything in the report, and it's been confirmed. It's just that, in the military, some events are better left unrecorded. I'll have an official copy for you to sign later."

"As you wish, sir."

Thompson rose and retrieved a map from a case. "Conditions are about to become uncorked again, Colonel." He unfolded the map and pointed. "Lee is somewhere about here, screened by these mountains. As we speak, General Meade is replacing General Hooker as commander of the Army of the Potomac. Our army is moving north to cut off Lee. Mr. Lincoln is understandably concerned with this new turn of events, as I am sure you will appreciate."

Wade nodded. "Unless Lee runs, there'll be a major battle. The General Lee I know would never run from a fight."

"Precisely," Thompson agreed. "Everyone is concerned. Confidence is low after the drubbing we endured at Chancellorsville." He folded the map and placed it back in its case. "By the way, Colonel, did anyone talk to you about Captain Clinton?"

"No, sir. General Jackson told me he was killed in an ambush."

"Well, he is very much alive and eager to see you. With you out of action he took the first opportunity to cross over to our lines. His information about troop dispositions and unit strengths was enlightening. It's unfortunate that General Hooker lacked the vision to make better use of the information. Convincing our generals that Lee doesn't have a quarter-million men is the most difficult task we face."

Wade smiled. "I'm pleased to hear Clinton is alive. He's a good man, sir, and capable of higher responsibility."

"So he is. He's due back from leave this morning. His promotion to major has already been processed. He will be meeting with you later today. But back to you, Sam. You deserve a reward, too. I am authorized to offer you the assignment of your choice."

"A field command, sir," Wade replied without hesitation.

"There's quite a demand for infantry commanders, but you're an artilleryman," said Thompson.

"I'd prefer the infantry, sir, if that's possible."

"I think it can be arranged. Will a regiment be to your satisfaction?"

"D-Do you think I'm qualified, Colonel?" Wade stammered in surprise.

"I'd trust my son to serve under your command, Sam—if I had a son."

"Begging your pardon, sir, but are you working in that direction?"

Thompson smiled, then shook his head. "Well, not directly—at least not yet. Have you met your new stepsister, Ellen Healy?"

"Haven't had the pleasure, Colonel, but from what I've learned about this new family of mine, you can't go wrong. If you don't mind the intrusion into your personal life, sir, am I correct in my understanding that you two are seeing each other?"

"Yes, well, conditions were a bit strained for a while," Thompson replied, "after I sent her father and brother South, but we continue speaking to each other, and sometimes a little more. I suppose, considering the events of the past months, I should find encouragement in that."

"About that regiment, sir?"

"You'll get it as soon as one becomes available. I'll have the orders cut immediately. There will be transport north later this afternoon. I assume you'll want Major Clinton along. He hasn't been assigned yet."

"Yes, sir."

"Consider it done. But before that, I have a brief diversion for you." Thompson walked behind his desk and unlocked a drawer. He withdrew a bound document and an envelope. He laid the envelope on the desk and handed the folder to Wade. "Read this, Colonel, then give me your comments."

Wade read the secret document, then returned it to Thompson without comment.

"Well, Sam?" Thompson asked.

"Well what, sir?"

"Do you agree with that assessment?"

"For the most part, Colonel."

"What are your objections?"

"I think the estimate of Lee's strength is too high—unless he received heavy reinforcements after Chancellorsville. Discounting teamsters and cavalry, this report estimates his strength at sixty thousand. If you subtract his losses at Chancellorsville, he should have fewer than fifty thousand men."

"If I told you he had received about twelve thousand reinforcements, would you consider this estimate accurate?"

"I would."

"Then I want you to go to General Meade and tell him that. Make him believe it. His comprehending this fact is essential to our success. If he believes these figures, he will know that he has Lee outnumbered by about four to three."

"Very well, sir, but generals often resist listening to colonels."

Thompson handed Wade the envelope he'd taken from the drawer. Wax had been spread along the seam of the flap. "Give him this, Colonel. Perhaps it will help him believe you." Thompson rose and extended his hand. Wade stood up and grasped it. "You've done a marvelous job, Sam. We were wrong about the importance of generals, you know. The ineptness of our own has demonstrated that beyond doubt." He retrieved another envelope from his desk. "Here. This authorizes you to get whatever you need from the quartermaster. Return here by three and my clerk will have your orders. Good luck if I don't see you before you leave."

Wade saluted and left the room. He proceeded directly to the supply depot to select a new uniform, then went to the finance office to sign for his pay.

Major Clinton was in Thompson's office when Wade returned. "Nice to see you in blue again, Major," Wade said as he hugged his friend. "Congratulations on your promotion."

"You look pretty damned good with that silver leaf yourself, Colonel."

Wade stepped back and looked at Clinton. "God, it's truly good to see you, Jim," said Wade. "I thought you were dead."

"So did I, more than once."

"They're giving me a regiment, Jim, and you are to be my executive officer. Given my rank, it most likely will be an understrength unit, but a regiment is a regiment."

"I heard just a few minutes ago. General Washburn told me."

"Give me a minute, Jim. I need to pick up my orders."

"Colonel Thompson had to leave for a while," Clinton said as he reached into his pocket. "He asked me to give you your orders. We're to report at the depot no later than six this evening. A supply train will take us north. Judging from the excitement at headquarters, all hell is about to break loose. Do you have to pack?"

"I have an extra pair of socks in my bag and my pistol is loaded," Wade replied. "What more is there?"

"Good," Thompson said as he entered the room and approached the two men. "I'm glad you're still here, Colonel Wade."

"We were about to leave, sir."

"Stay awhile," Thompson directed. "I may have something for you. Colonel Wade, Major Clinton, allow me to introduce Major Hamilton. Major Hamilton is with the War Department."

Thompson withdrew a map from his case. "Show me, Major Hamilton."

"Here, sir, just south of Rockville. Stuart attacked a column of our wagons this morning—right about here. Our best information places him somewhere just north of here now, at Brookville. It will be of immense value if we can keep him isolated from Lee's main force. Every hour is important."

Thompson studied the map. "What does the War Department have in mind, Major?"

Hamilton traced a finger along the map. "At present, Colonel, General Meade is here, at Frederick, Maryland, about forty miles south and a little west of Gettysburg. He has his engineers constructing a defensive line about fifteen miles northwest of his present position, along Little Pipe Creek. His plan is to block Lee from moving south toward Washington, but we doubt this is Lee's intention. Lee has moved his troops too far north to have Washington as his primary objective, at least for the present. Besides, Lee appears to be short of supplies. His men are living off the land. We see no way for him to sustain a siege of Washington, even a short one." Hamilton turned and looked at the broad glass panes at the front of the office. A constant flow of traffic moved in both directions down the long corridor. "May we close the curtains, Colonel?"

Thompson nodded, and Clinton drew the drapes together.

"That's better. At present Meade has columns strung out along this line from Frederick to Little Pipe Creek, with lead cavalry elements about thirty miles northwest of Jeb Stuart's cavalry. Advance elements of General Reynolds's corps are approaching the Pennsylvania border and should reach the outskirts of Harrisburg by the evening of the second.

"The situation is very fluid at present. We think Lee's main force is here, somewhere around Chambersburg, about fifty miles northwest of Meade's main force and twenty-five miles west of Gettysburg. We can't be sure about Lee, because his movements have been screened by the South Mountain barrier. But a large portion of Lee's army—Ewell's corps—is over here, in the Carlisle and Harrisburg area, north and east of Gettysburg.

"What it comes down to, Colonel, is that Lee is at the western corner of the triangle, Ewell is at the northern tip, and Stuart is here, at the southeast corner." Hamilton tapped the map for emphasis, then continued. "As Meade moves northeast, he will be in the center of the base of this triangle. If our calculations are correct, the Army of the Potomac will be moving closer to the separated parts of Lee's force than those parts are to each other.

"We think Lee made a serious mistake by letting Stuart strike out on his own. For the present, he is completely cut off from Lee. If Stuart can be diverted from this area, around Gettysburg, for seventy-two hours, Lee will be in the dark as to Meade's movement. Even if Stuart links up with Ewell, Meade will be in the middle and in position to keep the various components of Lee's force separated."

"What, precisely, do you expect of me?" asked Thompson.

"Divert Stuart, sir. Keep him moving north on a parallel route east of Meade and out of contact with Lee."

Thompson turned and looked at Wade.

Wade anticipated his superior. "Sir, General Stuart knows me."

"Will he recognize Major Clinton?" Thompson asked.

Wade turned to Clinton. "Will Stuart recognize you, Jim?"

"No, sir," Clinton said. "He's never seen me."

Thompson nodded, then turned and studied the map. Meade's army was strung out along twenty miles of unfamiliar road, he thought, vulnerable to attack. If Stuart reported that fact to Lee, the old Gray Fox was likely to strike first. What to do? he thought. A decision had to be made right away. Until that moment Colonel Thompson had always thought himself capable of much greater responsibility. But here, for the first time, he recognized the awesome burden that army commanders must feel a dozen times each day.

If Lee defeated Meade, sixty thousand infantry and ten thousand of the best cavalry in the world would be on the loose with nothing to prevent them from ravaging the whole Northeast. If, on the other hand, Lee moved east toward Gettysburg, Meade would be in position to converge his whole force there, with Stuart left wandering about the countryside out of sight and out of the fight.

The four officers stared down at the map, recognizing the advantage of diverting Stuart's cavalry, or just keeping it moving along in its present direction. But what if . . . ? What if . . . ?

"Do you have anything else, Major Hamilton, anything that confirms where Lee's men are heading?" Thompson asked.

Hamilton thought for a moment. "There's one piece of information, Colonel, but it's thin. We captured a prisoner, a lieutenant from General Ewell's corps, up here—near Carlisle." He pointed to the map. "That's about twenty miles north of Gettysburg. This prisoner bragged that the men in his regiment had heard about some shoes stored in Gettysburg, and that they meant to get those shoes before they marched on. If that's true, Ewell will have to come south toward Reynolds's corps."

"Thin information, Major?" Thompson snapped. "That's damned near invisible."

"Sorry, Colonel. It's all I have."

"Colonel," said Wade, "there *are* shoes there, or at least there were. My mother usually keeps a small stock in a warehouse. They're used to fill rush orders."

"How small a stock?" Thompson asked.

"About five thousand pairs. That's enough to shoe half a division."

Thompson shook his head. Had the state of the Confederate army sunk so low that conditions justified diverting an entire division simply to get some shoes? he thought. "Excuse me, gentlemen, I need to discuss this with General Washburn."

Thompson left them abruptly, closing the door on his way out. Twenty minutes passed before he returned. He stared thoughtfully at the map, then framed a portion of it with his hands. "Major Clinton, I'm sending you and Colonel Wade by train to Baltimore, then along this railroad spur up to Westminster. You will draw mounts and supplies there before moving east by southeast. With luck, you'll cross Stuart's line of march somewhere around Eldersburg. If you find Stuart, tell him you're a courier and that Lee is moving toward Carlisle, north of

Gettysburg. Inform him that he is to move through Dover before joining with Lee's forces at Carlisle. Convince him you were given a verbal message because you had to cross through enemy lines. If he accepts the order as authentic, he'll take a sixty-mile roundabout path, doubling his distance. That should delay him at least an extra day." Thompson studied the map as he thought. "He may just believe it, and his current circumstances support this action. Stuart's in a poor position to cross over to Lee anyway, considering that Meade's advance forces are strung out all along this line south of Gettysburg."

"I'd rather have something in writing to support the order," Clinton said.

Thompson thought a moment, then shook his head. "Too risky. Lee probably designated some identification mark for his written orders. Colonel Wade, you go with Major Clinton, but stay out of sight if possible. Set up a rendezvous before Major Clinton tries to cross Stuart's lines." He hesitated as he looked at Clinton, then turned to Wade. "If Major Clinton fails to return . . . well, you go on to General Meade and give him your best estimate of the situation. Major, Stuart knows Colonel Wade, so you'll have to ride in alone and do the best you can. Your life will depend on how convincing you are. When you complete the mission, the two of you ride back to the southwest and join with Meade. By that time, Colonel, word will have reached him advising him of your expected arrival, then you will have your regiment. Any questions? No? Then good luck, gentlemen."

From the diary of Caroline Wade-Healy:

June 29, 1863
I'm exhausted. Arrived at the Gettysburg Rooming House at nine this evening so tired I could hardly move. Rumor has it that General Lee is less than fifty miles west of here. I don't believe a word of it. What is there for him in this little town? I've decided to remain here until the day after tomorrow. I need supplies, and I want to inspect the warehouse.

....

The railroad cars were heavily loaded. One engine pulled as another pushed the long string of flatcars loaded with war materials. Wade and Clinton made themselves as comfortable as possible on either side of a cannon wheel. Neither spoke as the train raced across the country-side into the Maryland twilight.

Lee's army had finally surfaced. Word reached Washington just before their train built up a full head of steam. All the evidence suggested that Lee had moved from Chambersburg toward Gettysburg. Sporadic reports filtered in telling of terrified citizens streaming north and east to avoid being caught in the middle of a battle. Persistent newspaper reports depicting the horrors of Southern battlefields were enough to cause them to abandon everything except what they could pile in a wagon.

A forty-mile gap separated Meade's main force and Lee's invad-ing army, but Meade was feeling more certain by the hour that Lee was unlikely to turn south, and the distance between the separate parts of the army closed with each passing minute as Meade's corps com-manders urged their soldiers northward. As a hedge against a poor bet, the Army of the Potomac's engineers continued construction on the Little Pipe Creek fortifications, and Meade remained in the area to provide overall direction as elements of his army moved north and west toward Gettysburg. Protecting Washington remained his vital objec-tive, however, and the fortifications provided the only haven for his troops if the army had to retreat.

As midnight approached, the train sped past the tail end of one of Meade's auxiliary wagon trains as it moved northwest from Baltimore. The train pulled onto a siding and stopped for an hour as frantic sol-diers added new cars.

The twinkling lights of Westminster, Maryland, came into view just before dawn on June 30. Squads of sleepy-eyed quartermaster soldiers rushed toward the cars even before the train had fully stopped. Wade and Clinton jumped from the train and walked briskly toward the quartermaster depot. They selected two mounts to ride and two to take as spares before drawing their other supplies. They changed into cap-tured Confederate uniforms, then quickly ate a spartan breakfast. With a small cavalry escort to accompany them to the perimeter, the two men mounted up and headed southeast. Once in the open, Wade and Clinton were on their own.

Tension hung heavy in the warm morning air. Transport of every description was moving west. The ambulances were last in line—fifty or more, all of them new, with "U.S. Hearse" stenciled on their sides—rolling ominously toward the anticipated conflict. The unfolding events assured that they would soon be heading south, their mission to deposit the war's carnage at the doorway of every hospital between Gettysburg and Judiciary Square in Washington, before heading north again for another load.

At eight in the morning, Wade spotted Stuart's advance scouts. Clinton asked them for directions, then the two men rode at a gallop toward the advancing Confederate cavalry corps. The lead column, men riding eight abreast across the rolling countryside, came into view just after ten; they were at least four hours ahead of where Wade had expected to find them.

"Major," Wade said, pointing, "I'll wait for you over there. You ride ahead and try to find Stuart. I'll take your spare horse with me."

"Colonel," replied Clinton, "this is a long shot, and you know it. You get out of here if I'm not back by two."

"I'm the colonel, Jim, and you're the major. *I'll* decide when to leave. Now get going." He pointed west. "I'll wait on the other side of that small rise." He unfastened the flap on his holster. "Here, take my pistol. There may not be time to reload if events turn sour."

Clinton stuck the revolver in his belt. "Do you know what bothers me, Sam?"

"Besides the possibility of getting killed? No, what?"

"What the hell are we going to do for excitement when this war ends?" Without waiting for a response, he wheeled the horse left and rode off at a gallop.

Wade watched for a moment before riding toward a grove of trees two hundred yards west of the approaching horsemen's line of march.

Wade checked his watch impatiently. It was after 3:00 P.M. Throughout the late morning and into the afternoon, a stream of horsemen rode north and slightly east. Outriders approached close to his position on several occasions, but he remained hidden in the trees. He saddled his horse at quarter past three, then decided to wait a few minutes more.

Presently, two riders angled away from the main column and headed toward the trees. One was Clinton, the other a Confederate sergeant. Clinton said something to the sergeant, then stopped and dismounted. The sergeant sat for a moment before dismounting and stretching. As the sergeant turned slightly, Clinton placed his hands on the small of his back and stretched backward. Wade watched silently as Clinton moved one hand slowly toward the knife scabbard fastened to the back of his belt. He slipped the blade from its sheath, then lunged at the sergeant, driving the knife swiftly upward just under the man's sternum. The sergeant's knees buckled, his wide-eyed glare of surprise fixed on his killer, and he grasped Clinton's arms. Then the sergeant slumped to the ground in a heap. Clinton bent low and dragged the body by the arms to a shallow depression, where he covered it with brush.

Wade waited until Clinton finished concealing the body before riding down the shallow grade. "What was that all about?" he asked.

"He had orders to ride with me to report to General Lee," Clinton replied. "We couldn't have that now, could we? This eliminates any complications."

"I suppose it does," Wade replied. Still, the murder bothered him. *Do I have the coldhearted ability to kill a man so casually?* Wade wondered. He had struggled for more than two years to maintain his sense of humanity. He had even justified his own execution because he had, after all, directed another man's death. They could have tied the sergeant up, but he might have worked free, or others might have found him. But to just kill a man, without any preliminaries? The thought bothered him. *Am I qualified to lead men into battle?* he wondered. *Is Clinton a better soldier than I?* Then Wade remembered the man he had killed when he made his escape during the Seven Days' campaign.

"Let's get moving, Jim. We'll change clothes later." He grasped the major's arm. "Did Stuart believe you?"

Clinton shrugged. "What choice did he have? He's cut off from moving west by the whole Union army. I don't think he has any idea where Lee's army is. The order to meet up with Lee north of here made sense to him." He smiled. "It fit reality." The two men moved northwest at a canter. They faced a long ride to Meade's headquarters.

At 3:00 A.M. on July 1 Wade found Meade's headquarters a few miles south of Taneytown—still more than fifteen miles south of Gettysburg. Campfires sparkled as far as the eye could see in every direction. There was no evidence of anyone recognizing the emergency building a short distance beyond the northern horizon. More than anything, Wade wanted to sleep. But first he had to report to General Meade.

"Halt!" shouted a nervous sentry. "Who's there?"

"Lieutenant Colonel Wade with a message from Washington."

"Advance to be recognized."

Wade and Clinton slipped out of their saddles and moved wearily forward, leading their mounts. The sentry eyed them warily, then grunted as they approached the dim light of the fire, apparently satisfied that they represented no threat.

"The gen'ral's down by that creek," the sentry said, pointing toward a nearby cluster of campfires.

Too weary to walk, the two officers mounted their horses and rode up to where a captain squatted by a fire in front of a tent.

"Is this General Meade's tent?" Wade asked.

"It is," sighed the captain as he slowly rose and turned. "I'm the general's aide. May I assist you, sir?"

"I must speak to the general," said Wade.

"I'm sorry, sir, but that's impossible right now. The general needs his sleep."

"*Now*, Captain," Wade said sternly. "This is urgent."

"The general won't be happy about this, sir."

Wade stood firm. "Let me worry about that. Point him out to me. I'll wake him myself."

The captain lifted the tent flap and pointed at a cot. Wade pushed the officer aside and went in. He prodded the general's shoulder.

"Sir," he said, then poked the slumbering man again.

Meade sat up with a start. "Yes, what is it?" he asked groggily.

"Sorry to wake you, General, but I have an urgent message from Washington. You need to read it now, sir."

Meade rubbed his eyes as he swung his legs over the side of the cot. "Who the blazes sent this message, Colonel—what the hell's your name, man?" the general snapped.

"Wade, sir. The War Department, sir."

Meade took the envelope from Wade's outstretched hand and broke the wax seal on the flap. Then he stood and walked out to the fire. Wade followed and watched as Meade withdrew a folder from the envelope and began to read. A short note attached to the front of the folder by General Washburn informed Meade that Lee had emerged from the cover of South Mountain and appeared to be concentrating his army in the vicinity of Gettysburg and Cashtown. The note also mentioned a rumored attack on a Federal wagon train north of Washington by Stuart's cavalry the day before. The binder itself held the intelligence summary that Wade had read in Thompson's office. Meade finally looked up.

"General Hooker told me that Lee had half again as many troops as this report indicates. Why should I have any confidence in these numbers?"

"Begging your pardon, sir," Wade said, "but our commanding generals have consistently overestimated General Lee's strength." He paused and remembered the small envelope Colonel Thompson had given him almost three days before. He reached inside his shirt and pulled it out. "Perhaps this might shed some light on the subject, sir."

Meade took the proffered envelope. He broke the wax seal and pulled out a sheaf of folded papers. It was Wade's report of his activities behind Confederate lines. The general pursed his lips and muttered as he read. He stared curiously at Wade when he finished. "Are you the Colonel Wade mentioned in this report?"

"I am, General."

Meade cleared his throat. "I see. Well, damnit, what about Stuart's cavalry? There's no mention of them in the estimate of Lee's troop strength—"

Wade cut him off with a raised hand. "None of General Stuart's cavalry is with Lee, sir. I suspect old Jeb is somewhere between Westminster and Hanover by now."

"But—but," Meade blustered. "Why, that's absurd, Colonel. That puts him nearly fifty miles from Lee—*if* you are to be believed. Who's screening Lee's flank?"

"Nobody, sir." Wade spotted sudden movement near the edge of the firelight and saw Jim Clinton standing in the shadows. "General, may I introduce Major Clinton. He talked with General Stuart yesterday afternoon, just north of Eldersburg."

Meade glared skeptically. It wasn't hard to figure out why his troops called him "that old goggle-eyed turtle" behind his back. "Is that correct, Major?"

"It is, sir. I gave him a message from Lee directing him to proceed to Carlisle."

Meade studied the man carefully. "You speak like a Southerner, Major," he replied finally.

"Born and raised in Georgia, General," Clinton said with a grin.

"Tell me more about your acting as a Confederate messenger."

"It was a fake order, sir, contrived by Colonel Thompson and General Washburn in Washington—"

Meade burst out laughing. Clinton and Wade stared as the general wiped tears from the corners of his eyes. "Do you really expect me to believe you simply rode up to Stuart, told him to proceed to Carlisle, and he did just that—without any confirmation?"

"That's what happened, General."

"By God, Colonel," Meade snorted, shifting his fiery gaze to Wade, "are you asking me to risk my army on the word of a—of a goddamned Southerner?"

"Sir, please," Wade pleaded. "I saw Stuart's cavalry riding north and east yesterday afternoon. For four hours they rode past the spot where I was waiting for Major Clinton. We've been riding hard ever since then to get the word to you. The last report I heard confirms that General Ewell intends to bring his corps down from the north and link up with General Hill's corps outside Gettysburg. Apparently they're after the shoes stored in my mother's warehouse there. Sir, I don't think General Lee is even aware you're in the area."

"Do you have identification, Colonel?"

Wade handed Meade his orders and official identification.

Meade studied the documents in the dim light, then returned them to the colonel. He thought for a moment. "I seem to remember receiving a telegraph message mentioning you, Colonel."

"I hope so, sir. I'm to be given command of a regiment, if one is available."

Meade went back in the tent and pulled on his boots and buttoned his jacket. "Colonel, if I am to believe this report, I will have General Lee outnumbered by four to three if I get all of my troops up." A sudden urgency seemed to overcome him as he thought about the prospect. He removed his watch from his pocket. "It's three-thirty," he muttered to himself, "an hour before dawn." Meade struck a match and touched the flame to a lantern wick before moving to his map table. He studied the map for several minutes, then turned back to Wade. "I'm sorry, Colonel, but I don't have a regiment for you at present." Meade wrote a brief note. "Report to General Reynolds and give him this message. If your information is correct, there will be a number of regiments needing commanders before this campaign is finished."

"And Major Clinton, General?"

Meade glanced skeptically at Clinton again. "Take him with you, by all means."

"Sir, we haven't had any sleep since the day before yesterday. Might we stretch out here for an hour or two?"

Meade nodded absently as he shifted his attention to his map.

CHAPTER 22

· · · · · · · · · · · · · · ·

At dawn, Caroline Wade-Healy sat at the kitchen table chewing passively on a biscuit and jelly. Lingering fatigue impaired her attempts to concentrate, or even to worry much about the reports of approaching conflict. Rumors had spread wildly during the previous afternoon and evening. The more time that passed without anything happening, the less alarm successive murmurs caused. Sleep had been elusive. Twice during the night soldiers had knocked at the rooming house door to warn that advance columns of rebel troops were within a few miles of the outskirts of town. The soldiers had stopped short of ordering an evacuation, but the official ring of the warning suggested cause for concern. Somewhere around 2:00 A.M. Caroline had heard the sharp cracks of several rifle shots, but fatigue pushed the incident from her mind. It's probably nothing, she told herself as she drifted back to sleep.

An hour later a column of wagons rolled noisily down the street outside her open window. One thing after another kept her awake after that, until she finally abandoned all effort to sleep. She lay awake during the last hour before dawn; then she dressed and descended the stairs to the kitchen. She had just pulled her chair to the table when she heard a low rumbling sound. Her first thoughts were of rain. She looked out the window. Hardly a cloud in the sky, she thought. She finished the biscuit and walked outside. The still air seemed unusually muggy and warm for so early in the morning. She left her shawl behind and started walking the four blocks to the warehouse.

Although her body recently had been set free, her thoughts remained imprisoned. The first half of this year has been a living hell, she thought as she walked along the quiet street. The worst times were when nothing

distracted her, such as now. Tranquillity had become a curse, a time
for the distress of not knowing her husband's fate and the terror of
captivity to gain a foothold in her mind. The causes of her trepidation had been eliminated, but the curse remained. But, she thought,
July had finally arrived. Surely the second half of the year will be better.
I just have to get back to work, to return my life to normal. With each
new uncertainty, she felt her will to resist slipping and, with each slide,
the return of long-resisted depression.

For more than twenty years, she had moved steadily away from the
fears and uncertainties of her youth. It had required a journey across
half a continent to place enough distance between herself and the cause
of overpowering anguish. She had thought it gone forever; then, against
her better judgment, she had yielded to David's desires to return to
Chicago for their wedding. Less than seventy-two hours later her life
had been turned upside down. Her abduction and humiliation had shattered her carefully nurtured confidence.

Caroline busied herself in the lantern light, checking the dusty stock
in the small, stuffy warehouse. By seven her dress was drenched with
perspiration, and she walked to the door to get a breath of fresh air.
Then it happened. This time there was no mistaking the sound for thunder.
The booming seemed to rumble from east to west; then it began again,
rolling across the ground and through the streets as if a frantic bass
drummer had escaped from an insane asylum. The building shook as
distant cannon unloaded their terrible fury just west of town. The war
had come to Gettysburg. But why? What was here to fight over?

She turned toward the sound of galloping hooves and saw several
Union cavalrymen racing down the street. One peeled off and reined
in his horse, halting a few feet away from her.

"Ma'am, I'd get out of the street if I was you," said a young, smooth-
cheeked lieutenant. "All hell is about to break loose—beggin' your
pardon, ma'am."

"Surely our forces will hold them from the town," she replied hopefully.

"I think not, ma'am. Few of our forces have arrived. Only General
Buford's cavalry and a few brigades of infantry are here to hold against
all of Lee's army. The Rebs'll be shelling town before noon." He drove
a spur into the horse's flank and rode off.

Caroline Wade-Healy did not know—could not know—that events
conspiring to bring her directly into the conflict were in irreversible

motion. Major General Henry Heth, of Lt. Gen. Richard Ewell's II
Corps in the Army of Northern Virginia, had heard a rumor that Gettysburg
had a warehouse full of shoes. Shoes were among many items that
his men desperately needed. That rumor, coupled with a variety of other
fateful circumstances, had combined to place Confederate forces in
the area in the first place. Events were acquiring a momentum all their
own, however, and General Heth was leading his troops south with
the single-minded purpose of getting those shoes. Federal troops
placed advantageously in his way as a matter of chance might delay
his quest, but to deter him completely, more was required. Heth wanted
those shoes.

Still weary and saddle sore from their long ride, Wade and Clinton
rose at sunup. Although the activity in the vicinity was intense, there
was no sign of troop movement from the immediate area toward the
north. The principal efforts were still directed at the preparation of
the defensive line that Meade felt would be essential if Lee pushed
south toward Washington.

Wade poured a cup of coffee and handed it to Clinton, then poured
a cup for himself. "It seems we failed to convince the general of the
urgency for concentrating his troops," Wade said. "I know Lee's temperament well enough to believe he'll take full advantage of any opening
given him."

"We've done all we can do, Colonel," Clinton replied. "Generals
are a strange breed. They have to make up their own minds."

Wade nodded but could not shake the feeling of impending doom.
His agitation grew as he rose and walked to the rim of a small rise.
Columns of soldiers were marching with shovels and picks to the
unfinished trench line, efforts Wade was convinced would be a waste
of time. I must get to Gettysburg, he thought. I'm of no use here. He
walked to a nearby mess wagon and drew three rations each for himself and Clinton. He munched on a strip of hardtack as he returned to
where Clinton was squatting by the fire.

"Saddle up, Major. Let's head north."

Clinton gulped down the last of his coffee and pulled his suspenders over his shoulders. "Do you think we'll be alive when this day
ends?" he asked his friend as he lifted his saddle and flung it over
the horse's back.

Wade did not respond. He tightened the cinch on his own saddle and lifted himself into it. "Where's the road to Gettysburg?" he asked a sergeant leading a column of soldiers.

The sergeant pointed. "About a quarter mile over there, sir. You can't miss it."

Wade saluted and rode west. If they rode easy, they could cover the dozen or so miles to Gettysburg well before noon. A mile from camp the two men left the congested pike and rode into the open. They could make better time away from the seemingly endless line of wagons and marching troops. At least part of Meade's forces were moving north.

Caroline had managed to replace her conscious fear of Confederate soldiers with an undying hate: They had done their worst with her. But her hatred was on the conscious, rational level. Deep inside, fear of what they were capable of doing when left unchecked churned and knotted her stomach. The image of exploding cannon shells only heightened her sense of dread. Grinding steel and lead brought an impersonal horror to war, a horror that made no distinction between soldier and civilian. But where should she run? Was there any sanctuary, anyplace more safe than another? If so, she had no idea where it might be.

All around, panic gripped the townspeople. Now and again, a spent rifle bullet dropped from the sky and plunked against a building or kicked up a puff of dust in the unpaved street. A lamp hanging in front of a building gave way almost reluctantly to the depleted force of one of these wayward missiles. At first the globe simply cracked with the contact, then it shattered in a heap on the wooden walkway. Women screamed as they scrambled for safety. Old men and women, wondering what horror waited to dismantle their tranquil, twilight years, stood in the middle of the street or in doorways in numbed bewilderment. Only the small children seemed indifferent to the fear gripping those who had the sense to flee the horror now shattering their lives.

Columns of infantry, led by officers on fidgety horses held tight lest they bolt, ran at double step along the streets, moving toward the sounds of battle. The town had become a funnel channeling all movement north. The panic-stricken people, uncertain whether to demand irrationally that the soldiers leave or to pray that a thousand times their numbers would follow protectively in their path, scrambled to get out of their way. Events were moving too fast for anyone to comprehend their meaning.

With so many wayward bullets flying through the air, it remained only a matter of time before one of them found a living mark. It happened precisely as a column of men ran across the intersection next to the Wade warehouse. One moment a young, vigorous-appearing man of about twenty had been running breathlessly down the street. The next moment he sprawled with a thud in the middle of the column, dropped instantly, as if struck by an invisible mallet. A neat red hole just above his left temple marked the bullet's entry. As others in the column scrambled to avoid stepping on the soldier, Caroline instinctively ran to his aid. She arrived in time to hear him utter a futile cry for his mother, then he died.

It had been Caroline's plan to finish checking the inventory by noon before proceeding to the farm. Now there were two armies blocking her way. There was, however, one good sign: The Federal soldiers were all moving north, out of town. Perhaps the lieutenant had been wrong. It seemed to her that the rows of advancing infantry stretched endlessly toward the south edge of town. Such a force can hold back any army, she thought, even Lee's. Knowing of no safe place to retreat to, she reentered the warehouse. Work will take my mind off the noise, she thought. She picked up a lantern and moved to the back of the building.

The rider galloped along, just below the crest of Seminary Ridge southwest of town. He strained his eyes to see through the smoke. So far as he had the ability to determine from his vantage point, all the fighting seemed to be northwest of town. From the position of the sun, he judged it to be just after noon. If, as he watched the unfolding battle a mile to his north, even a semblance of sanity had prevailed, he would have turned and rode into the hills. But he had a mission, a personal mission, and what he saw suited his intentions perfectly.

Since before Christmas his captors had kept him locked away in a corner cell of the worst of prisons. He had lost thirty pounds in captivity, and only during the past couple of days had he regained enough strength to make it through a full day without feeling faint.

Everything changed a week before he was released along a mist-shrouded, isolated roadway somewhere between Richmond and Washington less than two weeks before. Shortly before his release, all that he wanted to eat suddenly became available. His captors provided him with a tub for bathing. They even permitted him to roam unattended in the prison yard. Color slowly returned to his ashen face and limbs. No one had bothered to explain the abrupt change in his treatment, and he chose to accept it without question.

On the last day of his confinement, a Federal colonel had opened his cell door and placed a faded but clean uniform on the floor. Simon Thornton had put it on reluctantly; he was only a major, and the insignia on the jacket was that of a Confederate lieutenant colonel. Three days later, there had been that strange exchange in the fog. Thornton realized, when he saw his mirror image in the middle of the clearing, that events of which he had no understanding were at work. Then he saw his father. They had talked awhile, mostly about nothing of importance; finally the general asked him what he wanted to do. The answer burst from him: He had to get back into the war, to be assigned to the first regiment with an opening. The elder Thornton understood and offered to help. Four days later Simon had boarded a train scheduled to make a roundabout trip to Winchester, down the Shenandoah Valley. Now, with instructions to report directly to General Lee, he rode his black stallion toward the sound of the guns.

He caught up with Lee, who was sitting astride his horse watching the endless line of soldiers march down the Chambersburg road, and saluted. "Lieutenant Colonel Thornton reporting, sir. I have orders to report to you for assignment, General."

Lee flinched as he looked at Thornton. The man's face sparked a flood of unpleasant memories. Oh, Thomas, he thought, how I wish you were here. But Jackson was dead. At that moment Lee would have traded half the soldiers within his sight to see Jackson, even absent his arm, ride jauntily down that road in their place. "I remember you," Lee said finally, shaking away the images, "from Chancellorsville."

"No, sir," Thornton replied. "I've never been there. That was my cousin. I've been in a Yankee prison for the past six months."

Lee sighed and nodded numbly. The whole affair had seemed totally implausible, yet the man in front of him was living proof. "What are your orders?"

"I have been declared fit for duty, General. I have been absent from this war too long. I request assignment to a regiment of the line, sir, if that's possible."

Lee examined the young man. Perhaps he had heard something. "What word have you of General Stuart, Colonel?"

Thornton appeared puzzled. "None, sir."

"I wish someone could tell me of Stuart's location. I need him now." The general seemed lost in his thoughts. "Report to my adjutant, Colonel. He'll find a place for you." Lee wheeled and rode toward Gettysburg.

The ride north for Wade and Clinton was peaceful enough for the first half-dozen miles. Then, as the two men neared the crest of a hill, they heard the dull roar of battle for the first time. It was as if all the guns in southern Pennsylvania had suddenly begun to fire. The sound grew louder with each stride north. Wade spurred his horse, prodding it to a gallop. Clinton raced to catch up. It was just past eleven when they reached the Baltimore Pike southeast of town. There was no questioning the fact: A major battle was in progress. The fire seemed concentrated in the immediate vicinity of the town. Wade knew the area well; he had spent most of his life within ten miles of the place. Sweat dripped from his nose as he guided his mount off the road just west of the Rock Creek crossing.

Hundreds of wounded soldiers were spread out in small clearings. An even larger number of skulkers stood in the shadows of the trees along the wooded banks of the stream. It was the same with every battle— the color of the uniform did not matter—as soldiers exerted maximum effort to stay out of harm's way for an hour, or even five minutes, taking such advantage as opportunity afforded to remain alive. Probably most of the unwounded men gathering here had volunteered to transport a wounded man on a stretcher, then they simply chose not to return to their units.

Wade drew to a halt at the edge of the woods. Culp's Hill was about a mile due north. Cemetery Ridge protruded a little more than a half mile to the west. The deafening roar made it difficult even to think.

"It appears we found the war," Clinton shouted.

Wade nodded. "Soldier," he shouted to a private crouched behind a tree, "which way to General Reynolds's headquarters?"

"I don't keep track of generals," the soldier replied before he faded into the underbrush.

Wade drew a deep breath. "Let's go, Major." The two men moved northwest at a gallop, riding in the direction of Cemetery Hill. They moved toward a cluster of tents pitched on the south side of a small knob of ground. Near the largest of the tents a pole was stuck in the ground with a small red flag with two white stars attached to its top. The men drew to a halt and Wade dismounted.

"I have orders to report to General Reynolds." Wade saluted as he spoke to a staff colonel. "Can you direct me to his headquarters?"

"*This* is his headquarters," the colonel replied, "but the general is dead."

"Who's in command?" Wade asked.

"General Howard has assumed command. His headquarters is over the rise near a large brick arch."

Wade walked back to his mount. "General Reynolds is dead," Wade said to Clinton as he swung his leg over the horse's back. "Howard is in command." Wade knew General Howard, or at least knew of him. He did not like what he knew.

An hour passed before they found Howard and his staff. It was obvious from the disarray all around that the battle was going poorly. There was little evidence of organized troop movement, and dozens of stragglers were moving south and east, away from the main concentration of soldiers. It was not quite panic yet, but unless order was restored, that was the obvious next step.

Wade rode up to General Howard and drew to a stop. "Begging your pardon, General," he said as he saluted. "Colonel Wade reporting with orders from General Meade." He handed an envelope to the general, who passed it to his aide. The aide withdrew the single sheet of paper and read it, then handed it to the general.

Howard looked at Wade after he read the orders. "When did you see General Meade last?" he asked.

"Early this morning," Wade replied.

"Well, Colonel, you are of little use here. I need regiments, not regimental officers. The troops that remain are digging in on the north side of Cemetery Hill. The best service you can provide at present is to find a rifle and assist with the defense of that position."

Wade had once before seen an army in which all semblance of control had been lost. He had watched the panicked retreat of Union forces at Chancellorsville back in early May, when Stonewall Jackson's corps had hit Howard's exposed flank. This was the same general, and the result seemed to be the same.

Wade saluted and, with Clinton close behind, rode toward the sound of the guns.

CHAPTER 23

• • • • • • • • • • • • • • •

By 3:00 P.M., the Federal lines had crumbled. The battle that had raged throughout the morning and into the early afternoon had produced terrible casualties. The famed Iron Brigade was decimated; one of its regiments had suffered 80 percent losses. As Confederate regiment after Confederate regiment moved east along the Chambersburg road and south down the Carlisle road, fear had gripped many of the Union soldiers. Finally, the numbers had overwhelmed them.

Caroline finally yielded to the stress of her confinement. As the battle moved closer, the sound became a continuous, massive roar. Her earlier hope that the Federal forces could hold the line evaporated as panicky Union soldiers ran and stumbled through the streets toward Cemetery Hill. She left the building as the last few stragglers of a retreating regiment ran down the street. For a few minutes she saw no one. All the townspeople had by now found sanctuary in cellars and basements. Then, to the north, she heard the steady tap of drums. The young drummers rounded a corner two blocks north of her warehouse. Why, they're nothing but small boys, she thought. Following the brief gap behind the drummers, a man on a tall gray horse turned the corner. He also wore gray. Caroline's shoulders slumped. As if they knew precisely where they were heading, the rebel soldiers entered the town, moving directly toward her.

The colonel leading the long column raised his hand and the column stopped. He motioned again and a squad of soldiers ran toward the warehouse. At three-foot intervals, rifles pulled hard against their chests at parade rest, they positioned themselves along the front of the building.

"What are your intentions?" Caroline demanded of the colonel.

"Is this the warehouse where the shoes are stored?" he asked.

"It is," she answered. "This is my warehouse and these are my shoes." She turned her head slowly and looked along the column of dust-covered men. They seemed as apprehensive as she. Many wore blood-stained bandages. A few wavered and appeared about ready to fall. Comrades had to steady them. Most were barefoot or wore shoes that were falling apart. "What are your intentions, Colonel?" she asked again.

"Begging your pardon, ma'am," replied the officer as he bowed slightly and tipped his hat, "but I have come to buy these shoes for my men."

"Buy, Colonel?"

"Yes, ma'am. I'm authorized to pay for the merchandise with Confederate currency."

"And what am I supposed to do with this currency, Colonel? It is worthless here."

"Those are my orders, ma'am. I'm authorized to pay a dollar a pair. How many pairs of shoes are stored here, ma'am?"

"I have recently concluded an inventory, Colonel. I have just under six thousand pairs."

The colonel motioned for a young officer to ride forward. They spoke in a whisper for a moment, then the colonel turned to Caroline. "We will take fifty-five hundred of them, ma'am. That's all the money I have."

"I see, Colonel. And how many men do you have?"

The colonel thought. "Can't say for sure, ma'am. There were nearly ten thousand this morning. Many have been wounded or killed in the fighting. Eight thousand is a fair estimate."

She sighed. The hardness she felt for this army, for the would-be nation it represented, began to soften. These people are such a dichotomy, she thought, a contradiction by their very existence. If they chose, they had the power to confiscate the shoes, for she had no means to stop them. Yet here they stood, offering to limit their procurement because they were short of cash. For the first time she was certain on one point: The South must eventually lose the war. Only the date and place of surrender remained to be determined. If its leaders lacked the capacity to provide even the barest essentials of self-preservation, no army had it within itself to achieve victory. Courage alone, of which they had an ample supply, was insufficient. In war, time was the only irreplaceable commodity. One uses what becomes available for the purpose at hand or loses it forever. Not thirty minutes before, in a desperate effort to escape the onslaught of these bedraggled, weather-beaten soldiers, the men of her own nation's army had scurried through these same streets. Now the Union officers were rallying their beaten troops and the time for conquering them slowly had slipped away.

Here, however, despite the urgency of keeping the Union army on the run, the war had ground to a temporary halt. And for nothing more important than shoes. Many of the shoes, she knew, were certain to go to waste. Even as they bartered—no other term applied—Union forces frantically began carving out fortifications on the north rims of Cemetery and Culp's hills. Freshly shod, these men intended to advance on those works. Many were doomed to pay with their lives in the efforts to drive back the Federal forces. It all seemed so futile. Everything in the warehouse had less value than the life of a single man. In an unavoidable sense, however, the war had progressed to this juncture by design—and thousands were dying, or suffering terrible wounds, for nothing more than some leather for their feet.

"I will accept five dollars, sir," she said firmly.

The colonel seemed startled by the demand. "That is more than I have!" he replied.

"For the whole lot, Colonel. Five dollars for the contents of the warehouse. It is only decent that your men should meet their maker wearing shoes." The old, deeply entrenched defiance had surfaced again. Pulling a trigger in defense of her property was pretentiously unrealistic. This was the only way in which she could express contempt for the system that she abhorred with every fiber of her being. It is, she thought, a terrible thing their government is doing to these young soldiers. Her thoughts drifted to another dusty street, a street in distant Alabama. There she had learned through distressing experience that people thought nothing of squandering $1,500 in gold for a slave. Now they were incapable of providing a decent pair of shoes for the soldiers asked to defend that wretched system. Give them the shoes, she thought, and let them get on with their dying, until the scope of the killing forces them to scream: "Enough!"

The colonel moved his hand to tip his hat, then thought better of the gesture. He reached into his pocket instead and withdrew a five dollar gold piece. He flung it to the street. Caroline made no move to retrieve the coin. Instead, she stood rigidly beside the doorway, clenched fists pressing firmly against her hips, as soldiers rushed by and entered the building. She only planted her feet more firmly when sev-

eral of the men bumped against her as they scurried into the street to
distribute their bounty. All the while, the colonel glared at her, and
she glared in return. In time, she won this personal battle. The colonel broke eye contact and sighed; then he looked briefly at her again,
this time more softly, before spurring his mount down the street. She
watched with disbelief as the excited soldiers hopped about trying to
put on the shoes. You would believe, she thought, that they had just
had their first woman.

Shortly before four in the afternoon on July 1, Col. David Healy,
Sr., rode in the company of two other officers and a small escort along
the depression separating the lower east side of Cemetery Hill from
the trees a hundred yards east. General Meade remained south of the
battle site, giving last-minute instructions for the construction of the
Pipe Creek defenses and organizing troop movements. He still believed
that Lee intended to move on Washington. Even so, Meade had sent
Maj. Gen. Oliver O. Howard's XI Corps ahead to join General Reynolds's
I Corps at Gettysburg. With Reynolds dead, General Howard was in
command, a condition that would not have given Meade peace of mind
had he known of this turn of events.

Major General George Sykes, commander of V Corps, who earlier
had been waiting east of Gettysburg, near Hanover, prodded his men
along dusty roads in an effort to reach the battlefield before sunup on
July 2. Sykes had sent his newest brigade commander, accompanied
by two of his personal staff officers, to survey the battle area and report
back as soon as practicable.

. About an hour before Colonel Healy began his ride along the ridge,
Meade received an unofficial but nonetheless inauspicious report from
a newsman. General Reynolds, the ranking officer at Gettysburg, had
been killed early in the battle, the reporter said. A short time later, a
rider arrived at Meade's headquarters tent with a message from the
cavalry commander, Brig. Gen. John Buford. The message outlined
the development of a disaster, noting that the rebels overlapped both
the right and left flanks of the beleaguered Union forces now attempting
to consolidate on a wooded ridge south of Gettysburg. The message
confirmed that Reynolds was dead and ended with an ominous postscript: "We need help now."

But Meade had already acted. He questioned the qualifications of
the other corps commanders already on the scene, or lacked sufficient

information about their overall qualifications to trust them with the army. He first thought of going himself to assume control of the fight before conditions got out of hand. Instead, upon first receiving information about Reynolds's death, he sent Maj. Gen. Winfield Scott Hancock ahead to organize the defenses. Hancock's corps would make a forced march and was expected to arrive at Gettysburg some time during the night. That was all Meade could do. Events were moving too fast for him to attend to everything personally. He had to put the best men in the most opportune place and trust to luck, a risky proposition when fighting Gen. Robert E. Lee. In the meantime, the two battered Union corps already engaged in desperate fighting would have to fend for themselves until the rest of the Army of the Potomac made its way over the dusty roads leading to Gettysburg.

Healy realized that more had happened here than his superiors had led him to believe. Smoke shrouded the whole north rim of the high ground and the shallow basin below. That a battle was in progress, or recently had been, was obvious. The incessant clatter of rifled muskets, accompanied by the steady boom of cannon, offered proof of the concentrated fury up ahead. The closer Healy approached, the more evident that appeared. Emerging from the smoke were steady lines of stretcher bearers carrying the limp, bloody forms whose war had ended for the foreseeable future, if not forever. From the chaotically random gathering of wagons and teams of agitated horses among which he now rode, more soldiers moved hurriedly toward the smoke. This endless procession of quartermaster troops carried boxes of ammunition and other supplies needed to sustain the fighting. Healy had never witnessed a battle before. Doubts about his courage weighed heavily on his mind as he moved into the smoke-covered clamor just out of sight.

He rode up to an unfamiliar general and saluted. "Colonel Healy, General, on a mission for General Sykes. Will you direct me to General Reynolds's headquarters, sir?"

"General Reynolds is dead, sir, killed this morning. Until General Meade arrives, General Howard is in command," Maj. Gen. Abner Doubleday replied. He hesitated, then asked, "Do you have any men with you, Colonel? I may have use for more men on this line."

"No, sir. My mission is to determine where best to place General Sykes's men when they arrive."

"And when will that be, Colonel?"

"Early tomorrow morning, General. They are still several miles to the southeast."

"I see. Ah, there's General Howard now, over by those trees."

Healy saluted and rode along the back side of trenches being dug along the crest of Cemetery Hill. Then he pulled to a stop. "Samuel Wade? Is that you, Sam?"

Wade turned at the sound of his name. He saluted. "Good afternoon, Colonel." He smiled. "Are you here on business, or just to visit my mother?" He wasn't sure he knew the colonel well enough to make light of Healy's recent marriage to his mother.

"It appears the pleasure of seeing Caroline will have to wait, Samuel." A cannon shell exploded thirty feet away. Healy instinctively jumped from his horse and ran to the shelter of a nearby tree. "I'm too old for this," he said, obviously embarrassed.

"It takes a bit of getting used to," Wade replied. "Congratulations on your assignment as a brigade commander, Colonel. Are your troops coming up?"

"No. They're several miles behind. I'm here at General Sykes's request to assess the situation and get a report back directing the movement of his corps." He hesitated. "I'm surprised you've received another assignment so soon."

"My request, sir. I've been promised a regiment, but none is available at present. I was ordered to report to General Reynolds, but he was killed this morning. For the present, I'm helping organize this defensive line."

Healy looked around to see if anyone was listening. "Are we in trouble here, Samuel?"

"You could say that, sir. General Ewell has his corps strung out across our front. My guess is we're outnumbered three to one. If he attacks in force we'll be driven from the field. Pardon my saying so, sir, but General Howard is not up to organizing our defenses here."

Healy did not respond. He ducked as another shell exploded nearby. "I suspect I'll see you later, Samuel. I have to report to General Howard and get instructions for General Sykes." He walked a few paces, then turned. "Is your mother here at Gettysburg?" he asked apprehensively. "When I left her in Washington she said she was coming here to inventory her warehouse."

Wade walked to his new stepfather. "Then I suppose this is where she is." He placed his hand on Healy's shoulder. "I know my mother fairly well, David. She's a very self-reliant woman. I think she'll find a way to take care of herself."

"I know. Still . . ." He clasped Wade's hand, then turned and mounted his horse. He saluted as he rode toward a gathering of officers two hundred yards west.

Healy approached the only major general on the scene. "General Sykes's compliments, General Howard. General Sykes is moving his troops forward from southeast of here. He requests direction for the disposition of his men."

"How far is he, Colonel?" Howard asked.

"Ten miles or more, General."

"Ten miles, you say, Colonel? Whatever is going to happen here will be settled before he arrives." A sharpshooter's Minié ball glanced off a nearby tree, ricocheting into a private's rifle, shattering the weapon in the process. Howard offered no reaction. Healy fought the impulse to wheel his horse and ride hard to the south, out of harm's way. His apprehension must have been obvious to Howard. "Your first time in battle, Colonel?"

"Is it *that* apparent, General?"

A second general, followed by his staff, rode up to General Howard and saluted. Healy recognized the general as Maj. Gen. Winfield Scott Hancock, known as "Hancock the Superb" to his troops.

Howard returned the salute. "Are your men here, General?" Howard asked.

"No, General Howard," Hancock replied. "General Meade sent me ahead. May I speak with you in private for a moment?" Howard nodded. Accompanied by a single aide each, the two generals rode a short distance away.

Healy leaned forward and rested his forearm on the neck of his horse. He watched as the two major generals talked and gestured. The conversation seemed to be less than friendly, but the noise drowned out the words. Then the two men returned. "This seems to be a strong defensive position, General," Hancock said as he pulled his field glasses to his eyes.

"I agree," Howard replied.

"Very well, sir. I select this for the battlefield."

Something had happened during the brief conversation between the two generals. When they departed, Howard had been in command. Now Hancock seemed to be giving the orders.

Hancock turned and looked at Healy. "Do I know you, sir?" he asked.
"Yes, General Hancock. My name is Healy, sir, Col. David Healy."
"Now I remember. You're a banker, am I correct?"
"Yes, sir. We met in New York City a few years back."
"Are you assigned to General Howard's staff?" Hancock asked.
"No," Howard interrupted, "Colonel Healy is a brigade commander
with General Sykes's corps."
Hancock looked surprised. "I didn't know General Sykes was up yet."
"Begging your pardon, sir," Healy answered, "but he isn't. He sent
me ahead to assess the situation and report back. My brigade is at the
head of the corps and will arrive at least two hours before the main
body—in about eight hours I would think. General Sykes requests
instructions for the placement of his men, sir." Uncertain who would
give him those directions, Healy looked at both generals.

Hancock turned in his saddle and studied the terrain and the troop
dispositions.

"Sir, begging your pardon, but can we hold?" Healy realized the
question might be interpreted as impertinent. Still, he had to know.
Judging from the general disorganization within his limited range of
vision, he wasn't certain there would be an army left to reinforce by
the time his men arrived.

Hancock smiled faintly as he turned his head slowly, field glasses
pressed against his eyes. "I think the answer to your question is largely
in the enemy's hands." He lowered the glasses and looked at Howard.
"What rebel force is that on our front?" he asked, pointing toward the
town.

"General Ewell's corps," Howard replied, "and I expect an attack
at any time. It is doubtful we have enough men to hold against a major
assault."

"Ewell's troops seem to have run out of steam for the present," Hancock
said. That assertion surprised Healy. Although there were no advancing troops in the immediate vicinity, the firing had grown louder since
his arrival. "Give my compliments to General Sykes," Hancock continued. "Tell him to bring his men along the west rim of the southern
half of the ridge. Tell him to stretch them as far as possible to the
south. If the rebels fail to break through here, I think they will attempt
to roll up our left flank before trying our center."

Healy looked down the hill. "General, there's a large column of Rebs
moving through those woods. Are you sure we can hold?"

"Don't worry, Colonel," Howard replied. "That's the Iron Brigade down there—at least what remains of it. They'll hold, or die in the attempt."

Healy's attention shifted to where he had talked with his stepson a short time before. "General Hancock, may I speak with you a moment in private?"

"I'm very busy at present," the general replied.

"It may be worth a few minutes, sir, but it's a matter of some confidentiality."

"All right, Colonel. Make it quick."

The two men rode a few yards to the right. Healy talked for several minutes, the general's attention growing more intense as the conversation continued. Healy pointed off to the line of trees where the defensive lines were being constructed.

"By all means," Hancock said finally, "bring Colonel Wade to see me."

Healy saluted and rode to where Wade and he had talked. He dismounted and moved in a crouch toward the safety of the tree line. "How are the works coming, Colonel?" Healy asked.

"Slow, sir," Wade replied.

"I think I may have something important for you to do. Will you come with me to talk with General Hancock?"

"I have to get my horse down in those trees. Can you give me five minutes? Is it all right if I bring Major Clinton?"

Healy nodded. Wade motioned for Clinton to follow and the men ran down the slope to their horses, dodging cannon fire as they moved into the open. They rode at a run back to where Healy waited in the relative shelter of the trees, then the three men galloped to where Hancock waited.

"General Hancock, sir," Healy said, saluting, "permit me to introduce Lt. Col. Samuel Wade and Maj. James Clinton." The noise of cannon and musket fire was increasing by the minute. Healy had to shout to be heard. "These are the men I told you about." Wade and Clinton saluted.

"May I take my leave of you now, sir?" Healy asked as the general turned his attention to Wade. "I must report back to General Sykes as soon as possible." Healy had left his brigade in command of his deputy. He felt a sudden urgency to get back to it.

"By all means, Colonel, and thank you for your assistance here today."

The two men saluted and Healy rode off, eager to put distance between himself and intensifying fire.

Healy rode the short distance to the two staff officers who had accompanied him. He informed them of the substance of his conversation with General Hancock. "Find General Sykes," Healy directed, "and inform him of General Hancock's instructions. I will return to my brigade alone." The others rode off as Healy directed his field glasses toward the town. He could see only the top of the tallest building over the trees. I wonder where Caroline is? he thought. I pray she left Gettysburg before the battle began. He lowered his glasses and turned the horse east.

Wade and Clinton had made a wide swing around the left flank of General Ewell's Confederate corps. They had been escorted by a small cavalry troop until they had passed beyond the Union lines. This was to prevent them from being shot. The two men were wearing the captured uniforms of a Confederate colonel and captain. The two rebel officers had protested loudly when ordered to strip, but to no avail. Wade tugged at the too-tight collar of his jacket. Clinton's uniform hung like a sack around his solid small frame. They rode captured rebel mounts.

"This is, without a doubt, the dumbest thing yet," Clinton said as they threaded through the dense stand of trees.

"You could have declined to go," Wade replied. "This is a volunteer mission."

"Did you ever hear of a lieutenant colonel and a major saying no to a request from a major general?"

Wade smiled. "Now that you mention it, I can't say I ever did."

"Halt," said a voice with a stout Southern accent. "Advance and be recognized."

"Colonel Thornton, of Lee's staff, with a message for General Ewell."

"Lee is off to the west," the sentry replied. "What are you doin' comin' from the east?"

"We got lost," Wade replied. "Where is the general?"

"Should find him about a thousand yards over yonder," said the sentry, pointing.

"Carry on, Corporal." Wade spurred his horse to a gallop.

Shortly, they rode into a small encampment. "I have a message for

General Ewell from General Lee," Wade said to a young officer. "Can you direct me to him, Lieutenant?"

"That's him, lookin' through the field glasses over by them trees."

Wade rode on. Wade did not know General Ewell by sight. The general had been badly wounded and was out of action before Wade replaced his brother on General Jackson's staff. But that did not diminish the possibility of an encounter with others who might have known him during the period of his impersonation, or knew his brother, which would be just as fatal. He pulled his hat low over his eyes. Clinton did the same.

With muskets at the ready, soldiers were moving in regimental strength to the right and left of this central position a quarter mile north of a rail fence at the base of Cemetery Hill. Even with all the smoke, Wade could see the frantic digging by Union soldiers along the military crest of the hill. As Wade watched, a fresh regiment climbed down the grade and came to the ready position within the freshly dug trenches. From here the position appeared more formidable than from the other side, where he had been engaged in its construction less than ninety minutes earlier.

It was nearly 6:00 P.M. as Wade rode to General Ewell's front and saluted. "General Lee's compliments, sir. The general has sent me with instructions."

"General Lee, sir? Another courier left here not twenty minutes ago." Ewell hesitated. "Very well, Colonel, hand me the message."

"It's verbal, sir. General Lee reports that Union reinforcements have arrived and are moving into the defensive position to your front. The general says that unless you can be certain of success, you should delay your attack until all of your forces are up, perhaps until morning."

"My God, Colonel, what am I to do?" Ewell shouted. "First I'm instructed to attack with all possible haste, and then I'm told to delay unless success is certain." The general's eyes were fixed on the regiment moving into the enemy trenches. From this distance they seemed fresh and confident. For all he knew, the Federals were moving another division—perhaps a whole corps—into the trenches to his front. His ammunition was low from a day of hard fighting and sundown was only ninety minutes away. One of his two divisions was badly mauled and would be of little use in an all-out frontal attack up a steep hill. All of this was on his mind as he considered the conflicting orders. Certain of success? he thought. When is success in attacking entrenched forces ever certain? The question seemed rhetorical. His own battered body offered ample evidence of the softness of flesh when confronted with steel and lead. Every advantage rested with the enemy, and he wasn't even certain that he had General Lee's confidence in the success of this attack.

He watched intently as one of his regiments filed into position for the planned attack. Willing though they might be, it had been a tiring day for his men. They had experienced one success after another. Now he had the option of ordering them forward and perhaps ending the day with a humiliating defeat, or waiting until tomorrow. Already a thousand or more of his young soldiers lay in crumpled heaps from the woods north of Gettysburg to the hill in his front.

Lee had left the decision to him. This could only mean that Lee also had second thoughts about the wisdom of a late-evening attack against a stout position. Doubt clouded his mind.

"Very well, Colonel. Tell General Lee I will evaluate conditions on my front and decide what I must do."

"Yes, sir. I will inform him." The general seemed in doubt, not yet certain he should delay the attack. Wade looked up through the trees. "It's growing late, General. Before I left Seminary Ridge I saw several fresh Union brigades moving north along Cemetery Ridge. They must be nearing the trenches by now." He shook his head. "Tomorrow will be a rough day, sir. Good luck."

Wade wheeled his horse and rode west. Out of sight of the general and his staff, he turned north toward Gettysburg. He resisted the temptation to keep riding through the town to his home. At the south edge of the small community, he and Clinton, uncertain that their effort had served any useful purpose, headed east to make the long swing around the Confederate left flank and back to Union lines.

An hour later, at seven, General Lee mounted his horse for the ride to General Ewell's headquarters, to check for himself why the corps commander had decided not to mount the late afternoon attack he had personally encouraged but had not ordered in the message sent at 5:00 P.M. Lee had acquired one anxiety and had another relieved. Shortly before he mounted Traveller, a messenger rode into the headquarters and informed him that General Stuart's cavalry was riding hard from Carlisle and should arrive some time the next day. This may have softened his feelings about Ewell's failure to attack.

*   *   *

From the diary of Caroline Wade-Healy:

11:55 P.M., July 1, 1863
  This day, the longest and most dreadful of many long and dreadful days these past two years, is about to end. The warehouse is a wreck. Not a single pair of shoes remained after the rebels ravaged the place. But there are more important things than shoes. It seems every man in both armies has converged on our tranquil little town. If that is so, then David and Samuel must be here someplace.
  I never knew there could be so much noise. The landscape has been in perpetual explosion since seven this morning. A soldier told me that less than half of our forces have arrived, and that what has transpired previously is hardly more than a skirmish. My God! What will it be like when the battle begins in earnest?
  The town is awash with rebel soldiers. Wounded and dying fill every house and barn. There must be thousands, and it has hardly begun. Oh, what havoc we have wrought upon ourselves. I watched a young lieutenant, with stubs where his arms used to be, scream and flail at the air as they cut off his right leg. When everything suddenly became quiet, I knew for sure there is a merciful God. The boy died, and his passing bestowed God's blessing.
  It is mostly quiet now. Even soldiers have to rest sometime. I shudder at the thought of what morning will bring.

....

  All through the long night, columns of soldiers converged on the once peaceful village. They seemed drawn by a powerful magnetic force eager to elevate the killing to such a fearful level that all involved would eventually beg for it to stop.
  By nightfall the Union lines traced a rough outline that resembled a gigantic fishhook. Culp's Hill formed the barb of the hook; the north rim of Cemetery Hill formed the bend. The long ridge extending south from the graveyard on the hill formed the shank. Little Round Top, two miles south, formed a prominent eye. Most of this formation, except for the barb and the hook, had few defenders at this early hour. In a desperate effort to solve that problem, the generals would lead their troops into position throughout the long night. But even at this late hour, not a single soldier occupied Little Round Top.

David Healy, Sr., eager to resume his position as commander of a three-regiment brigade, had arrived and departed, performing a small service in the interim. Now he reversed course a second time and presently approached a point five miles distant from the field. Colonel Healy's new stepson, assigned as deputy commander of a reserve regiment in Hancock's corps upon his late evening return from his mission into enemy lines, was directing his men into the seclusion of the trees down by Rock Creek, on the lee side of Cemetery Ridge, for a couple of hours of much needed sleep.

Simon Thornton had been placed in reserve. On the far side of the field, beyond Seminary Ridge, he slept fitfully under a giant oak tree. He awaited the last of Longstreet's divisions, which was expected to arrive late during the coming day, or later. Lee's adjutant had assigned Thornton to George Pickett's division. Pickett's arrival, in time for the battle everyone expected to climax during the approaching day, seemed doubtful.

All the way around, it had been a heartbreaking, bone-splitting, bloodcurdling yell of a July 1. Nearly three men, North and South, had fallen for each pair of shoes secured by a five-dollar gold piece flung gratuitously into the dust. About a fourth of those, with many more destined to follow, were dead. All day long, General Lee had asked the same question of approaching riders: "Have you seen General Stuart? What has happened to Stuart?" No one knew. As a result of Stuart's absence, Lee had, in a very real sense, been fighting blind. He had no reliable means for evaluating the strength or disposition of the force confronting him on the hills across the small valley. Without that information, confined as he was in a very small place in a foreign country, he had opened himself to a disaster of the first magnitude. The fate of his fledgling would-be nation hung in the balance, or nearly so, although it is doubtful he had analyzed his situation from that perspective. What had occurred up to that point had been to his advantage. His forces had routed the enemy and driven them into a prevail-or-die position. That accomplishment alone could have been counted a Southern victory. Lee had learned the virtue of patience when constructing a defeat for the Union army.

One thing Lee did not fully realize, although he, more than any man alive, would have understood its significance: More than a thousand miles away, a disaster seemed imminent for a hard-pressed portion of his beleaguered people's armed forces. A month earlier, Maj. Gen. Ulysses

S. Grant had surrounded the Mississippi River city of Vicksburg. The siege had driven the people there to the brink of despair. Lee had to win in Pennsylvania, or the South would be forced to measure its survival in long, desperate months rather than the generations its people considered nearly an established certainty.

As the first day of July ended, that responsibility lay heavy on the Southern commander's mind. He no longer fought to defend hearth and home. Now he led an invading army. As he had learned during the long months of the Virginia campaign, men somehow fight harder when defending their homes—except that there his soldiers had been the defenders.

Across the way, General Meade, himself a Pennsylvanian, faced a different problem, one certain to be recognized when he arrived a few hours later. Circumstance demanded nothing of him other than to hold. Although Lee had to win or retreat in defeat, for the Union commander a draw would serve the purpose of outright victory. In the bargain, Meade had one significant advantage: He enjoyed the luxury of fighting from the defensive with a superior force. All he needed to do was absorb the blows Lee would surely unleash with the next light.

At least one of Lee's burdens was lifted now that Stuart had been found. At his present location, however, he remained as much out of the war as if his troopers were camped on the far side of the moon. All the while, on the Union side of the battlefield, the balance tipped further in favor of the North as thousands of soldiers concluded their long marches from a dozen points on the compass by filing exhaustedly into hastily prepared positions.

Lieutenant Colonel Sam Wade sighed as he stood alone on the crest of Cemetery Hill. Confederate campfires as numerous as stars dotted the countryside before him. It looks so peaceful, he thought, for there to be so much malice here. He had no illusions about the approaching conflagration. He had lived with that army across the way, eaten its food, experienced its medical services, joked with its officers, watched in awe as its commanders had wreaked havoc on the Union forces now facing it. He knew those soldiers, and he knew that none gave a moment's thought to the idea of defeat. But having been in their midst and survived to record it, he, perhaps better than anyone, knew they were not invincible. He also knew that their dedication had no limit. If need be, they were willing to die by the thousands to promote their cause. That was enough to know about any army, about any man.

CHAPTER 24

·················

The first published report of the second day of battle at Gettysburg did not appear until July 5. By then the issue had been settled. Partly because events were spinning out of control for all concerned, and partly because what was happening was unfolding on too grand a scale for mortals to fully understand, the report's author, Joseph Pickering of the Boston *Globe,* struggled to find words to describe what had happened, or what he thought had happened. But the message was there, the part that was important. His dispatch attempted mainly to make some sense out of the bludgeoning administered equally by and to Union and Confederate soldiers at the southern end of the battlefield, but the scale of conflict, confined though it was, was too huge to capture on paper—except when filtered through long-term analysis. That would follow. But it is the first three paragraphs of Pickering's report that are worth mentioning, for in them the writer made an effort to make sense of what really happened that day at Gettysburg, as well as in the larger sense of the war, and why it was so important in determining what followed:

At present, our self-flagellating nation is fighting on two fronts. General Grant has a Confederate army sealed in at Vicksburg, hard against the Mississippi River. It is an open question how long that Confederate army can sustain itself against hunger and constant bombardment. Here at little Gettysburg, Pennsylvania, the outcome is less certain.

Long after dark today, July 2, 1863, the second day of the Gettysburg battle, the Federal army under the able leadership of

Gen. George G. Meade, and the Confederate army, under the leadership of that incomparable military genius Gen. Robert E. Lee, concluded a day of utter carnage. The day began as the day before had ended, with Union forces stretched out along a three-mile-long curving line that resembles in one's imagination a giant fish hook. At first, it seemed nothing much would happen. Lee's main line, on Seminary Ridge, faced Meade's main line, on Cemetery Ridge. All morning, and into midafternoon, it remained fairly quiet. The pressure seemed too intense to endure. More than one man screamed, "For God's sake, why don't they attack?" It seems strange that men grow so eager to die.

From the impartial point of view of this reporter, it was impossible not to notice the subtle change that has occurred here—on both sides. The change was not in the gruesome outcome of the second day of epic struggle—that remained the same. The change was in the approach to the killing. Lee, the hard-charging genius of the offensive, seemed uncertain, lacking in conviction. Meade, on the other hand, seemed committed to stand and fight, regardless of the cost or the risk. But perhaps more important, there is the observation that both armies are still here: Lee because he has not won; Meade because he refuses to run. It is as if the Army of the Potomac came of age today, refusing to be intimidated on its home ground. This change does not bode well for the Army of Northern Virginia.

There it was for all to see, for anyone who bothered to look: The Army of the Potomac, battered and bruised though it may have been, remained on the field at the conclusion of two of the most difficult days of fighting ever seen by any army. It is difficult to emphasize too strongly what it meant for a man such as General Meade, in command of the army for less than a week, to stand virtually toe-to-toe and slug it out with the likes of Gen. Robert E. Lee. The Army of the Potomac had always possessed everything it needed for success, save one thing: A commanding general had never been found with the qualities necessary to fully manage this body of men. Perhaps such a man had been found at last, the men dared to hope. As tired as they were of fighting, they were more tired of losing, and it was enough to give them a resurgence of pride simply by observing that their new general had sufficient confidence in them to let them stand and take the best, or worst, that General Lee could throw at them. On this second day of battle, the gray-clad general did not disappoint them.

Pickering could not have known the underlying reason for what he observed or, more precisely, what he did not observe. The day dragged on as the tension grew. On the west side of the valley, the prevailing condition was more one of confusion than lack of resolve. The Confederate command structure was at odds, a condition created by disagreement between General Longstreet, who had replaced Stonewall Jackson as Lee's chief lieutenant, and Lee himself. Miscommunication added to the confusion as Lee tried to maneuver Longstreet's corps into position for an attack at the southern end of the battlefield. As the day progressed, most soldiers on the Union side of the valley concluded that Lee believed Meade's forces had too firmly entrenched themselves for an attack to be successful. Sam Wade, like the others, waited.

Wade had slept uneasily the night before, troubled by equal concerns that he might have arrived too late for the main battle and by the pressing fear that the coming storm would diminish the significance of all that had happened until now. He kept himself busy getting to know the officers in his regiment and checking the men to see that they had sufficient ammunition to endure against a dedicated attack against the center of the Union line. The soldiers tried to convince themselves that Lee had suffered enough and that he was preparing to withdraw. "Do you think they'll pull out?" the men would ask hopefully as Wade moved along the line. "I guess we showed 'em we'uns can take as much lead as anyone," they would add, or something like that, in the effort to give Lee a reason to save his men to fight another day. But it was just talk, and everyone knew it. The bustle of activity across the way increased with every hour. Something was in the works.

Just before four in the afternoon, General Hood's division from General Longstreet's corps moved out of the trees at the southern end of the battlefield. They moved first at an angle, north along the Emmitsburg Road, toward Meade's men on the ridge; then they turned east toward the two hills at the southern end of Meade's extended line. In less time than is required to describe the intricate maneuvering, the two armies collided in a fierce clash of arms. For more than an hour, the battle raged on and around the lower of the two hills, called Little Round Top by local citizens. The rocky ground across from the hill came to be known as the Devil's Den—justifiably so, for the devil himself could not have devised a more perfect killing ground, or a worse place to fight.

Wade knew the place well. He had imagined himself as a courageous captain of a great sailing ship as he'd climbed over rocks as large as cabins as a boy of ten. He had fought many a successful battle there in his youth, but the enemy had been imaginary, usually a band of hostile Indians trying to drive him from his defenses. The imagined impregnability of the place came to mind as he watched the Confederate regiments storm forward, only to slam against the invincible rocks and the Union soldiers who fought among them. The rebels obviously had an indomitable will to accomplish their task, or they would not have kept at it so long, but the rocks and the sweltering defenders were more than their doggedness could overcome.

At 5:00 P.M., General McLaws's division moved against General Sickles's forces in an exposed orchard and wheat field and drove them running back toward Meade's main line. Then a third division moved onto the plain and advanced toward Meade's main line at the lower end of Cemetery Ridge. There followed a fearful loss of lives as, one by one, Confederate brigades moved across the valley and collided with Federal forces. For more than an hour, the outcome hung in the balance. Wade's excitement grew in anticipation of his regiment being sent into the battle. Reserves were called up, and only by deftly moving fresh troops into the battle did General Meade avoid total collapse and defeat. At one point, a single regiment of Minnesota volunteers charged an entire Alabama brigade as it moved toward a break in the Federal lines. Most of those brave men paid with their lives to buy the scant ten minutes Union officers needed to move troops forward to repair the breach. In the end, the Confederate forces ran out of steam and fell back. A thousand or more dead, and as many too maimed even to crawl from the field, marked the path of this brave but futile charge.

As this phase of the battle ended, General Ewell's corps attacked the Federal forces dug in on the two hills at the north end of the Union line. A few thousand more dead and dying fell before fresh troops again sealed the breach. Wade's regiment waited anxiously in the center as the attacks hammered both ends of the Union line, but the Confederates did not advance against them.

Nearly twenty thousand men were dead, wounded, or missing by sundown, about equally divided between the two armies. Still, neither side had moved much from the positions they had occupied as the day began.

*   *   *

"There is nothing here worth fighting for," newspaperman Pickering wrote at the conclusion of his report on the second day of the battle. "Rumors have circulated that the rebels' only interest in coming here was to take some shoes stored in a small warehouse in the town. Now the purpose of this, the greatest battle of the war, seems nothing more than to determine which army can outlast the other.

"With one more day such as today, the reason may have no importance. There may be no one left alive to carry the dead from the field."

Once armies are set in motion, sergeants and privates win or lose battles. Until that time, however, everything depends on the generals: on their preparedness, on their state of mind, on their willingness to commit their troops along the paths leading in harm's way. A simple phrase—"Go get 'em!" for example—sets everything in motion. But someone has to say the words.

On the first day at Gettysburg, General Ewell of Lee's army neglected to say the words. With his troops securely positioned at the bases of Culp's and Cemetery hills, a dedicated attack most probably would have crumbled the hastily constructed defenses of the now dead General Reynolds's corps. If that had happened, events during the next two days would have taken a different course. There would have been no bitter struggle in the Devil's Den and on Little Round Top. The peach orchard and the bloody wheat field would have remained untrammeled. There would have been no need for George Pickett to lead his division in a futile charge up Cemetery Ridge. Ah! for the might-have-beens.

Instead, more than nine thousand gray-clad soldiers lay wounded or dead as a result of combat on the second day of battle. An equal number of blue-clad soldiers joined them. The armies squared off for the final round, like a pair of punch-drunk fighters who had bludgeoned each other thus far without gain. In the process, the tide began a slow turn in favor of the Union. On the practical level, however, nothing had changed—except the diminished sizes of the two armies. For all their effort in two days of fighting, the Confederates still clung to the barest slice of Pennsylvania countryside. No one dared try to take that slice from them, but neither could they drive Meade from the field. Failing that, Lee's men would have given better service if they had remained in Virginia, for the purchase price of that useless small sliver had been cripplingly steep; thus far, nearly one Confederate had been killed or otherwise removed from action for each foot of Lee's three-mile front.

The failures of Lee's generals, at least some of them—enough to matter at a time when failure proved most costly—were beyond dispute. In the short period since Chancellorsville, the Army of Northern Virginia had acquired some of the least desirable tendencies of the Army of the Potomac. Everything seemed just a little late, somewhat off balance, chronically out of focus. Hood's attack had developed late, then had moved in the wrong direction, toward the Devil's Den, instead of around the Union flank.

The attack on the main line had evolved disjointedly, with some of the generals failing to advance their troops at all. One of Ewell's subordinates failed to have his division in place to support the late evening attack on Cemetery Hill on the second day. The squandering of a thousand more lives had followed.

Yet with all the carnage that had gone before, there remained one imponderable. That was the absence of Gen. Stonewall Jackson, a man General Lee sorely missed. Jackson's absence, it has been forcefully argued, changed everything at Gettysburg. In an immeasurable sense, a young officer sleeping on Cemetery Ridge had done his part to win the battle even before it began.

The accolades for brilliance belong to the bold assailants who prevail. Otherwise, the tributes accrue by default to the defenders. All through the war, for more than two long years, Lee's army had prevailed in the face of ever-increasing odds. A fair share of the credit for that success belonged to Stonewall Jackson. But that ethereal warrior had departed forever, and his pure instinct for war had vanished with him.

Where General Longstreet had resisted the idea of a frontal attack across the mile-wide plain on that second day of battle, Jackson would have been ecstatic at the opportunity to deliver, once and for all, the decisive, mortal blow to his enemy. Although Lee felt no reluctance at all in rejecting Longstreet's proposed turning movement, he would have listened to and responded to Jackson's instincts. Lee had done more than listen two months earlier when he had agreed to release most of his army to Jackson to have it work its way to the Union right flank and rout the hapless Federals at Chancellorsville. With the wily Jackson gone, Lee stood alone—or might as well have. That, in combination with a Union army that seemed to have shed its inclination for running, brought to the minds of many the idea that, somehow, Lee's stars had become crossed on the hard road to Gettysburg.

To prevail against the heavens, one must take desperate chances. There remained nothing for Lee to do but to fight: headlong, all out, using every resource at his disposal.

Colonel David Healy, Sr., fumed as he and his brigade spent July 2 guarding the roads leading south and east from Gettysburg. He had resisted joining this conflict, but now that he was in it, his natural competitive tendencies had taken charge. A monkey has the ability to command soldiers assigned to guard roads, he thought. A wise general, however, secures his lines of retreat. Too many times in the past, General Meade had seen long lines of blue-clad soldiers scampering to escape the fury of Lee's advances. If their use became necessary, Healy's assignment to guard these avenues might be his most useful service during the battle or its aftermath.

Six miles west, an hour before sunset and two hours before dark, as the battle in the Devil's Den sputtered to a close, Lt. Col. Simon Thornton saddled his horse and rode off to report to General Pickett's camp slightly west of Gettysburg, along the Chambersburg Pike.

CHAPTER 25

· · · · · · · · · · · · · ·

Sam Wade found sleeping impossible. He rose just as the first pale streaks of dawn stretched across the valley. As he looked north, to where the frail light extended long shadows from the markers on Cemetery Hill, he rubbed the stiffness from his legs and the sleep from his eyes. He mused to himself at the sight of so many sleeping soldiers stretched out among the tombstones that speckled the hilltop graveyard. A prophetic symbol, he thought; how cheap life has become these past two days that now the dead and the living keep such perfect company.

No one had taken a more circuitous route to this battlefield than he. Two days of hard fighting had passed before he reached the forward slope. So far as he could determine, neither army had taken one step in preparation for retreat. One sensed such things, even before the action moved toward its climax. There was no boldness evident in the dispositions of his commanders, but neither were there, by this stage, the signs of panic in the Union ranks he had witnessed in other battles—panic he had seen from the other side. Wagons remained empty. Large piles of ammunition boxes and ration cartons remained stacked behind protective dirt and log barriers. Horses grazed unattended in woodland seclusion. There appeared to be a grim resignation in all of this, a hard resolve to prevail or perish. By pushing the conflict onto Northern soil, Lee had gone too far.

The battle must continue, Wade knew, regardless of the cost, and there seemed to be no way possible for anyone to remove him from it now. He stretched again. Except for the stationary frames of sleeping soldiers and the rubble of war, the grove of trees a hundred or so yards to the north provided the only object blocking a clear view in that direction. During his youth he had played among those trees. He had chased butterflies in the fields below. He remembered being ten when he had, for the first time, ridden his pony down to Sugar Loaf Hill—which the soldiers now referred to as Big Round Top. He had frolicked among the large boulders of the so-called Devil's Den, where so many men had died the day before. He had dreamed, as he slashed with a crooked stick that served as a pretend sword, that he was captain of a great ship. Once, on a warm fall day, his mother had brought Jefferson's children and him to the spot where he now sat for a picnic.

A three-foot-high rock wall, built parallel to the flow of the terrain, stretched along the side of the ridge toward the Confederate lines. Immediately ahead of Wade, the wall reached a temporary bend, turned down the slope for fifty yards or so, then continued on its southward path before ending abruptly a quarter mile beyond. He had thought, during his youth, as he slithered behind the structure hiding from imaginary savages, that the farmers who had built it must have continued their labor with no thought in mind other than to use up the rocks in the field. For no apparent reason, the wall stopped in midconstruction. There, at the south end, it pressed against emptiness. A modest jumper with ambling stride could clear the obstacle with minimum effort. It will require more than that, he thought, to stop a serious assault.

That, in part, worried him, or at least caused doubt. The day before, the rebels had tried and failed in an assault across a shorter distance against less well-entrenched forces. Might he miss the battle, after all, if Lee decided to send his main attack against the flanks again— or against less well-defended segments of the ridge?

Soldiers, moving like so many snakes in the early morning shadows, began to stir. As men disturbed the embers by throwing logs on the smoldering fires, faint, swirling sparks rose in a jagged course toward the heavens. Then the hell of war returned to shatter the tranquillity. Just out of sight, on the north slope of Culp's Hill, an earsplitting cannonade let loose, sending shot and shell crashing into the distant trees. It sounded as if someone lit a match and the hill exploded. Wade flinched; the conditioning rendered by total war demanded nothing more. The rumbling clamor, however, ended all attempts at slumber by the prostrate soldiers. Officers and men scurried to their defensive positions in anticipation of a dawn attack.

As Wade watched the men scramble, moving without orders, each seeing to his own defense, his thoughts drifted back to Bull Run. It occurred to him that conditions now were different. At Bull Run, when the first shells began crashing all around, the men had cowered in uncontrollable fear and wet their britches. More than a few ran with the first shots. Those who remained had looked to their officers for direction. When the officers began to waver—few of them had any more conditioning to the terrors of war than the soldiers they led— the men saw no need to stand firm. No more. The men had learned to take care of themselves. Here, as soon as they realized that the attack was a short half mile up the ridge, they relaxed, uncocked their weapons, and began to rummage through their packs. The war could wait until after they lit their pipes and ate some breakfast.

Franklin Sill, the regimental commander, approached his deputy. "Anything moving out there, Samuel?"

Wade shook his head. "Not to the west, sir. Up north. I suspect that General Slocum is attempting to drive the rebels from the trenches they captured at dusk."

"Most likely," said Sill nervously. "Most likely. Still, it's best to be prepared. Let's get all the men into position. Have them eat their breakfast in shifts, one platoon at a time from each company."

Wade saluted, then moved along the ridge informing the company commanders of the colonel's orders. Finished with his chore, Wade brought his field glasses to his eyes. He turned his head slowly as he scanned the far ridge. He detected plenty of movement but nothing resembling preparations for an attack. He lowered the angle of his glasses for a closer view of the valley. Here and there, a wounded soldier from yesterday's battle moved an arm or a leg. During the night mercy squads had removed most of the dead and wounded from the field. A few were inadvertently left behind. As soldiers in blue and gray came within easy shouting distance, a number of verbal jabs had been exchanged.

"Don't worry about gettin' any sleep, Yank," one yelled. "After tomorrow, you'll sleep for eternity."

"Think again, Reb," answered a Northern counterpart. "It's *you* who'll be spending eternity under Northern soil. I s'pose you'll make the corn grow as well as any other shit."

Those in the rescue parties knew they might find themselves in a similar position the next day, stretched out and unable even to crawl from the field. So, despite the harsh words, both sides held their fire.

By late morning, the clatter to the north subsided, then ceased completely. Union forces had recaptured their trenches.

"You must be familiar with this area," said Sill to his new deputy as they leaned on a cannon.

"Yeah," Wade replied. "My mother owns a farm less than ten miles from this spot." He looked pensively toward the north. "I sure hope she made it to safety before this began. This war has been hard on her. She spent several months as a captive of the rebels."

"How did that come about?" asked Sill.

"I don't know. She refuses to talk about it."

"Do you plan to return here and farm after the war?"

"No, sir," Wade replied emphatically. "I'm West Point. I suppose I'll remain in the army, if there's a need for one after this is finished."

"I'm not a professional soldier, myself," replied Sill. "I practiced law in New York until '61. Guns always frightened me when I was a kid growing up in the streets." A long pause followed. "What do you think will happen today, Samuel?"

"I don't know, sir, but whatever it is, this battle will be over by nightfall."

"Why do you think that?"

"Soldiers can take only so much battering. Something has to give. Either we'll win or they'll win, but it will end today."

"How old are you, Samuel?"

"Twenty-four, sir."

Sill smiled. "Before the war, there wasn't one twenty-four-year-old that I would have trusted to take ten dollars of mine to the bank. Now I entrust much younger men with my life. The war has changed me— for the better, I think."

Wade touched his fingers to the colonel's hand. "Haven't we all changed, Colonel?" He looked into the man's soft blue eyes and smiled. "I never thought I'd have any use for a lawyer. Now I find I have one for a father and another as my commander."

Sill started to ask something, but thought it too personal.

General Pickett led his soldiers through the woods shading the west side of Seminary Ridge. He smiled as he sat ramrod stiff in the brightly polished saddle. Nothing becomes a man so much as glory, he thought. As the sun washes over a ripe wheat field on a cloudless day, so did Pickett expect glory to wash over him that day. Although the rumors persisted that his rapid elevation within the army had re- sulted from privilege rather than meritorious performance on the field,

the insults no longer mattered. Lee had recently directed him to prepare to lead this day's attack. Pickett still had no opportunity to examine the battlefield, but that did not matter, either. General Lee believed
in the plan, and Pickett believed in Lee—almost as much as he believed in himself.

Pickett had an excess of field grade line officers, so he had assigned
Colonel Thornton to General Armistead's brigade staff as temporary
assistant adjutant.

Thornton's thirst for battle seemed doomed to go entirely unquenched.
He had received orders to remain in reserve and to record from afar,
when victory was in hand, the exploits of Pickett's charge. The orders directed Thornton to remain on the ridge, out of the fight. To him,
the assignment seemed a waste of his talents. All of his training had
been for one purpose: to teach him how to lead men into battle. Besides, he considered himself less than skilled with a pen.

The soldiers of the brigade clattered and banged along the narrow,
dusty road. As the sun rose overhead, the heat grew more oppressive.
Water became scarce, and the men complained. The most common
complaint was that Pickett meant to see them all dead, that he had it
in mind to march them to death. They never spoke of this to officers,
and the officers pretended to ignore the discordant groans. All anyone expected of the soldiers was to fight, when the time came, and
these men, from commander to the lowest private, hailed from Virginia. No one doubted their fighting ability. From that perspective,
Thornton, an Alabaman, was nothing more than an interloper.

Until the brigade reached the jump-off point, Thornton rode his horse
at the side of the road. There, he dismounted and had just lifted the
saddle from his mount when an unfamiliar officer rode by. Thornton
looked up briefly. Their eyes met for a moment; then he returned to
his chores. The officer, a lieutenant colonel, rode a few yards beyond;
then he stopped and turned his horse. He looked menacingly at Thornton.
Even before seeing it, Thornton sensed the hostile glare; then, turning, he reacted with surprise. Thornton forced himself to look away,
but the man continued to stare. The man seemed to be pondering some
unknown but hostile action. Thornton had never seen him before, at
least not that he could remember. It made no sense for the man to stare
at him like that. Shortly, the rider wheeled his horse and rode off without
saying a word, leaving Thornton to wonder about the meaning of this
strange, silent encounter.

Thornton placed his saddle next to a tree and stretched out on the grass. He adjusted his position several times until he settled into a space free from the sunbeams drilling their way through the branches. He pulled the brim of his hat down over his face, closed his eyes, and dreamed of the glory he seemed destined never to achieve.

"Is this the man?"

"That's him," said another voice. "That's Wade."

Thornton pushed his hat back and opened his eyes. Four musket barrels pointed menacingly at his chest. The bright sun shining in his eyes prevented him from distinguishing the features of the men who stood over him.

"Colonel," said the first speaker, "please come with me."

"What's this all about?" asked Thornton, shading his eyes to see. Upon hearing Wade's name he knew he was in trouble.

"You are to come with me, Colonel," the lieutenant standing in front of Thornton said more sternly. "Colonel Benning wishes to speak with you."

Thornton rose to his elbows. He saw the lieutenant colonel who had stared at him a short time before. "Who are you?" Thornton asked.

The man, stern faced and resolved, remained silent.

The soldiers with rifles surrounded Thornton as the lieutenant led the small party down the parched road. The mysterious officer followed close behind. They stopped in front of a tent in the process of being stretched into a standing position. A stout, imposing man, a half foot taller than anyone around, turned. He wore the three stars of a Confederate full colonel. He also stared menacingly at Thornton, but said nothing.

"Sir, this is the man," said the lieutenant. "Colonel Pollard identified him."

"I don't remember ever seeing you before, Colonel," said Benning.

"You haven't, sir," Thornton replied. "I just arrived today. I'm temporarily attached to brigade staff."

"It's Wade, Colonel," said Pollard. "Everything about him is the same, even his voice. Only the beard is missing. Tell him to take off his hat, let's see if he has the birthmark."

"Do it, Colonel," said Benning.

Thornton's anger flared as he ripped the hat from his head. "He is mistaken, sir. Goddamned mistaken. Colonel Pollard must have confused me with my cousin." Thornton told his story, condensing it where possible in the interest of time. All the while, he watched his accuser. The man's features gradually softened; then his eyes dropped.

"May I, Colonel?" Thornton asked as he moved his hand toward his jacket. The colonel nodded. Thornton unbuttoned his jacket and withdrew a copy of his orders. The colonel read them quickly before handing the papers to Pollard. Pollard also read them. A brief, official-looking document had been attached to the back of the orders. It explained about Thornton's recent release from a Federal prison, where the enemy had held him captive since December. It mentioned that he had been part of a prisoner exchange less than two weeks before.

Pollard sighed. "I'm sorry, Colonel, I thought you were Wade and had escaped execution, only to come back to try and work more devilish mischief," he said as he looked at Thornton, his menacing expression gone. "Please forgive me."

From the start, Pollard had been hesitant to report Thornton. He still graphically remembered those long minutes in the Wilderness when his life hung in the balance, where the next breath depended entirely on the goodwill of a Yankee prisoner to keep a finger pressed tightly against the pulsating artery in his neck. He had even argued in that man's defense at his trial, but conceded that his enthusiasm had been less than fervent, for by then General Jackson was dead. Never had a single death had such an impact on an army. Seeking to find a way to adjust for the loss, General Lee had launched into a top-to-bottom reorganization of the Army of Northern Virginia. In the process, Pollard had been given command of a regiment.

When he found time to examine everything in retrospect, Pollard realized that his gratitude for life had turned to hate for the man who had preserved it, then to guilt for being so thankless. Until that moment, he had remained uncertain whether his increased responsibility suited his purpose. Back there in the Wilderness, he had realized the fragile quality of life, and clinging to it acquired new importance. The life expectancy of a regimental commander had grown quite short, especially in Longstreet's corps in Lee's army. Now he had another uncertainty. Was it the hate or the guilt that had finally compelled him to report this man? Logic convinced him of the improbability of the army's making the same mistake twice. Even more unlikely was the chance of this man placing himself in the same situation for a second time.

Thornton thought for a moment. He recognized a chance to get into the battle. "There's nothing to forgive, Colonel Pollard," Thornton answered with a forced smile. "I commend your vigilance." He turned to the other colonel. "Sir, if I might have one more moment of your time."

"One minute, Colonel. I have a battle to prepare for."

Thornton explained his assignment; then he explained the importance of his getting back into the fight. Although he had done nothing wrong, the suspicions and mistrust remained. This most recent event offered sufficient proof of that. He desperately wanted a chance to prove his loyalty.

The colonel listened impassively. "Yours is an important assignment, sir."

"Yes, sir, but one that any of a thousand men is qualified to perform. Surely you do not have so many trained line officers that you fail to see the merit of my joining in this attack. My honor will continue to be questioned until—"

The colonel raised his hand. "I see your point, Colonel." He turned to Pollard. "I seem to remember that your deputy strained his back this morning and is unable to walk."

"Yes, sir. I have temporarily elevated the regiment's senior captain to replace him."

"Colonel Thornton seems to be qualified. I think that is the least you must do."

"If that is your order, Colonel."

"I'll work it out with headquarters. Now, gentlemen, if you will excuse me."

Conditions differed on either side of the valley. On the eastern side, anxiety grew because no one had the slightest idea what might happen as the day progressed. Anxiety also grew on the western side, but for a different reason, for there, everyone had recently learned with certainty what was about to transpire. Lee had already given his final orders to Longstreet, whose corps would make the assault. Longstreet, in turn, had informed his division commanders—the revelation that had prompted General Pickett to ride so high in his saddle upon receiving orders to lead the assault. Longstreet had counseled against the prior day's attack, and done so vigorously, without positive result. This time, he spoke even more forcefully in opposition, but with the same result. "General," Longstreet had said to Lee that morning, "I have been a soldier all my life. I have been with soldiers engaged in fights by couples, by squads, companies, regiments, divisions, and armies, and should know as well as anyone what soldiers can do. It is my opinion that no fifteen thousand men ever arrayed for battle can take that position." His reference to "that position" meant Cemetery Ridge, which Lee had ordered him to capture.

The common soldier knew nothing of this exchange, nor was it likely to have made any difference if he had. For him, every advance against the enemy was the same: There was no difference between dying in a minor skirmish or a major battle, no advantage to be gained. But here, if he had bothered to think about it, with nearly a mile of open ground to cross and an equal distance back if the assault failed, the odds for survival were slim.

There existed no cover at all. It was Fredericksburg in reverse, except the Federals at Fredericksburg had to cross less than half the distance. Here, the Confederates would face twenty minutes or more of concentrated frontal and flanking fire by cannon and rifle. Even if the men miraculously survived the long walk, there awaited them on the other side a force several times larger than their own. Meade had the advantage of being able to move troops to threatened areas. No one seemed to have considered that, including Lee.

Something about that army across the way had changed, even in the short time since Chancellorsville, but awareness of this apparently had escaped Lee's notice. They had engaged, these past two days, in as brutal a battle as either army had suffered through all this long war. No one on Seminary Ridge could say for sure that their army had experienced the least of this suffering.

At precisely 1:07 P.M. the Confederate artillery opened fire. More than a hundred guns on either side proceeded to pound the respective ridgelines. Never before in a single engagement had so many cannon been arrayed for and used in a bombardment. For an hour and more, thunder answered thunder. If not for the lay of the land, the effect might have been much worse. As each cannon fired, it gouged a little deeper into the ground and slid a little backward. The length of the barrage exaggerated the overall effect of this gradual transformation. The slight movement had the effect of elevating, and thus extending, the line of fire. Within a short time, the elevated trajectories of the shells fired from Seminary Ridge began crashing to the ground on the far side of Cemetery Ridge. Although the effect on the support troops proved most devastating, few of the front-line soldiers were hurt by the barrage.

Just the opposite occurred on Seminary Ridge. The assault troops crouched out of sight in the woods and along the roads on the far side of the slope. Before the battle rightly began, more than four hundred of these unlucky combatants died or suffered wounds. The immediate effect was to jangle the survivors' nerves and lower their resistance to what they were about to experience.

As ammunition grew scarce, the order for the assault moved from regiment to regiment. Eager to escape the oppressive heat held in by the trees and the pummeling by the guns still out of sight, the rebel soldiers climbed and stumbled up the ridge. For most, this provided the first view of the task now expected of them. Pickett's men had moved onto the battlefield just that morning. Their approach had been along the west slope of the ridge, and the ridge shielded their view of the open plain beyond. They had seen nothing of the broad, open field east of the ridge, nor had they even guessed at the strength of the army that faced them across the way. Seeing all of this for the first time was an experience guaranteed to make a man gasp in dismay. This they did, all along the line. As the smoke from the bombardment began to clear, and as the full scope of the task emerged more clearly, few failed to share Longstreet's sentiment—that no fifteen thousand men ever arrayed had it within them to take that position. By that time, as a result of attrition by shot and shell, and from miscalculation about the number available from the start—so many had fallen from the ranks during the previous two days—there were only 12,500 available to attempt the assault. Still, General Lee had said it was possible, and those men all had an abiding, undying faith in their general.

"Sir," screamed Wade, "look at those fools! They're about to cross that field."

"It will be Fredericksburg in reverse," replied Sill. "Let them come."

"The center of their line will come straight at our position," cried Wade. He felt his blood rise with the excitement—or was it fear? No matter, the effect was the same. He watched in breathless awe as the seemingly endless ranks tromped from the woods and onto the level ground below. A man had to respect an enemy such as this, an enemy who displayed no fear in defending his cause. But in addition to the grandeur, it was insanity, sheer madness.

"Advance the regiment to the wall," Sill said calmly. "There is nothing to do now but let them come at us." He turned and looked into Wade's sparking eyes. "What are you thinking, Colonel?"

Without shifting his stare from the spectacle beyond, Wade replied in contradiction, "I'm absolutely terrified, sir—and I wouldn't have missed it for the world." With the rush of battle surging through his veins, he pulled his saber and walked stalwartly to the wall.

The men in Pickett's division were on the far right flank of the advancing mass. Theirs was the shortest distance to cross. As they marched onto the valley floor, they made a left oblique and advanced to close the gap separating them from Maj. Gen. James Pettigrew's division to their left. At about the same time, the full intensity of the Union guns bore in on their ranks. The effect was immediate and catastrophic. As shot and shell exploded in their midst, gaping holes appeared in the ranks. As many as ten men crumpled from the explosion of a single shell. Their orders had been to keep the ranks closed. Considering the distance and the holes rapidly expanding all along the line, this soon became impossible.

Across the way, on the lower, near face of Cemetery Ridge, Union soldiers cheered. No one ever asked if their elation expressed admiration for the sheer beauty of the sight, or was an expression of delight for the approaching opportunity to repay in kind what they had suffered so many gruesome times before. Soon, however, as the men's expressions changed and as grim-faced determination drove them toward the inevitable collision, the cheers subsided.

At five hundred yards the front ranks of the three advancing rebel divisions came together to form one vast line nearly a mile long. By then they were approaching within comfortable range of the riflemen crouched on the ridge, especially those Union soldiers assigned to defend the lowermost level of the rock wall that traversed the side of the gentle slope. Correspondingly, the cannoneers on the crest of the ridge changed their load to canister, a round composed of hundreds of jagged-edged, slicing bits of steel. This type of shell was designed to perform its lethal task at a range so short that it became impossible to avoid striking flesh with every shot. Men slumped to the ground by the dozens. Yet still the rebels advanced, their officers urging them onward to do their duty, the light shimmering on their bayonets, their shuffling, shoeless feet carrying them forward because Bobby Lee had said they had a chance.

The rebels faced the massed fire of Union soldiers who blasted away at them as fast as flying arms could stuff cartridges into hot rifle barrels. After the battle was over, an examination of weapons recovered from dead men revealed that a few had as many as five or six cartridges stuffed down the barrel. In their excitement, some men had neglected a necessary action for firing the weapon: They had failed to employ percussion caps, without which their weapons would not fire. Amidst the noise and confusion of battle, and feeling the urgent need to knock men from the approaching ranks, they didn't realize that their rifles had failed to shoot.

At first, Sam Wade ordered his men to fire by volley. Out on the flat plain, the strain became too much, as volley after volley slammed into flesh. At two hundred yards, the rebels began to trot. This soon gave way to long, loping strides, then to an all-out charge. As this evolved, the long delays between volleys became too much for the Union commanders. Then it became every man for himself. By that time the number within the rebel ranks had permanently dwindled by five thousand or more, with many more reluctant to move a step closer. Still, the main force of the tide streamed forward.

Colonel Wade felt the surge of rushing blood against his temples. He screamed to ward off the terror building in his chest. Despite every effort to prevent it, the inevitability of the gray tide's reaching the lower level of the rock wall was becoming apparent. Wade raised his sword and jumped to the wall at the corner where it bent sharply at a ninety-degree angle toward the lower wall. The mighty collision moved toward a crescendo. "Bayonets at the ready, men," he screamed. "Charge!" No one heard the final order. His lurching motion gave the only signal required. With a bellowing roar that rivaled any ever uttered by the onrushing rebels, the men flowed like a towering wave down the slope toward the crossroads of eternity.

At precisely that moment, the men of Confederate Brig. Gen. Lew Armistead's brigade reached the lower wall. Wade observed, out of the corner of his eye, a fresh brigade running down the slope. A glance back down the hill confirmed to him that they would arrive too late to close the breach, unless something more was done immediately. Already, the will of the blue-clad soldiers defending the lower wall had crumbled. Many had abandoned their positions and were running up the hill. Firing the pistol in his left hand and waving the saber with his right, Wade ran down the rough stone top of the wall.

A hundred or more rebel soldiers who had circled around the wall's lower corner were moving to filter in behind the remaining Union defenders. Wade screamed the order to attack, but again it was unnecessary. The momentum of his regiment's downhill charge—it was his regiment by now, for Colonel Sill had fallen—carried the men forward in an irresistible surge. Steel and flesh collided with steel and flesh. Sharp screams accented the lower-pitched roar of the struggling mass.

No one realized it at the time, but the battle had all but ended. There was no chance for the relatively small rebel contingent now climbing over and running around the wall to succeed. What remained of the struggle at that point became intensely personal, with no immediate or long-range objective other than survival. At no other point along the long line had a single rebel soldier reached a Union defensive position. Many already were fading back across the ground they had crossed at such terrible cost only minutes before. But at the angle in the wall, the men knew none of that. The slicing and the hacking continued with the frenzy of massed, famished sharks feeding on a thrashing whale.

Wade pointed his pistol and fired his last round into the face of a lunging private. The impact spun the man half around and the dead soldier's momentum carried him forward, knocking Wade from the wall. Wade struggled to rise through the forest of churning legs and stomping feet. Blood gushed from his forehead as the butt of a dropped rifle ripped his flesh. He pulled himself over the wall and fell on his back before struggling to his feet. Although he had dropped his pistol, his right hand clung desperately to his sword.

Through the scarlet haze he glimpsed a rebel officer charging forward with saber extended. With his last remaining energy, Wade lifted his own weapon and prepared to fend off the approaching blow. He never saw the second gray-clad soldier running up the slope at an angle. The blurred figure flung himself between Wade and the rebel officer just as Wade lunged forward with his blade. At exactly the same moment, the onrushing rebel officer drove his own arm forward. Wade's locked elbow held the limp figure at arm's length as he observed the point of the other sword exit the man's chest. The dying man slumped. The force of his fall pulled Wade's blade free from his hand. As the falling figure pulled Wade forward, the more distant man stumbled and fell.

As the last of his strength drained from him, Wade wiped the blood from his eyes. Uncaring for what might follow, he sank to his knees.

He lifted his weary head slowly and gazed with recognition into the piercing eyes of the soldier kneeling less than three feet away. The man's sweat-soaked hair lay flat on his head; a large, dark red stain revealed where a bullet had entered his side. The man gasped for breath as he lifted both arms over his head. An expression of pure agony distorted his features, then the air wheezed slowly from his lungs. With a soft groan, he clutched at his side before toppling slowly backward. There, under the warm Pennsylvania sun, Lt. Col. Simon Thornton erased the stain from his record.

Wade began to weep and, in his despair, leaned forward on both hands. As the battle ended, his sight blurred by tears, he examined the cold, dead eyes of the man who had stepped between him and onrushing death. A stiff hand clutched at the gleaming steel blade extending from his chest. For the first time, Wade realized that the god of battle could not be cheated. The twisted form before him had the face of a man he remembered from what seemed a thousand years in his past, a man named Emerson Pollard.

At that moment, war's fierce waves drove the high tide of the Confederacy against the unremitting sands of time, yet the final barrier proved no more tangible than an insubstantial rock wall. With the mournful retreat of beaten men across that Gettysburg field, the desperate hopes of a rebel nation began to fade.

When Samuel Wade boarded the train for Baltimore on the eve of the battle of Gettysburg, only two copies of the report describing his actions existed: Colonel Thompson retained one, and Wade took the other with him to show to General Meade.

When Thompson gave his copy of the draft to General Washburn for approval and instructions on disposition, Washburn read through it quickly; then he read it again, only more carefully.

"I need to clear this with the president," Washburn told his energetic subordinate. "There is material in here that could seriously jeopardize our relations with the South when the war is over."

Later, as the rebel tide receded from Cemetery Ridge, Washburn and Thompson met with President Lincoln at the White House. As Washburn finished his explanation of what the report contained, there was a knock on the door. An excited aide rushed into the room.

"Mister President," he exclaimed, "a telegram from General Meade at Gettysburg! The rebels have been repulsed with great losses."

Lincoln thanked the man, dismissed him, then asked to see Wade's report. Like Washburn, he read it twice—first quickly, then again with care.

When he finished, the president squinted his eyes and massaged the bridge of his nose with thumb and index finger. He slumped in his chair and stared out the window for several minutes, lost in thought. Finally he let out a sigh, got up, and walked slowly to the fireplace on the other side of the office. Taking a match from the mantle, Lincoln lit it and ran the flame along the edge of the document. As the flames spread and the pages began to blacken and curl, he tossed the report into the fireplace.

Washburn and Thompson watched silently as Lincoln stared into the flames. As last he turned to them.

"Well, gentlemen," Lincoln said, eyeing the two officers carefully, "let us hope that this matter never comes to light—for all our sakes. This war will end soon enough, no doubt in our favor thanks to the events at Gettysburg and Vicksburg this week. When that time comes there will be many wounds to heal. We can only hope that those who know of this operation on the other side will feel the same way and choose to remain silent as well."

Neither of the officers replied.

"Thank you, gentlemen," Lincoln said softly as he sank into an overstuffed chair facing the window. "I appreciate your forebearance in this matter. Now, if you will excuse me, the war lays heavy on my mind."

From the diary of Caroline Wade-Healy:

July 4, 1863
God help us. I have just concluded a tearful walk along the blood-soaked slopes of Cemetery Ridge. At times I knelt beside the dying to offer soft words of comfort. One young soldier grasped my hand and called me Mother as he died. I can endure no more.

Meade's army waits in silent apprehension to see what General Lee might try next. The only activity is that of the gravediggers as they scoop dirt on the bloated faces of dead soldiers being placed in mass graves.

Numb of mind and weary in spirit, I have looked at this page for nearly an hour now. It has been a hard day, and my only options for describing what I have seen are an avalanche of words—or silence.